TEMPTING DR DAISY

BY
CAROLINE ANDERSON

MILLS &
BOON

First published in Great Britain 2011
by Mills & Boon, an imprint of Harlequin (UK) Limited.
Harlequin (UK) Limited, Eton House, 18-24 Paradise Road,
Richmond, Surrey TW9 1SR

© Caroline Anderson 2011

ISBN: 978 0 263 88609 2

Harlequin (UK) policy is to use papers that are natural, renewable and recyclable products and made from wood grown in sustainable forests. The logging and manufacturing process conform to the legal environmental regulations of the country of origin.

Printed and bound in Spain
by Blackprint CPI, Barcelona

Dear Reader,

When I was asked to write a duet of two closely linked books, I thought 'How close can people be?' And the answer? Identical twins who are both gorgeous guys and amazing doctors—my LEGENDARY WALKER DOCTORS. But they're not just normal twins, but twins who'd shared the same amniotic sac, who'd been in touch with each other from the first moment and who now, 34 years later, were still very close emotionally and in their working lives. You really can't get closer than that—and for both Ben and Matt, their journeys have been paved with tragedy and pain.

But then Ben moves to Yoxburgh, where Daisy and Amy, dear friends and colleagues, are waiting in the wings.

Ben has a daughter, little Florence, who is the centre of his world—until he meets Daisy. He just has to find a way for both of them to trust again, so together they can give Florence the family they all long for in TEMPTED BY DR DAISY.

For Matt and Amy, the past is so painful they can't bear to go there again, but when Ben and Daisy fall in love, her best friend and his twin are brought together again and circumstances conspire to force them to face their past and deal with the loss that drove them apart in THE FIANCÉE HE CAN'T FORGET.

Writing their stories was heart-wrenching but wonderful, and I hope you enjoy reading them as much as I enjoyed coaxing them along each step of the way.

With love,

Caroline

**Praise for
Caroline Anderson:**

'From one of category romance's most accomplished
voices comes a beautifully told, intensely emotional
and wonderfully uplifting tale of second chances,
new beginnings, hope, triumph and everlasting love.
Caroline Anderson's WEDDING OF THE YEAR is
an engrossing, enthralling and highly enjoyable tale
that will move you to tears and keep you riveted
from the first page until the very last sentence.
Kate and Nick's story is sure to satisfy all those readers
who have been waiting with bated breath for their
story. Moving, heartbreaking and absolutely fantastic,
with WEDDING OF THE YEAR Caroline Anderson
is at her mesmerising best!'
—*www.cataromance.com* on
ST PIRAN'S: WEDDING OF THE YEAR

CHAPTER ONE

SHE could hear water running.

Her new neighbour, whoever he might be, was up and about already. Well, she hoped he'd slept better than she had, she thought grumpily. He'd kept her awake until midnight moving things, and the cat deciding she was hungry at five thirty *really* didn't help.

To be fair, he hadn't been that noisy, but she wasn't feeling fair after *another* hen weekend, and *another* of her friends settling down to matrimonial bliss. That left her and Amy, but she couldn't see Amy letting anyone close, and as for her—well, where *were* all the decent single men without a ton of emotional baggage? Not in Yoxburgh, that was for sure, and even if they were, she wasn't sure she was quite ready to dip her toe in that particular pond again.

She fed Tabitha, made herself a cup of tea and went out to the conservatory. Dawn was breaking, the sky washed pale pink above the rooftops to the east, and she curled up on a chair overlooking her pretty little garden, pressed the mental 'reset' button and let herself come to slowly.

It was her favourite time of the day, before the rest of the world got up, and she cradled her mug in her hands, snuggled further down into the chair and listened to the sounds of the glorious spring morning.

The birds were singing, and she could hear boards creaking next door, more of those masculine footsteps running down the stairs, a muffled exclamation—and an almighty crash that sent Tabitha fleeing for the hills and made Daisy spill her tea.

'Oops!' she murmured, trying to tune out the man's voice as she blotted uselessly at her dressing gown, but it was hard to ignore. What on *earth* had he done? Something pretty drastic, judging by the expletives seeping through the thin party wall.

And then there was silence.

'Are you OK?' she called warily—although she didn't really need to raise her voice.

'Um—yeah. Sort of,' he replied, his voice muffled by the wall. 'Sorry. Minor crisis.'

'Anything I can do?'

A despairing laugh, then, 'Not unless you're a plumber.'

She heard footsteps striding down the hall, then a door opening, and a knock at her front door.

She opened it, and her mouth sagged. Wow, he was…

Well, he was many things. Tall. Broad. Gorgeous. Young enough to be interesting, old enough to have something about him. And there was *plenty* about him. He was covered in filthy, sodden debris, his suit drenched and splattered, his hair full of bits of stuff, his once-white shirt a dirty, streaky grey. In the striking, really rather fabulous blue eyes lurked a hint of irony that made her smile.

Then the eyes tracked down her dressing gown and stopped on the huge tea-stain. 'What happened to you?'

he asked incredulously, and she gave a stunned little laugh.

'I thought that was my line,' she said, trying not to laugh any more because it really, really wasn't funny, but his mouth quirked.

'Ah. My ceiling came down,' he explained unnecessarily, and Daisy had to bite her lip. To her surprise his eyes creased in a smile.

'Sorry about the noise. And the language. I'm Ben, by the way,' he said, holding out his hand, then withdrawing it and wiping it on his trousers, scanning it before offering it again. She took it, noting that as well as being a little wet and gritty, it was warm and firm. Strong.

And his voice—a hint of something that could have been Yorkshire? A little gruff. A little blunt. And a *lot* sexy.

'Daisy,' she said, and let herself smile properly. 'Welcome to Rivenhall Villas. May it get better.'

He gave a slightly desperate laugh and closed his eyes, dragging his hand over his face and smearing the dirt into it. A streak of blood joined the dirt, welling slowly from a thin cut over his eyebrow.

'I can only hope. I don't suppose you know a plumber?'

She tightened the belt of her saturated dressing gown, hopped over the low fence between the diamond-patterned paths and peered down his hall at a scene of utter devastation. His kitchen had disappeared under a sea of sodden lime plaster and broken laths, and there was a slow, steady drip from a dangling lump of ceiling. The rush, she sensed, was over, but...

'Just a plumber?' she murmured thoughtfully, and behind her she heard another wry laugh.

'A plumber would be a pretty good start. An electrician might be a handy second, that light's hanging at a jaunty angle. And a plasterer, perhaps?'

'Mmm. It seems to have stopped, though.'

'Yeah. I reckon it was the waste. I'd just had a bath.'

'Ah. Very likely, then. I tell you what,' she said, turning back to him and finding him right behind her. She took a step back, and a nice deep breath, because under the plaster filth and the wet dog smell coming off his suit was the lingering remains of some seriously interesting aftershave. Citrusy, with a touch of amber…

'You were about to tell me something,' he prompted, and she collected herself.

'Um—yes. Why don't I throw on some clothes and come and help you clear up? I've got an hour before I have to leave for work.' And a nice long shower planned, but she could feel that going out of the window rapidly.

'Lucky you. I have to leave now. Let's face it, it can't get any worse, but I can't do anything about it and I've got bigger fish to fry. It's my first day in a new job, I don't have another suit or any way of getting the filth out of my hair, and there's no way I'm turning a tap on! I guess I'll just have to make do with spitting on a handkerchief.'

Obviously he hadn't looked in a mirror yet.

'This is going to take more than spitting on a hankie to sort out,' she said drily. 'And you've got a cut over your left eye. Do you have another shirt?'

He fingered his eyebrow gingerly and nodded. 'And trousers and a jacket, but not the power suit, sadly.'

'Can't help you there,' she said, giving up all hope of starting her day with any kind of normality. 'However, I do have a shower. Why don't you grab some clean stuff and sort yourself out while I find you a plumber?'

'Really?'

'Really. Find your clothes, I'll get dressed and I can make a start on the clean-up, too. I have a vacuum that's very good for sucking up spills.'

'Spills?' He choked on a laugh, and the smile that crinkled his eyes made her stomach turn over. 'There's a bathful of water on that floor.'

'No problem. It can cope. I'll just have to empty it lots—if I can find the sink.'

He frowned. 'Daisy, are you sure? It's a hell of an imposition.'

Well, at least he realised it. Her morning was running away with her, but she couldn't just leave him like this. She found a smile—not as hard as she'd thought, because those eyes were really quite...

'I thought you were in a hurry?' she said, and squeezed past him, hopped over the fence and ran upstairs, dragged on her gardening clothes, put a towel in the bathroom for him and had just hauled the vacuum up from the cellar as he appeared at her door.

'Look, you really don't have to clean up—'

'Don't be silly, it's nothing. Bathroom's at the top of the stairs, straight ahead of you. I've put you out a towel on the side of the bath and the plumber's calling me back.'

He didn't believe it.

He should. Things like this seemed to happen to him these days. He tipped his head forwards so it was under the stream of hot water and let out a tired, frustrated sigh. He'd known moving into the house before it was fixed was rash, but—this rash?

Thank God for Daisy. The shower was bliss. He could have stood there all day under the streaming hot water, but he didn't have time. He borrowed some of her shampoo and washed the filth out of his hair, and discovered some interesting lumps and bumps on his scalp. The cut over his eyebrow was stinging, too. Damn. He sluiced the grit and grime off his body, gave himself a very hasty rub-down with Daisy's borrowed towel, then dressed in record time, scowled at the cut on his eyebrow, frowned at a mark on his shoes that wouldn't shift and gave up.

There was nothing more he could do. Nothing he had time to do. His ruined suit was lying in a soggy heap in the bottom of Daisy's pristine and rather beautiful bath, and he left it there. He'd sort everything out with her later, once he'd got today out of the way.

He could hear the vacuum going next door, sucking up the water. Bless her heart. Of all the days—and of all the neighbours, he thought with a bemused smile. What a star.

A small black cat with huge ears and brilliant green eyes watched him disdainfully through the banisters as he went downstairs. He stretched out a hand to her, and after a second she turned away, and he carried on down with a wry chuckle, dismissed.

He hopped over the pointless but decorative little fence and went into his house, to find Daisy in the middle of the kitchen somehow bringing order to the chaos. The water was largely gone, and she was shoving debris to the side with a broom.

'Daisy, you don't have to do that! I'll clear it up later.'

'I'm nearly done. I've cleared the rubble off the boxes to give them a chance to dry out. I think you might have lost some crockery or glasses—that one tinkled a bit.'

He shrugged. Glasses he could live without. At least he was alive. He fingered the cut again, and she peered at it.

'You need a plaster on that.'

He shrugged again. 'No idea where they are, but I'm sure I'll live. I don't suppose you've heard from the plumber, have you?'

'No, not yet. Take my mobile number and give me a missed call, and I'll send you a text when I hear from him.'

He keyed it in, then slid the phone back into his pocket and ran a hand through his damp hair. 'Look, I'm sorry, I've left my suit in your bath, but I have to go now. I'll deal with it later, and all of this. You don't have to do any more—'

'Go. I'm nearly done. I'll see you later. Can I just drop the door shut on the latch?'

'That's fine. Thank you so much. I owe you, big-time.'

'Too right. I'll expect a slap-up dinner at the least,' she said drily, swiping an armful of soggy plaster rubble off the worktop onto the filthy floor.

'Consider it done.'

She flashed a smile at him, a streak of dirt on her cheek giving her the impish, mischievous look of a little girl having way too much fun—and he didn't really want to start thinking about Daisy having fun, because it was a long, long time since he'd had fun with a woman, and for all she might look fleetingly like the little girl she'd once been, there was nothing but woman under those clothes. And he was taking her out to dinner?

He cleared his throat, nodded curtly and went.

'Phew.'

Daisy straightened up, blew the hair back out of her eyes and looked around. Utter chaos, but at least it was organised chaos now. The rubble was swept into a heap, the boxes had been blotted dry and the water sucked up—and she was going to be late for work, today of all days!

She fled, grabbing the quickest shower on record and dragging on her clothes. Her hair would have to do, she decided, pulling it back and doubling it into a loose bun in an elastic band. No time for makeup. No time for anything, and the new consultant was starting today.

Great start, she thought. Please God he wasn't an arrogant snob—or a tedious box-ticker. One of them on the team was more than enough. She ran to the car, paused in the street to shut her garden gates and headed for the hospital.

On the way she took a call from the plumber, then dropped Ben's suit into the cleaners in the hospital reception area, instructing them to be careful. She'd seen the label, and it had made her wince.

Then she legged it for the ward.

By the time she got there, people were clustered around the nursing station. She could see a man's head slightly above the rest, hear a quiet voice giving some kind of team-leading chat, and her heart sank. Damn. He was here already, doing the meet and greet. So much for making a good impression.

Evan Jones, the specialist registrar, gave the ward clock a pointed look as she squeezed into the group.

'Sorry I'm—' she began a little breathlessly, and then stopped in her tracks as the man turned and met her eyes, and if she hadn't been so busy staring at him in shock she would have missed the quickly masked flicker of surprise.

'Mr Walker, this is Dr Fuller,' Evan said, sounding and looking unimpressed, but Ben's professional smile did something utterly different in his eyes, and he brushed Evan smoothly aside.

'Yes, we've met. Dr Fuller's very kindly been doing something for me,' he explained, cutting him off at the knees, and then turned back to her. 'Any joy?'

Still shocked, running on autopilot and ready to fall in love with him for saving her from another tedious lecture, she nodded. 'Yes, it's sorted,' she told him without missing a beat. He'd found a plaster, she thought, staring at the cut above his eyebrow, but apart from that you'd never know how his day had started. He looked cool, calm and in control—more than she was.

'Thank you. I don't think you've missed much,' he said with a wry smile, then he looked back at the group. 'As I was saying, I'm looking forward to working with you all, and I hope you'll forgive me when I ask silly, irritating questions and don't know where things are or how they're done here. I'll do my best to make this transition as painless as possible, if you'll just bear with me, and if you've got anything you want to talk about, my door's always open, so to speak.'

He smiled at them all. 'Right, that's it, everybody. I know you've all got plenty to do, so I won't hold you up. Dr Jones, rather than keep you from our patients any longer, why don't I get Dr Fuller to show me round? I need to speak to her anyway, so she might as well give me a quick tour and I'll introduce myself to her properly, then I suggest we meet for coffee at nine thirty, if that's all right, and you can fill me in on anything she might have missed and show me the department in detail. Any problems with that, either of you?'

Evan looked a bit startled, but conceded with a stiff little nod. 'No, you go ahead, Mr Walker. I'm sure Dr Fuller can tell you everything you need to know. I don't really have time, anyway. There are some patients I need to see urgently.'

'Clare Griffiths,' she said, worrying about her as she had been all weekend. 'How's she doing?'

'I've seen her already. Don't worry, I can manage without you,' he said dismissively, and Ben frowned. He didn't like the sound of that at all. In fact, he was beginning not to like Evan Jones…

'Fine. We'll catch up with you later,' he said, and without pausing for breath, he ushered Daisy towards the doors.

'Doing something for you?' she muttered under her breath, and his laugh, low and soft and inaudible except to her whispered over her nerve endings and made her shiver.

She gulped as he swiped his ID over the sensor and pushed the door open for her.

'Well, you were, it wasn't a lie. OK, first things first. I want you to fill me in on everything there is to know about the department and its politics—starting with the location of the nearest decent coffee.' His mouth tipped into a wry grin. 'Breakfast was unexpectedly cancelled.'

She had a vision of him covered in his ceiling, and grinned back. 'Indeed. Full English, Mr Walker, or would you rather have something sweet and sinful?'

His eyes flared slightly, and for a second her breath hitched in her throat. 'Oh, I think sweet and sinful sounds rather promising, Dr Daisy, don't you?' he murmured, and followed her out of the ward while she tried to remember how to breathe.

'So—the plumber's coming at seven?' Ben said as they sat down with huge mugs of coffee and wickedly sticky buns—sweet and sinful, she'd said, and he had to try very, very hard to keep his thoughts on track as he watched her bite into hers. 'Is that seven today or in three years' time?'

'No, today,' she said with a laugh, taking down her hair and twisting it back up again into a knot. Pity. He preferred it down. It looked soft, silky, and he could almost imagine sifting the long, dark strands through his fingers—

He stirred his coffee for something safe to do with his hands and dragged his mind back in line again. 'So how come he's available this quickly? Usually if a tradesman's any good, you have to wait weeks. Do you know him?'

She nodded. 'Yes. He's doing it as a favour to me, and he is good. He refitted my bathroom for me.'

'Ah. Yes. Your lovely bathroom. I'm afraid I left it in a horrendous mess.'

'Don't worry, it's fine, I'll deal with it later.'

'So did he charge a fortune, or did your landlord pay?'

'Landlord? I don't have a landlord,' she said ruefully. 'It's my house, and he was very reasonable, as plumbers go.'

'You're buying it alone?' he added, fishing, although it was none of his business and utterly irrelevant, he told himself firmly. He was *not* interested.

She nodded and pulled a face. 'Although sometimes I wonder how I got myself in this situation. I must be mad. I wanted my own house because I was fed up with unscrupulous landlords but I'm not quite convinced I'm really grown up enough!'

Oh, he was sure she was. She was certainly grown up enough to satisfy his frankly adolescent fantasies, he thought. She was biting into the sticky bun again and it was giving him heart failure watching her lick her lips.

And they were colleagues *and* neighbours? Sheesh, he thought, and was hauling his mind back to work when she spoke again.

'So how about you?' she asked, her clear green eyes studying him curiously. 'I mean, you're a consultant, so clearly you're old enough to have a house, but—well, without being rude, what's a consultant doing buying a run-down little semi in a place like Yoxburgh?'

Good question—and one he had no intention of answering, but at least it had dragged his mind out of the gutter. 'What's wrong with Yoxburgh?'

She shrugged. 'Nothing. I love it. It's got the best of both worlds—good hospital, nice community, the sea, the countryside—it's a lovely town.'

'Exactly. So why should I be flawed for wanting to be here?' he asked, curious himself and trying to divert attention back to her and off his personal life.

'Oh, no reason. It's not Yoxburgh, really. It was just—I would have expected you to have a better house. Bigger. More in keeping…' She trailed to a halt, as if she felt she'd overstepped the mark—which she probably had, but she'd rescued him before six o'clock in the morning without batting an eyelid, lent him her shower, cleared up his mess, got him a plumber…

'I'm divorced,' he admitted softly, surprising himself that he was giving so much away to her, and yet oddly knowing it was safe to do so. 'And it might be modest, but the house suits my needs perfectly—or it will, when the plumber's been and I've thrown a whole lot of money at it. Besides, maybe I don't want to live in anything flashy and ostentatious—more "in keeping",' he added, making little air quotes with his fingers.

She coloured slightly, her thoughts chasing each other

transparently through her eyes, and he had to stifle a smile as she gathered herself up and sucked in a breath.

'Sorry. None of my business,' she said hastily. 'And talking of suits, I dropped yours into the dry cleaners in the main reception on the way in, and it'll be ready at five—and before you panic, I told them to take good care of it.'

'Chasing brownie points, Daisy?' he murmured, and she laughed.

'Hardly. I didn't know who you were then. I'm just a nice person.'

'You are, aren't you?'

'Not that nice. I've still got my eye on dinner,' she said with a teasing grin that diverted the blood from his brain, and he wondered how the hell he was going to keep this sudden and unwanted attraction in its box.

With huge difficulty. Damn.

He turned his attention back to his coffee, and then she said quietly, 'Thanks for covering for me so smoothly, by the way. Evan's a stickler for punctuality, and he was getting all ready to flay me later.'

'It was the least I could do. I was hardly going to throw you to the wolves for bailing me out—literally! And Evan doesn't strike me as the friendliest of characters. He was pretty dismissive when you asked about that patient.'

A flicker of what could have been worry showed in her eyes. 'Oh, he's OK really. He can come over as a patronising jerk, but he's a good doctor. He's just a bit miffed that you got the job, I think. He was advised to apply for it, and I reckon he thought it was a shoo-in.'

'And then they had to advertise it by law, and I applied. And with all due respect to Evan, I would imagine my CV knocks spots off his.'

'Exactly. So he won't welcome you with open arms, but you should be able to rely on him.'

He gave a choked laugh. 'Well, that's good to know.'

Her mouth twitched, and those mischievous green eyes were twinkling at him again. 'So, I hope you've got some good ideas about what I was supposedly doing for you?'

He leant back in his chair and met her eyes with a twinkle of his own. 'Oh, let's say finding me some statistics on twins on the antenatal list. That should cover it. Anyway, I thought it was pretty good for a spur-of-the-moment thing. Sorry if it sounded a bit patronising, but I thought it was better than explaining I'd already had a shower in your bathroom,' he said softly, and then felt his legs disintegrate when a soft wash of colour touched her cheeks.

He cleared his throat.

'Tell me about Yoxburgh Park Hospital,' he suggested hastily, and she collected herself and gave a tiny shrug.

'It's old and new, it's on the site of the old lunatic asylum—'

'How delightfully politically incorrect,' he said drily, and she chuckled.

'Isn't it? Nearly as politically incorrect as locking up fifteen-year-old girls because their fathers or brothers had got them knocked up and if they were put away here for life then the family could pretend they'd gone mad and carry on as normal.'

'Lovely.'

'It was. It was a workhouse, really, and the pauper lunatic label was just a way of covering up what they were doing, apparently. I mean, who's going to go near a lunatic asylum? You might end up inside, and so they got away with murder, literally. But life was cheap then, wasn't it?'

'So was building, which I guess is why the old Victorian part is so magnificent.'

'Oh, absolutely, and the other plus side is that because they wanted it isolated, we've got glorious parkland all around us, tons of parking and plenty of room to expand. The locals have access to it for recreation, we have a lovely outlook—it couldn't be better, and the hospital's great. Quite a few areas of it are brand new and state of the art, like the maternity wing, and it's earning an excellent reputation. We've got a bit of everything, but it's still small enough to be friendly and it's a good place to work. Everybody knows everybody.'

'Is that necessarily a good thing?'

She gave a wry smile. 'Not always. You wait till they find out we're neighbours, for instance.'

'You think they will?'

She laughed. 'I give it three days—maybe less.'

Oh, that laugh! Musical, infectious—it was going to kill him. And then she flicked the tip of her tongue out and licked the icing off her lips, and his eyes zeroed in on them and locked.

'So—guided tour?' he suggested hastily, because if he had to sit there opposite her for very many more minutes, he was going to have to strap his hands down by his sides to stop himself reaching out and lifting that tiny smear of icing off the corner of her mouth with his fingertip.

'Sure. Where do you want to start?'

'Maternity Outpatients?' he suggested wryly. 'Then you can ask about the twins, so it's not a lie, and there's an antenatal clinic with my name on it later today, so

I'm told, and it would look better if I could find it.' His eyes twinkled. 'Can't have me turning up late, clearly. Evan would have a field day with it.'

CHAPTER TWO

IT WAS a hectic day, with very little time to think about her new boss and neighbour.

She took Ben for a quick walk through the hospital—the antenatal clinic, as they'd discussed, and other key areas that he might need to visit as well as the location of the dry cleaners, and then armed with the twin statistics she took him back to the maternity unit and gave him a lightning tour of the department—the gynae, antenatal and postnatal wards, the labour ward, the theatre suite, SCBU as well, just for information, and then handed him over to Evan Jones on the dot of nine thirty and went back to the gynae ward to check her patients from last week. She had three to discharge before the afternoon antenatal clinic, then it was back to the antenatal ward and the young first-time mum with pre-eclampsia that she'd been worrying about.

Evan had said he'd already looked at her, but she wanted to see with her own eyes, and she was glad she did. Clare wasn't looking so great. Her blood pressure was up, her feet and hands were more swollen and she was complaining of a slight headache.

Daisy had thought they should deliver her on Friday, Evan had wanted to give her longer for the sake of the baby. He'd won. And now it was looking as if it might have been the wrong thing to do.

'Right, I want you much quieter,' she told her softly, perching on the bed and taking Clare's hand. 'I guess you've had a bit of a busy weekend, and we're going to have to slow things down for you and make you rest much more. So the telly's going, the visits are down to hubby only, once a day, and I really want you to sleep, OK?'

'I can't. I'm too scared.'

'You don't need to be scared. We're taking good care of you, and all you need to do is relax, Clare. I know it's hard, but you just have to try and find that quiet place and let go, OK? Try for me?'

She nodded, rested her head back and closed her eyes.

'Good girl. We'll keep a close eye on you, and I'm tweaking your drugs a bit, and you should feel better soon. If anything changes or you feel unwell, press the bell, and I don't want you out of bed for anything. OK?'

Clare nodded again, and Daisy left the room, closing the door silently behind her, and was repositioning the 'Quiet, Please' sign more prominently when she became aware of someone behind her.

'Is this the woman you were concerned about?' he said softly.

'Yes—Clare Griffiths. She's got pre-eclampsia.' Daisy's voice was a quiet murmur. 'Actually, can I have a word with you about her?'

'Sure.'

They walked away from the door, and Daisy filled him in. 'I don't know if she's OK to leave. I was going to order another ultrasound. She's only 32 weeks, and Evan wants the baby to have as long as possible, so I've told her not to move a muscle, to close her eyes and rest, but it's easy to say and much harder to do, and today her hands and feet are more swollen and she's complaining of a headache. She's got a urinary catheter and we're monitoring her fluid balance.'

'Are those the notes?'

She handed him the file, and he scanned through it, and met her eyes. 'Gut feeling?'

'I think we're going to end up delivering her today.' She bit her lip. 'I wanted to do it on Friday, but Evan—'

'Evan wanted to wait. And you disagreed. He said something about that.'

She frowned. 'What?'

'Oh, just the implication that you were over-cautious.'

Daisy shrugged, disappointed that Evan had thought that rather than respecting her judgement, but maybe he'd been right. Maybe she was overreacting now. 'Do you want to examine her?'

'I thought you'd just done it?'

'I have, but—'

'But nothing. The notes tell me what I need to know. I don't want to stress her by going in straight away. If she sees me, she'll think she has to panic. And I trust you, Daisy.'

'Is that wise? You know nothing about me.'

'I know you're thorough and meticulous with the notes. Evan thought you lacked confidence. That implies to me that you should have more confidence in your judgement, not less.'

She nodded and bit her lip. 'OK. Well, we can watch her if you're happy to. She's had steroids, the baby's as ready as it can be. I'm thinking that waiting much longer's probably not an option but I could be wrong.'

'Or you could be right. So alert Theatre, have SCBU on standby, order another ultrasound and hourly obs, and we'll give the drugs time to work and wait and see. We aren't fortune-tellers, we just have to watch and wait. Keep me up to speed.'

She nodded, and with an encouraging wink, he handed her back the notes and walked away.

There wasn't time for lunch, and she arrived at the antenatal clinic at the same time as Ben and Evan.

They were seeing the tricky patients, the mums with known problems, and she was working her way steadily through the more routine cases and trying not to think about her new neighbour and boss when her pager bleeped.

Clare Griffiths. Damn. She must have deteriorated. Handing her patient over to the clinic midwife to refer to Evan, she went straight up to the ward and found Clare looking pale and sweaty. Her face was looking more bloated, and she was clearly wretched.

As soon as she saw her, Clare started to cry.

'I'm so glad you're here. My feet really hurt, and I can't bend my fingers, my headache's worse, and I can't really see—there are flashing lights and it's as if I've got worms wriggling about all over the inside of my eyes. I'm so scared.'

Retinal haemorrhages, Daisy thought, scanning the monitor and her test results and fluid balance. The ultrasound result showed that the baby hadn't grown since the previous Thursday, and that meant it wasn't getting enough nutrition. She perched on the bed and held her hand, feeling the difference in her fingers even in two short hours. Have more confidence, Ben had said, and he trusted her. Well, let's hope I'm not overreacting now, she thought.

She rubbed her fingers soothingly. 'Don't be scared, Clare, we're looking after you,' she said, trying to inject some of that confidence into her voice, 'but I'm afraid your blood pressure's gone up again, and your blood results show your kidneys are struggling and the baby's not growing. Let me call Mr Walker and ask him to come and look at you.'

'Is this it?' she asked, sniffing and looking even more worried. 'Are you going to have to deliver me?'

'I think so,' Daisy told her honestly, and Clare swallowed.

'But it's so early—what about the baby?' she asked, welling up again.

'The baby should be all right, but if we leave it where it is it certainly won't be, and nor will you. I'm sorry, Clare, we haven't got any choice in this. I'll get Mr Walker, and I'll ring your husband and get him to come in. You might want him with you.'

She asked the midwife with them to prep her for Theatre, rang the antenatal clinic and then Clare's husband, and two minutes later Ben was in with Clare examining her. To her relief he backed her without hesitation.

'Dr Fuller's absolutely right, Clare, we need to deliver your baby now. We'll get the anaesthetist to do your epidural, and then we'll take you into Theatre. You should start to feel better almost immediately, and we have lots of babies born at this stage without any problems. We'll go and scrub, and we'll see you in Theatre in a minute. And don't worry. I know it feels scary, but it's pretty routine for us, and we'll look after you.'

His smile was kind, his manner firm and confident, and Daisy felt herself relaxing. He was right, it was routine, but Clare had every right to be scared, and he'd been good with her. Very good. It was the first time she'd seen Ben with a patient, and any reservations she might have had about their new man disappeared instantly.

'Do you feel ready to lead?' he asked Daisy as they scrubbed. 'I want that baby out fast—I think she's heading for a crisis so I don't think we should hang about. Are you up to it, or would you rather I did it this time?'

'Will you? Not because I don't think I can, but because I know you can, and it's not about pride, it's about Clare and her baby.'

He gave a gentle, understanding laugh and turned the tap off with his elbow.

'Wise words. Right, let's go.'

He was slick, and Daisy was glad she'd opted to assist rather than lead. His hands were deft and confident, and within moments, it seemed, he had their baby cradled securely in his fingers, his tiny mewling cry music to their ears.

'Hello, little one, welcome to the world,' he said softly, and then met Clare's eyes over the drapes. 'You've got a son,' he said, smiling, 'and he's looking good.'

He was—small but strong, and after a brief introduction to Clare and her flustered and emotional husband, he was whisked away to SCBU and they were able concentrate on Clare.

As much as Daisy was able to concentrate on anything except those strong, capable hands that worked so deftly, and the magnetic blue eyes that from time to time met and held her gaze over their masks for just a fraction of a second longer than necessary...

Ben made it back just in time for the plumber. He'd left Daisy settling Clare back onto the ward after he'd kept an eye on her in Recovery and then gone back to his antenatal clinic, and then she'd paged him with a message that she'd collected his suit and Clare was fine.

Brilliant.

He walked through the door, stripping off his tie and hanging his jacket on the end of the banister, and before he had time to do anything else there was a knock on the door behind him.

The man on the doorstep had a toolbox in his hand, and reassuringly grubby fingers. 'Steve, the plumber? Daisy said you'd got problems.'

The temptation to laugh hysterically nearly overwhelmed him. 'You might say that,' he offered drily, and took Steve through to the kitchen.

Daisy let herself into the house, hung up his suit, kicked off her shoes and fed the cat. She could hear Ben moving around next door, and she sat down at the table and signed the card she'd got for him in the supermarket, propped it up against the bottle of bubbly she'd also bought and ran upstairs to shower. The bath was calling her, but she was too hungry to dawdle and she wanted to know how Ben had got on with Steve.

She rubbed herself briskly dry and went back into her bedroom. Jeans? Or sweats?

Jeans, she decided, running the hairdryer over her hair and brushing it through. Jeans and a pretty top, because a girl had her pride and he'd seen her in a dressing gown covered in tea, in her gardening clothes, in her professional 'trust me, I'm a doctor' clothes, and when she popped round with his housewarming present it would be the first time she could show him who she really was.

Which was ridiculous, because she was all of those things, and in any case, why the hell did it matter what he thought of what she was wearing? He was divorced, with no doubt all sorts of emotional baggage. And he was her neighbour, and her boss. Three very good reasons why she should keep him at arm's length and have as little to do with him as possible, she reminded herself fiercely.

And washing her hair and leaving it down was all part of shedding the working day, she told herself. Shoes off, hair down, sweats on.

Except in this case it was jeans, and a pretty top, and the makeup she hadn't had time to put on first thing, because a girl had her pride.

'Oh!'

The knock on the door made her jump, and she swiped the blob of mascara off the side of her nose and ran downstairs, pulling the door open.

He was propped against the inside of her porch, one ankle crossed over the other, hands in his pockets and wearing a pair of jeans and a cotton shirt that looked incredibly soft. She really wanted to touch it.

He smiled at her and shrugged away from the wall, and she folded her arms and propped herself up on the door frame and tried not to grin like an idiot. 'So how did you get on?' she asked.

'Fine. He was amazing. He fixed it in two minutes, he's coming on Monday to fit a new suite and he's getting me a plasterer. And an electrician's already been and fitted a temporary light, so at least I can see in the kitchen, even if I can't really use it.'

'Told you he was good. Any idea why it happened?'

'The bath trap had pulled apart. He thought the seal might have perished, but you'd think the previous owner would have found that out.'

She shook her head. 'Mrs Leggatt couldn't get upstairs. She washed in a bowl the whole time I knew her, and she never had visitors. She used the shower downstairs before that, she said.'

'Did she? Well, that doesn't work, either, which might explain the bowl.'

'Not having much luck, are you?' She shifted and smiled at him, ridiculously aware of his strong, muscled body just a foot or so away. 'I was going to come and see you later to find out how you got on. I've got your suit and a little something to try and compensate for the horrendous start. Come on in.'

He followed her, and she handed him the bottle and the card. 'It's nothing special, but I thought it might help to balance things out.' He gave a quizzical smile, and shook his head slowly. 'Ah, Daisy, I think you've done far more than a bottle of bubbly ever could. I just can't thank you enough for today,' he said softly. 'You've been amazing. Bless you.'

She felt her cheeks heat, and flashed him a quick smile before turning away and heading for the kitchen. 'It was nothing,' she said, grabbing the kettle like a lifeline and shoving it under the tap. 'You're welcome. To be honest, I'm hugely relieved you aren't a property developer or crazy DIY-er who's going to do something awful to devalue my house! Well, at least I hope you're not.'

He chuckled. 'Well, I'll try not to, but I'm not having much luck so far! This is a lovely house, though. It gives me hope for mine.'

'They've both got most of their original features. That's really rare. I hope you're going to keep them?'

'Oh, definitely. That was one of the reasons I bought it. Luckily I'd budgeted for the kitchen and bathroom.' His mouth quirked, and she felt her heart hitch. It was ridiculous! They'd been working together all day without a problem, but here, in the intimate setting of her kitchen…

'So—how's Clare now?'

'Fine,' she said, clutching the change of topic like a lifeline. Work she could deal with. 'She's settling, her blood pressure's already coming down, her urine output's up and she's feeling a lot better. And the baby's doing well.'

'Good. For what it's worth and off the record, I would have delivered her on Friday, too, looking at the notes in more detail. Just in case she'd flared up at the weekend. She was lucky.'

She spun round, eyes wide, and stared at him. He agreed with her? 'Really?'

'Really. You were justifiably cautious.'

She felt something warm unfurling inside her, and she smiled. 'Thank you,' she said softly.

'My pleasure. Have you eaten?'

'No. I picked up a ready meal on the way home and I'm just about to cook it, but it's only enough for one or I'd offer to share. Sorry.'

'Don't worry. I was going to take you out. I owe you dinner, remember?'

She flushed again. 'Ben, I was joking.'

'Well, I wasn't, and you'd be doing me a favour. I've got no food in the house, my kitchen's destroyed and I'm starving. I haven't eaten anything today except that sticky bun, and low blood sugar makes me grumpy.'

'Oh, well, we wouldn't want you grumpy,' she said, going belly-up with a grin, and tried to tell herself she was only doing it as a favour to her boss and her pathetically easy submission was nothing to do with those gorgeous blue eyes, or the rippling muscles she'd seen as he'd pulled off his scrub top on the way through to the changing rooms after he'd delivered Clare.

Nothing to do with that at all...

They went to the bistro on the waterfront.

It had uninterrupted views of the sea, good food and it was close enough to walk to.

Not that they could see the sea, really, this late in the evening, but they could hear it as they walked along the prom, the soft rush of the waves surging up the shore, the suck on the shingle as the water receded, and they could smell it, the tang of salt sharp in the moist air.

'I love the sea,' she told him. 'I don't think I could live anywhere landlocked.'

'You want to try the Yorkshire Dales. It takes a good hour or more to get to the coast.'

'But it's worth it when you get there, surely? Doesn't Yorkshire have lovely beaches?'

'Oh, yes. Gorgeous. And Lancashire, on the west coast. It's just a bit of an expedition. London wasn't any better.'

'Is that where you've just come from?' she asked, trying not to be nosy but failing.

He grinned, his teeth flashing white in the street-lights. 'For my sins. How about you? Are you Yoxburgh born and bred?'

'No. I've only been here two years. I've got a friend working here, and she persuaded me to come.'

'Good move?'

'Oh, yes, for all sorts of reasons. Nice town, and the hospital's great, much nicer to work in than my previous one, and—well, further from someone I needed space from.'

Now why had she brought that up? Idiot! She could see the question forming in his eyes, but she was saved from having to explain by their arrival at the restaurant, and by the time they were seated and the waiter had given them menus and water and a basket of warm, squashy bread, they'd moved on.

Thankfully.

'So why obstetrics?' he asked her, reaching for the bread.

'I love it. Less keen on the gynae, except some of the surgery's quite interesting and technically challenging, but mostly it's the babies. Making a difference, saving such vulnerable little lives—I'm a sucker for it. The friend I told you about's a midwife, and I guess she influenced me a bit. You?'

He shrugged. 'All sorts of reasons, really. My father's a vet and my brother and I used to go out with him on calls sometimes when we were kids. We helped with the lambing and the calving, and sometimes there'd be a foal, and I just loved it. And of course all the cats and dogs had litters, and we always watched them giving birth, and my mother's a midwife, so when I went into medicine it just seemed the obvious choice. My brother's an obstetrician, too, but he's a bit more focussed on his career than me.' He gave a wry smile. 'It's been a bit difficult recently. Life sort of threw a spanner in the works.'

'That's divorce for you,' she said without thinking, and could have bitten her tongue off, but he just shrugged again and smiled sadly.

'Yes, it is. Are you divorced?'

'Me? No! Single and proud of it,' she lied. Well, not about the single part, because she was, profoundly, since Mike had walked away, but she wasn't proud of it. She was more—well, lonely, really, she admitted, but she'd rather be single than in the situation she'd been in. And for all the difference it would have made, in many ways she felt divorced. Would have been, if Mike had ever got round to asking her to marry him instead of just stringing her along for years. She scraped up a chirpy grin. 'Mad spinster lady, that's what I am. Didn't you notice the cat?'

'I thought you had to have more than one to be a mad spinster?' he said softly, his eyes searching even though there was a smile teasing his lips, and she felt her heart turn over.

No! No no no no no!

'Oh, well, I've only got the one, so that's all right, then, I'm not a spinster, just mad,' she said lightly, and turned her attention to the menu. Fast.

Ben watched her. She was distracted, not concentrating. The menu was the right way up, but it could have been in Russian or Japanese for all the difference it would have made, he was sure. She was flustered—by him?

Interesting—except that she was a colleague, and his neighbour, and he'd just got out of one horribly messy relationship and he was in no hurry to get into another.

Even if she was the most attractive, interesting and stimulating person he'd been near in what felt like decades.

He shut his menu with a snap, and her body gave a tiny little jerk, as if the sound had startled her. 'I'm having the pan-fried sea bass,' he said briskly. 'What about you?'

'Um…' She stared at the menu, blinked and nodded. 'Sounds nice,' she said, and he would have laid odds she hadn't even seen the print, never mind made sense of it.

'Wine?'

Stupid. Utterly stupid, on a week night, with work the next day.

'I could have a glass, I suppose,' she said thoughtfully.

'Sauvignon blanc?'

She nodded, and the light from the candle caught her hair and it shimmered like rich, dark silk. He wanted to reach over and catch a strand between thumb and forefinger, wind it round his fingertip and reel her in, tugging her gently towards him until those soft, full lips were in range, and then—

'Are you ready to order, sir?'

He straightened up, sucking in a slow, silent breath and raising an eyebrow at Daisy. 'Have you decided?'

'Oh—um—the sea bass, like you?' she said, saving him from the embarrassment of admitting he'd forgotten everything except the shimmer of her hair and the soft sheen of her lips.

'Sounds good,' he said, and added the wine to the list. A couple of glasses wouldn't make any difference...

'That was really nice. Thank you, Ben,' she said, hesitating by her front gate.

They'd walked back side by side, fingers brushing from time to time, shoulders nudging gently. Not holding hands, but not far off it, and she wondered, just idly—well, no, not idly at all, really—if he was going to kiss her goodnight.

Madness! Too much wine. She shouldn't have had the second glass.

'My pleasure. I'd offer you coffee, but the cafetière was in the box that jingled,' he told her ruefully, and she smiled.

'I've got coffee,' she told him before she could stop

her mouth, and their eyes locked and he lifted his shoulders in an almost imperceptible shrug.

'Coffee would be nice. Thank you.'

She unlocked her door, and he followed her in, all the way through to the kitchen. It was open to the dining area, and she directed him to the table to get herself a little space.

'Make yourself comfortable,' she said, and switched the kettle on, glancing at the clock as she did so. Heavens, they'd been out for well over two hours. It was after eleven o'clock, and she had to be on the ward tomorrow at eight. Silly. She shouldn't have invited him in. Too late, and way too dangerous.

She frowned into the freezer, searching for the coffee, and then gave up and opened a new packet. She had no idea how long the other one had been open and her mind didn't seem to want to work it out.

'Black or white, and hot or cold milk?' she asked, sloshing hot water into the cafetière to warm it.

'Black, one sugar,' he said.

Of course. That was how he'd had it in the bistro, although he'd had a latte in the hospital that morning. Heavens. Was it only that morning? It seemed aeons ago!

Her thoughts miles away, she picked up the tray and found herself heading automatically to the sitting room at the front of the house. She'd meant to put it down on the dining table, but before she could change tack he'd stood up and was following. Damn! It would be too cosy in there, much too intimate, and the wine was fogging her brain.

The wine, and the company...

'Oh, this room's lovely, Daisy,' he said warmly as

she put the coffee down, and she felt herself glow with his praise.

'Thanks. Do you want some music on?'

'Shall I?' He was crouching down in front of her iPod dock without waiting for an answer, scrolling through her music collection, making himself at home. He put on something soft and romantic, and she could hardly tell him she didn't like it, as it was her music. And she'd sat down already, so it was impossible to choose the other sofa when he sat at the other end of hers, a perfectly respectable distance from her and yet just close enough that her nose could pick up the scent of that citrusy cologne he'd been wearing this morning.

It had been teasing her nostrils all evening, and she could have leant against him and breathed him in.

Except that it wouldn't make any sense at all, and if she knew what was good for her she'd drink her coffee and send him on his way.

Except it didn't quite work like that.

They talked and laughed until long after the coffee was finished, and then finally he sighed and got to his feet.

'I ought to go.'

'Yes, you should,' she said, and stood up, but she'd kicked off her shoes and she tripped on one and he caught her, his hands strong and steady on her arms.

'OK?' he murmured, and she lifted her head and met his eyes and everything seemed to stop dead.

Her heart, her lungs, the clock—everything froze in that moment, and then as if someone had thrown a switch and set him free, he bent his head, so slowly that she had all the time in the world to move away, and touched his lips to hers.

She sighed his name, her heart kicking back into life

like a wild thing, and then his arms were sliding round her and he was kissing her properly.

Improperly?

He tasted of coffee and after dinner mints, his tongue bold and persuasive, coaxing her, leading her, then retreating, making her follow.

She was putty in his hands, all her senses short-circuited by the gentle, rhythmic stroke of his tongue, the soft brush of his lips, the warm whisper of his breath over her face as he sipped and touched and lingered.

If he'd led her upstairs, she would have followed, but he didn't. Instead he lifted his head and rested his chin on her hair and cradled her gently against his chest.

'I really ought to go,' he said again, but his voice was gruff this time, the soft Yorkshire burr teasing her senses, and his arms stayed wrapped around her.

She lay there another moment listening to the steady, insistent thud of his heart against her ear, and then reluctantly she dropped her arms from round his waist and stepped back.

'Yes, you should. Thank you for taking me out. You really didn't need to, but it was lovely. I really enjoyed it.'

'So did I. I'd like to do it again, but I'm not sure if that's wise. We work together, we live next door. It could get messy.'

She nodded, struggling against an inexplicable urge to cry. 'Yeah. Lousy idea.' And he was divorced. She didn't do that. Didn't do anything. Not any more.

He took a step towards the door, then turned back, his eyes lingering on her face. 'Thank you for everything today. You've been amazing.'

She tried to smile. 'Any time.'

He lifted a hand and his knuckles grazed her cheek

tenderly. 'Goodnight, Daisy. Sleep well. I'll see you to-morrow.'

She nodded. She couldn't speak, because for some ridiculous reason she was on the verge of tears, and as if he knew that, he gave a sad, fleeting little smile and let himself out.

CHAPTER THREE

WORKWISE, Tuesday was a day like any other.

On a personal level, Daisy thought she was going to go out of her mind. She'd hardly slept, and by the time she arrived on the ward, she'd convinced herself that working with Ben was going to be impossible.

In fact, it was easy.

He greeted her with a smile, and if it hadn't been for the lingering heat in his eyes, she wouldn't have known anything had happened between them. It was just business as usual.

No cosy coffees today, just the normal routine of a busy surgical list, including an elective Caesarean on a woman with an old spinal injury who had to have a general anaesthetic rather than an epidural. It was a good chance for him to see what she could do, and he could talk her through it without worrying the patient or her partner.

Although, in fact, he hardly said anything, just nodded reassurance and made the odd suggestion, and then stripped off his gloves and walked out. 'You're doing fine. You close, I'm going to get a coffee. Bit of a late night.'

Evil man. Thank God for a mask she could hide her

smile behind, and the scrub nurse and anaesthetist deep
in conversation about another colleague.

She finished, stripped off her gloves and went out to
the staffroom, to find him pouring another coffee and
holding it out to her as she approached.

'Nice,' he said. 'Good hands. You remind me of my
father.'

'Is that a good thing?' she asked, not sure she was
flattered.

'It is if you're a good vet.'

'Like James Herriot? All stone barns and stroppy
farmers?'

He chuckled. 'Things have moved on since the for-
ties. You've got the makings of an excellent surgeon,
though.'

'Just don't get me delivering calves.'

The silly banter was just what she needed to take
her mind off what had happened last night—or not
happened. Except of course the tension between them
was still there, the incredible sexual chemistry striking
sparks off her every time she was within twenty feet of
him. And of all the people for it to happen with—

'Hey, it's OK,' he murmured softly, as if he realised,
and then the anaesthetist stuck his head round the door
and gave them the thumbs up.

'She's round, she's fine. Ready for the next?'

He got to his feet and went to scrub, and when she'd
drained her coffee she joined him and the awkward,
sensitive moment was gone.

For now.

Ben closed the front door behind him, rolled his neck
and cradled it in his palm, massaging the tight muscles.

He'd been operating most of the day, and on top of

lugging boxes all weekend, it was getting to him. Not forgetting lying awake thinking about Daisy all night.

He groaned and shut his eyes. He really, really didn't need to think about that. It had been difficult enough having to work alongside her all day without coming home and fantasising about her all evening as well.

He put the kettle on, rang the plumber back about the electrician and the plasterer, and made himself a cup of tea. He'd just dropped into a chair in his sitting room to drink it when his mobile rang.

'So how's the new house?'

He gave a slightly strangled laugh and looked around at the hideous 1970s wallpaper and the dangling paper on the ceiling. When he closed his eyes, all he could see was the trashed kitchen. 'Let's just say it's got potential.'

'Oops.'

'Yeah. The bath waste wasn't properly connected.'

'And?'

'I don't have a kitchen ceiling now.'

'OK...' His brother was stifling a laugh, he could tell, and he could feel his own lips twitch.

'You ought to come up and see it.'

Matt didn't bother to stifle the laugh then. 'You have to be kidding. You'll have me stripping wallpaper and pulling out kitchen units before I've taken my coat off,' he said drily, and then added, 'So, how's the job? Any good?'

'Yes, very good. The SpR's a bit of an old woman, but the registrar's excellent. Good team.'

'And your neighbours? Met them yet?'

'Ah—yes. Actually, the registrar's my neighbour. She's in the other half.'

'Is *she*, now?'

Ben closed his eyes and leant back. 'Yes, *she* is. And she was very helpful about the leak. I took her out for dinner to say thank you,' he added rashly, and he heard Matt's curiosity crank up a notch.

'And?'

'And nothing.'

Matt was laughing. 'Oh, come on, bro, I know you better than that. I thought you were sounding pretty chipper. So let's have it. What's her name?'

'Daisy.'

'*Daisy*! What kind of a name is that?'

'Don't mock, you're only jealous.'

'Ooh, defensive—that's interesting! So what's she like?'

'Average height, curvy, long dark hair, green eyes, sexy mouth—'

'Really? How sexy?'

Damn. He sighed and shut his eyes. 'Didn't mean to say that.'

He heard a low chuckle. 'I'll bet. How sexy?'

He gave up. 'She kisses like a goddess,' he admitted, and there was a second of startled silence on the other end.

Then, '*When* did you meet her?'

'Yesterday.'

'And you know how she *kisses*? *Already*? Sheesh, that's fast work! And she's a *colleague*? You're normally much more circumspect. She must have really lit a fire under you.'

Oh, yes. For all the good it'd do. 'It's not going anywhere. You know I'm not in the market for a relationship, Matt, any more than you are.'

'So who's talking about a relationship?' Matt asked with his usual bluntness, and he sighed again.

'She's a nice girl, not someone you take to bed for the hell of it.'

'I thought you grew out of that years ago.'

'Yeah, well, I nearly forgot.'

Matt blew out his breath. 'It must have been some kiss.' He sounded incredulous, and Ben ran a hand round the back of his neck and sighed.

'Yeah. Big mistake, kissing her. We—uh—we got a bit swept along on the moment, and we shouldn't have done. I should have had more sense, and I know it's crazy, and I keep telling myself it can't go anywhere, but—hell, I was so tempted to stay, Matt. I was that close…'

He heard her front door shut, and shook his head to clear it. 'Look, I've got to go, she's home now and these walls aren't exactly soundproof. I think I'm going round there to talk to her—tell her why it can't ever go anywhere before she gets ideas.'

'Are you sure it can't?' Matt prompted, his voice soft. 'Maybe it's time to move on—find some time for yourself.'

And because he wanted it to be otherwise, because he was blown away by Daisy and wanted to be able to follow through but knew he couldn't—or wouldn't—Ben bit back.

'I don't see you moving on with your life,' he said, and he heard Matt suck in his breath again.

'Back off,' he warned softly.

'Sorry, ignore me. Well, no, don't ignore me. Come up here and stay for a few days. It would be really good to see you and I promise I won't make you strip wallpaper.'

'I don't believe a word of it, but I might come anyway, just to get a look at this Daisy. Good luck with her. I'll look forward to meeting her one day.'

The line went dead, and he stood up and went out to the kitchen with his mug. He'd give Daisy a few minutes to change and feed the cat, and then he'd go round there.

And stop this thing in its tracks.

She wanted a bath. She'd wanted a bath since Sunday night, and nothing that had happened in the meantime had changed that.

She stared at it, sitting there taunting her with its promise of gentle, lapping water and utter relaxation. She still hadn't unpacked from the weekend, there was washing waiting to go in the machine, and—

'Oh, damn it,' she said, and turned on the taps, poured in a generous dollop of bubble bath, and while the delectably indulgent Victorian claw-foot bath filled with water, she put on some music, turned down the lights and lit a scented candle, then dropped her clothes into the laundry basket, stepped into the bath and slid under the bubbles.

'Oh, yes,' she groaned. Bliss.

Except she was twitchy. She could hear Ben moving around next door, unpacking probably. He was going to come round, she just knew it, and catching her in the bath really wouldn't help. She'd have to run down to the front door looking like a drowned rat, and what little was left of her pride would go straight out of the window.

She rinsed her hair in clean water, dragged herself reluctantly out of the bath, dried and picked up her dressing gown. It still had a tea stain all the way down the front, and there was no way she could wear it again until it had been washed. She really *had* to do her laundry.

She contemplated her baggy old sweats, and then put on jeans and last night's top, because she just had a feeling he'd be round. No reason. He hadn't said he would, but better to be prepared. And she resisted the urge to change the top for one he hadn't seen.

She'd dry her hair, and put on a touch of makeup—just a flick of mascara and some concealer under her eyes to hide the bags, because two nights without sleep showed on her fair skin—and then she'd unpack and tidy her room.

Not that she needed to worry about Ben seeing it, anyway, she thought with irony as she dabbed on the concealer. He'd been the one to walk away, while she'd been teetering on the brink.

And in any case, what on earth was she *thinking*? She didn't *want* him in her bedroom! There was no way she was getting involved with another divorced man, because she was still dealing with the devastating emotional fallout from the last one. And he was her boss! *And* her neighbour!

'Huge great big fat no, Daisy,' she said firmly, and picked up her mascara.

She heard him run downstairs, then the sound of his door closing. A moment later, there was a knock on her own door, and even though she'd tried to convince herself it was the last thing she wanted, her heart raced with anticipation and her hands started to shake.

She put the mascara down before she could poke her eye out, went downstairs and opened the door.

He had flowers. A huge bunch of pure white longiflorum lilies, the scent astonishing, and he held them out to her.

'Are you trying to soften me up or is this a peace offering for trying to take advantage of my innocence?'
she asked, taking them from him warily, and he felt his
mouth kick up in a wry smile. If he'd wanted to take advantage of her innocence, he wouldn't have had to try
very hard, she'd been with him every step of the way…

'Neither. I thought they'd mask the smell of damp
plaster clinging to me.'

She gave a disbelieving little laugh and walked off,
and he followed her through the door she'd left open—
presumably for him—to the kitchen. She was putting
the flowers in a tall vase and fiddling with them, pulling off leaves, trying to arrange the stubborn stems, and
he could tell she was nervous.

Why? In case he tried anything again? No way. She
was safe on that front, at least.

'Have you eaten?' he asked, and she felt her brow
crease in a little frown.

'No. Not yet. I was going to have that ready meal.'
Don't ask me out again, Ben, please, don't ask me out.

'Can I change your mind? I thought maybe we could
find a pub somewhere, grab something to eat and have
a chat.'

Her stomach fluttered, and she squashed the quiver
of anticipation ruthlessly. 'I don't really want to go out.
I could do with an early night, to be honest,' she lied,
and jammed another lily stem into the vase.

He watched her thoughtfully. 'Is that, "Ben, sling
your hook," or "I don't want to go out but we could
have a takeaway"?' he asked, trying to read her body
language.

She gave up on arranging the flowers and dumped
the vase in the middle of the dining table. 'Neither. Ben,
why are you here?' she asked a little desperately.

He propped himself up against the table next to her, hands thrust into his trouser pockets, and sighed quietly.

'I think we need to talk about what happened last night.'

'Nothing happened last night.'

His laugh was low and mocking. 'Get real, Daisy. We were *that* close.' He held up his hand, his thumb and forefinger almost touching, and she felt heat pooling in her at the memory.

She made herself meet his eyes, and then regretted it, because they were glittering with an intensity that should have terrified her.

It *did* terrify her.

She looked away. 'Well, spit it out, then, because you've obviously got something to get off your chest,' she said briskly, and she felt the huff of his quiet laugh against her cheek.

'It's—complicated.'

She gave a derisive snort and straightened one of the lily stems. 'The last man to say that told me he was going back to his wife and family,' she said drily, and he found himself wondering about the bastard who'd hurt her.

'I'm not going to say that, exactly.'

She felt relief try and break free, but sensed it was a little early and squashed it. And that 'exactly' was hanging in the air like an unexploded bomb. 'So what *are* you saying, *exactly*?' she prompted. 'That you're my boss and it's a bad idea? You're divorced? We're neighbours? I've already worked all that out, and I absolutely agree.'

'I have a daughter,' he said, dropping the bombshell of all bombshells without preamble. 'She's nearly three, and she's called Florence. That's why I'm here, why I'm in Yoxburgh. My ex moved back to be near her family and friends, and I've followed.'

Here we go again, she thought, and her heart sank. 'Because you want to get back with her and she won't play ball?'

'No way. To be near Florence, so I can take an active role in her day-to-day life. There's no way we're getting back together—'

'I've heard that before, too,' she said bluntly, still curiously reeling with disappointment, but that was silly. He'd said nothing, done nothing. No lies, no promises. He hadn't spun her any kind of line at all, unlike Mike. He'd just been himself, easy, charming, relaxed, funny, and she'd—what? Fallen for him? Even though she'd known he was trouble?

'But *I* mean it. We won't be getting back together. Our marriage was a disaster and I have no intention of revisiting it. The only reason I've moved up here is for Florence, and she has to come first before anything.'

'Well, good. It's refreshing to hear a father say that,' she said with feeling, 'but I can't see what it's got to do with us.'

'It's why there won't be an "us", in any meaningful way,' he said gently. 'I owe it to Florence to make her life as uncomplicated and normal as it can be for a little girl with two parents who can't live with each other, and amongst other things, that means no "aunties" drifting in and out of her life, so if you're harbouring any illusions about this going any further, then I'm sorry, Daisy, I'm not in the market for it.'

Harbouring any illusions? The only illusion she'd harboured was the notion that he might be free and unencumbered. Not *a father*! How could she have been so naïve that it hadn't even occurred to her?

And now she knew he had a daughter, there was no way she'd touch him with a bargepole! She'd been here before, and two little girls had been desperately hurt when he'd decided he loved his wife after all and she was going to forgive him for his endless indiscretions and have him back.

'Don't flatter yourself, I'm not harbouring anything,' she told him straight. 'And the last thing I need in my life is another relationship with a man with a ton of emotional baggage, so relax, Ben. You're safe. I'm not even slightly interested.'

He gave a soft laugh. 'Well, that's me told,' he said, and wondered why on earth her emphatic rejection should matter quite so much.

'You don't need to be too injured. Without the baggage I could have been very interested,' she added rashly. 'I just don't have a death wish, so I don't do family men. One of my rules. Out of curiosity,' she went on, 'why didn't you tell me about your daughter yesterday?'

He frowned. 'I'm sorry, I didn't realise it would be such a big deal to you,' he said. 'I wasn't deliberately keeping her a secret, although I don't talk about her or any other aspect of my private life to people I don't know, but by the time we'd reached a point when I might well have told you, I wasn't exactly thinking clearly, and neither were you, if you remember.'

Oh, didn't she just—but he'd walked away, in the nick of time.

'Nothing happened, Ben,' she reminded him firmly, 'and I don't expect anything to. As I said, I'm not interested.'

His shoulders dropped, and he nodded slowly. 'Good. I think.'

'You think?' she asked warily.

He shrugged, his mouth twisting into a fleeting, rueful smile. He ought to leave it alone, really, to drop the subject and move on, but honesty compelled him to explain.

'I'm torn, Daisy,' he told her. 'And it sounds like you could be, too. It's a lousy idea, as I said last night, but I'm not made of stone, and I really like you. And in an ideal world—well, it might all be very different. It would be nice to see you outside work, get to know you, spend time with you, but I don't think it would be fair on you. You aren't the kind of girl for a casual fling, and I can't offer you anything more serious at this point in my life. I don't want you getting hurt—I don't want either of us getting hurt, come to that, and I won't have Florence hurt under any circumstances, but there's no future in it for us, and I'm still your colleague—'

'Well, if we're going to be brutally honest you're my boss,' she pointed out frankly, and he felt his mouth twitch again.

'I'm still your *colleague*,' he repeated, 'we have to work together, and I can't afford to jeopardise that. I have to make a success of this job, for my sake and for Florence's, and there's no way I can give you any kind of happy ever after. My marriage really screwed me up. I put everything I had into it, even though I knew it wasn't perfect, but it wasn't enough, and it nearly tore me apart. I'm never going there again.'

Oh, Ben, she thought. She'd been there, felt the same way when Mike had walked out and taken his daughters with him. She'd done everything she could, and it just hadn't been enough.

'I'm sorry,' she said softly. 'I know how that feels, I really do.'

He nodded, and reached out a hand, squeezing her shoulder gently. His touch warmed her, and she wanted to lean into him, to lay her head against his chest and stay there.

Instead she moved away, going to the kettle to put it on.

'So that's both of us nursing a broken heart.'

'Nursing a whole heap of disillusion and disappointment,' he corrected quietly, but making a very large and clear note to himself that her heart was broken. 'And the last thing I need is to get involved with someone with the same history.'

Especially after Jane—Jane, who'd been on the rebound when he'd met her. Never again.

'You're right. It would be crazy. Ben, I'm hungry, I need to eat,' she said, wondering if it was low blood sugar making her feel a little light-headed, or the conversation. 'I'm going to heat up this ready meal.'

'Or we could share a takeaway,' he said, changing tack, not quite ready to end this time with her, needing to get their relationship as friends and colleagues and neighbours firmly on track and lay the ghost of that kiss. 'I have an ulterior motive. I want to ask your advice about my house.'

She stared at him, bit her lip, shrugged. 'I don't know that I can be much use, I know very little about your house. Apart from the other day, I've only been in it a few times, and I've never been upstairs except to fetch something for Mrs Leggatt once.'

'But you know this house, and I love what I've seen of it, which let's face it is pretty much all of it. Come and have a look. I'll order a takeaway, and while it's coming, you can cast your eye over it and tell me what you'd do,' he coaxed. 'Unless you'd rather not?'

She laughed softly. 'I'd love to see round it,' she said honestly, and tipped her head on one side. 'Can we have Chinese?'

'Sure. Got a menu?'

'Of course I have. I've got a stack of them. They get put through the door all the time. We're quite civilised round here.'

'Great. And we can wash it down with the bubbly you gave me yesterday. It seems only fair to share it.'

'I don't think that would be a good idea,' she said carefully.

'Maybe not,' he conceded with a rueful smile, and held his hand out. 'Let's have the menu, then. I'm ravenous.'

He saw Florence the following evening.

He couldn't bring her home for the night, which was the eventual plan for Wednesdays, because it was in chaos following the ceiling collapse and would be for some time, so he spent the evening with her at Jane's.

Difficult, because although they'd parted on reasonable terms, it was her house, and technically speaking her night off.

'Do you mind if I go out?' she asked, and he agreed readily. It would be easier without her, would give him a more relaxed and focussed time with Florence, and would mean less of a change when she did eventually come to him.

So he stayed there with Florence, and he cooked her supper and bathed her, and then tucked her up into bed and lay beside her with her snuggled into the crook of his arm while he read her a bedtime story.

'Again,' she said when he'd finished.

He read it again. It was easier than arguing, and easier than reading her another book—because that could lead to another, and another, and another—and he'd been suckered before. Not yet three, and she was a clever little minx.

He adored her.

'Again,' she said, but sleepily this time, her thumb in her mouth. She'd started nursery school full time because Jane wanted to go back to work, and she was loving it, but she was tired by the end of the day and he guessed that if Jane had been reading the story, she would have fallen asleep sooner.

Bedtime with Daddy was a novelty, though, her time with him limited, and she was often clingy.

So he read it again, and then eased his arm incredibly carefully out from under her head, lowering it to the pillow and kissing her softly on her rosy little cheek as she slept.

'Goodnight, my precious,' he murmured, smoothing the hair back from her face as his eyes filled. 'Sleep tight.'

He kissed her again, and left the room, her door ajar and a nightlight on in case she woke, and then he went downstairs and sat on the sofa they'd had in London and watched his old television until Jane came home at ten.

'Everything all right?' she asked brightly, and there was something in her tone of voice that made him search her face as he got to his feet.

'Fine. She's asleep. We read *Goldilocks and the Three Bears* three times.'

'Oh, Ben, you have to learn to say no.'

'No, I don't. I have to make her happy and bond with her, so she feels secure with me. We spent too much time apart before I moved up here, and I've got ground to make up. Anyway, reading to her isn't exactly a hardship.'

She nodded, then as he was leaving she said carefully, 'So, are you planning on sleeping here this weekend?'

'Yes, if that's all right, otherwise I won't be here when she wakes up, so she'll disturb you and that's not fair.' And he'd miss that lovely morning snuggle. 'I can't have her at the house for ages, but if it's a problem I can maybe sort something out.'

'No, it's not a problem. I was just wondering—if you're going to be staying over anyway, do you mind if I'm not here on Saturday night? Well, from Saturday morning to Sunday evening, really.'

There was definitely something different about her. She looked—what? Happier? He shrugged. Why should he mind? It was easier than feeling guilty about ruining her life, and he resisted the urge to ask where she was going. It was none of his business, unless it affected Florence—and it didn't. 'That's fine. Do whatever. I might bring some washing over to do, if it's OK?'

'Of course it is—you pay the bills, Ben. And I might have got a job lined up, by the way, which should make things easier. It's not certain yet, but—who knows?'

She smiled, and he realised she did look happy—maybe because of the job, or maybe not. And he also realised he'd never really seen her look this happy before.

What a sad indictment of their marriage. No wonder it had failed so spectacularly.

'Well, I hope it works out for you,' he said, fishing for his keys in his pocket. 'Right, I'm off, I'll see you on Friday.'

He drove home, his heart aching at leaving his little

daughter behind. He hated not being part of her every-day routine—not sharing her bathtime and bedtime, her breakfast, taking her to nursery, not being there to cuddle her when she woke in the night.

Just not being there for her.

Still, he'd have the weekend alone with her, or most of it, and they'd be able to stay at the house and just chill out together. Maybe he'd buy her a swing and put it up in the garden—or maybe he'd do that at his own house in a few weeks' time, once it was a bit more sorted. Then she'd have a proper home with him here, too, with toys and things, and maybe she'd be a bit more settled.

He pulled up outside, cut the engine and stared long-ingly at Daisy's house.

The lights were on, and he was so tempted. He hesi-tated by his front door, debated stepping over the silly little fence and going to see her, and crushed the urge. He couldn't keep going round there. It was self-indulgent and intrusive, not to mention downright dangerous. He was drawn to her like a moth to a flame, and the *last* thing he needed was another woman on the rebound.

And he needed to find something more mentally in-volving to do at work than have Daisy assist him in Theatre. It gave him too much time to think about her while he operated on auto-pilot.

He'd let her lead tomorrow. He'd have to teach her, then, and there were some interesting cases on his gynae list.

And maybe it would keep his mind a little more firmly on the job and off his obsessive preoccupation with his registrar…

CHAPTER FOUR

It was odd not seeing him after work on Wednesday. Wednesdays were his night for Florence, he said, and he'd be back late.

She didn't miss him. Of course she didn't! She'd only just met him, so how could the house feel empty if he wasn't there? She was just bored, and catching up with the washing—never her favourite task but she needed her dressing gown back and she was running out of underwear. And she'd finally eaten the ready meal, the solitary little portion underlining her pathetic single status.

Not that her status was any different to this time last week, but it somehow *felt* different. It was the kiss that had done it, she thought. The kiss, and talking to him, sharing smiles and the odd joke at work. Going round to his house last night and seeing the full extent of what he'd taken on.

Making friends slowly, day by day.

Actually, not that slowly, and working with him was a privilege and a joy. It was living next to him and wanting the man and not the doctor that was so hard, because if the doctor was wonderful, the man was downright off the scale.

She heard him come in at ten, and she wondered if

he'd knock on her door. Bring round a bottle of wine, or ask her to go there for coffee. And then maybe he'd kiss her goodnight…

She slammed the washing machine door shut, put the iron away and shoved the basket into the corner. She'd deal with the sheets and towels tomorrow, she decided, and went to bed, irritated that he had the power to affect her both with his presence and his absence. Ridiculous!

Anyway, she needed an early night, and the next day she was glad she'd had one. Ben had a busy gynae list and asked her to assist—which meant in practice he got her to lead on several of the ops, so that she did most of the surgery and he held instruments and handled the suction and told her what to do.

It was his job to mentor her after all, and she appreciated it, but he took it very seriously and stretched her to the limit, testing her ability all through the day so that she was exhausted by the time the last patient was in Recovery.

Exhausted and proud of herself, she thought as she showered. She'd done far more than she ever had before, and she'd been able to do it because he had confidence in her.

Unlike Evan, who still double-checked her work and seemed unable to delegate.

She raised it with Ben as they sat in her conservatory drinking tea after she'd got home, and he shrugged. 'That's his problem,' he said. 'I don't have any problem delegating to you. I think he lacks confidence in himself, to be honest, and I don't think he's ready to be a consultant. What do you think of this one?'

He'd brought round a bunch of kitchen brochures the plumber had dropped in, and they were flicking through them while they waited for the takeaway to be deliv-

ered. Thai, this time, for a change. His choice. His bill
again, he said, as he was commandeering her time to
get her advice on his kitchen refit.

It was a safe topic, well clear of the minefield of his
personal life—and hers, come to that. Not that she had
one, unless you counted the cat. Safer than talking about
her feelings, anyway, because she certainly had *them*
and they were getting more complex with every passing day.

The food arrived, and it was getting cooler in the
conservatory so they ate in the dining room, with soft
music in the background and the lights on low.

A mistake, she realised, because it made it very intimate, and suddenly it began to feel like a date, all over
again.

He'd brought the bubbly with him as a bribe for her
input into his kitchen, and whether it was that, or the
intimate atmosphere, or just that the chemistry between
them was so all-consuming that it wiped out everything
in its path, she didn't know.

All she knew was that everything he said made her
laugh, and when he smiled his eyes lit up and his whole
face joined in. And he was just so *nice*, so ordinary and
yet extraordinary, unlike all the other men she'd ever
met before.

They drained the bottle between them—foolish, she
thought, on a work night, but after the first sip she was
past caring—and she made some coffee and they took
it through to the sitting room.

Was it that? Returning to the scene of the crime? Or
was it the bubbly? She didn't know, but when at last he
looked at his watch and got to his feet, she followed him
to the door and he turned and took her in his arms and
hugged her briefly.

'Thank you, Daisy. You did amazingly well today. And you've been really helpful over all this kitchen planning nonsense. I couldn't have done it without you, I wouldn't have thought of half those points.'

'You're welcome. I have just done it, so I know what the pitfalls are. And thank *you*, anyway. You bought the dinner—again. And you shared the bubbly.'

His mouth twitched into a smile. 'But I stole your brains. Fair exchange.'

He had. Stolen her brains. All of them. If he hadn't, she wouldn't have gone up on tiptoe and kissed him, touching her lips lightly to the corner of that smiling mouth, the slight rasp of stubble on his lean, male cheek making them tingle. She wouldn't have turned her head so that their lips collided.

And when he groaned and slid his arms around her, she wouldn't have curled hers around his neck and threaded her fingers through his soft, silky hair and given him her mouth.

He took it with a low moan, sipping and tasting and coaxing, and by the time he lifted his head she was beyond coherent thought.

'Daisy, I have to go,' he said, his voice a little roughened.

No! Stay. Please stay. Make love to me.

Their eyes locked, and he let out a shaky sigh. 'Don't,' he whispered soundlessly.

'Don't what?' she croaked, wondering for a hideous second if she could have said it out loud.

'Don't look at me like that.'

Her heart stuttered. 'Like what?' she whispered.

'Like *that*,' he said fervently, cradling her cheek in his palm, his thumb tracing her cheekbone. 'As if—oh, hell, this is such a lousy idea,' he muttered as his mouth found hers again, and she went up on tiptoe and opened her mouth to him and whimpered as he took it in a kiss so hungry, so urgent, so fiercely needy that it rocked her world.

'Daisy...!'

The groan tore through him, echoing in her body, ricocheting around inside it and unsettling all her fragile resolve.

She wanted him. It was sheer lunacy, but he was perfect, everything she'd ever wanted in a man, and she needed him *so much*...

'Ben...'

He lifted his head and searched her eyes, his own almost black with this incredible need that seemed to have sprung up out of nowhere and caught them both in its grip.

She moved away a fraction, to give him a chance, and waited, her hand held out to him. For a breathless, endless age he stood there, those dark eyes trapping hers, and then, just when she thought he was going, he lifted his hand, threaded his fingers through hers and locked them tight.

She led him upstairs to her bedroom on legs that could hardly support her weight.

Her case was still lying on the floor, there was a pile of clean underwear on the top of the chest of drawers and her work clothes were scattered all over the carpet where she'd dropped them, but they picked their way through the chaos to the bed, and then he turned her into his arms and brushed his lips lightly over hers.

His eyes were serious. 'Are you sure you want to do this?'

Sure? Not really. Want? Absolutely. It was the

craziest thing she'd done in years, but if she couldn't hold him, touch him, feel him—

She nodded, and he slid his wallet out of his pocket and pulled a little foil packet out and put it on the side. Her lids fluttered closed. He wasn't going. He was going to stay, going to make love to her.

And how. His fingers gathered up the hem of her top and drew it carefully over her head, his breath catching as he looked down at her, and she was glad she'd washed her favourite bra.

The clip gave to the touch of his hand, and then her breasts were spilling into his hands, and with a deep groan he ducked his head and grazed his lips over the soft, sweet flesh he'd exposed.

He didn't know what he was doing here. He was past caring, past thinking rationally. He just knew he needed Daisy as he'd never needed any woman, and if he didn't have her in the next few minutes, he was going to explode.

And he had a feeling it was mutual.

Her eyes were wild, her soft, sweet lips parted, her head tipped back as he suckled deeply on first one taut, pebbled nipple and then the other.

'Ben…!'

'I'm right here, Daisy,' he grated, his breath heaving, his heart trying to escape from his chest, and her hands were on him, pulling his shirt out and flattening her palms against his ribcage, gasping as he tugged down the zip of her jeans and eased them over the ripe, sweet swell of her hips so he could cup her bottom and drag her up against him.

Oh, lord, she was going to go up in flames! His skin was hot, taut over the muscles beneath. She wanted more, wanted to feel the rest of him, wanted to touch him, hold him, look at him, but her fingers were struggling with his belt, and she was whimpering with frustration. If she couldn't get his belt undone—

He swatted her hands aside gently and ripped the shirt off, dealt with the belt and the stud and the zip and shucked the lot in one hasty and desperate movement, and her legs buckled.

She gasped as he pulled her back into his arms and their bodies came firmly into contact from top to toe. Well, knee. Her jeans were still there, but not for much longer, apparently. He lifted her as if she weighed nothing, dropped her into the middle of the bed, stripped off her jeans and came down beside her, the condom in his hands.

'Let me,' she said, taking it from him with her trembling, uncoordinated fingers. The first intimate touch of her hands made him suck in his breath in a shuddering groan, and then he was rolling her under him and sinking into her, filling her, and her scream cut through the air.

He shifted up a gear, drove into her and felt her rising to meet him, her body straining against his.

'Ben, please! I need…'

'I'm here,' he growled. 'I'm right with you, Daisy. Come with me—please, come with me.'

He felt her body tighten, heard her breath catch as she bucked against him, and then he was lost in a climax so devastating that he thought he might have died.

As the last shudders faded from their taut, sweat-slicked bodies, he rolled them to their sides, gathered her into his arms and closed his eyes.

He felt in shock. Never before. Not like that. He heard her breathing slow, and then another shudder, a tiny one, almost a sob, ran through her and he cradled her gently against his heart and held her while the last of the emotions roiling through them faded to a more manageable level.

Then, and only then, did he open his eyes and move his head so he could see her face.

It was streaked with tears, her eyes soft and luminous, her mouth swollen and rosy from his kisses, and he brushed his knuckles lightly over her cheek.

'Are you OK?' he murmured.

'I think so. Not sure. If you let me have my brain back, maybe I can work it out?'

It was so ridiculous he started to laugh, and once he started, he couldn't stop. Neither could she, and they lay there all but sobbing with laughter as the last dregs of emotion ebbed away. Then she lifted her hand and touched his face, her fingertips brushing lightly over the tiny cut above his eyebrow.

'That was amazing, Ben,' she said softly, and her eyes were so nakedly revealing he felt guilt tear through him, because he shouldn't have done it, shouldn't have touched her, held her, taken that sweet, precious gift she'd offered.

They were destined for disaster. What the hell had he been thinking about?

He closed his eyes and rolled away from her. 'I need to deal with this,' he said, and headed for the bathroom, leaving her lying there feeling a little foolish and vulnerable in the aftermath of so much raw emotion. She scooted under the quilt and sat up, hugging her knees, waiting for him to come back from the bathroom and tell her it had all been a mistake.

As if she didn't know that!

Or she could get up, put on her dressing gown and go downstairs and clear the dining table.

'Daisy.'

Damn. Too slow.

She looked up, her eyes lingering on his body, making an inventory, storing up the memories. This wouldn't happen again. She knew that. He was about to tell her that, just as soon as he'd pulled on his clothes and that beautiful, perfectly honed body was hidden from her eyes.

Or partly. Dressed only in the jeans, he sat on the edge of the bed and took her hand, pulling it away from its death-grip on the quilt and folding it inside his own.

Here we go, she thought. *The gentle put-down.*

'That was incredible,' he said softly. 'And I want to stay, to make love to you all night, but it isn't going to happen. It can't happen. I'm going home to get a decent night's sleep, and in the morning we'll go to work and act as if nothing's changed, and then afterwards we'll talk about it, OK?'

She swallowed. 'It's OK, Ben, I know it was a mistake.'

His thumb stroked her wrist. 'It was, but we've done it now, and it's changed things, and I don't think we can really just put them back the way they were. We have to find a way to move forwards from this.'

She nodded. They did, but she couldn't imagine how. She didn't know what she wanted, she just knew nothing so special had ever happened to her and she was in no way finished with it, but of course nothing had really changed. It was just different, but it still had no future, and a feeling of impending loss settled over her.

'We'll talk tomorrow,' she agreed. 'I'll cook for you.'

'No. It's Friday tomorrow, isn't it? Damn. I'm at Jane's with Florence, and Jane might have plans to go out. It'll have to be Sunday night, after I've put Florence to bed and come home. We can get a takeaway or something.'

'I can cook, you know,' she said, finding a smile from somewhere.

He smiled back, his eyes troubled and yet tender. 'I'm sure you can. Don't go to a lot of trouble, I don't know how late I'll be. Jane's away for the weekend and I can't leave till she's back.' He sighed softly. 'I have to go now, it's getting really late and if I don't leave I'll end up staying and I don't think that's a good idea, but I'll see you in the morning. Maybe we can grab a coffee.'

He leant over and kissed her, his lips tender and lingering, and then he straightened up, gave her a tiny, slightly sad little smile and then went out, and she lay and listened as he closed her front door behind himself, opened his own, went up the stairs and into his bedroom.

She heard him moving around, then he went still, and she could swear she could hear him breathing on the other side of the wall.

'Goodnight, Daisy,' he said, his voice soft but clear in the quiet.

She didn't answer. She was too busy wondering what the future held. She didn't have a clue, but she was pretty sure she wouldn't like it...

They didn't have time for a coffee on Friday morning, and they didn't have time for lunch, either.

He disappeared off her radar that afternoon to see Florence and reappeared on Sunday night at seven, by which time she'd had plenty of opportunities to think about their relationship and where it was going. And she'd come to exactly no conclusions.

'You look bushed,' she said, letting him in, and he gave a tired laugh and hugged her.

'I am. Florence was exhausted, too, that's why I'm so early. We've had a busy weekend, and she crashed at six, and Jane was back so I thought I'd get away.' He sniffed the air and smiled. 'Something smells tasty.'

'I made a casserole. I just have to heat it up when we're ready.'

'Great. Stick it on now, I'm ravenous. And then maybe we can talk.'

They needed to. There was no way she'd intended to go to bed with him on Thursday night—or any other night, come to that. Her boss, her neighbour—and another divorced father? No way. But that night—that night had been something she'd had no defences against, and she didn't think he had, either, thinking back. And she'd had all weekend to do that.

What to do?

'OK, fire away,' she said after she'd switched the heat on under the casserole.

'You aren't going to make it easy, are you?' he said wryly, meeting the challenge in her eyes.

'I need to know, Ben,' she said softly. 'I need to know where I stand with you. I know we shouldn't have done it, but as you said, we have now. So where do we go from here? I haven't got a clue.'

'I don't know. I've been thinking about it all weekend, and I wondered—maybe if we had some kind of framework,' he suggested.

'What—like rules?'

He felt himself frown. 'I don't like the word rules. Parameters, maybe.'

'Such as?' she asked, trying to be rational because

the idea of never holding him again was hard to take, however sensible it might be.

'Separate compartments,' he said honestly. 'I have to keep Florence out of my private life, for everybody's sake. You won't ever see her—well, not in any relationship context, anyway. As far as Florence is concerned, you'll be my neighbour. That's all. The lady next door. Not Aunty Daisy. But she isn't what this is all about. This is about two consenting adults who've both been hurt in the past, having a relationship with clearly understood boundaries, and Florence doesn't come into it at all.'

She was relieved about that, but in another way gutted, because there was a quantum leap from what he was offering her now and the way she was starting to feel about him. That little flicker of hope that maybe, finally, her luck was changing.

Stupid. She knew perfectly well it wasn't. They'd talked about that, about the fact it was going nowhere, long before they'd scrambled their brains and ended up in bed.

'So what are you suggesting?' she asked a little warily. 'We just—' she shrugged '—carry on?'

'If you feel we can. But I don't want anyone knowing about it at work. Not about this. I want them kept utterly separate, to protect both of us when—'

He left it hanging, but she knew what he was saying. When it came to an end, which it would. Of course it would. But maybe not for years. She was only twenty nine. She could afford to take time out to dally with a man who made her feel like no man had ever made her feel before, but not an indefinite amount unless she wanted to give up all hope of having a family of her own one day. And Ben—well, Ben hadn't wanted this. Not with her. Too messy, in so many ways.

Oh, lord. It was all her fault. If only she hadn't kissed him. If only she'd kept her hands to herself, not held them out to him in that blatant invitation—

She shut her eyes. 'I'm sorry. I shouldn't have taken you upstairs.'

'Let's not play the blame game, Daisy,' he said softly. 'I kissed you first, on Monday night. I couldn't help it. And I couldn't help it on Thursday either. I needed you, and I think you needed me. And we still do. Well, I do, anyway. And it *is* about more than just sex, much more, but we can't let it grow into anything dangerous. You just have to understand that this can never be anything other than what we had the other night, no matter how amazing it was. If you can accept that, then we can carry on.'

'As what? Lovers?'

He shrugged. 'If you like. Lovers, friends. It would give us someone to do things with—have dinner, go to the cinema, chill out in front of the telly—just ordinary stuff, but not alone. I'm sick of being alone, Daisy, of having no one to share things with, nobody to tell a joke to or unload on at the end of a rough day. And I would very, very much like to do that with you, but it's your call. If you tell me to go to hell, I'll quite understand, and you don't need to be afraid that it'll affect our relationship at work. I wouldn't do that to you.'

She held his eyes, saw the regret, the need, the sadness, and felt her eyes fill. She was lonely, too, and having someone to share the little things with would be wonderful.

And even though she knew it was the stupidest thing

in the world, the last thing she should be doing, she nodded.

'OK. But only so long as Florence is right out of the picture. I can't lose my heart to another little girl, Ben. I've done it before, and I swore never again. Mike's girls came to us every other weekend, and for holidays. And when he went back to his ex, I lost contact with them. And I vowed never again—not a man with children.'

'Oh, Daisy, I'm sorry,' he said softly. He could see the hurt in her eyes, the wariness, the soul-deep pain the breakup had caused her. 'I had no idea you were in so deep.'

'Oh, yeah,' she said with a brittle laugh. 'So if we're going to do this, well, just keep her away from me, please.'

'I will. So—do we have a deal?'

'What—fun dates, hot sex and no complications?'

He winced. 'Daisy, don't,' he said softly, but she wasn't in the mood to be toyed with.

'It's the truth, Ben. If we can't have anything else, then let's for God's sake have that.'

'OK,' he said softly, after a silence that had stretched on altogether too long. 'Fun dates, hot sex and no complications. And one more rule. No using the "L" word.'

She swallowed, nodded, then tried to smile. 'Done,' she said. 'So—is eating a complication, or a fun date? Because I'm starving and that casserole must be warmed through by now.'

He started to laugh, then pulled her gently into his arms and hugged her close. 'Oh, Daisy. I'm starving, too, and it smells fantastic. Actually, I've got an idea. Can we take it with us next door? I've got one or two things I have to do, and I've got a nice bottle of wine in the fridge and half an apple pie.'

'Home-made?'

He winced. 'Yes. By me and Florence, so it's not amazingly elegant, but it's tasty.'

She smiled at him. 'Tasty sounds good. Lead the way.'

They ended up in his bed.

Not then, not until they'd eaten the casserole on their knees in the sitting room—the only room apart from his bedroom that was in any way in order, if you didn't count the dangling ceiling paper.

He opened the wine he'd had chilling and poured it into champagne flutes, 'All I seem to have left,' he told her wryly, and they toasted his house, and the plumber's health, which made her laugh.

And then, when they'd eaten her casserole and the endearingly inelegant and tasty apple pie, he pulled her to her feet.

'Come to bed,' he said softly, and her breath lodged in her throat as she followed him up the stairs and into his room. He undressed her slowly, his hands sure and gentle, but then she met his eyes and saw the fire blazing in them and realised he was hanging by a thread, holding onto his control so he didn't rush her.

He didn't need to bother, but it was an interesting notion. She returned the favour, unbuttoning his shirt with agonising slowness, driving him to fever pitch. She slid the shirt off his shoulders, and as it fell to the floor, she looked past his shoulder to the bedside table and saw the picture.

A little girl with a tumble of dark curls, a tiny turned-up nose and laughing eyes.

Her father's eyes.

She turned her head back and unfastened his belt, then the stud of his jeans, then the zip, tooth by tooth.

Florence was nothing to do with them. This was about them, not her. Fun dates, hot sex and no complications, remember, Daisy? And absolutely no 'L' word.

Taking care not to look at the photo again, she moved into his arms and lifted up her face to his kiss.

She didn't stay.

'The plumber's coming at seven thirty tomorrow,' he reminded her, 'so I need to empty the airing cupboard and sort some stuff out.'

She wanted him to ask her to stay, wanted to tell him she'd help him sort it out in the morning, they could do it together, but that was crazy, and she was still trying not to let herself fall for him. And she certainly wasn't going to beg for crumbs.

'That's fine, I've got things to do as well. Feel free to use my bathroom while yours is out of action,' she offered instead, and he nodded his thanks and dropped a slow, lingering kiss on her lips as she left.

'No, no, no,' he groaned, dragging himself away. 'I have to get on. I'll see you tomorrow at work.' She nodded, and he kissed her again.

'Sleep tight,' he murmured as he let her out, and she went home and made a cup of tea and took it to bed, reading her book and listening to the sound of him shifting things around next door, emptying the airing cupboard and moving the boxes off the landing, and she lay there and tried not to feel cheated.

'Oh, stop it! You knew the rules,' she reminded herself, and clearly spending the night with her came under the heading of complications. She would soon get used to the routine.

And as routines went, it sounded pretty straightforward. If she was in, and he was in, they'd see each other. If not, they wouldn't.

Wednesday evenings with Florence, he'd told her, were utterly sacrosanct, and from Friday to Sunday nights he would have her to stay, once the house was ready, but until then he'd stay with his ex at the weekends, as he had this weekend.

She tried not to imagine them together. It had been plaguing her all weekend, but he said she'd been away, so they couldn't have spent the weekend in a passionate clinch. Unless he'd lied? He'd seemed keen enough to make love to her after supper, but he hadn't wanted her to stay the night, and her old insecurities came back to haunt her.

Was monogamy one of the rules?

Not that she was about to ask, but it was hard telling herself it was none of her business, because for all they had very strict rules, that was surely one of them?

It hadn't been for Mike. He'd been sleeping with his wife off and on the whole time they'd been together, she'd eventually discovered. And he wasn't Mike, she reminded herself fiercely.

Whatever, on Wednesday, Friday and Saturday evenings he'd have Florence, and on all the others he'd be free—free, and ready for some adult conversation and recreation. Especially the recreation, she thought with a twinge of sadness.

And that was all she wanted from him, she reminded herself sharply. No complications, no painful, heart-wrenching involvement with little children who'd been so easy to slot into her life. No 'L' word. She didn't want declarations of undying love, like she'd had from Mike, followed by the inevitable excuses and gradually cool-

ing and then the bombshell, just when the children had
started calling her Mummy Daisy.

She turned over and thumped the pillow, blinking
away the tears. It still hurt so much to think about.
Two years! Two years she'd been with him, living with
him, giving him everything she had of herself, and he'd
thrown it back in her face. And the stupid thing was,
she'd *known* something was wrong. She just hadn't
known what.

No, she didn't need another relationship like that to
suck her dry. Once was enough, for any woman.She
propped herself up and looked at the clock. Midnight.
Too late to phone Amy in Crete. She'd be back on
Wednesday. She'd talk to her then, get a little sensible
perspective on it. God knows she could do with some.

And in the meantime, she needed sleep.She flopped
back down onto the pillows, stared at the ceiling and
finally drifted off, the picture of Florence on his bedside table haunting her dreams.

CHAPTER FIVE

THE plumber arrived on the dot the next morning, and Daisy bumped into him on her way to the hospital a few minutes later.

'He's got his work cut out with this one,' Steve said, jerking his head towards the house, and she laughed.

'Tell me about it. Look after him for me, won't you, Steve?'

'Like that, is it?'

She rolled her eyes. 'He's my boss. I don't want to be in trouble because my plumber takes the mick out of him with the bill.'

'I wouldn't do that, Daisy, you know that,' he said. 'Besides, the wife's due in a few weeks. Don't want to upset the delivery driver!'

'No, you don't,' she said with a grin, and left him to get on. She met up with Ben in the antenatal clinic later in the day and relayed the conversation.

'I'll get the staff to look out for her. What's her name?'

Daisy shrugged. 'Mrs Steve?' she offered, and he sighed and smiled.

'I'll ask him. With any luck she won't need us. I thought Evan was on with me this afternoon?'

'He was, but he's been called to the labour ward, so he thought you might want me.'

Unfortunate choice of words. She felt herself colour, but Ben just smiled, one eyebrow tweaking a fraction, and stuck to the script.

'Good. Could you give me a hand? It's a bit hectic.'

'Sure.'

She was out in the waiting room calling for her next patient when a woman caught her eye and all her antennae went on red alert. She didn't like the look of her at all.

Pale and sweating, she was obviously in pain, and she was waiting to be assessed when Daisy spotted her. Veering away from her next patient, she asked her who she was, picked up her notes and took her into her room to examine her.

She said she'd come in because she thought she was in labour, but Daisy didn't think she was. Her abdomen was rigid, her pulse was raised, her blood pressure was falling and even though she had no external signs of bleeding, Daisy had a thoroughly bad feeling about her.

'I'm just going to get Mr Walker to look at you, Debbie,' she said with a smile, and leaving the door open and the midwife in attendance, she went in search of Ben.

'Excuse me, could I borrow you for a moment?' she said calmly, and he turned from his patient and met her eyes.

'Can it wait a minute?'

'I don't think so, no.'

He gave a curt nod and joined her outside the door a moment later, one eyebrow raised in enquiry.

'Placental abruption, 34 weeks,' she said succinctly, and he wasted no time.

'Call Theatre, get Evan in there if he's free yet, if not we'll do it. Where is she?'

'Cubicle 2. Her name's Debbie Haynes.'

She paged Evan, discovered he was still up to his eyes with a tricky delivery and went to tell Ben. By the time she got there Debbie was on a trolley and heading for the lifts, phoning her husband en route, and Ben was with her putting a line in as they moved. He waved her over, and she ran and joined them as the lift doors closed.

'Good call. Can you assist?'

'What about the clinic?'

'It'll run late,' he said candidly.

'OK.' She smiled at the woman. 'It's all right, Debbie, you're in safe hands.'

Normally, it would have been a platitude. This time she meant it—assuming they were in time.

She had a general anaesthetic, because time was of the essence, and even though Daisy thought she'd seen him do a section fast before, it was nothing on this. Like the well-oiled machine that it was, the team had sprung into action at her call and were ready for them. A runner with blood was on the way, a SCBU crib was in the room and an army of neonatal specialists descended on them, just in time to receive the dark, floppy baby from Ben's hands.

He swore softly, but there was no time to worry about the baby when the mother was bleeding out. He dealt with the placenta, then held a pressure pack firmly against the site while the drugs worked to contract her uterus, and gradually her blood pressure picked up.

And then, out of the blue, she arrested.

Ben swore again and looked at Daisy. She had the

paddles in her hands already, the pads stuck on, the defibrillator charging.

'Clear,' she said, and he let go of the pressure packs and stepped back. Debbie arched off the table, and their eyes all locked on the monitor.

'OK, we've got her back,' the anaesthetist said, and in the background they heard the thin, mewling cry of a newborn baby.

An audible sigh of relief filled the room as the tension was released.

Ben put the pressure back on and shut his eyes briefly, and when he opened them they were brighter than she'd ever seen them. 'OK, let's make sure this bleeding's sorted and then close,' he said matter-of-factly. 'Sounds like Debbie's got a baby to meet.'

'Well spotted.'

'It was pretty obvious.'

'No. You were observant,' he said, giving praise where it was due—something he was sure Evan didn't bother with. 'She was going downhill fast, and you spotted her in the nick of time. Thank God she had the sense to come to the hospital for a check-up and didn't just wait and see. It saved her life, not to mention the baby's.'

'No, you saved both of them,' she said quietly. 'I've never seen a section done so fast.'

Nor had he. 'It's not the neatest.'

'It didn't need to be neat. It needed to save two lives, and you did it. Thank God you were there. And anyway, it *was* neat. You wouldn't let it be anything else.'

'Rumbled.' He smiled down at her and dropped the last set of notes on top of the pile. 'What are you doing now?' he asked as they left the clinic.

'Going home,' she told him wearily. The clinic was finished—well over time, due to their abrupt departure with the emergency, but that was the nature of obstetrics. Some things—some babies—couldn't wait.

His voice was a low murmur. 'Fancy celebrating?'

'Debbie's baby?'

'Debbie's baby, my first week in a new job—us?'

'I thought there wasn't an "us"?' she said quietly.

'Of course there's an "us".'

There was. Of course there was, he was right, but there wasn't really supposed to be.

'There's a pub in Woodbridge,' he suggested. 'We could try that.'

Rather than go public in their own patch?

'Sounds good,' she said.

'I'll book a table, then. Is it OK if I come round and have a shower before we go out?'

'Of course it is.'

Except they ended up sharing the shower, and he had to call the pub and move their reservation.

They went in his car, which was, of course, a much nicer car than hers, and she guessed he'd had it since before the divorce. She settled back against the leather upholstery and sighed. 'Nice,' she said, and he laughed.

'Yes. Luckily I managed to keep Jane's hands off it. She doesn't like automatics.'

She found herself speculating again about their weekends. Speculating too hard, apparently, because he reached across and took her hand.

'What's the matter?'

'I was just thinking about your wife.'

'Ex-wife. What about her?'

She shrugged. 'I know it's stupid, and it's none of my business, but—when you stay there, at the weekends…'

He slowed abruptly, hitched up on the kerb and cut the engine. 'No way,' he said firmly, sounding appalled.

'Did you seriously imagine—hell, Daisy! You think I'm *sleeping* with her?'

'Well, it wouldn't be that unreasonable, would it?' she said, trying not to let her insecurities show. 'I mean, it's not as if you haven't done it before.'

'Daisy, it's over!' he said, even more firmly, and he took her hand and wrapped it in both of his. 'Jane and I are finished. We hardly even started. We never really loved each other, and the only reason I have anything to do with her is for Florence. Believe me, there is no chance of us ever having anything to do with each other ever again, not in a personal way. Besides, I've got a sneaking suspicion her old flame might be on the scene.'

'Really? Does Florence know?'

'Not as far as I'm aware. She shouldn't. Jane knows that and she's promised she'll keep any relationships discreet. Not that it would be hard, if it is him, because he's in the army and he's away a lot of the time. And trust me, when he is, it's no part of my duties to fill his shoes. I've tried that once before, and Florence was the result.'

'They were still together?'

'No. She was on the rebound from him, and very far from over him. I was there. She got pregnant. End of story.'

Yikes. That was a bit of an info-dump she hadn't expected, and she filed it away to think about later and told herself to relax. 'Sorry. I was just—I mean—we didn't specify anything in the rules about monogamy...'

'Daisy, there aren't any rules!' he said, his thumb grazing the back of her hand gently. 'Not really. We're making it up as we go along, but—absolutely, monogamy is key. I'm not and never have been promiscuous, and I don't intend to start now. You're the best thing that's happened to me for years, and I'm not going to sacrifice what I have with you by revisiting a relationship that was a disaster from start to finish!'

She stared at him, and then started to smile. 'I'm the best thing that's happened to you for years?'

'Without doubt, and with the exception only of Florence. And as you know, she has to come first.'

'Of course she does. I wouldn't want it any other way. I couldn't respect you if you felt any different—and for what it's worth, you're the best thing that's happened to me, too.'

Their eyes locked, and he gave a soft sigh and leaned over and kissed her gently on the lips.

'Bless you,' he said quietly. 'You're a sweetheart. I'm so sorry it can't be more than this. You deserve so much more, and I just can't give it to you, but I'll never lie to you. That much I can give you.'

She touched his cheek. 'That's all I want. I'm not really ready for more yet myself, and I'd rather have this than nothing,' she told him honestly, and wondered how long she'd feel like that. A year? Two? Ten?

Forever?

She felt her future drain away, subjugated to the love of this man, and she straightened up in her seat and looked ahead. Love? Oh, God, no. The 'L' word was banned!

'We'll be late,' she said, and he put the car in gear and pulled away, while she sat there and contemplated the fact that while she'd been keeping her head focussed on the 'no complications' part of the deal, her heart had apparently had other ideas.

She was in love with him, and it was going nowhere, and all of a sudden she wanted to cry.

Clare Griffiths, their pre-eclampsia patient Ben had

delivered on his first day, was improving rapidly and now spent all her days sitting by her little son in SCBU, watching over him as he slowly grew stronger. They bumped into each other in the café on Wednesday, and Clare bought her a coffee.

'Just to say thank you, although it seems a pretty pathetic thank-you for all you did.'

'I didn't do anything special,' Daisy protested, but Clare shook her head.

'It may not have felt special to you, but to me—you just took the time to talk to me, to explain what was happening, and Mr Walker—well, he was brilliant. So quick, so decisive, and I just—well, I felt safe with both of you looking after me, so thank you.'

'My pleasure,' she said, touched by Clare's words. 'I'll pass that on to him.'

'Oh, I've already told him. He thinks you're special, too.'

'Does he?' Daisy was startled, amazed that he'd discussed their private feelings with a patient, but Clare just smiled.

'Oh, yes. He said so. He said he was very lucky to have you working with him, and that you were excellent.'

She felt a little wash of relief. Of course he was praising her and backing her up to the patients. She was a member of his team. What else would he do? But she still felt a little glow of pleasure to know that he'd done it.

'Well, you're looking a lot better than, what—ten days ago?' she said, changing the subject swiftly. Ten? Was that all it was since she'd met Ben? Amazing. 'So, tell me all about Thomas. How's he doing?'

'Really well. Why don't you come and see him on

your way back?' she asked, and Daisy hesitated for a second and then folded.

'Do you know what? I'd love to,' she said with a smile, and they walked in to find Ben there, standing by the crib chatting to one of the nurses as he looked down at young Thomas Griffiths with a tender smile on his face. He glanced up as they approached and his smile widened.

'Clare—hi. Hello, Daisy. Come to see Thomas?'

'I have. I thought I'd play hooky for a moment as it's quiet. Is that OK?'

'Of course it's OK. He's looking good, Clare, isn't he?'

'He is. I'm just about to get him out and feed him. Want to give him to me? I know you're itching for a cuddle.'

He chuckled. 'Sit down, I'll get him out for you.'

He snapped on gloves and reached into the incubator, juggling the tubes and wires with careful, gentle hands while the nurse supported their weight, and little Thomas lay there cradled securely, fast asleep in Ben's outspread fingers like a tiny doll.

'There you go, little man,' he murmured. 'Here's Mummy.'

He settled the tiny baby gently in Clare's arms, pausing to run a gentle finger over his soft, transparent cheek, and Daisy felt a huge lump in her throat. She'd seen him in Theatre with slippery little babies in his capable hands, passing them swiftly to the midwife— very swiftly, in Debbie's case. She'd seen him deliver Thomas a little more slowly, but no less carefully. She'd seen him in the delivery rooms wielding the forceps or Ventouse with ludicrous ease and then handing the babies over to their mothers as if it was all in a day's work—which of course it was.

But here he was for no good reason, sneaking a cuddle with little Thomas, his big, strong hands cradling a tiny infant with such exquisite gentleness that she felt her eyes fill.

Was he like this with Florence? Yes, of course he was. He'd be a fantastic father, devoted, patient, gentle—Florence was a lucky little girl.

'He's beautiful, Clare,' she told her softly. She was aching to hold him, but he didn't need over-handling, and besides, they had work to do, so they left her feeding him and headed back to the ward.

'You know she thinks you walk on water,' she said to him as they went, and he chuckled.

'We aim to please,' he said. 'She's looking good, isn't she?'

'Very. And the baby's gorgeous.'

'Utterly. Why do you think I went up there? Although having said that, I think they're all gorgeous. I was talking to Debbie's baby's nurse a minute or so before you came in. He's doing well, too, and she seems to be getting there, thanks to you. He's much stronger than Clare's baby, but even so, that was too close for comfort.'

'So where are you going now?'

'Paperwork—unless there are any deliveries that need me? Any more babies I can legitimately cuddle?'

'You're just a softie under that big tough Yorkshire front, aren't you?' she said to cover her own emotions, and he laughed.

'Absolutely. Why do you think I do the job? Right, I've got a huge pile of paperwork needing my attention, then I'm off to pick up Florence, talking of babies.' He lowered his voice. 'What are you doing later?'

'Nothing. Well, that's a slight exaggeration. I'm on call to the labour ward from nine tomorrow, so I'll probably have an early night. If it's anything like last time, it'll be hellish.'

'I hope not.'

'Don't rely on it. I probably won't get away till late.'

He nodded acknowledgement, then with a rueful grin he headed for the mountain of paperwork in the office, and she went home. Amy was back, and she had so much to tell her. She couldn't believe so much had happened since Laura's hen weekend, and she needed Amy's take on it.

And at some point in the future, she was sure, she'd need Amy's support.

Not that she was going to let herself think about that now. For now, she was happy just to be happy, and when it was over—well, she'd worry about that when the time came.

'Are you home? I've got lots to tell you.'

'Sounds exciting. Bring some food.'

She raided her fridge and freezer, drove round to Amy's house and let herself in, hugging her friend and standing back to look at her.

'Wow, you're brown! So how was Crete? Was it gorgeous?'

'Utterly fabulous. What's in the bag? I'm famished.'

'Pizza and salad.'

'Great. Stick it in the oven and tell me whatever it is you have to tell me. And you can tell me all about the new consultant, as well. Forewarned is forearmed and all that!'

'Ah. Yes, well, it's one and the same thing, really,' she admitted, and Amy's eyes narrowed.

'I'm—um—seeing him?'

'What!'

'Off the record.'

Amy plopped down on a stool at her breakfast bar and gaped. 'So—come on, tell me more! What's he like? And how on earth did this happen?'

'His ceiling fell down?' she offered, and Amy's eyes widened. 'He's also my new neighbour. Did I mention that?'

'No, you damn well didn't! Come on, you can't stop there!'

So she told her—all of it, only keeping back the intimate details because they belonged solely to her and Ben, but leaving Amy in no doubt. And then she delivered the punch line.

'He's got a *daughter*?'

'Yup. That's the catch. She comes first, last and everything in between. No relationships that involve her, he says he's never getting married again, at least not while she's so vulnerable, and to be honest he sounds so adamant about it I don't think he'll ever go there again. So there we have it—the perfect man, utterly ruined by a disastrous marriage and an even worse divorce, reading between the lines.'

'And you love him.'

She rolled her eyes. 'Oh, God, is it so obvious?'

'Well, to me it is, but you *are* spilling your guts so it's not hard to work out. How does he feel?'

She swallowed. 'He says I'm the best thing to happen to him for years.'

'Except his daughter.'

'Except his daughter. How did you guess? But that's

fine. I have no issues with him being a good father. How could I? And anyway, that's not what it's about.'

'No. Well, be careful,' Amy said, and peered past her at the oven. 'So how's the pizza?'

'Doing better than the washing. You might want to stop bullying me for the gory details and press the start button.'

She didn't get her early night in the end.

She and Amy ended up watching a movie until midnight, and by the time she got home Ben's lights were out and she slipped quietly into the house and went straight to bed.

And of course she overslept, woken only by Ben phoning her to say he'd knocked on her door to use the bathroom but couldn't get an answer and was she at home?

She ran down, tripping over the cat, and limped to the door to let him in. 'Sorry, a friend of mine got back from her holiday yesterday and we ended up watching a movie and I didn't get home till late, and then the cat hijacked the bed so I overslept.'

'So why are you limping?'

'I just fell over her. She has this knack on the stairs.'

'The friend?'

'No, the cat,' she snapped, and he started to laugh, then thought better of it.

'Oh, dear,' he chuckled, and pulled her into his arms. 'You're really not a morning person, are you, sweetheart?' he said, and it was on the tip of her tongue to suggest that if he stayed the night he'd have a better chance of judging that, but she thought better of it. No bickering. That was probably in the rules, too.

'I'll make tea. You shower first,' she told him, letting

him go reluctantly, and headed for the kettle, feeding the cat on the way. She could hear him in the shower overhead, and the need to be near him was just too great.

She walked into the bathroom, dropped her pyjamas on the floor and stepped into the cubicle behind him, sliding her arms around his waist and resting her cheek against his back.

Heat shot through him, and he turned, tilting her head up to his and taking her mouth hungrily. How could he want her so fast? One touch, one kiss and he was ready—

'We can't,' he said, dragging his mouth away.

'No time?'

'No condoms.'

She gave an impish smile. 'So we improvise,' she said, and he felt her hand curl round him. The breath whooshed out of him, and he nudged her knees apart, slid his hand up her thigh and found the crucial spot with unerring accuracy. Her eyes widened, her mouth dropped open and he cursed his lack of foresight as she climaxed for him.

'That's just for now,' he promised, and then gritted his teeth and bit down on the groan as she took him over the edge.

The labour ward, as she'd predicted, was hectic.

Amy was working there, and she never called for help unless it was essential, but midway through the morning she paged for assistance.

Daisy found her in a delivery room, with a labouring woman lying on the bed and her partner rubbing her back with a worried expression on his face.

'What's up?' she asked softly.

'The baby's back-to-back, and I can't shift it. Mum's

knackered, the baby's big, she's been in labour for hours and I think we might need a more experienced hand. Talk about easing back gently into the job!'

Daisy nodded. She'd used the Ventouse before, but never forceps, and if the baby was very stuck or very high, it might need more than suction to help to shift the head.

'You just want to meet Ben,' she murmured out of earshot, and Amy chuckled.

'Oh, yes. But seriously, we might need him.'

'I'll page him.'

He couldn't have been far away, because he walked in a moment later and winked at her. 'Morning, ladies. What can I do for you?' he asked, and Amy spun round, gave a horrified gasp, stripped off her gloves and fled, leaving Daisy standing there staring after her in astonishment.

'Amy?'

'Amy?'

She turned at the sound of Ben's voice, seeing a much milder version of Amy's shock on his face, and her heart sank. No. This couldn't be the guy who'd broken Amy's heart. Could it?

'Back in a minute,' Ben said to the patient, and they went out into the corridor and stared after her.

'Do you know her?' she asked, dreading the answer, but it wasn't in any way the one she'd expected.

'Yes. She had a relationship with my brother.'

'Your *brother*? So—why did she look at you like that?'

'Because we're identical twins,' he said softly. 'I need to talk to her. Where will she have gone?'

'The emergency stairwell, I'd guess. It's our usual retreat for a crisis.'

'Right. Lead the way—and come with me, if you know her well enough.'

'I do. She's my best friend. And for what it's worth, she's never got over him.'

He said something very quiet and very rude. She'd heard it before, when his ceiling came down—which would indicate the seriousness of this situation and the extent to which he was ruffled.

Not as ruffled as Amy. She was crouched on the bottom step of the stairs, waiting for Daisy, and she sucked in her breath as Ben followed her into the quiet space.

'Amy, it's me, not Matt,' he said softly, and crouching down, he took her hands. 'I'm sorry. I didn't mean to shock you like that. I had no idea you were here or I would have warned you.'

She studied him for a second, and the tension drained out of her, leaving her limp and shaken. 'It's OK, Ben, it's not your fault. It just—I didn't—at first glance I…' She broke off, shook her head. 'It took me by surprise, that's all. I'm OK, really.'

'Are you?' he murmured, and then to Daisy's horror Amy started to cry. Ben swore again and sat down beside her, slinging a solid arm round her and hugging her hard against his side. She burrowed into his chest, and Daisy, helpless, unable to do anything, sat down on the other side of her and waited until Amy's tears stumbled to a halt.

'Sorry,' she mumbled, groping for a tissue in her pocket. Daisy handed her one.

'OK, my love?' she asked softly when Amy had blown her nose and shaken her head as if she was trying to clear it.

She nodded. 'He's—'

'I know. He said.'

She sucked in a shaky breath. 'We ought to get back,' she said. 'My delivery…'

'Don't worry, take your time,' Ben soothed. 'Go and have a cup of tea. We'll find another midwife to help us.'

'No. It's OK, I'll do it. I'd rather. I can't bail on her.'

She got shakily to her feet, and with another hug from Ben, she pulled herself together, swiped the tears from her cheeks and followed them out of the stairwell.

CHAPTER SIX

'Is SHE all right?'

'I think so. I caught up with her later and we talked for a bit. She didn't say a lot—she never does.'

He grunted. 'Nor does Matt. Do you think it's going to be a problem, her working with me?'

'She says not, and I'm inclined to believe her.'

He came up behind her and put his arms round her, resting his chin on her shoulder.

'I think she was just a bit shaken up to see me.' He nuzzled her cheek. 'Do you really want coffee?'

'Not really. I thought you would.' She turned in his arms, fully expecting to see a glint in his eye, but instead there was a curious sadness.

'Do you mind if we just go to bed? It's been a long day.' He'd only just got in, and he'd grabbed something to eat in the hospital, he said, but it was more than that, she sensed.

'Of course I don't mind,' she said softly, going up on tiptoe and kissing him with infinite tenderness.

He stayed that night, making love to her with exquisite care and then holding her in his arms all night, and she wondered if it was something to do with Matt and Amy, or if it was something that had happened with

Florence yesterday. They hadn't really had time to talk, and in any case, he never talked about Florence to her.

Sticking to the rules?

Whatever, it was lovely to have him hold her all night, and to wake up in the morning with a crick in her neck from sleeping on his shoulder with his arm round her and her leg wedged between his powerful thighs.

'I need to move,' she whispered, and he opened his eyes and smiled.

'Thank God for that. I think my arm's going to drop off.'

She laughed softly and shifted out of his way, and he rubbed his arm and winced while she stretched her neck out and sighed with relief, then rolled back to him and propped herself up on her elbows.

'Good grief, what a fuss! Are you all done whinge-ing on about a few pins and needles?' she teased.

He moved faster than a striking cobra. One second she was laughing down at him, the next she was flat on her back with his lean, muscled body sprawled over her and her arms pinned to the bed above her head.

'No! No, I'm sorry, I'm sorry,' she laughed, but he just raised an eyebrow, clamped both her wrists together with one large and inescapable hand and trailed his other hand slowly and tormentingly over her body.

'Too late,' he growled. Last night's thoughtful mood was clearly gone, replaced with a playful lust that was much more in keeping with their rule book, and taking his time, he finished what they'd started.

It was all going like clockwork until the following weekend, when she heard his front door open and close during the course of Saturday morning, and then the sound of little running feet.

It stopped her in her tracks, and she stared at the wall

in horror. No. He'd said she wouldn't be here until the house was finished, but it was nothing like ready for Florence to stay, and nor was she! She wasn't prepared, her defences were down, her emotions far too close to the surface. Why hadn't he *warned* her?

And then her phone rang.

'Daisy, hi, it's me. Look, I'm really sorry, I've had to bring Florence back here. Jane's got a migraine and she needs some peace, so I've come to get my walking boots so we can go out for a bit of a yomp in the woods, then we might come back here. I hope we don't disturb you.'

Disturb? 'She's not a virus,' she said sharply, even though she'd been mentally chastising him for not warning her, and then felt evil for bitching at him. 'Sorry. Thanks for the heads up. I'll keep out of your way.'

'OK. We might see you later.'

'No!' she said, but he'd hung up. So what now? Should she go out? Leave the house and come back after dark? 'Oh, don't be ridiculous, she's just a child, she's not poisonous! Get a grip,' she told herself, and finished the pile of ironing, then made some lunch and went out into the garden and started weeding.

She'd been there half an hour when there was the sound of the back door opening, and Ben's voice saying, 'This is my new garden—or it will be. It's a bit of a jungle.'

'It's very messy,' a childish voice piped, and Daisy's heart turned over. She sounded so like Freya…

'Yes, it is messy, isn't it? Shall we make it tidy?'

'Yes! Me do it, Daddy! Me do it!'

She stayed there, frozen, trowel in hand, listening to the soft rumble of his voice as he talked to Florence. Should she go inside? Say something? Tell him she was there? Or carry on and say nothing? No. He'd hear her then. Would he talk to her?

She stuck the trowel in the ground and brushed off her hands. Maybe she'd just creep inside and pretend—

'Hi.'

She lifted her head and saw Ben leaning over the fence, a tentative half-smile on his face as he searched her eyes. He must be standing on something, she thought, and got stiffly to her feet.

'Hi. How was your walk?'

'Great. We saw lots of bluebells, and a squirrel, and then we had some lunch, and now we're going to clear up the garden. I don't suppose you've got a broom, have you?'

'Sure.'

She found it in the shed and passed it over, waiting for the invitation to meet Florence, hoping it wouldn't come yet longing to see the little girl who was so excitedly helping her daddy clear up the messy garden.

No invitation was forthcoming. Instead he smiled and disappeared behind the fence, and left her standing there staring into space.

'Basket case,' she muttered, heading for the conservatory, and she went inside and put the kettle on. Ten seconds later she got a text from him.

Tea would be nice if you're making one.

She rolled her eyes. Tea, indeed. And no doubt biscuits, and something healthy for Florence. Apple juice? She opened the fridge and found an unopened carton of apple juice, and poured some into a little mug, then made two mugs of tea and put the chocolate biscuits on the tray and took them out.

'Tea's up,' she yelled, and he appeared at the fence,

his little mini-me on his shoulders, both of them grinning happily.

'Daisy, this is Florence. Florence, meet Daisy. She's my neighbour. She has good biscuits.'

Florence giggled and squirmed on his shoulders, and he clamped her legs firmly in his hands and disappeared while Daisy tried to get her breath back and unclamp the hand that was pressed over her mouth.

Why on earth had she done this? She should have refused to make the tea, told him to sling his hook and gone out—or just gone out earlier and let him sort his own broom and refreshments.

He was at her gate, letting himself in and holding Florence by the hand. She had one arm round his leg, which was obviously making walking difficult, but he just went slowly and accommodated her as she giggled and hung on, and Daisy's heart squeezed. She was *so* like him!

'We've decided the garden's a bit much for us,' he said with a wry grin. 'We think it needs a gardener.'

'I think it needs a chainsaw and a gang of landscapers,' she said drily, unfairly angry that he'd had to catch her outside and trap her like this.

'Sounds like a plan, and then we'll have a lovely garden for you, won't we, Florence?'

'I like *this* garden,' Florence said shyly, looking around her with eyes like saucers. 'It's pretty. Look, Daddy, a froggy! Daisy's got a froggy!'

Oh, lord, she was so sweet. Her eyes were like huge blue saucers, and Daisy wanted to scoop her up and hug her. She found her voice.

'Yes, I have, but he's not real.'

He was a hideous little concrete frog she'd found in the flowerbed and been meaning to throw out, but now she was glad she hadn't, because Florence sat down on the path and had an earnest conversation with him that had Daisy desperate to laugh out loud. Either that or cry.

'She's delicious,' she mouthed to Ben, and he nodded, watching her with pride and love in his eyes.

'Froggy wants a biscuit,' she said, and Ben crouched down beside her.

'Does he? He has to say please.'

'Please.'

So 'froggy' had a biscuit, and Ben had a handful, and Daisy watched Florence puggling about in the flower-bed and chatting to the frog and feeding him bits of her biscuit, and she watched Ben watching his little daughter, and all the time she could feel the thin, fragile defences around her heart cracking and crumbling in the gentle onslaught.

'I have to get on, I've got things to do in the house,' she said abruptly. 'Feel free to stay in the garden as long as you like.'

And without another word, she got up and went back inside before the wall around her heart came down in a million pieces...

They disappeared later in the day, and he rang her that night, something he didn't usually do at the weekend.

'Thank you for this afternoon,' he said softly. 'I'm sorry we imposed. I just didn't know what to do with her. I thought the garden would be all right, and it was only when we went out into it I realised how many dangerous things there were out there.'

Namely Florence, as far as she was concerned, with him running a very close second! 'It's fine, don't worry,' she said firmly. 'She was no trouble.'

'But I promised I'd keep her out of your way, and then

we didn't have any milk or any juice for her because I wasn't expecting to be there, and that was really pushing it. I'm sorry. I should have just taken her to the playground or to a café but she was tired after our walk.'

She swallowed.. 'Ben, it's all right, it was only the once. She's just a child. It's fine.'

Except she wasn't just a child. She was the flesh and blood of the man she loved with all her heart, and seeing his little daughter made her all the more real. Seeing them together. Seeing the love between them, the way his eyes never left her.

He was a good father. A brilliant father. Loving, caring, thoughtful, aware of the dangers but happy to let her get well and truly grubby and be a real child. When she'd got bored with the frog she'd climbed all over him and sat on his shoulders, peering down into his eyes and laughing, and she wished she'd had a camera to capture the moment.

Silly. It was nothing to do with her. *Florence* was nothing to do with her. And she needed to remember that. She went to the drawer where she kept her sentimental things, and pulled out the photo of Millie and Freya. She stared at it for a long time, wondering how they were, if they were happy, who they were living with. Mike and his wife, still? Or had she thrown him out again so they had a different mummy for the weekends? She stroked her finger lovingly over the image. They'd be older now, three years older, so they'd be nine and seven.

Gosh. How time passed.

She stuck the photo on the front of the fridge under a magnet, so she'd see it every time she made a cup of tea and got the milk out, and it would remind her of all

the reasons why she was keeping Florence firmly off
limits.

There. Now she'd remember. All she had to do was
make sure Ben did.

The house being in chaos was doing his head in. Not just
because it was messy, but because it meant he couldn't
have Florence there.

And then finally, almost four weeks after the ceiling
fell down, the kitchen was plastered, the house rewired
and the kitchen could go in.

He couldn't wait. Staying at Jane's every weekend
had driven him crazy, and the prospect of doing it for
weekend after weekend was intolerable, he thought as
he packed and set off there yet again. But he had no
choice, not if he wanted to see Florence, and their time
together was so short, so fleeting, and she was growing
like a weed. Her childhood would be gone in the wink
of an eye, and the fact that he was missing so much of
it gutted him.

But he missed his home, too, while he was at Jane's.
He missed having his own things around him—and he
missed spending time with Daisy. And the first thing he
did after he had a shower when he got home on Sunday
night was to go round and see her.

'God, it's so good to be home and get back to normal,' he said, burying his head in her hair and holding
her tight. 'I love her to bits, but Florence can be so de-
manding, and we had to spend the day out because Jane
had a headache again today.'

'Is she ill?'

He laughed and let her go, following her into the
sitting room and settling down on the sofa with her in
his arms. 'Not really. I'm sure she wasn't feeling great,

but I took Florence out for hours so she could rest, and when I got back she was on the phone and looked fine. The moment she saw me she had a relapse, curiously.'

'Looking for sympathy?'

'I don't know what she was looking for, but she won't get it. Not from me, anyway. Not in my job description.'

'So you left.'

'After I'd fed and bathed Florence and put her to bed and read her a story. It was the princess and the frog tonight—again. She's got frogs on the brain now, thanks to you,' he told her, tapping her on the nose.

She smiled. 'Sorry,' she said, although she wasn't sorry for him at all for having such a delicious little daughter, and then she reminded herself that she wasn't going to think about Florence. Hard, when Ben was talking about his precious little mite, but if she wasn't careful she'd end up hurt again.

And more to the point, because she was the most vulnerable one, so might Florence.

'Have you eaten?' she asked him, changing the subject.

He gave a hollow laugh. 'If you count fish fingers and peas.'

'Doesn't sound as if you do.'

'Don't worry, I'm fine. I had lunch.'

'What?'

He shrugged. 'A sandwich?'

'I know you and your sandwiches. You had half a cheese sandwich and a banana on Friday, and I don't think you finished the banana,' she reminded him. 'Fancy scrambled eggs on toast?'

'That would be amazing,' he groaned, and she left him slouched on the sofa while she went to make it. When she came back, he was asleep, but she woke him up to eat it, then cleared away, turned off the television and took him up to bed.

Tabitha was curled up in the middle of it, and gave him a disgusted look as she jumped down and stalked off.

'I don't think she likes me stealing you,' he said with a grin, but Daisy just laughed and hugged him.

'Tough,' she said, lifting her face up to his. 'I've missed you. It's been a long weekend.'

His smile was tender. 'It has. Much too long.'

He tunnelled his fingers through her hair, sighed in contentment and rested his forehead on hers. 'Oh, I'm so tired. Florence was really on form today. Can I sleep in my clothes, please?' he asked, and stifled a huge yawn.

She laughed, undressed him and toppled him into bed, then snuggled in beside him and fell asleep. It was the first time they'd gone to bed without making love, and there was something settled and homely and *right* about it.

And if she hadn't been tired, if it hadn't been late, if she'd been thinking clearly, it probably would have worried her. But it didn't. Instead she curled into his side, her hand over his heart, and went to sleep.

Clare Griffiths took her baby home that week, and came to say goodbye. He was still small, but he was a little fighter and he was a lot bigger than he had been and the paediatricians were happy to let him go home.

Ben sneaked a cuddle—a proper one this time, and it stopped Daisy in her tracks. He looked so comfortable and at home with Thomas in his arms, as of course he would. He handled babies all day, he'd had Florence to practise on, and it seemed that every time she looked up these days he had a baby in his arms. Her emotions were in uproar when he looked up and met her eyes and she thought, *What if that was our baby?*

No! Was she going *mad*? Fun dates, hot sex and no complications, remember? Not *babies*! They were *definitely* a complication!

'Here—he wants to say thank you to you, Daisy,' Ben said with a smile, and passed her the tiny infant.

Oh, heavens. As he'd settled his head in the crook of her arm, his fingers had brushed her breast, and it felt so intimate, so—realistic? As if Thomas was theirs, and he'd handed him over for a feed.

Sudden tears scalded her eyes, and she handed him back, gave Clare a hug and said a hasty goodbye and excused herself, disappearing onto the gynae ward to check the post-ops and make sure they didn't need their pain relief adjusted, but Evan had already done it and she wasn't needed.

Pity. She could have done with a good, solid reason to stay out of Ben's way. He was sneaking up on her blind side and it was all Florence's fault for being so utterly delicious. She'd managed to keep children off her radar since Mike, and the babies at work had been just that—babies at work. But not now. Not since Florence. Now they were real, tiny little children, part of a family, and each and every one seemed to tear a hole in her heart.

Florence, quite by chance, had found the chink in Daisy's armour, and the crack just kept getting wider and wider.

By the next weekend, Steve's wife still hadn't had her baby, and so Ben had a kitchen—or at least enough of it to have Florence to stay. He'd stayed up late on two nights painting her bedroom—nothing special, just a

quick coat of emulsion over the wallpaper to freshen
it up for now, and some curtains and bedding from the
local DIY store, and he showed it off to Daisy when he'd
finished on Thursday night.

'So what do you think?'

'Wow! It looks tons better. Well done,' she said, looking around it critically and nodding.

'Do you think she'll like it?'

Daisy just laughed at him softly. 'Of course she'll
like it, Ben. It's pink. Little girls all love pink.'

He grinned. 'So the woman in the shop told me.
I asked—just to be sure—and she said I couldn't go
wrong with that.'

'You haven't. And the curtains and bedding are
lovely.'

'Well, they'll do for now. I looked for something with
frogs on, but they were a bit thin on the ground.'

Daisy chuckled. 'Don't worry. I expect she'll grow
out of frogs soon.'

He rolled his eyes. 'I live in hope. There's only so
many times I can read her *The Princess And The Frog*
without losing my marbles, but it makes a change from
Goldilocks, I suppose.'

Daisy made a mental note to look out for frog books,
because Florence's birthday was coming up at the end
of June, just a few weeks away—and then she realised
what she was doing. Stupid. So stupid.

'What?' Ben asked, looking at her thoughtfully, and
she shrugged and smiled.

'Nothing. Just remembered something I have to do,'
she lied, and vowed to put frogs and books and little
girls right out of her mind before she lost it completely.
'I should go and get on.'

'Really? Can't I talk you into staying? I was hoping

we could look at colour schemes, and maybe have a glass of wine,' he said softly, but his eyes were searching hers, and he was too astute to miss the emotions coursing through her, and he sighed before she could answer.

'Daisy, I'm sorry. I'm making assumptions—taking you for granted. You go, do whatever it is you have to do. I'll see you tomorrow at work.'

So maybe not that astute. He'd realised she didn't want to be there, just not why. Well, that was fine. She didn't need an in-depth analysis of her emotional weaknesses.

She kissed him goodnight—hovered on the brink of changing her mind, but left anyway, and lay in her bed alone and wished she could find it all a little easier to be sensible and keep her distance.

She'd stay out of the way this weekend, she vowed. No going out into the garden if they were there, no listening through the wall to the sound of childish laughter—Florence's and Ben's—and absolutely no impromptu tea-parties with Froggy in attendance.

And maybe—just maybe—she'd get that wall back up again, brick by brick, to keep them out of her heart...

CHAPTER SEVEN

SHE went to London for the weekend. Laura's fiancé was away for his stag weekend, and she invited Daisy down at the last minute. She went, and spent the whole weekend talking weddings and helping Laura make the favours for the tables.

Just what she didn't need, but it was probably better than listening to Florence and Ben through the wall, and he'd got the garden landscapers coming to make a start, as well, so she couldn't even have retreated to the conservatory for peace and quiet.

She got home on Sunday evening, and almost immediately her phone rang.

She wasn't surprised. His lights had been on and he must have heard her come in. And he was always ready to see her on Sunday evenings, after the undiluted conversation of a not-quite-three-year-old. After spending the weekend listening to Laura panic about the wedding, she was more than ready to see him, too.

'Hi, there. Good weekend?' he asked.

'If you like wedding planning,' she said with a laugh. 'What did Florence think of her bedroom?'

'Oh, she loved it. You were all so right about the pink. So, what are you up to? I've got a bottle of wine in the fridge and a seafood paella on the go. Fancy dinner?'

Of course she did. 'Mmm, paella?' she mused out loud, teasing him. 'Are you trying to bribe me, by any chance?'

'I can only hope,' he said softly, and she could tell he was reaching out to her, trying to undo whatever it was he felt he'd done on Thursday night when she'd left him and come home, and she felt guilty for letting him stew. After all, it wasn't his fault she'd been letting herself get ahead of the game.

Into another game entirely, in fact, but not any more.

'It sounds lovely. Give me ten minutes for a shower.'

She went round and walked straight into his arms.

'I've missed you,' he said, gathering her to his chest and hugging her gently.

'I've missed you, too,' she murmured, and went up on tiptoe and kissed him, and he made a soft sound deep in his throat and threaded his fingers through her hair and kissed her back. Endlessly.

'I've been thinking about Tabitha,' he said when they came up for air.

The cat? Well, that was unexpected. 'I'm flattered,' she said drily. 'What about her?'

He chuckled and kissed her nose. 'She's been alone all weekend, and the landscapers have been trashing her playground. She might feel the need of a bit of company and reassurance, and I feel guilty for stealing you, so why don't we take dinner back to yours?'

She smiled at him, amazed at his thoughtfulness towards the cat who'd done nothing but treat him with disdain.

'You do realise if we take anything fishy round there, she'll be all over us for it?' she warned.

'Maybe I'm trying to bribe *her* to like me?' he said with a chuckle, and she grinned.

'Oh, it'll work. She's a hussy—just so long as there's fish on the plate.'

Tabitha thought it was Christmas.

She mugged their plates, was thoroughly spoiled by Ben and spent the evening with them, snuggled on his lap with her claws in his knee and purring like a diesel engine while Daisy enjoyed having her legs to herself for once, but she didn't get the ultimate reward. There was only so much he was prepared to do to earn Tabitha's love, he said with a smile, and sharing the bed was above and beyond the call of duty, so they shut her out of the bedroom and tuned out her protests.

And yet again, he stayed the night.

He had an interesting case in the antenatal clinic the next afternoon, and he went and tracked Daisy down.

'What do you know about MCMA twins?' he asked, and her eyes widened. He could almost hear the cogs turning and for a second he thought she was going to disappoint him. He should have had more faith.

'OK. MCMA stands for monochorionic monoamniotic—they're identical twins that split at late embryo stage hence share placenta and both foetal membranes, unlike other twins. They're also known as momo or mono twins.'

'Incidence?'

'Tiny. One in a hundred twin pregnancies, maybe?' she tried. 'Stats aren't my best thing.'

'Complications?'

She was surer on this. 'Cord entanglement or compression, twin to twin transfusion, premature delivery and low birthweight.'

'Management?'

'Aggressive,' she said firmly. 'Close supervision, frequent scans, possibly drug therapy from 20 weeks to reduce the level of amniotic fluid. In-patient from 28 weeks with aggressive monitoring by Doppler up to three times a day, and daily scans as well at 30 plus weeks? Guessing now, but elective delivery from 32 weeks or as soon as viable in the event of an earlier emergency?'

'Death rate?'

'High.'

'How high?'

'Lord, what is this, an exam?' she said with a wry laugh. 'Very high. Fifty per cent? Much less with aggressive management?'

'Excellent. You passed.' He grinned at her. 'Want to come and see some on a 3D scan? Mum and Dad are waiting for us.'

Her eyes widened and she felt a little leap of professional excitement. 'You've got MCMAs in the clinic?'

'Yup—and I want you to work with me on their care. She's twenty-eight, first pregnancy, 13 weeks' gestation. The first scan wasn't clear, so she's had a 3D ultrasound and the radiologist's just phoned me with the result. I'm just about to give them the news and I thought you might like to be involved as it could be the only time you get to see them in your career.'

'You thought right. Wow. Shouldn't they be referred to a specialist unit, though?'

'What, and give my brother the satisfaction? Not if I can avoid it. Anyway, I've worked with him in the same department.'

She tilted her head on one side and stared at him, confused. 'Your brother?' she asked blankly.

'Matt's a twin specialist.'

'Ah.' It made sense, as they were twins, and explained

his choice of twin statistics as a cover for her errand on his first day. 'Well, come on, then, what are we waiting for?' she asked impatiently, and he chuckled and led her into the consulting room, introducing her to the patient and her husband, then he brought up the ultrasound images on his computer and swivelled the monitor so they could see it.

'Right, let's start at the beginning, because I don't know how much you know about twins and I want to make sure you understand the baseline, if you like,' he said, and then while Daisy, knowing what was coming, studied the 3D image on the screen, he explained everything she'd just recapped, but slowly, thoroughly and in great detail and without scaring them half to death. Tricky, considering the statistics and the fact that they'd clearly been doing their research.

'Is that the same thing as momo twins?' Melanie Grieves asked, and Ben nodded.

The colour drained from her face, and she grabbed her husband's hand. 'They could—'

She broke off, and Ben gave them an understanding smile.

'OK, first off, I don't want you to panic. I know you will have been trawling the internet, so let's talk it all through, because the stats can look a bit scary until you break them down.'

'Scary? Half of them *die*!' she said, her voice wobbling, and he shook his head.

'Only if they're not monitored properly to keep an eye on the cords and make sure they're not getting tangled or compressed. The next few weeks are probably the most critical, because there's nothing we can do if they get tangled now, but once they've survived to 20 weeks, we can do more, and with aggressive management the odds of surviving rise considerably.'

He went on to explain the management of her pregnancy in detail, and far from being frightened by the intensive nature of the monitoring, she seemed reassured.

'So—where will I be treated?' she asked.

'This is where you get a choice,' he explained. 'It's up to you whether to want to be treated here, locally, or go to a specialist centre in London, and I won't be in the least offended if you choose to do that. All I can promise is that if you stay here with us, I'll do everything I can to make sure that you end up with two healthy, normal babies at the end of your pregnancy.'

'But if I go to a specialist centre, can they do more?'

'Not necessarily. I was working there until I came here, and I do have a special interest, but obviously they deal with more cases as they're a referral centre. The care, however, wouldn't be any different, I'd make sure of that.'

'So are you as good as the consultant there?' Mr Grieves asked, and Ben chuckled. Daisy, on the sidelines, stifled a smile.

'I would have to say yes, but then I am his older brother, by about a minute,' he told them with a grin, and then shocked her. 'We were monoamniotic twins, and we survived, and that was nearly thirty five years ago. Hence our mutual interest.'

'You're momo twins?' Mrs Grieves said, echoing Daisy's incredulous thoughts, and he nodded.

'Yes—and we'd work closely together on your case, so although he might have a little more experience than me, you have to juggle that against the disruption of being treated away from home. In any case the early part of your care would be here, and I'm sure my brother would be happy to review all the scans if I ask him.'

He let that sink in, then added, 'It's a lot to think about. I want you to be scanned every other week for now, and we'll then scan you weekly from 20 to 28 weeks, then admit you to whichever centre you choose for even closer monitoring. Go and think about it, and let us know your decision in the next few days.'

'I want to stay here,' she said firmly. 'I don't want to travel, and if I'm going to have to be an in-patient for weeks, I don't want it to be miles from my family. And I trust you. You've worked there, your interest in the condition is much more than academic, and as you say, your brother will pass anything new on to you. I'd like you to look after me—if you will? If you think it's safe?'

Ben smiled at her and gave a soft laugh. 'Of course I will, Mrs Grieves, and I don't think you'd be any safer there, but I think you should talk it over with your husband.'

'I don't,' he said instantly. 'If she's happy, I'm happy. If you're confident that you can do it as well as them, and it'll save Mel all that stress of the travelling, then I think it's a much better idea. And thank you for taking the time to be so helpful.'

'My pleasure. Take it steady and get plenty of rest. And if you've got anything else you want to ask, you can talk to me at any time. Just ring up and I'll phone you back as soon as I'm free, or you can make an appointment and come in. And I'll arrange to have some literature sent to you. I don't want you to feel you're on your own with this. Any questions?'

There were a few, and he answered them patiently and comprehensively without hesitation. He clearly knew his subject, Daisy thought, and she could see the parents relaxing as their confidence in him grew.

He said goodbye and showed them out, and Daisy turned to him with new eyes.

'That's amazing. I can't believe you and Matt were MCMA twins. How early were you?'

'Just over a month. They picked it up on ultrasound at 18 weeks, and Mum was transferred to a specialist centre two months later when we were still both alive and mothballed for weeks. She nearly went nuts, apparently, but she got away with it, and so did we. I guess we were very lucky.'

'Evidently.'

'Anyway, I'd like you to read up on it, and if there's anything you want to know, just yell. I've got all sorts of literature at home. Just remember they may very well die if things go wrong in the next few weeks.'

'That's so sad.'

'It's a fact of twin pregnancy. Everyone thinks it's great, but it's not, it's often complicated and it's always riskier than a singleton pregnancy, but with any luck we'll be able to give them two healthy babies. How do you fancy dinner later?'

She blinked at the change of subject. 'Sounds great, my fridge is empty. What did you have in mind?'

'Fish and chips on the seafront while we watch the sunset?'

She laughed. 'That sounds amazing.'

'I thought so,' he said cockily, and winked. 'Come on, then, pull your weight, Dr Daisy. Haven't you got patients waiting?

The sunset was glorious, and they sat on a bench on the clifftop eating their fish and chips out of the paper while they watched the clouds change colour.

'This was a great idea,' she said as she finished, and leant over and gave him a greasy little kiss on the cheek. He laughed and rubbed it off, then slung his arm round her shoulders and they stayed there, heads together, staring out to sea until the reds and golds faded to the purple and silver of moonlight.

The temperature plummeted as the sun went down and Ben felt her shiver, so reluctantly they strolled back to her house and sat in the conservatory drinking tea while he emailed Matt from his phone about the Grieves twins and she flicked through the literature he'd given her.

'You were so nearly conjoined twins! If the embryo had split any later you would have been,' she said, looking up at him, and he gave a hollow laugh.

'Tell me about it. Damn good job we weren't, we would have killed each other. Close as we are, we're not that close and we're both far too opinionated and independent.'

'It must be so weird to be that close to someone,' she said thoughtfully. 'Snuggled up in the womb, really able to touch each other—odd. It must make a bond like no other.'

'I guess it does,' he said thoughtfully, putting his phone down. 'I don't really think about it and I don't know what it's like to have a normal sibling of a different age. There's only the two of us. I think by the time my mother had got over the shock, she didn't want any more. I think we were a bit of a handful.'

'I'll bet. Did you live in town?'

'No—well, on the edge of town, with fields behind the house, and we had a million rescued cats and dogs and rabbits and goats and God knows else what to keep us occupied.'

'Why weren't you a vet?' she asked curiously, and he laughed.

'Because I didn't want to spend my life up to my knees in mud and worse, freezing to death in a stone barn in January with my arm up the back of a cow. Next question?'

She laughed with him, and then gave it serious thought. 'With Matt, do you hurt when he hurts?'

'Gosh. That's a deep one. Do you mean physically?'

'Whatever.'

He nodded slowly. 'Maybe. I was sick when he had appendicitis. We share a lot—tell each other things we wouldn't tell another living soul. But then, don't all siblings?'

'I don't know, I'm an only child. Mike's kids were close, though, poor little things, and I'm glad they were, because at least they had each other. They didn't deserve what he did to them—to all of us.'

His eyes were sympathetic, and he nodded slowly. 'Is that them, on your fridge?'

'Freya and Millie. Yes. I still miss them. If Mike had been half the father to them that you are to Florence, things would have been fine, but he wasn't, he was weak and self-centred and I should have seen it sooner, then none of us would have been so badly hurt.'

'I'm sorry,' he said softly, and she shrugged and got up, shutting the windows.

'One of those things. It was years ago now—nearly three.'

'And he went back to his wife.'

'Yes. He never really left her. They were still sleeping together, all the time he was with me. I had no idea.'

She saw the realisation in his eyes, the explanation for her insecurity over him staying at Jane's.

'Oh, Daisy. I'm sorry. Was that when you moved away?'

'Yes. I didn't need to hear any more about him, and he started phoning me, sucking up again. Bored, I expect. Time to cut and run.'

'Sounds like it was a good move.'

She turned and looked at him, her eyes sad. 'I thought it would be, but I'm not so sure now. Out of the frying pan and all that.'

He felt sick. She looked defeated, resigned, and he'd done this to her. 'Oh, hell, Daisy, I'm sorry. I shouldn't have let this go so far. It was always going to be too complicated. I'm being selfish.'

'No, you're not. I went into this with my eyes open.'

'No, you didn't. I didn't tell you about Florence until we'd almost slept together.'

'I could have stopped it there,' she said, but they both knew she was lying. It had been too late the moment they set eyes on each other, him covered in plaster, her covered in tea. Their eyes had met and that had been it, and their first kiss and everything that followed it had been inevitable.

He shifted the cat off his lap and stood up. 'Do you want me to go?' he asked, wondering if this was the end, if she was finally coming to her senses and kicking him out, as she probably should have done weeks ago, but she shook her head.

'It's too late, Ben,' she said simply. 'I already love you.'

He felt as if she'd punched him in the solar plexus, and he closed his eyes. 'Daisy, no. Not that.'

'What, the "L" word? I thought we'd agreed on honesty?' She reached out for him, taking his hand and cradling it against her heart. 'I know the rules, Ben, and

I'm not trying to change anything. I'm just telling you the truth. I just wish it could be different, less complicated, but it isn't and I don't have the strength to walk away from you now.'

God help him, he didn't have the strength to walk away from her, either. He folded her against his chest, rested his face against her hair and breathed in her fragrance. To hell with the rules.

'For what it's worth, I love you, too,' he admitted softly, his voice gruff with emotion. 'And I wish—'

'I know.' She stepped away. 'Come to bed.'

Their loving was heartbreakingly tender, and when it was over Daisy lay in his arms, silent tears leaking from her eyes.

'Don't cry.'

'I'm not,' she lied, her voice clogged with tears.

'I thought we were being honest.'

'We are.' She squeezed her eyes tight shut and hugged him. 'I'm sorry.'

'Me, too. You deserve so much more.'

'Ben, I don't want more, I want you, and if this is what we have, then I'll treasure it for as long as it lasts. And I know that won't be forever, but let's just enjoy it while we can.'

His arms tightened, and he pressed his lips to her hair and wished—hell, he didn't know what he wished. That she'd never met Mike? Oh, yes—but then she wouldn't be here and he wouldn't have met her. That Florence didn't exist? Impossible to wish that.

That Daisy was her mother?

The ache that gave him in the region of his heart nearly took his breath away.

* * *

Steve's wife was admitted the following day in labour, and Amy called for Daisy.

'She's breech and I'm not sure she's going to be able to deliver. Want to try, or do you want to send in the big guns?'

'Ben's on call this week. I'll find him,' she said, reluctant to take the responsibility. She'd tell him what was going on and hand over, but she didn't want to work with him today, she was still feeling fraught after last night.

She shouldn't have told him she loved him. She should have let sleeping dogs lie, but no, she'd had to confess, and now it seemed they were both in deeper than they'd wanted to be, and their light-hearted affair was turning into an emotional minefield.

He was in his office struggling with paperwork, and he was only too happy to leave it—but he was taking Daisy with him. 'You need the experience,' he said, and she couldn't argue with it, so she went. 'Any idea what kind of breech?' he asked as they walked down the ward.

'No. I haven't seen her. The baby turned last night.'

'Really? That's late. I wonder if I can turn it back.'

'Are you good at it?'

'I'm good at everything—except relationships,' he added quietly, and pushed the door open and ushered her in.

'Hello, Steve. Marian, isn't it? Hi, I'm Ben.' He shook their hands, and Steve looked relieved to see him.

'Glad it's you, guv,' he said anxiously. 'Can you sort it?'

'I'm sure we can,' he said, snapping on gloves and feeling Marian's abdomen. 'Amy, can I have an update?'

'Slow progress, she's 3 centimetres dilated and that

hasn't changed for over an hour. Heartbeat's normal, but labour's just not progressing.'

'Your baby's obviously got a skinny little bottom,' he said with a smile, then asked Daisy to feel the baby's position.

'What do you think?'

'It's a frank breech, I think. I'm sure I can feel at least one foot up by the head.'

'Yes. I can only feel one, but the other one won't be far away. So it's a good position for a natural delivery, or I could try and turn it. How frequent are the contractions?'

'Every five minutes,' Amy said, and they then paused while Marian breathed her way through one.

'It doesn't feel as if it's doing anything,' she complained afterwards. 'It's not like my other labours.'

'How many babies have you had?'

'This is the fourth—and the last. That's what you get for going on holiday to somewhere uncivilised.'

'It was only Turkey! She was on the pill and got sick,' Steve chipped in.

'It happens,' Ben said wryly, and Daisy frowned. Was that what had happened to Jane?

There was no time to think about it, though, because he was feeling her abdomen again, apologising as he dug his fingers in deeply around her pelvis and flexed them a little. 'I think it might be possible to persuade this youngster to right itself. Want to give it a go?'

'Will it hurt?' Marian asked.

Ben pulled a face. 'Not hurt, exactly. It don't think it'll be very comfortable, but all I want to do is push the top and bottom in opposite directions to try and spin it. The baby often joins in and kicks, and that seems to help. Either it'll work, or it won't, and then we think again. Want to try?' he said, and she nodded.

Without wasting any time, he laid one hand on the back of the baby's head, the other low down on the other side, and as he pushed and jiggled and coaxed, there was a shift, her abdomen changed shape and Ben's hands followed through as the baby somersaulted into the right position.

He straightened up, grinning, and gave Marian a broad wink.

'There you go. One baby, the right way up, and settling nicely into your pelvis. Go on, down you go, little one,' he said, giving it an encouraging little push, and her eyes widened.

'Oh—gosh—that feels a bit more like it,' she gasped, and grabbed Steve's hand, panting furiously.

Amy was at the business end, and she looked up a minute later. 'OK, Marian, that's lovely, keep breathing. Your waters have broken and you're doing really well.'

Daisy and Ben stayed. Technically they weren't needed, but things had moved on so fast that a second midwife hadn't come yet, so they were there when a squalling baby slithered into Amy's waiting hands, bright red with indignation and screaming the place down.

She laid her on Marian's front as she sagged back against the pillows, laughing and crying and trying to get her breath, and as she stared down, her eyes welled over.

'It's a girl!'

'Of course it's a girl,' Steve said, trying and failing to hang onto his masculine pride as the tears coursed down his cheeks. 'Only a woman would change her mind that late, and then change back again!'

They all laughed, and Daisy leant over for a closer look at the new arrival. She'd stopped crying now and she was staring up, transfixed, into her mother's eyes, and Daisy felt an unexpected lump in her throat.

'Oh, she's lovely. Congratulations,' she said. 'Has she got a name?'

'Yes—Tommy,' Marian said drily, and they all laughed again. 'I didn't let myself get carried away with girls' names, because I just knew she'd be a boy like the others.'

'Apparently not,' Amy said with a smile as she clamped and cut the cord. 'Still, you've got a few days.'

'Oh, it seems wrong not having a name for her,' Marian said, stroking her baby's face with a gentle finger. 'Who are you, sweetheart, hmm? What's your name? Are you a Katie?'

Another midwife arrived, so they left the little family in their capable hands, trying out names on their daughter.

Outside in the corridor, Ben hesitated.

'Coffee?' he said, but Daisy shook her head. Just watching Marian and Steve with their beautiful little girl gave her a hollow ache inside. She was getting broody, she realised, and that was so, so dangerous. So easy to get lulled into a fantasy world, now the 'L' word was out of the box. She should have kept her mouth shut.

'I've got loads to do—patients waiting. I'll see you later.'

Except it was quiet, for once, and she had altogether too much time to think about Ben and the fact that he loved her, too—and that still, even so, there was no way forward.

CHAPTER EIGHT

THE status quo persisted between them for the next couple of weeks. The landscapers had taken down the fence between them, and that weekend, he'd got Florence as usual.

Which would have been fine, except that it was getting hotter as spring moved towards summer, and Daisy needed to plant her containers. And because it was warm, because the landscapers had carefully pruned the trees and left a shady canopy over part of the garden, Florence was out there with Ben, running around in the fresh air and playing games with him.

Daisy wanted to join in.

Well, no, she didn't. She wanted him to take her away, she corrected herself, but of course he didn't, and Florence, being the delightfully friendly little girl that she was, kept coming over to her with things she'd found—a wood louse, a pretty stone, a flower she'd picked her—endless little visits that scraped away at the sore place in her heart until it bled.

'Can Froggy come to my garden?' she asked after yet another trip to show something off. 'I want him to see it.'

'Sure,' she said, and Florence picked him up, very

carefully in case she hurt him, and carried him back to Ben, chattering to him all the way.

Daisy turned her back on it all and carried on potting up her containers, but all the time her ears were tuned to the sound of their voices, and she reached for the last pot with an element of desperation.

Thank goodness for that, she thought as she crammed in the last scrap of lobelia and picked up the hose. A good soaking and they'd be done and she could go back inside and make herself scarce.

'They's very pretty!'

She turned the hose off and smiled down at Florence. 'Thank you. They'll be prettier when all the flowers come out, and some of them will smell lovely.'

Her chubby little fingers touched a blue brachyscome flower with exaggerated care. 'Is that a daisy like you?'

She laughed softly. 'Sort of. It's called a Swan River daisy, and these are verbena, and this is a geranium. Here, squash this leaf in your fingers and smell them. You have to rub your fingers together—there. Can you smell it now?'

Her little button nose wrinkled, and she giggled. 'It smells funny—like lemons!'

'That's right. It's called a lemon-scented geranium, and it has really pretty pink flowers like your bedroom.'

'And the daisies are blue.'

'They are. And the verbena's going to be a lovely purple colour.'

She fingered another plant. 'What's this?'

'That's lobelia, and this is an ivy-leaf geranium, and this is called Creeping Jenny—'

'Daisy, I'm so, so sorry, I had to take a phone call,' Ben said, reappearing beside them. 'Florence, come on, darling, leave Daisy alone. You can see she's busy.'

'No, she's finished!' Florence said. 'Aren't you?'

Her little face was tilted earnestly up to Daisy's, and she felt her heart squeeze. 'Yes, I am. It's OK, Ben.'

But it wasn't. Her heart was being invaded by him and his little daughter, slowly but surely taking up residence in every nook and cranny of it until it was bursting with love for them.

She looked down again, and Florence was stroking the flowers in the last little pot tenderly.

Oh, what the hell, she thought, and bent down, pressing her hands between her knees and smiling at the little girl.

'I tell you what, why don't you have this little one, and you can water it when you're here at the weekends, and look after it and watch it grow. I'm sure Daddy can find a place for it in your garden somewhere.'

She lifted it up and held it out to him, and after a second's hesitation, he took it.

'Thank you,' he murmured, as if he knew what it had cost her, that it wasn't the plant she was giving his daughter but a gift infinitely more precious. 'There, Florence. Your own pot! What do you say?'

'Thank you,' she piped, beaming at it and then at Daisy, making her heart turn over. 'Can Froggy look after it for me when I'm not here?'

Ben sighed. 'No, he belongs to Daisy, Florence, you know that.'

'She can have him. That's fine.'

He gave a rueful chuckle and thanked her. She knew perfectly well that he thought the little concrete frog was as hideous as she did, but Florence adored him, and that was all that mattered.

He put the pot down in his garden, out of the way of the landscapers, and she put Froggy down beside it.

'Come on, Florence, time to wash your hands. We're going to go to the playground now.'

Florence ran to the outside tap and turned it on carefully, running her fingers under the dribble. 'Washed them!' she said, wiping them on her once-pink dungarees, and then bent over, sticking her little rump in the air and telling Froggy very seriously to look after her plant. Daisy watched her, torn between laughter and tears, and she was very much afraid the tears would win.

She'd just managed to suppress them both when Florence straightened up and bounced over to Ben and said, 'Ready!'

She waggled her fingers at Daisy, and she waggled hers back and squashed the little pang inside. 'Have a lovely time,' she said, wishing she was going, too. Wishing so many things that were just so dangerous to wish...

Ben, watching the interchange between them, saw the sadness in her eyes just before she masked it, and before he could stop himself, he said impulsively, 'Why don't you come, too?'

'Oh, yes, Daisy come! Please come!' Florence squealed, bouncing up and down with her little curls flying, and he watched the brief internal battle before she crumpled.

She looked up at him, reproach in her eyes, and was on the point of refusing when Florence ran up to her and took her hand. 'Please come? It will be much funner if you're there and you said you're finished,' she begged with wide, pleading eyes just so like Ben's it hurt, and Daisy gave up.

'I'm not dressed for it,' she said a little desperately, but Florence didn't care.

'You can change,' she said with three-year-old logic. 'We'll wait for you. Please please please *please*?'

Cursing him silently, she stripped off her gardening gloves and ran upstairs, changing into clean jeans and a T-shirt. She caught sight of herself in the mirror and was reaching for the makeup when she stopped herself.

No! They were taking the child to the playground, against her better judgement, and she didn't need to tart herself up for it! The sooner they went, the sooner they'd be back, and the sooner it would be over. She ran back down, and found Florence and Froggy in earnest conversation about the plant.

'I'm sorry,' Ben said softly as she reached his side.

She made a small, 'just you wait' sort of noise, and fell in beside them as they headed to the little park just a couple of streets away, Florence dancing around between them like a puppy, oblivious to the atmosphere between the adults.

'Can we go on the see-saw?' she asked Ben hopefully.

'Maybe, if Daisy doesn't mind.'

Daisy did mind, but there wasn't a lot she could do about it. The problem was that although Ben weighed more than she and Florence put together, he was much, much heavier than Florence alone, so without Daisy to balance they didn't have a hope of making the see-saw work.

Simple ergonomics—except there was nothing simple about this equation.

Ben + Florence + Daisy = Disaster, she thought, and she was right. He went on one end, and she went on the other, with Florence cuddled up against her tummy and hanging onto the handle. He sat down carefully, and they lifted up into the air, but not so far that Daisy's feet were off the ground.

And Florence loved it.

Up and down, up and down, faster and faster while Florence shrieked with delight, her little body snuggled safe against Daisy's and making her want to cry. So sweet. So precious. So very, very easy to love.

She could have scooped her up and cuddled her to bits, but she kept on pushing, up and down, and up and down, until finally Ben stopped the ride by bracing his legs and bringing them to a halt.

'More!' Florence pleaded, but in the middle of laughing with Florence and having fun, Ben had caught Daisy's eyes and seen the pain in them, and he'd felt gutted.

What the hell were they doing? What on earth was he doing to her? To Florence? To all of them? He'd promised Daisy he'd keep Florence out of her way, and he'd done nothing of the sort.

'No, that's enough see-sawing,' he said firmly but gently, and got off. 'Come on, I'll push you on the swing. You like that.'

He lifted her clear of the see-saw and carried her to the swings, settling her in the seat safely before pushing it high. The see-saw forgotten, she shrieked with delighted laughter, and Daisy went over to a bench and sat down and watched them, wondering how on earth she could have got herself into this position again.

'I'm sorry.'

He'd lifted her out of the swing and left her on a bouncy little rocking horse nearby, and he sat down heavily beside Daisy and propped his elbows on his knees, his hands dangling between them, looking the picture of dejection. 'I should have thought before I opened my mouth.'

'Yes, you should. You shouldn't have asked me in front of her,' she said quietly. 'You knew I'd have no choice. I couldn't refuse a child, could I? Not without sounding mean.'

He tilted his head so he could see her, his eyes searching. 'You could have done—but I didn't think you wanted to. You looked so sad—as if you couldn't bear to be left out.'

'And this helps?' she asked incredulously. 'I can't *do* it, Ben. It was supposed to be about us—about fun, remember? Fun dates, hot sex and no complications, that's what we said. But it's not fun any more, Ben, it just hurts. I'm sorry. I thought we could keep this in its box, but we can't. It just spills over into everything else, and we're all going to end up hurt. It's just hopeless. You can't keep her away from me while you're living next door, it just isn't possible, and I'm not playing happy families all over again. I'm not ready for this, and I don't know if I ever will be.'

His eyes met hers, the naked emotion in them tearing through her, and then he masked it and sat up straight, his hands braced on his knees as he dragged in a deep breath. 'So where does that leave us?' he asked, dreading her answer, and she gave a sad little shrug.

'We both know it's going nowhere, so why drag it on?'

He opened his mouth, closed it and pressed his lips into a firm line. How could he have been so stupid? It was never going to work. She was on the rebound, he'd known that, and this was resurrecting all that old hurt. Well, he couldn't say he hadn't been warned.

'You're right. I'm sorry. Look, why don't you head

on back, and I'll bring her back in a little while. And
we'll keep out of your way.'

She nodded and got unsteadily to her feet, then with
a little wave to Florence, she walked away.

Something she should have done weeks ago…

'Daddy, why's Daisy going?'

Ben could hardly answer her. The lump in his throat
was huge, and he swallowed hard, then again.

'Uh—she's got lots to do,' he said eventually, and
wondered if it was his imagination or if his voice really
sounded as if he'd swallowed a handful of rusty nails.

'Can I go on the slide?'

'OK. Come on, then.'

He helped her up, over and over again, dredging up a
smile from somewhere until he thought his face would
crack, then he called a halt and took hold of her hand.

'Come on, let's go back now. It's time for supper.'

'Can we see Daisy?'

'Daisy's busy,' he said, his voice catching, and he
cleared his throat and headed for the gate, Florence in
tow. He wasn't really concentrating on Florence, just
putting one foot in front of the other, his thoughts tum-
bling in free-fall.

We both know it's going nowhere.

But he needed her so much, and it seemed to have
been going so well. For the first time in years, he'd been
truly happy.

'Daddy, look at me!'

She was walking along the top of a little low garden
wall—something that under normal circumstances he
would have stopped her doing, but he just smiled absently and tightened his grip on her hand in case she
toppled.

And then a loose brick twisted away under her foot, and she fell off the wall and he jerked her arm up without thinking to steady her.

The thin scream cut through him to the bone, and he dropped to his knees beside her, gathering her gently into his arms as a sickening wave of guilt rushed over him. 'No! Don't touch!' she screamed, backing away, her arm hanging awkwardly in front of her, held in place by the other one, and he stared at her, shock holding him rigid for a second.

He'd dislocated her elbow! He couldn't believe he'd done it. So easy, so stupid. And he knew what to do now, but he couldn't do it alone, and she was his daughter, for heaven's sake, and if he'd only been paying attention…

'It's OK, sweetheart. It's just in a crick. It'll be fine soon. I'll call Daisy, she'll come and help us.' It would have to be Daisy, because Jane was away with Peter. Of all the weekends to decide to go away with him…

He fumbled for his phone, his fingers shaking so much he could scarcely operate it, and when it went straight to her voicemail he could have wept. He was about to call the house phone when she rang him back.

'Ben, I—'

'Daisy, help. She fell off the wall and I grabbed her, and I've dislocated her elbow, and Jane's away, so I can't ask her.'

There was a fraction of a second of silence, in which she must have heard Daisy sobbing, then she said, calmly and firmly, 'OK, stay with her, I'll bring the car and we'll take her to A and E. Where are you?'

'Um…' He looked around. 'Just—just at the end of the road. We're nearly home, but I can't carry her, she won't let me touch her. Daisy, I can't—'

'It's OK. I'll be with you. Don't move.'

It probably only took her a couple of minutes, but it felt like forever. He thought he was going to throw up, and he couldn't stop shaking. 'Florence, darling, I'm so sorry—come here. Sit on my knee and wait for Daisy.'

She sat, leaning her shoulder against his chest and holding her arm very, very still, the quiet sobbing more telling than any screaming would have been. She was shaking like a leaf, her tiny body racked with tremors, and guilt was crippling him.

If only he'd been paying attention, he would have seen the state of the wall and stopped her before she'd hurt herself. She shouldn't have been on it anyway, it didn't belong to them and he would never normally have let her walk on it—so why had he? Because he'd been selfishly obsessing.

'Ben?'

He lifted his head, and saw Daisy crouched in front of him, her eyes concerned. She lifted a hand and touched his cheek, then stroked Florence's hair gently. 'Come on, darling, let's get you and Daddy to hospital so they can make your arm better. OK?'

Florence shook her head. 'Don't want to go to hospital,' she sobbed unevenly. 'Want to see Froggy!'

Oh, no. Daisy's heart contracted, and she stroked the child's hair with all the love she'd been suppressing for weeks. 'You can come back and tell him all about it very soon. You don't want to make him worried, do you?'

She had no idea if she was saying the right thing or not—not, probably, but if it got her in the car then she'd worry about it later, and frankly Ben looked as if he was past coping with this situation.

'Come on, poppet,' she murmured, helping her to her feet, and then she lifted her incredibly carefully into the car on his lap, shut the door and went round to the front and drove to the hospital as if she was on eggshells.

She let them out at the A and E entrance, then parked the car and ran back.

She could hear Florence sobbing quietly, hear Ben's gruff, tender voice trying to reassure her, and she went in and crouched down beside them.

'Have you checked in?' she asked, and he nodded. 'I'll go and find someone,' she said, and opened the curtain as Andy Gallagher walked up.

'Daisy, hi.'

Thank goodness. She'd met him on several occasions over emergency patients, and he was brilliant. She smiled in relief.

'Hi. Can you take a look at Ben Walker's daughter? She's got a radial subluxation. She fell off a wall and he caught her.'

'Ah,' he said softly, smiled at her, and followed the sound of sobbing.

'Hi, Ben,' he said, and crouched down in front of them. 'Hello, young lady. Who are you?'

'F-Fl-Florence,' she said, sniffing and sobbing.

'Well, Florence, I'm Andy, and I work with your daddy and Daisy here in the hospital. And Daisy tells me you've hurt your arm. Can you show me where it hurts?'

She sniffed again, let go very carefully and pointed to her elbow region.

'Oh, dear. That's not very nice. Shall we fix it, then?' he asked, warning Ben, and taking her elbow firmly in his left hand, he took her hand in his right and with a quick twist and flex, it was done.

There was an audible click, Florence sobbed hysterically for a second or two, then whimpered for a moment before she got off Ben's knee and ran to Daisy, throwing her arms round her shaking legs and hugging her tight.

'Fixed, I think,' Andy said with a smile at Daisy, and Ben shut his eyes, dropped his head back and went chalk white.

'Oh, no, you don't,' Andy said, grabbing Ben's head and dragging it forward over his knees.

A long moment later he straightened up, blinked and pulled a face, and then shook his head. 'Sorry, it's just the shock. I just can't believe I was so stupid. One minute she was on this wall, the next she was screaming in a heap, and it's all my fault.'

'Rubbish, it's easily done. She's fine now. We'd probably better have another look at it, maybe take a picture. Can we do that, Florence? Can we take a picture of your arm?'

'For Mummy?' she asked.

'Oh, God,' Ben said faintly in the background, the implications dawning on him, and Daisy took over.

'It's a picture of the inside—it's very clever. It shows all your bones.'

'Does it hurt?' Her little chin wobbled, and Daisy smiled.

'No. It doesn't hurt at all. It's just like having your picture taken, but you have to keep very still so it doesn't go all blurry.'

'Will you come with me?'

'No, Daddy wants to,' she said firmly, handing responsibility back to her father. He got to his feet and held out his hand to her, then thought better of it and picked her up, cradling her in his arms for safety.

'I'm going to buy her toddler reins so I don't have to hold her hand ever again,' he growled, and Andy chuckled softly.

'Don't beat yourself up. You aren't the first, and you won't be the last, but you will need to be careful for six weeks or so until it's completely recovered, and it may well recur.'

'Fabulous. That's going to take some explaining to her mother,' he muttered, and they went off to X-Ray clutching the form.

'So how come you're here? Have we got a maternity case in that I don't know about or are you switching specialties?' Andy asked.

'No, I live round the corner from the park where they'd been playing—we're neighbours. I gave him a lift. It was just lucky I was around,' she explained glibly, feeling a twinge of guilt for lying.

'Yes, driving her would have been tricky. Can you take them home?'

'Of course I can.'

Even though I'm not supposed to be having anything to do with them, she thought wryly.

Why did *nothing* go according to plan?

'I want Froggy,' Florence said as soon as they got back. She'd been saying it all the way home, but the last thing he wanted to do was give her the heavy little concrete frog to cradle in her recently dislocated arm.

Ben sighed. He was at his wits' end, exhausted with the emotional roller-coaster of the afternoon, and he just wanted to crawl into a corner.

'Froggy's gone to sleep,' he said softly, 'and it's time you did, too. Come on, let's give you a bath and put you to bed.'

The bath was a nightmare. Lifting her in and out suddenly became fraught with danger, and he gripped her firmly under the arms and hoisted her out, wrapping her in a huge, fluffy towel and snuggling her dry on his lap. The arm was tender, although he couldn't see any swelling or bruising, but when he patted it carefully dry she pulled it away.

'I want Froggy,' she said again, and started to cry.

He should just go out and get it—it was in his garden, he remembered, guarding the little planted pot that Daisy had given her.

His dearest, darling Daisy. Only not his Daisy any more, apparently, because he'd pushed her too hard and he'd blown it.

Pain washed through him, and he crushed it ruthlessly. This was all his fault. He shouldn't have asked her to go with them.

He was dressing Florence and still debating getting the frog in from the garden when he heard her voice call softly from the bottom of the stairs.

'Ben? Can I come up?' she said, and he swallowed hard. She must have come in through the back door from the garden, he realised.

'Sure. We're in the bathroom. Hang on.'

He moved the soggy towel from in front of the door and opened it, to find her standing there with a carrier bag.

'I got these for her for her birthday,' she said in a quiet undertone, 'but I wondered if she should have them now. It's a frog cushion and a story book. I thought, she's had a rough day…'

Hadn't they all?

'Daisy, that's so kind,' he said, feeling choked, and Florence appeared at his side and gave her a wobbly smile.

'Daddy says I can't see Froggy's 'cos he's sleeping,' she said, and the smile wobbled a little more.

Daisy's smile wobbled, too. She crouched down so

her head was on the same level, and delved into the bag.
'I know, but I've brought you something else instead—
it's a froggy cushion, look. You can rest your sore arm
on it while Daddy reads to you, because there's a Freddie
Frog book, too.'

Her eyes lit up, and she cuddled the small pink and
green cushion to her chest and eyed the book.

'Daisy read it.'

For a second he thought she was going to refuse, but
then he saw resignation settle over her, and she held out
her hand to Florence and led her back to her bedroom.

'All right, then. Just this once, because of your arm.'

She tucked her in, rested her arm on the cushion,
then sat down beside her pillow so Florence could see
the pictures. And then she started to read.

'Once upon a time…'

Ben sat quietly down on the other bed, and listened
to her soft, musical voice telling the story.

The cushion seemed to be doing the trick, Daisy
thought, and she'd snuggled down, the painkillers making her sleepy, and insisted a little tearfully that Daisy
read the book again. Common sense would have stopped
her, if she'd had any, but she'd given up the unequal
struggle, and so she read it again, while Ben sat on the
other bed and listened, tears in his eyes, his face drawn.

Then at last her eyes drifted shut, and after another
page, Daisy put the book down and tiptoed out. Ben followed, leaving the door ajar, and they went downstairs.

'I'm so sorry. It's been a hell of a day.'

They were standing in the hall, both of them a little
uncertain because they had no established protocol for
this. A few short hours ago, she'd broken off her relationship with him, supposedly, and yet here they were,

hovering midway between the sitting room door and the back door, and all she wanted was to get away.

She didn't think Ben was enjoying it any more than she was. He still looked awful, and he was apologising?

'Don't,' she said softly. 'It's not your fault, it's fine.'

'No, it's not, and nor are you,' he said quietly. 'I've asked far too much of you, and you've just done it without a murmur. I don't know how to thank you.'

'I took you to the hospital, Ben, that was all.'

'I'm not talking about that. Well, I am, but I meant much more. All the endless kindnesses—the silly things. Mopping up my floor on the first day. Getting me the plumber. Getting my suit cleaned. Letting me trash your garden while they change the fence. The pot for Florence. Just being there for me, sharing the downtime on bad days when things have gone wrong, sharing the good times. Just sharing everything without question. Letting me into your life and asking for nothing back. And the cushion and book for Florence—it must have taken you hours to find them.'

'No. There's a craft shop in town, and they had the cushion in the window. The book was in the charity shop next door, it's not even new, but it had Florence written all over it. And tonight seemed like a good time to give it to her.'

'It was. It was an amazing time to give it to her. Thank you for being so thoughtful.' He dragged his hand over his face, and when he dropped it to his side, his eyes were bright. 'You're always thoughtful, though, aren't you? Always kind, always willing to put other people first. I don't deserve you, Daisy. You were right today. We can't go on like this. Everything we do makes you unhappy, and I can't bear to see you unhappy.'

'You make me happy,' she said, her voice hollow

with pain. 'It's the situation I can't deal with. It's just too dangerous, Ben. Too messy. I'm glad I could help today, and if I can again, please ask, but otherwise—Ben, I really don't want to see Florence again.'

'Or me,' he said rawly.

Or him. Of course it would be easier if she didn't have to see him again, either, but that was too much to ask for, and possibly more than she wanted, sucker that she was for punishment. 'That's not possible,' she said.

'But it would be easier if I didn't live next door. I'll move,' he said heavily. 'I'll get the house finished and put it on the market, and we'll find somewhere else and leave you in peace. Will you be all right with me at work?'

All right? She doubted it, and as for him moving away and leaving her in peace, she knew that would be a long time coming. The move might happen, but the peace? She doubted it. 'I'm sure we'll cope. And I'll move, not you. I'll look for another job—there's bound to be one coming up. And so long as it's in Suffolk, I can still see Amy regularly. And you'll be close to Florence, and you can settle here and build your career. It makes more sense for it to be me.'

His face contorted briefly, and she hesitated at the door, then leaned over, touching a tender, lingering kiss to his lips.

'Goodbye, Ben,' she said softly, and then opened the back door and went out, closing it quietly behind her. She picked her way carefully through the gardens and made it all the way to her sitting room, with the door closed and her face buried in a cushion, before the first sob escaped.

CHAPTER NINE

SHE'D lied, of course. They weren't all right at work.

Oh, they fudged through, but they avoided each other whenever possible, and Amy took her under her wing and comforted her with girly chats and cake when it all got too much.

There were times when they couldn't avoid each other, of course, and in those times it was excruciating.

The antenatal clinics on Mondays were usually safe, which was just as well because after the weekends with Florence running about all over the house and garden, her nerves were fraught anyway.

Every other week, though, they met inevitably over the Grieves and their MCMA twins. The scans showed the babies tangling, then untangling, then tangling again, and at 20 weeks they had a couple of twists in the cords.

'Will they be all right?' Daisy asked, standing next to Ben and trying to concentrate on the almost photographic 3D scan of the tiny little girls, and he shrugged.

'I don't know. I'm going to put her on drugs to limit the fluid. We've got them this far. Another six weeks and they'll be viable—maybe less, at a push. We'll see. But they're both OK so far.'

'So where are we now? Weekly scans?'

'Yes. Weekly till 28, maybe as little as 26, and then I'll admit her. It depends what these two are up to by then. I'm going to play it by ear.'

She nodded. 'Right. Well, unless you need me in the consultation, I've got lots of patients to see still,' she said, desperate to escape from him, and he shrugged.

She didn't want to be with him, he realised, and he could understand that. It was sheer torture being in the same room as her and unable to touch her, unable to look forward to the evening, when they'd be alone and he could take her in his arms and hold her.

God, he missed holding her. Missed everything about her.

'You go, I'll talk to them. I'll let you know if anything changes.'

'OK.'

She went and he closed the door, rested his head against the wall and sucked in a steadying breath.

Bad idea. He could smell her—not perfume, but something more subtle. A hint of her shampoo, perhaps? Whatever, it dragged him straight back to happier times—times when he had the right to bury his head in her hair and breathe in the sweet, fresh scent. Times when she'd trailed it over his face while they were making love, and he'd lie and look up at her and wonder what he'd done to deserve her.

Nothing, was the answer. He'd failed in his marriage, failed to give his daughter the security she deserved, and he'd failed in his promise to keep her away from Daisy—he was a walking disaster area as far as relationships were concerned, and the best thing he could do was keep himself and Florence as far away from her as possible, even if it was too late.

He wrenched the door open and went to find Mr and Mrs Grieves.

'So what are you wearing to Laura's wedding?' Amy asked her.

She was on call to the labour ward, and she'd just done a Ventouse delivery. They were 'debriefing' over a cup of coffee and a shared slab of sticky gingerbread, and at the mention of the wedding Daisy lost her appetite.

'I don't want to think about it.'

'It's in ten days! You have to think about it!'

She shrugged. 'I don't really feel like going.'

'I know you don't, hon. I don't, either. But she'd be gutted if we didn't go, and she's relying on us. Why don't we go to Cambridge this weekend? Have a properly girly day out together. We haven't done it for ages.'

They hadn't, and Daisy felt a pang of guilt. 'OK,' she said, and then tried to inject a little enthusiasm into her voice, but she couldn't summon any enthusiasm for it.

For anything, really. Without Ben, her life was drained of colour, and she wondered if it would ever be the same again—

'Oh, Daisy. I'm sorry,' Amy murmured, and she realised there was a tear sliding down her cheek. She scrubbed it hastily away.

'Don't be nice to me. I really can't cope with it at the moment. I just need to get through the days.'

'But it's been weeks,' Amy pointed out gently. 'Three weeks? Four?'

'Four weeks and three days. I'm going to move, I think. I told Ben I was, but there haven't been any jobs.'

'You're going to move hospital?' Amy said, her face falling. 'Gosh, I'll miss you.'

'I'll miss you, too, but I can't cope with this. He's just always there, and even when he isn't, I'm looking for him. I'm really sorry, Amy.'

Damn. The tears were welling in earnest now, and she fumbled for a tissue and squeezed her eyes shut.

She could hear Amy moving, shifting her chair, but when she opened her eyes Amy was gone and Ben was there, his eyes tortured.

'What's wrong?' she asked. 'Why are you here?'

'Nothing's wrong. Well, nothing else, apart from you. I can't bear to see you like this, Daisy.'

'Well, hopefully you won't have to for long. I'm going to start applying for jobs further away. Maybe I'll go back to London.'

'I'll ask Matt if he needs a good registrar.'

'Please don't bother. I don't need to be looking at your doppelganger all day every day.'

He sighed. 'I'll ask around. Maybe there's somewhere else local.'

'You know what? Don't worry. I'll do it myself. It's fine.'

And getting up, she walked away from him, head up, back ramrod straight, and he cursed the day he'd ever set eyes on her and upset the fragile equilibrium of her life.

Cambridge was busy, as bustling as ever, but at least she was away from Ben and Florence, and she found a dress for the wedding.

She needed a smaller size than usual. She was losing

weight, because she couldn't summon up the energy or enthusiasm to eat.

'That's fabulous,' Amy said firmly. 'Buy it, and let's go and get lunch. I'm starving.'

Maybe it was the fact that Ben wasn't around, but suddenly Daisy felt—well, not starving, exactly, but certainly hungrier than she had for a while.

Maybe I'm getting over him, she thought hopefully, and then they turned a corner and there was a man ahead of them who, for a fleeting second, looked like Ben, and her heart crashed into her mouth.

Over him? Not in this lifetime.

She drove them back, dropped Amy off and went straight home. Her feet hurt—funny, she was on her feet all day, and yet shopping made her feet hurt like nothing else—and she wanted to shut her front door behind her, kick off her shoes, pull on her sweats and curl up in the corner of the sofa with a cup of tea and the door shut, so she didn't have to listen to Ben and Florence.

But Ben was there, sitting on his doorstep, deep in thought.

Or was he? She opened her mouth, shut it and stood stock still as he got to his feet.

'You must be Daisy,' he said in Ben's voice, and she felt her heart start again.

'Matt?'

He smiled Ben's smile, the smile she hadn't seen for weeks, and held out his hand. 'It's good to meet you—especially since my brother seems to be out. I don't suppose you've got a key?'

'No.' Not any more. And she couldn't leave him standing on the doorstep. 'Why don't you come in?' she offered reluctantly. 'I'm just about to put the kettle on. Is he expecting you?'

'Sort of. I said I'd ring when I got here, but I couldn't give him a time. I've been at work all day.'

'Twins again?'

'No, just paperwork. I gather you've got MCMA twins. That's why I'm here, to see them in the clinic on Monday. I thought, since things were quietish at work, I'd skive off.'

She'd have to warn Amy, she thought. Send her a text, tell her to steer clear. She opened her door, and he stepped over the little fence and followed her in.

How odd. They were almost exactly the same to look at, she thought, eyeing him as he settled at her table and made himself comfortable, and yet there wasn't that tension there that she felt with Ben.

Just what Amy had said, in reverse.

She sent her a text while the kettle was boiling and then reached for the mugs.

'Tea or coffee?'

'Coffee, if there's a choice.'

'Real or instant, caf or decaf?'

He laughed. 'Whatever. Black, one sugar.'

Just like Ben.

She made a pot of real coffee, and sat down at right angles to him at the end. 'Are you hungry? I've got some biscuits.'

'Yes, Florence has told me about your biscuits.'

Did something happen to her face? Because he leant forwards slightly, propping his elbows on the table, and turned his head towards her, his eyes searching hers as she sat down again and slid the biscuits towards him.

'Ben hasn't told me what's happened, but he's stopped talking about you, so I can only imagine it's not going well,' he said quietly. 'Tell me to butt out, but he sounds unhappy.'

She swallowed. Tell him to butt out? How tempting.

'There are reasons,' she said instead.

'There always are.'

'I've warned Amy you're here,' she said, watching him carefully, and he went very still.

'OK. I won't pry if you don't.'

'Deal.'

'He told me you kiss like a goddess, by the way,' he said casually, and she nearly dropped her coffee. So much for the deal!

'When did he tell you that?' she squeaked.

'The day after he met you. Which is unlike him. He's usually much more circumspect.'

'Aren't we all?' she muttered, wondering when Ben was going to get back and take his brother away. 'Why don't you send him a text—tell him you're here?'

'No. He'll be here in ten seconds if I do that, and I'm actually quite happy getting to know the woman who seems to have broken my brother's heart.'

She swallowed. 'What makes you say that?'

He just laughed, as if she'd said something hilarious, and she sighed. 'OK, you can read his mind.'

'I don't have to. He just shuts down. It's easily recognisable.'

'Because you do it?' she asked, and he gave a wry little smile. Funny, she could read him just like she could Ben. The same slight facial movement, the same almost indiscernible shift in expression, and she knew what he was thinking.

'It's a shame, you know. I think he really loves you.'

'I know, but we have reasons.'

'Back to that again,' he said with a faint sigh, and then looked around. 'Nice house. I can see what he saw in his now.'

'I'm moving,' she said, and his eyebrows twitched together.

'Because of Ben?'

Because of Ben, because of Florence. Because her heart couldn't cope with being shredded all over again, a year or so down the line when he'd decided he couldn't handle their relationship after all.

'He says he's good at everything except relationships.'

'False modesty. He's actually very good at relationships. Jane was a one-off, and he never should have married her, but I wasn't much use to him when they started going out.'

She wanted to ask more, but she heard a key in his lock, and the door open and close, then Florence's little voice saying, 'Can we go and see Daisy, Daddy?'

She bit her lip and turned away, but not before he'd seen the anguish on her face, and with a soft sigh he got to his feet, pressed his hand on her shoulder and thanked her for the coffee.

'Stay there, I'll let myself out,' he said gently, and then he was gone.

She rang Amy.

'Where is he?' she asked, and Daisy could hear the fear in her voice. Fear? Dread?

'He's just gone round to Ben's. He was out, so Matt came and had coffee with me while he waited for him to get back.'

'Um—did he seem OK?'

Except that he'd promised not to pry if Daisy didn't. So no, not really.

'He seemed fine,' she lied. 'He's come up to see the

MCMA twins' parents at the clinic on Monday.' And meet the woman who'd broken his brother's heart. As if it wasn't mutual...

'Pity about Daisy.'

Ben froze, the kettle suspended, and shot his brother a killing glance.

'Don't go there.'

'I did. She gave me coffee. She's a lovely woman.'

'Yes—and one day, she'll make someone a wonderful wife.'

'You think?'

'I'm trying *not* to think about her, and you're not helping,' he growled, putting the kettle on to boil. 'So, are you going to see Amy while you're here?' he asked, and turned just in time to see the pain flash in his brother's eyes.

'I don't think that would be a good idea. Daisy's warned her I'm here, anyway, so I imagine she'll make herself scarce. She usually avoids confrontation.'

'Do you want to confront her?'

'Not especially. Look, can we leave this? Some things are just too deep, Ben. Even for us.'

He looked at Matt, at the lines sorrow had carved in his face, and with a rough sigh he turned away, propping his hands on the worktop and staring blindly down the garden.

'I love her,' he said softly, his voice clogged. 'I can't get over her. I fell in love with this house, and then I found her there next door, sexy and funny and kind— so kind, Matt. She's the kindest girl I've ever met. And the sexiest.'

He sucked in a breath, then went on, 'It was all working so well, and being next to her was just perfect. Too perfect, maybe. It was all I could handle, all either of us was ready for, and it was going so well, but then we fell in love and now we've got too much to cope with, too much love, too much emotion. We were burning ourselves out with emotion.'

'And you don't do emotion.'

He raised an eyebrow.

'OK, *we* don't do emotion,' Matt amended.

'I need her in my life, Matt. I can't have her, I can't deal with it, but I sure as hell can't cope without it. Without her.'

Matt propped himself up beside him and stared down the garden with him. 'You are ready to move on, you know. I know you denied it, but you've really fallen for her hard, and she has for you, judging by the look on her face when you and Florence came in. So how are you going to get her back?'

'I can't. She has issues about being a stepmother. She's almost been one, but he was a bastard and the relationship's scarred her, so it's all a bit déjà vu for her, and for me, too. I think she's afraid to trust her heart to anyone else, especially anyone else in the same situation, and I can understand that. Maybe if I'd been single, unencumbered, it might have been different.'

'So she was looking for a clean slate, and she found you?'

'Something like that.'

'So is Florence the stumbling block?'

'Not really. She adores Florence. It's the similarities, for both of us. It plays on our insecurities. I'm another single father with an ex-wife in the background, like the man who broke her heart, and she's on the rebound.'

'Just like Jane.'

'Pretty much. Except Peter's a decent man, unlike

Daisy's Mike. And you're right, I am ready to love again. I didn't think I was, but I am, and it was only when she bottled out that I realised how much. But as I say, she's not ready.'

'Could you wait for her?'

He gave a gruff laugh. 'There's no danger I'll be looking around for anyone else, Matt. I've never felt like this before, certainly not with Jane. She's seeing Peter again, by the way. It's looking serious.'

'Ah. Is he still in the army?'

'Yup. He's coming out in three months, and she's hoping they'll get married. It's what she's always wanted, anyway. What she should have had in the first place.'

Matt gave a quiet sigh. 'And you really don't think there's any hope for you and Daisy?'

'No, because she won't have me. She's told me that, in black and white. Look, can we drop this?'

For a moment Matt said nothing, then he levered himself away from the worktop and frowned at the hob.

'Are you doing anything with that kettle, apart from filling the kitchen with steam?'

'What do you suggest?'

'How about ordering in a curry?'

'I was going to make one.'

'Got beer?'

'Of course.'

'Done. You make the curry, I'll grab a shower, and then we can talk over these twins.'

She didn't see Matt again.

He and Ben dealt with the Grieves case, and she dealt with the others, and by the time she'd finished, he'd left for London.

It was a pity, she thought, that he hadn't taken his

brother with him, but she gritted her teeth and they got through the week, and then it was Laura's wedding— just to rub salt into the wound.

She droved to Nottingham with Amy, and despite her reservations, she had a good time. It would have been better if she'd been happier, but it was good to see the old crowd again and good for her morale to have to fend off the single men. And some who weren't.

They left the next morning after a long breakfast with everyone in the wedding party, and she dropped Amy off and went home, glad it was over. Maybe she could have a bit of peace from weddings now for a while.

As she put her car away, she realised that Ben's car wasn't there, and felt a twinge of disappointment.

Silly. So very, very silly. The sooner she moved, the better.

She let herself in and found her phone blinking, and scrolled through the call log. Ben had rung her and left a message. So why not her mobile? Because it was still switched off since the wedding, she realised, and stared at the blinking light. For a moment she nearly didn't pick the message up, but then she weakened. It would be something about work, she was sure of it—the MCMA twins, perhaps?

It wasn't.

'Daisy, can you call me as soon as you get this? I'm at the hospital with Florence.'

Oh, dear God. Whatever had happened? Her fingers trembling, she rang him without questioning it. She'd told him to call her if he ever needed her again, and he hadn't. Until now. And if he needed her, for whatever reason, she'd be there for him.

CHAPTER TEN

BEN paced the tiny room, his nerves on edge.

Jane had called him at five thirty that morning, to tell him she felt dreadful. Another migraine, he'd thought dismissively. It wasn't a migraine. It was something much worse, something frightening and potentially threatening to Florence and the status quo.

She was lying in the dark when he got there, and when he went in she moaned and flinched away from the landing light.

'Are you OK?' he asked, instantly concerned.

'No, I feel so ill. I think my head's going to explode,' she whispered. 'Ben, it's never felt like this. I'm scared.'

He didn't mess about. It could have been nothing, or it could have been something very sinister—a bleed, a tumour—or meningitis. Fear clawed at him. What if Florence hadn't just been tired yesterday? She'd been grizzly, fretful, and he'd pretty much dismissed it. But what if…?

He called an ambulance. Then he called Jane's mother, but she was away on holiday, he remembered as the phone rang and rang and rang, and he had no idea how to get hold of Peter. He might even be on a posting abroad, or on some operational exercise.

He found her handbag, her phone and her house keys,

threw some basic essentials into a bag and went to let the paramedics in.

Jane was admitted to MAU, and they sent him with Florence to the Paediatric Admissions Unit to be on the safe side. She had bloods taken and all manner of tests and examinations, and now he was waiting for the results, his nerves stretched taut.

And he needed Daisy as he'd never needed her before.

He called her, but her mobile was off, so he left a message on her house phone. Please get it, he thought desperately. Don't go back to Amy's and stay there till the evening. Please go home and find the message and ring me.

She didn't ring, and he tried again. No reply.

He didn't have Amy's number. He could have pulled rank and got it from HR, but it wasn't really necessary, and the only reason he wanted Daisy was for moral support. Well, he'd just have to tough it out.

His ringtone—the one he'd reserved for her—shattered the fraught silence, and he grabbed the phone from his pocket and stabbed the answer button. 'Daisy—thank God,' he said, weak with relief.

'Ben, what's going on? What's happened to her?'

He stepped out of the door so he didn't wake his daughter. 'It's Jane. She's been admitted. She might have meningitis. They're checking Florence to make sure she's OK, but she's been grizzly, and...'

'Do you want me to come?' she asked without hesitation, and he felt his eyes burn. Always thoughtful. Always putting others first. God, he loved her so much.

'If you don't mind.'

'Of course I don't,' she said, and he told her to come to the PAU. Florence was in a vacant side room, just as a precaution, and would stay there until they knew the outcome of both Jane's and her investigations. And now, after a few hours of it, he was tearing his hair out.

Till Daisy walked in and wrapped her arms around him and hugged him hard. He hugged her back, hanging on for dear life, and after a moment she lifted her head and stared up at him, concern transparent in her eyes.

'Any news?'

He shook his head. 'No. They're waiting for the results of Jane's lumbar puncture. If it's bacterial meningitis, then Florence could still be at risk, but they can't find anything wrong with her at the moment except what's most likely a slight cold, so we're probably going to be sent home to watch and wait. I need to distract her because she's worried about Jane and keeps asking for her, but I'm going crazy. I daren't take my eyes off her till I know what it is.'

'What can I do, Ben? Tell me what to do, what you need,' Daisy offered instantly, to his amazement.

He couldn't ask it of her. She'd found the last few weeks incredibly difficult, and he was still feeling guilty—always would—but Daisy assured him it was fine, and he had to believe her because he'd never needed her as he did then.

He wasn't convinced, but he had little choice. 'I need to try and get hold of Peter for her. I'm not sure where he is, but his number's bound to be in her phone and she's got it with her. I ought to check on her, too, see if I can find anything out while I'm there.'

'So go,' she said.

Jane was awake, dazed with pain but coherent enough to speak, and she was desperate to see Peter. 'His number's in my phone,' she said, her voice slurred, and he rang him and filled him in.

'Can I talk to her?' he asked.

'Sure.'

He handed the phone over, and Jane started to cry. He looked away. She loved him, that much was obvious, and from the sound of his voice, Peter loved her, too. He wondered what the future held for them, because it would have a knock-on effect on Florence, and he might end up picking up the pieces.

Suddenly weary, he took the phone back from her when she held it out, and gave Peter directions in the hospital to find the ward.

'He's coming now,' Jane whispered. 'You need to get back to Florence. Who's with her?'

'Daisy,' he said, and she closed her eyes and sighed.

'That's good. Florence loves her—but I thought—'

'Yeah, well, she offered.' Ages ago, but today he'd needed to take her up on it, and she'd come, without a murmur.

He so, so didn't deserve her.

And he wanted her so much.

'Go back to her,' Jane murmured. 'I'll be all right. He'll be here soon.'

He squeezed her hand and left her, hurrying back to the PAU to find Daisy sitting in the chair with Florence on her lap, looking at a book.

'Daddy, Daisy's reading to me!' she announced when he went in, and she sounded much, much better.

'*Freddie Frog?*' he said with a smile, and Daisy shrugged and smiled.

'It was here.'

'I know. Thank goodness I had the foresight to bring it. It's the only book she likes now.'

Her smile was apologetic. 'I'm sorry.'

'Don't be,' he said. The book was the biggest success story of the year, as far as he was concerned, and he often found her showing the pictures to Froggy in the garden, sitting on the lawn in the shade of the little apple tree and telling him the story.

She'd asked him once if he thought Froggy missed Daisy, and he'd somehow managed to answer her coherently.

Froggy? No. As for Ben himself, that was a different matter, and Florence, too. They both missed her, and the hole in their lives was huge.

They got the all clear to take her home under strict observation, and they went back in convoy. He took Florence inside and got her a drink and a biscuit, and Daisy joined them a few minutes later in the garden.

'I thought you might need some moral support,' she said softly, and settled down cross-legged on the grass next to Florence. She snuggled up to Daisy, her head on her lap and her thumb in her mouth, while Daisy ran her fingers gently through her hair and told her a story.

To look at her, you'd never know there was anything wrong, he thought, staring longingly at Daisy, that under that serenely smiling exterior her heart was in turmoil, but he knew it must be, because his was, too.

When the story was finished, she helped him with the weeding, and Florence kissed Froggy and hid him for Ben to find, and then ran giggling behind Daisy and hid herself from him, too, and Daisy played along with it like a trouper while Tabitha watched them over the fence from the safety of the conservatory roof.

Florence tried to coax her, but Tabitha just settled down, folded her paws under her chest and watched them play, and Ben, out of the corner of his eye, watched them all and wished that it was real, and all the time the fear was eating at him.

And then the hospital rang him.

He took the call in the kitchen, watching Florence out of the window, feeling as if his whole life was hanging in the balance as he waited for the verdict.

It wasn't bacterial meningitis, it was viral meningitis. Not transmissible in that form, all Florence would get was a cold, if that. Probably the one she had, the little niggle that had made her crabby yesterday and sleepy today.

The relief nearly took the legs out from under him, and he felt his eyes prickle with tears. God, she was so precious to him, so incredibly precious.

'Are you OK?'

He nodded, ended the call and hugged Daisy hard. 'It's viral,' he mumbled into her hair. 'She's fine. They ruled it out with the lumbar puncture, and she's staying in hospital on IV opiates for the pain, and they're going to do scans and blood tests and numerous other things just to be sure, but it's definitely not bacterial meningitis, so Florence is safe. She's just got a little cold.'

'Thank goodness for that,' she said, her voice relieved, and he hugged her again for caring, and for her support, and just because holding her felt so damn good he couldn't let her go.

She eased away. 'So what happens now?'

'God knows. I'll have to wing it. Will you and Evan be able to manage the antenatal clinic without me? And the Grieves twins' check-up? I'm not sure what time their appointment is, I might be able to make it,' he added, thinking on his feet.

'I'm sure we'll cope,' she said calmly. 'I can email

the scans to Matt, can't I, and get his verdict, if necessary. The clinic will be fine.'

'It's not just Monday, Daisy,' he said, troubled. 'I'm
on call all week, and Jane's mother's away till Tuesday
and in any case she can't do the nights because she takes
sleeping pills. It could go on for weeks. What the hell
am I going to do?'

'Accept my help?' she said simply, although there
was nothing simple about it and they both knew it, but
there was no choice for her, Daisy realised. She'd just
have to protect her heart as well as she could, but she
couldn't walk away from them when they needed her.
'I'll stay with you and cover you when I'm not on call
myself. We'll get through this.'

He wanted to hug her again, but it didn't somehow
seem like a good idea, so he just thanked her, sighed
with relief and went back out to the garden to Florence.
She was sitting on the edge of the path talking very seriously to Froggy, and he stood and watched her for a
moment, overwhelmed by his love for her.

'She's going to be fine,' Daisy said softly from his
side, and he nodded.

She was. But how about them? Daisy was going to be
staying here, in his house, so near and yet so far. How
on earth were they going to cope with that?

Jane came out of hospital on Tuesday afternoon, at
which point his life went back to normal. Well, his work
life, anyway. His home life was a different matter.

Florence stayed with him as planned, and he dropped
her off every morning at nursery and picked her up from
Jane's when he finished work. Jane wasn't well enough
to cope with Florence after nursery school, her head
still aching constantly, so her mother did the afternoon

nursery school runs and fed her, but she couldn't really cope with much more.

And then there were the nights, and because he was on call for the week, and because nobody was able to swap, it was Daisy who picked up the pieces.

Dear, beloved Daisy, who kept out of the way in her own house all evening unless he had to call on her, and then slept on the sofabed in his sitting room from midnight to six and was gone before Florence woke.

He had to call her back on Thursday morning, because he was paged by the hospital, and she came round with her hair wound up in a towel and her dressing gown on.

'I don't know if I'll be back in time to take her to nursery,' he said apologetically. 'I could be a while in Theatre, by the sound of it. Nasty RTA. I don't know what I might have to do.'

'Don't worry, I'll take her to nursery, I know where it is.'

'Thanks. I owe you. I'll put the car seat by your car.'

And without thinking, he leant over and kissed her. Just lightly, but it was enough to shock her immobile. Him, too. Their eyes locked, and after a breathless second he moved away, grabbed his keys and went out of the back door.

She sucked in a breath and went upstairs to wake Florence and take her back to her house, armed with her clothes and toothbrush, her lips still tingling.

'Shall we have breakfast?' she asked when they got there, and Florence nodded. They looked in the cupboard and found some cereal, but it was a bit ancient. Daisy tasted it and pulled a face.

'Is it horrid?' Florence asked.

'Very horrid. It's like yucky cardboard. Shall we have toast, instead?'

'I like toast.'

'Good. So do I.'

'Have you got peanut butter? I love peanut butter.'

'No. I've got chocolate spread, though.'

Florence's eyes widened, and Daisy spread it liberally on her toast and then winced as Florence managed to get it all over the table and her face and hands.

While Tabitha licked the table clean, Daisy cleaned her up, swiping the wriggling, giggling child with a damp flannel, and then she took her upstairs to dress them both, wondering as she did so how Ben was getting on.

'I don't want to go to nursery,' Florence told her as they pulled up outside, her bottom lip sticking out. 'I want to stay with you.'

She'd been expecting it. One of the life-skills she'd acquired during her time with Mike had been taking the children to school on occasions, and they'd always tried it on.

'It would be nice, wouldn't it?' she said placidly. 'But I have to go to work and help all the mummies have their new babies, and you have to go to nursery and see all your friends. I tell you what, though, it'll soon be the weekend, and if Daddy has to go to the hospital, if you're a good girl now I'll take you to the playground, and maybe we can take a picnic. How about that?'

She brightened instantly. 'A picnic? Can we take Froggy?'

She stifled a laugh. That wretched concrete frog was destined to feature in every conversation!

'I expect so. Go on, in you go, darling. I'll see you later.'

Florence took two steps up the path, then ran back and reached up, and Daisy bent and kissed her good-bye, her heart contracting as Florence cuddled close for a second before running off again.

Dear, sweet child. She loved her so much. If only she could dare to trust in this love, could trust herself not to fail, could trust Ben not to leave—so many if onlys.

She got back in the car and hurried to work, to find Ben just coming out of Theatre.

'How is she?'

He shook his head. 'Rough, but we saved the baby—thirty seven weeks, perfect little boy and he's doing well. But Mum's got a nasty tear in her liver and massive blood loss. They're working on her now but I don't know if she'll make it, and Dad's got a fractured femur.'

'Oh, Ben, I'm so sorry.'

'Yeah. Life sucks sometimes. I'm just going to find him and tell him he's a father. I'll leave the rest of the news till after he's had his leg pinned. They might know more by then. How's Florence?'

'Fine. She's at nursery, but I had to bribe her with the offer of a picnic in the playground at the weekend.'

He gave a soft huff of laughter, and unexpectedly, his eyes glazed. 'You're such a star,' he murmured, and then dragging in a breath, he walked away to find the father.

She didn't envy him but she knew he'd handle it well, because for all he managed to keep his emotions to himself most of the time, he was very sensitive to other people's feelings.

It was one of the very, very many things about him that she loved.

They met up for coffee, and he was looking happier. 'Sheena Lewis made it,' he told her.

'Your mum with the liver?'

'Yeah. Baby's fine, she's going to recover, Dad's been pinned and plated and the grandparents are on their way to look after the kids. They've got five, apparently—four of his, and this one. They've only been married just under a year.'

'And she's taken on his four children?'

'Mmm. She must be a saint.'

'Or very brave,' she said softly, wishing...

She met the mother later that day, resting quietly in a side room with her baby beside her looking none the worse for wear, and while she was checking Sheena, her mother-in-law came in with two of the children.

'Hello, darlings,' Sheena said weakly, her eyes filling with tears, and they leant carefully over and kissed her cheeks, one each side, their little faces worried.

Bless their little hearts, Daisy thought, and was on her way out when their grandmother stopped her with a gentle hand on her arm.

'Are you attached to her doctor? Ben something, I think?' she asked quietly, and Daisy nodded. Attached? You could say that, she thought, and resisted the urge to laugh hysterically or burst into tears.

'Yes, I'm his registrar. If you want to talk to him I'm sure he's around.'

'Oh, no, don't disturb him. I just wanted to thank him for saving the baby, and keeping Dan so well informed. He was so worried, and he kept him right up to date apparently and really put his mind at rest. And he didn't lie about how serious it was. Dan was really grateful for that—it meant he could trust him.'

How like Ben. Tell the awful truth, but do it so carefully, so sensitively that it didn't break the person receiving it.

'I'll tell him. Thank you. Please don't make her too tired, will you? She's been through an awful lot.'

'No, we won't, but the children were desperate to see her. My husband's got the younger ones downstairs in the café keeping them amused for a minute, and then we're taking them home.'

'Well, good luck with it. I don't envy you.' *Liar*!

'Oh, we love it, and we'd do anything for them,' Mrs Lewis said with a doting smile. 'Sheena's been a god-send to the family. We all love her to bits.'

'I'm sure you do.'

Daisy summoned a smile and left. If only Mike's family had felt like that. If only *he* had felt like that, instead of just making use of her until he'd convinced his wife to have him back.

No! Stop thinking about the past. It's done. Forget it.

And move on?

She felt a shiver of something. Fear? Anticipation? Hope?

If only…

Their arrangement worked fine until the weekend, and then all hell broke loose at work and it all got much more complicated.

He was in and out all Friday night, and then again in the morning, and it became obvious to Daisy that she was going to have to be there all the time. And that brought guilt, because Tabitha was getting lonely.

But maybe she didn't need to feel guilty, because Tabitha was also getting braver, and while Daisy was in the kitchen making a picnic to take to the playground, she looked up and found Florence sitting on the lawn with Froggy on one side and Tabitha, just out of reach, on the other, as if she was trying to decide if Florence was OK or not.

She smiled, but it was bitter-sweet. There was no point in Tabitha getting used to Florence, because they were going to move. At least, that was the plan, but she'd done nothing about it. There weren't any jobs, or none that she wanted, and she wasn't going to move until she found one. That would be foolish.

Only marginally less foolish than being here like this with Florence.

Her phone rang, and she glanced at the display as she answered it. 'Hi, Ben. How's it going?'

'OK. Where are you?'

'In the kitchen, making a picnic. Why?'

'Because I'm done here. Are you about to go?

'Yes—five minutes?'

'Make me a sandwich. I'll be with you.'

She slid the phone back in her pocket and sighed. He was hijacking their picnic, taking it and making it something it wasn't meant to be, and she felt sweat break out on her palms.

She could do covering Florence, because that was babysitting in an emergency. But—picnicking with her and her father, in the playground? That was lunacy. Playing happy families, for heavens' sake. Not wise. So, so not wise.

She shut her eyes briefly, then opened them again and reached for the bread, and as she did so, she saw Tabitha curl up beside Florence and settle down, the little girl's hand stroking her incredibly gently, and without warning hot, scalding tears spilled down her cheeks.

He got back just as Daisy put the last few things into a bag.

'Perfect timing,' she said crisply. 'You can carry the lunch. Or Froggy. Take your pick.'

He felt his eyebrows crunch together. 'Froggy?' he said incredulously, and then started to laugh. 'Oh, God, Daisy, we've made a monster.'

'*We* haven't made anything,' she said flatly, and hoisting the bag off the worktop, she went out into the garden, leaving him to follow in confusion.

'Is it time? Are we going?' Florence asked, dancing from foot to foot, and they set off three abreast with Florence skipping in between them.

'Can we do "One two three whee?"' she asked, holding up her arms, and in unison they both said, 'No!'

Their eyes met over her head, remembering her elbow, remembering the conversation they'd had shortly before, in the very playground they were going to. Daisy's eyes clouded, but he was the first to look away.

'We have to be careful with your elbow. You can go on the swing,' he told her firmly.

'Will you push me *really* high?'

'*Really* high,' he promised.

'Can Froggy come on the swing?'

And to think that last week she'd been so subdued, and he'd been worried! Whatever had been wrong with her had clearly passed and left her full of beans, and he wondered what kind of a day Daisy had had with her. Hellish, probably, judging by her rather short greeting.

Oh, damn. Was she mad with him because he'd gate-crashed their picnic? He'd thought it would help, dilute her interaction with Florence, but maybe he'd been wrong. Maybe it just made it worse.

He took Florence on the swing with Froggy watching safely from the sidelines, and he watched Daisy setting out the picnic out of the corner of his eye. She was kneeling on a rug under a tree, unloading all the goodies, and then she looked up and waved them over.

'Is it time for our picnic?' Florence asked, and she nodded, so Ben lifted her out of the seat and she ran over, settling down cross legged on the rug and patting the space next to her for Froggy—which left a space for him beside Daisy.

Damn. He'd hoped—what had he hoped? That a concrete frog would be enough to keep them apart? Hardly. A brick wall would be more like it. And this had been his idea. He could just as easily have stayed at the hospital, but it didn't seem fair, and after the week they'd all had, he'd just longed to do something normal.

Something a family would do.

He picked up a sandwich at random and bit into it, then stopped in his tracks, his mouth rebelling.

'What...?'

'Chocolate spread,' Daisy said. 'Florence chose it.'

He looked at it in a mixture of confusion and disgust, and she took pity on him. 'I suppose you'd rather have ham and cheese and chutney?' she said, trying not to laugh, and he handed Florence the chocolate spread sandwich, swallowed the single bite reluctantly and took the sandwich Daisy was offering him.

'Thank you,' he said fervently. 'For a moment there, I thought I was going to have to eat it or starve.'

'Would I do that to you?' she murmured, but he just grunted and ate his sandwich, and she watched Florence chomping her way through the chocolate spread sandwich and a small banana and some crisps, in no particular order, and wished she could bottle this moment and get it out, in the long dark days ahead after she'd found another job and moved away and Florence and Ben were in the past.

She picked a daisy out of the grass, and then another, absently slitting the stem of the first and threading the other through it, then adding another, and another—

'What are you doing?' Florence asked curiously, and she blinked and dragged herself back to the here and now.

'Making a daisy chain. It doesn't matter if we pick them, the daisies are weeds, really, they don't belong here.' Funny, that, she thought. Another Daisy that didn't belong. 'Look—if you slit the stem with your nail, and you're very careful, you can thread another one through, and if you do it enough times you can make a necklace.'

Florence's little fingers couldn't manage, but she could pick them, very carefully. 'Keep the stems as long as you can,' Daisy asked, 'and mind you don't squash them.'

And as Ben watched and Florence brought her the little white flowers that didn't belong, she made a necklace for Florence and put it over her head. 'There you go, Princess. Your very own daisy chain.'

Her eyes were huge blue saucers. 'It's *really* pretty,' she said, stroking it as carefully as she would a tiny bird. 'Daddy, look!'

'I'm looking,' he said gruffly, and Daisy glanced up and caught his eyes, and her breath jammed in her throat.

Oh, no. No, no, no! They weren't supposed to be doing this! Where was his pager when she needed it? Not that she wanted some poor woman to have an emergency, but if anybody was planning one, now would be a good time.

Nobody was.

And Ben, lounging back on one elbow so he was

half facing her, plucked a daisy off the little pile that Florence had created and fingered it thoughtfully.

'I can remember, when we were kids, the girls would get a daisy and pull the petals off, one by one, and as they did it they'd say, "He loves me," then "he loves me not," each time they'd pull a petal out, like this, until they got to the last one, and then they'd pull it out, too, like this—"He loves me",' he ended, pulling the last few petals out in one and looking straight into Daisy's eyes.

He loves me.

She swallowed and looked hastily away.

'What does he loves me not mean?' Florence asked.

'It means he doesn't love me,' Daisy told her, and looked pointedly at Ben, who just smiled sadly and got to his feet.

'Come on, Florence. Let's go on the see-saw.'

'With Daisy!' she squealed, getting to her feet and pulling Daisy up, and what was she supposed to say to that?

Staring daggers at him, she sat on the end of the see-saw, Florence cuddled up to her as she'd been before, all those weeks ago, and damn him, he just smiled sadly at her and rocked them gently up and down, up and down, singing, 'See-saw, Marjorie Daw, Johnny shall have a new master,' his deep voice soft and warm and curiously comforting. Daisy closed her eyes so she didn't have to look at him, but she could still hear him, could imagine him quietly rocking a baby and singing nursery rhymes, and her heart was splintering as he sang, and the see-saw rose and fell, and rose and fell, until at last she couldn't bear it any more.

'I want to get off,' she said firmly, and he stopped, so her feet were just off the ground and their eyes were locked.

'Count the petals on a daisy, Daisy,' he said softly, and let her down.

She got off. 'They have an even number,' she said expressionlessly, and walked away.

He watched her packing up the picnic, and with a quiet sigh he got off the see-saw and took Florence to play on the slide. He didn't know what to do. He loved her. She loved him, and she loved Florence. If only she could believe in them, then maybe he could dare to hope…

CHAPTER ELEVEN

His pager went off just as Florence was settled in her bed.

Daisy had gone home as soon as they'd got back from their picnic. 'Call me if you need me,' she'd said, and walked out, leaving Florence confused and disappointed, because she'd wanted Daisy to read her a story. Even Tabitha, sunning herself in the garden, had looked confused when she disappeared.

And it was his fault, apparently. Well, that didn't surprise him. The atmosphere between them had been fraught since the moment he'd come home from the hospital, and apart from a brief interlude in the playground, it hadn't improved since.

So she'd gone home—to regroup, presumably, and rant about him in private—and he'd put Florence to bed. He'd really hoped he wouldn't need her, so that she could have some time away from the situation to chill out and destress, but the pager wasn't on their side.

He was reaching for the phone to call her when she knocked on the door and walked in. 'I heard the pager,' she said flatly. 'I hope you aren't going to be long, I wanted a bath tonight.'

'Have one here. I could be ages, judging by the look of this. It's a breech that's on a go-slow, so fill the bath and take your time. There's wine in the fridge and Florence is in bed.'

Wine. That was all she needed, on an empty stomach. But the bath? Oh, yes. She went back to her house, grabbed her things—bubble bath, her razor, deodorant, moisturiser, body butter—she was really going to go for it, and if he was back in ten minutes, tough, because she wasn't in the mood to hurry. At all.

She ran the bath, thought why not, went and got a glass of wine and slid under the bubbles. Bliss. There were no candles—maybe not a good idea with a child in the house, but a luxury she longed for. She glanced mournfully at the wall, picturing her bathroom on the other side of it, her sanctuary.

This room was clean, efficient and masculine, dominated by a huge walk-in shower, and his things were all over it. His dressing gown on the back of the door, his toothbrush on the basin. A pair of jeans had been chucked in the corner, next to Florence's tiny little pink knickers and a T-shirt with a frog on it.

Oh, damn you, Ben Walker, damn you and your gorgeous little daughter and your 'he loves me, he loves me not' nonsense. She had no idea how many petals there were on a daisy, and she was absolutely *not* counting them!

She sipped the wine, sighed and slid a little lower under the bubbles. Mmm. Better. Half an hour of this, and maybe she'd feel a lot less fraught and a little bit more reasonable.

'Daisy?'

The house was in darkness, except for the nightlight spilling from Florence's room. He put the hall lights on and went up to check, but there was no sign of her, just Tabitha curled up in a ball at the foot of Florence's bed, next to the frog cushion. He ought to move her, he thought, but then he shrugged. He'd had cats on the bed all his childhood and they'd never done him any harm. He pulled the door to, and paused outside the bathroom to listen.

Nothing.

'Daisy?' he murmured, and tapped very lightly so as not to wake Florence, but there was no reply.

Where the hell was she? She was supposed to be looking after Florence, and she'd clearly gone home— and some time ago, because it was dark outside now, and it was three hours since he'd left, so she hadn't just nipped out to fetch something from next door or the lights would still be on.

But there were no lights on in her house, either, and she wouldn't just leave Florence, she wasn't irresponsible. Had she had an accident? Surely she couldn't *still* be in the bath?

He opened the door quietly, and his breath left him in a soft huff of relief, mingled with regret and a deep and painful yearning.

Oh, Daisy.

She was in the bath, her eyes closed, fingers loosely wrapped around a wine glass balanced precariously on her sternum, and through the very few bubbles that still floated on the surface, he could see her chest rising and falling gently, rocking the half-full glass with every breath.

Sleeping Beauty meets the Siren on the Rocks, he thought, and walked up to her, perching on the edge of the bath and staring down at her, mesmerised. God, she was gorgeous. Even like that, with her mouth hanging slightly open and her fingers round a wine glass, looking for all the world like a lush.

He smiled fondly and eased the glass out of her fingers, waking her abruptly. Startled, she sat up, clutching her arms across her chest and staring at him with wild eyes as the water sloshed and settled. Then she let out her breath on a gasp.

'Ben! Gosh, you scared the living daylights out of me. Is Florence all right?'

'She's fine,' he said, stifling a smile. 'Why don't you get out of there and dry off and come downstairs and I'll get you another glass of wine. Have you eaten tonight?'

She shook her head. 'No, not yet. What's the time? The water's freezing.'

'I'm not surprised, it's ten o'clock. I'll call a takeaway. What do you fancy?'

She looked at him, her lips parting slightly, her eyes unreadable in the soft flood of light from the landing. He thought she might be blushing, and it made him want to smile. Or kiss her.

'Anything. Go away, Ben—and shut the door behind you!' she squeaked, her modesty returning as she woke up properly.

He left her with the tatters of her dignity, changed his trousers because they'd got soaked when she sat up so abruptly, and went downstairs to phone for a takeaway. Even if he had to go out again before it arrived, she could eat, and if she was feeling mellow maybe she'd even save him some.

She came down a few minutes later, wrapped in her dressing gown and looking tousled and delectable. She smelt gorgeous, and he wanted to pull her into his arms and just hold her.

'I'm sorry I've been crabby,' she said, before he could

do anything so rash. Just as well. And maybe it would make sense to talk.

'Why have you? Because I gatecrashed your picnic?'

'Partly,' she admitted. 'It took it from me babysitting to something else, something we'd agreed we wouldn't do any more. And then when we got there, there was all that silly *nonsense* with the daisies.'

'What silly nonsense was that?' he asked, perfectly serious, and her heart thumped in her chest.

'You were pushing my buttons, Ben.'

'I was telling you that I still love you.'

She felt her eyes fill, and looked hastily away. 'Ben, we can't—'

'Why can't we? I've been thinking about it a lot—endlessly, in fact. About why you're so worried about us. And I don't think it's anything to do with Florence—'

'I don't want to hurt her!'

'But you won't. She adores you, Daisy, and you adore her. And I know you'll never hurt her.'

'But she will be hurt—when we split up, she *will* be hurt.'

'What if we don't?'

She turned slowly and looked at him. 'What are you saying?'

'I'm saying maybe we didn't give ourselves enough time. Maybe we didn't get to know each other well enough. As far as Daisy's concerned, you're just a friend of mine who lives next door and does stuff with us occasionally. If we give ourselves another chance, spend some time alone together, without changing anything with Florence, then maybe we could learn to trust each other. Maybe we could make it work.'

'And if we can't?'

'Then she won't be hurt any more than she is now, and at least we will have tried.'

She felt a tiny stirring of hope, but she didn't dare let it grow. Not just yet.

'What about Jane? What will she think?'

'Don't worry about Jane. I saw her yesterday when I picked Florence up, and Peter arrived while I was there. He's there for the weekend, and he scooped Florence up and gave her a big kiss hello, and she hugged him and called him Uncle Peter. And Jane took me on one side and told me that they're thinking of getting married. And Florence doesn't seem even slightly fazed by him being around.'

'Are you?' she asked, reading his eyes carefully, because Mike would have gone into orbit if his wife had even looked at another man, but Ben just shook his head.

'Why would I be? Except in so far as it affects Florence, and it really doesn't seem to. She clearly likes him, and Jane's been in love with him for years. He wouldn't marry her before because he was in the army bomb disposal team, and he didn't want her ending up a widow. We met at a mutual friend's wedding a few months after they split up, and I think she'd decided then that it was time to move on. And I was there, physically and mentally sound, single, ready for a permanent relationship, and I had decent career prospects. And if she couldn't have Peter, then I ticked all the necessary boxes. And then she forgot to take her pill one day and got pregnant.'

'So you married her.'

'Yes. She was having my child, and to be honest she ticked the boxes for me in the same sort of way. Matt tried to warn me that it wasn't enough, but he had his own problems at the time and I ignored him, because following his heart didn't seem to have done him any good. And after we were married, I realised he was right. Jane was lonely, she wanted to come back here to be near her family, and of course she missed Peter. He's from round here, too, and I think that was a big part of her wanting to come back.'

'Did you know about him?' she asked, appalled that he might have found out after they were married—or at least, after it was too late.

'I did by then. She'd realised she didn't love me, and she didn't want to be with me. She said it wouldn't be good for Florence anyway to have unhappy parents who were stuck with each other in a relationship that was going nowhere. I didn't agree at the time, I thought she was using me and maybe had all along, but maybe I agree now, now I can see that it works. Anyway, we split up and she moved up here, and as soon as I could get a job in the area, I was to move closer so I could share Florence's care. And in the time it took for that to happen, Peter came back into her life.'

'But I thought he was still in the army?'

'He is, but he's just reaching the end of his commission and he'll be UK based now to the end, but you've only got to see them together to see how well it works for them. I know they'll be all right, and he's a thoroughly decent guy.'

Her heart was thumping. 'So—you're not worried about Florence being upset by you having a relationship with me? If—if we felt it could work? I mean—*really* work.'

He gave a fleeting smile, and grazed her cheek gently with his knuckles. 'No. Not at all. Not now I know you, because I know you'd never hurt her. Jane says she talks about you all the time and seems very

fond of you, and if we don't involve her any more than
we already have until we're both utterly sure about it,
then I can't see it'll do her any harm. And I can't go on
like this, Daisy. I really miss you, and I really want to
see if what we've got could work. I'm not on call after
tomorrow, and Jane's better now, so Florence will be
back there from tomorrow night.'

And they could be alone. It was written in his eyes,
in the longing and hope she could read there so clearly,
and it echoed the longing she didn't dare give a voice
to.

'Please give me a chance,' he went on, his voice serious. 'Let me prove to you that this can work. Give me
this coming week—and next weekend. Maybe Jane can
have Florence and we can spend some time together
doing fun stuff.'

'I might be working.'

'You aren't. I changed the rota.'

She opened her mouth to tell him not to interfere,
and then she caught the uncertainty in his eyes.

'OK,' she said, capitulating, but with reservations.
'We'll try. This week. I don't know about the weekend
yet.'

'Just don't rule it out.'

He hugged her briefly, but before her arms could
come up and circle him and hold him to her heart, the
knocker sounded.

'That'll be our food,' he said, and let her go, and she
sucked in a deep breath and closed her eyes.

What on *earth* had she just done?

She woke up on Monday morning tingling with anticipation. Ben had been called out again Sunday night and
he'd sent her home.

'Tomorrow. I don't want any interruptions,' he'd said, with a promise in his eyes, and she'd gone home to bed alone. It was lovely to sleep in it again, after a week on Ben's sofa bed, and she woke refreshed and looking forward to going to work for the first time since their breakup.

Ever since then she'd been avoiding him, trying to keep out of his way, and when they'd been forced together there'd been a tension that she was sure everyone would have felt.

But now—now it was back to how it had been, working together seamlessly through the ward round and the routine of the morning, then Mel and Adrian Grieves came into the antenatal clinic for their check-up scan on the monoamniotic twins. They were twenty four weeks now, and although there was a loose tangle that didn't seem to want to untangle, both twins were growing well, their heartbeats were strong and healthy, and Ben was happy.

So were the parents.

'Are they viable now?' Mel asked, and Ben pulled a face.

'At a push. I wouldn't want to deliver them yet, not for at least eight more weeks, but they would stand a chance now, yes.'

The tension went out of her, and her husband squeezed her shoulder as her eyes welled with tears. 'I've been so scared for them. It just seems to have been such a long time.'

'Well, it isn't over yet, but we'll have you in in a few more weeks—maybe two? The cords *are* tangled, and I do have a little bit of concern, but at the moment they're fine and I'm happy to leave them. If they get another loop in that tangle, I'll want you here, so maybe from next week have a bag in the car with you, just in case. OK?'

She nodded, looking almost excited, as if for the first time she dared to let herself believe it could be all right.

'Do you think they'll make it?' Daisy asked Ben when they'd left.

'I hope so. I want you in charge of them when she's admitted. Daily scans, Doppler three times a day, at least, and really close scrutiny. If she feels they're moving a lot it could be because there's a problem, so I want her checked again then, day or night.'

He broke off and met her eyes searchingly. 'You will be here, won't you? Until we deliver them? I really want you in charge of the day-to-day running of this case, even if we…'

'Don't you trust Evan?'

'Trust? Yes, of course I do, he's a box-ticker and he wouldn't let anything happen to them, but I don't think he's right for Mel. I want *you*,' he said quietly. 'Mel knows you, and so do I. And you don't have an ego so you won't try to go it alone if you're worried.'

She gave a wry little laugh. 'Fair point. But there aren't any jobs for me to go to anyway, so even if we decide it doesn't work, you'll be stuck with me for a while, so, yeah, I'll be here.'

His gaze didn't flicker from her eyes. 'Good, because I feel we could be getting somewhere now. Give us time, Daisy. Please. And have a little faith in me.'

She felt her smile slip, and nodded. 'I will. And whatever happens, I'll stay for the twins at least.'

He levered himself off the edge of the desk and took her shoulders in his hands. 'Thank you,' he said quietly, and folded her into his arms for a brief and gentle hug. Then dropping a kiss on her hair, he eased away and swatted her lightly on the bottom. 'Off you go, Dr Daisy, before I do something unprofessional to you halfway through the antenatal clinic. And I'm cooking for you tonight, by the way.'

'I'll look forward to it,' she said, and went off to find her next patient, her heart lighter than it had been for weeks.

He sent her off for a relaxing bath in her lovely sanctuary when she got home from work, and when she came down, the dining room was transformed.

He'd cooked her a meal, laid the table, lit candles—but they didn't get that far. He poured her a glass of wine, handed it to her and kissed her fleetingly, then the wine glass ended up on the table and she ended up in his arms.

'Oh, Daisy, I've missed you so damn much,' he said raggedly into her hair, cradling her close. 'Missed having you to myself, missed spending time alone with you doing nothing in particular, just being with you. And it feels *so* good just to hold you.'

She lifted her head and looked up into his eyes. 'Will supper keep?'

He went over to the hob, drained the potatoes, turned off the heat under the casserole and came back to her. 'It will now,' he said, smiling as he cradled her face in his hands and kissed her lingeringly. 'Did you have anything special in mind?'

They ate later, with the candles burned down and the casserole well and truly tender, and Tabitha mugged him for scraps which he gave her without question.

'You shouldn't feed her at the table,' she said disapprovingly, but in fact she was glad he did, glad he didn't mind the cat, because she was spending more and more time next door, and on Saturday night she'd slept on Florence's bed. And if—

Don't jump the gun! she warned herself, and put another scoop of his delicious casserole on her plate.

'No!' she told the cat and put her on the floor. 'You see what you've done?'

His eyes twinkled. 'Mmm. Turned her into a normal cat. What a shame. Do you want these green beans, or shall I finish them?'

Sheena Lewis was making steady progress after her car accident, and Daisy went in to check her on Tuesday afternoon just as her husband and the children were leaving. He was in a wheelchair, and the oldest two were squabbling good-naturedly over who was going to push him back to the ward.

'Hey, take it in turns or you won't be allowed to push it, because you'll hurt him,' Sheena said. 'Lucy first, she's oldest. And where's my kiss goodbye?'

The children ran to hug her, not a sign of the dutiful about them, both of them obviously devoted to their stepmother. She'd seen them before, last Friday, and they looked a great deal happier now that both their parents were on the mend.

'Come on, horrors, let's leave Sheena with the doctor,' Dan Lewis said, and they left. Sheena flopped back against the pillows with a weary smile and sighed with relief, and Daisy chuckled as she turned back the covers and had a look at her wound.

'That's coming on really well. It looks lovely and clean. You should be able to go home soon.'

'Good. I think Dan's parents are finding it all a bit much. Still, he'll be home tomorrow so he can help to keep them in order.'

'They're quite a handful, I imagine,' Daisy said, wondering how she coped, but she just smilingly agreed.

'Oh, they are, but I wouldn't change them for the world. They're the sweetest things, and they lost their mother four years ago, so they've been really upset by this accident. I think they wondered if it might not all happen again, and the fact that we're both all right and the baby's here is just a bit much for them on top of the shock, so they're a bit like a bottle of fizzy drink that's been shaken—open with care! But they're such good kids. Dan was saying earlier that if he'd died, he wouldn't have had to worry about the kids because he would have known they'd be all right.'

'It's a lot to take on. They're lucky to have you,' Daisy said quietly, and she shrugged.

'I fell in love with Dan, and the kids are part of him. How couldn't I love them? It hasn't all been easy, don't think that, but I wouldn't give back a minute of it. It's been wonderful, and it's just got better, and I'm just so grateful that I'm alive to share it.'

'I bet you are,' Daisy said softly, and left her in peace. She told Ben about their conversation later, over dinner, and he winced.

'I didn't realise their mother was dead. Poor little things.'

'Mmm. She said Dan feels he doesn't have to worry about anything happening to him because they'll be all right with her.'

'I can understand that,' he said, surprising her. 'If anything happened to me and Jane wasn't around for any reason, if you were there I'd know Florence would be safe and secure and loved.'

He trusted her that much? Feeling choked, she laid a hand over his and squeezed it. 'Thank you.'

He turned his hand over and caught hers, threading their fingers together. 'What for? It's the truth, Daisy. You love her, and given the slightest encouragement, she'll love you, too. She probably already does. It's not hard, after all.'

'Too hard for Mike.'

'Tell me about him,' he urged softly, and she shrugged.

'Oh—what's to tell? He just messed me about. He kept saying we'd get married one day, maybe, but he just wouldn't set a date. He never really asked me, and he certainly didn't give me a ring. I don't think he had any intention of doing it, he was just looking for someone to help with the kids at weekends, and then he realised how busy I was and how much he was still having to do, so when his wife said she'd have him back, he dropped me like a hot brick—but he'd talked about us getting married in front of the children, so they were really confused because it just didn't happen. Kids are too immediate. If you tell them you're getting married, they want to know when, and they want it to be in the foreseeable future. "Sometime" just isn't good enough, it's like saying "Maybe" when they ask if they can do something. It means no. I should have realised that, pinned him down and forced his hand, and it would have been over earlier.'

'No,' he said flatly. 'He should have been more straightforward with you. And if he wanted to marry you, he should have asked you properly. He was just wasting your time, using you, and I'd quite appreciate a few minutes alone with him.'

He let go of her hand and cleared the table, and they made tea and took it into the sitting room in front of the television and watched the news with Tabitha lying sprawled across them both, Ben's arm around Daisy's shoulders, snuggling her close and making her feel safe and wanted.

Loved.

It was a wonderful feeling. Dare she trust it? She was still afraid of making a mistake, of doing something that could hurt an innocent child as Freya and Millie had been hurt—as she'd been hurt—but there were lots of people who made second marriages work.

Take Sheena Lewis. She was amazing with her stepchildren, and Ben had said he felt the same way about her and Florence as Dan did about Sheena and the children.

He trusted her that much. He trusted her with his beloved child. Could she trust him?

Yes. Surely, yes.

She snuggled closer, and he turned off the television and lifted the cat off onto the floor. 'Bedtime,' he said, a smile flickering in the back of his eyes, and she slipped her hand through his and let him lead her up to bed.

'Jane and Peter can't have Florence this weekend, they're going away,' he told her on Thursday morning, when she'd been looking forward to it for days.

'Oh. Well, it doesn't matter,' she said, surprised at how disappointed she felt, but Ben just smiled and pulled the rabbit out of the hat.

'I've got a better idea. Let's go to Yorkshire and see my parents. We'll have resident babysitters, and it's ages since they've seen her, and I can show you where I grew up.'

He was taking her to meet his parents? Wow. That was progress. She'd never met Mike's parents—but then, as she'd realised belatedly, he'd never been serious about her, so why would she have done? She'd never been that important.

But she was important to Ben. Very important, and this weekend suddenly took on a whole new meaning of its own.

They were leaving at four on Friday afternoon, straight from work.

'Bring a dress,' he'd said. 'I've booked a table for Saturday night, and it's quite smart.'

'How smart?'

He shrugged. 'I'll wear my suit, since you rescued it for me and it's survived. Probably not a tie.'

The dress she'd had for Laura's wedding? She'd only worn it once, and it was lovely. She felt really good in it, and it was the sort of material that packed well. 'What else?'

'Jeans and walking shoes. And just normal stuff. We'll take my parents and Florence to Bettys for tea.'

'Oh, I've heard of Bettys tearoom! Can we really go?'

'Yes. I've booked that, too.'

'You're a marvel of organisation,' she said with a smile, and packed. Then repacked, because she was taking far too much, and she realised she was nervous.

They set off promptly, leaving Evan in charge with strict instructions to contact Ben if anything happened with the twins, and they arrived at eight, just as the sun was going down.

It was a stone farmhouse, right on the outskirts of Harrogate, with spectacular views over the Yorkshire countryside. She could see the sun setting in the distance as he turned onto the drive, and as he pulled up outside three dogs came running towards them, tails lashing.

'Hello, girls,' he said, getting out of the car and greeting them, and then they rushed round to greet Daisy as Ben lifted Florence out of her seat in the back. 'I'll get the luggage in a minute,' he murmured, Florence's head lolling on his shoulder, and putting his arm round Daisy, he led her into the house, the dogs at their feet.

She felt ridiculously nervous.

Was her hair a mess? Her makeup smudged? She'd probably got cake crumbs round her mouth from snacking in the car—

'You look fine,' he said, his eyes laughing as he pushed the back door open and went in. 'Hi, Mum.'

His mother was lovely. Warm and homely, practical, no-nonsense, with an apron tied firmly round her middle and a kitchen that smelled of heaven. 'You must be Daisy,' she said, beaming. 'I'm Liz.' And without hesitation, she hugged her. 'Andrew's about somewhere— ah, there you are, darling. They're here.'

'Dad, this is Daisy. Daisy, my father Andrew.' Ben kissed his mother's cheek, handed her the sleeping child, hugged his father and put the kettle on.

'If I don't make Daisy a cup of tea soon, she'll kill me,' he said mildly. 'But if you're opening a bottle of wine, Dad, I'm with you all the way.'

'It's done.' He shook her hand firmly. 'Hello, Daisy, it's lovely to meet you.'

'You, too. I've heard a lot about you. Apparently I have "good hands" like you when I'm operating.'

His father chuckled. 'Oh, dear. I hope you weren't too insulted.'

'I told her not to be. Mum, that is seriously good chilli,' he said, putting the lid back on the pot and licking the spoon. 'I'm starving.'

'You're always starving. I've made plenty.'

'Good. Where have you put us?'

His mother's face was bland. 'I've made up the guest room and your room, and Florence is in the little room. Take your pick. Bring your bags in and you can put her to bed before we eat. She's exhausted, poor little mite. Has she eaten enough?'

'Plenty,' he said, laughing. 'Dad, can you give me a hand?'

'So where *are* we sleeping?' she asked later as they were going up to bed.

'If Florence wasn't here, I'd say my room. As it is, I think I'd better show you to your room and kiss you goodnight.'

Pity. She could have done with a cuddle.

She got one. Too brief, but a very definite cuddle.

'They're lovely,' she mumbled into his shirt.

'They are. They think you are, too.'

He kissed her, then kissed her again, just in case she'd missed it the first time, and she had to push him away laughing.

'Go on, go to bed. What are we doing tomorrow?'

'Breakfast, walking the dogs, light lunch, then afternoon tea in Bettys, and then back here to get ready for dinner. And then after dinner,' he said, his eyes twinkling, 'I might have to introduce you to the hay barn.'

'Gosh, you know how to treat a girl,' she laughed, and pushed him away again. 'Go on, out, before you have any more silly ideas.'

He went.

CHAPTER TWELVE

IT WAS, as he'd said, an action-packed day.

They left Florence feeding the animals with her grandparents and walked for miles over the Yorkshire Dales, the dogs trotting happily alongside them. The weather was glorious—not too hot, and with a light breeze to cool her skin, but he'd smothered her in sun screen just to be on the safe side, and found her a hat.

He swiped it off and sang, 'On Ilkley Moor Bar T'at' to her in his lovely rich, deep voice with a good helping of Yorkshire, making her laugh, and they sat down under an outcrop of rocks to rest for a while. He wrapped his arm round her and hugged her against his side, and she sighed with contentment.

'It's beautiful,' she said, looking out across the moors, and he made a soft sound of agreement.

'I love it here. I often come here, when it's all too much.'

'Is it, often?'

His smile was pensive. 'It has been. It's getting a whole lot better,' he said, and kissed her.

After a very light lunch they went into Harrogate and had the most wonderful afternoon tea at Bettys, served on three-tier silver cake stands, to the sounds of the resident pianist playing softly in the background. Florence was in her element, and she wriggled to the edge of her seat and ate her sandwich, then two tiny fondant fancies, and another sandwich.

'Someone won't want any more tonight,' Andrew said with an indulgent smile, and Ben chuckled.

'You'll be amazed. The child has hollow legs.'

'More than I have,' Daisy said, wondering how she'd get through dinner, but by the time she was dressed and ready, her stomach was churning a little.

With hunger? Or something else?

Florence was downstairs with Ben in the kitchen when she went down there, and there was no sign of the others.

'Will I do?' she asked, and his eyes softened.

'Oh, yes. You'll do,' he said, and smiled down at Florence. 'Shall we sing Daisy that song?'

'What song?' Daisy asked, expecting another silly Yorkshire ditty, but he crouched down, sat Florence on one knee with the other one on the ground to steady himself, and counted Florence in, then started to sing.

'One, two, three, "Daisy, Daisy, give me your answer, please."'

Daisy laughed. 'It's not please.'

'Oh, yes, it is. Hush now, listen. Ready? "I'm half crazy all for the love of these."'

She laughed again. 'It's not—'

He lifted a warning finger, his eyes twinkling, and Florence shushed her. 'It's very hard, don't laugh!' she said seriously.

So Daisy stopped laughing, and listened to them, Ben coaxing Florence along as she stumbled on the words.

'"It won't be a stylish marriage, I can't afford a carriage, but you'll look sweet, upon the seat of a bicycle made for three."'

She stared at him. He was kneeling on one knee, looking up at her intently, and her heart began to pound.

The laughter was gone, his eyes deadly serious.

'Ben?'

'Did you like it?' Florence asked, running up to her and grabbing her hand, her eyes alight. 'Did you like our song?'

'Um—yes, it was lovely, darling.' Utterly charming, and she felt a strange sensation all over her body, a tingling, fizzing sensation, like champagne bubbles bursting through her veins. Was he—?

He was on his feet now, brushing off the knee of his horribly expensive suit and smiling at her. 'Come on, our taxi's here. Off to bed, poppet. Go and find Grannie and tell her we'll see her later. Kiss!'

He bent down and kissed her, and she hugged Daisy and kissed her, too, and then skipped out, humming the tune a little off-key.

'Got a cardigan in case it's cold later?'

'Um—I've brought a wrap,' she said, still slightly stunned and a little off balance.

'Great. Come on, then, let's make a move.'

He seemed oddly tense suddenly, and he was quiet all the way there. He paid the taxi driver, then threaded his fingers through hers as they walked to the restaurant.

'Oh, Ben, it's lovely.'

'Hope so. I've never been.'

They were ushered to a table in an alcove, and the service was incredible. Swift and unobtrusive, and the food was amazing.

'I've chosen the menu—I hope you don't mind,' he said as they sat down, but she just shrugged, a little puzzled but prepared to go along with him, because there was something about him...

They had a starter of fish and chips—a tiny cone, with minute goujons of sole and the sweetest little French fries.

'Gosh—the portions are a bit more delicate than the ones we got the from the Yoxburgh chippy,' she said with a delighted laugh.

His eyes were strangely intense. 'That was the night you told me you love me,' he murmured, and her breath eased out on a sigh.

Oh, Ben. You sentimental thing...

The starter was followed by sea bass.

She looked at it, then at him, and he just smiled. 'I fell in love with you over the sea bass,' he said softly, as if that explained everything, and her heart started to beat a little faster.

She smiled at him, her heart full. 'I think I fell in love with you when I opened the door and saw you covered in soggy plaster. It was the power suit that did it, of course. It looks good on you. I'm glad it survived.'

He laughed softly and topped up her wine.

'Eat up. We've got a special dessert coming.'

'Really? I'm going to struggle.'

'I'm sure you'll cope. It's very light. It's carrot based.'

'Carrot?' She laughed, fascinated, but she ate up as instructed, savouring every mouthful, the butterflies settling down now as he started to talk to her about his childhood.

And then his marriage.

'I think the problem with it was that it wasn't real. We didn't really love each other—there was no deep-rooted connection between us, and I don't think there was between you and Mike. I don't know how you feel, but it's as if I've never really been married—never known before I met you what it is to get to the end of the working day and long to get home to see the person I was sharing my life with. And when it all disintegrated, I wasn't that gutted, really. It didn't seem such a great loss.'

'Oh, Ben, that's so sad,' she said. 'And you're right. I didn't know Mike. I thought I did, I thought I loved him, but I just wanted to, really, and wanted him to love me, so we could make a life together for the girls, but he didn't care about any of us. Not like you.'

'I didn't want to love you. No, I did. I was afraid to,' he said honestly, and signalled to the waiter. Their plates were whisked away, and he reached over and took her hands in his, his eyes curiously intense.

'I'd decided I'd be alone. It was easier that way, less complicated, and it meant I could concentrate on Florence. I never expected to find anyone like you. It's the first time I've ever met anyone I want to spend the rest of my life with, and it's just utterly different. I didn't know what love was until I met you, Daisy, and now I do, well—I don't want to let it go.'

He glanced up and let go of her hands, and a waiter placed a dish in the centre of the table between them. It was covered with a silver dome, and he bowed slightly and lifted it away with a flourish.

It was a pile of ice chips.

Very pretty ice chips—a little heap, decorated with rose petals, the one in the middle sparkling in the candlelight.

She leant over, frowning slightly, not quite sure...

'I thought you said it was carrot based?' she murmured, puzzled.

Ben reached into the pile of ice and drew out the centre one, the one that sparkled. Only it wasn't ice at all, it was—

Carat, she thought, not *carrot*, and her heart did a little skitter.

The waiter removed the dish, and Ben took her hand in his. 'I love you, Daisy Fuller. I think it was the sea bass, but it could have been the tea all down your dressing gown,' he said, making her laugh. Or cry. She wasn't sure. And he was humming now, the tune he'd sung with Florence. Just a few bars, and then he broke off.

'I don't want to go down on one knee in front of everyone, but I will, if it'll make a difference. So what's your answer, Daisy?' he asked softly. 'If I promise to keep the plumbing in order and not complain about chocolate spread sandwiches, will you marry me? Will you be my wife, and give me and Florence all the love I know is in your heart?'

His mouth was smiling, but his eyes were uncertain, and she couldn't let him struggle. 'Yes,' she said softly, tears filling her eyes. 'Oh, yes, Ben, of course I will. I love you—I'll always love you. And I'll love Florence as if she's my own.'

He let his breath out on a shuddering sigh, smiled and slipped the ring onto her finger, then stood up and pulled her up into his arms, laughing and hugging her until she thought her ribs might break. And then he let her go, just a little, and looked down into her eyes and kissed her.

'Time to go somewhere a little more private,' he murmured, and she realised that everyone was clapping and cheering.

Ben let her go. A little. He still kept his arm around her firmly, but he smiled down at her, his eyes glowing.

3 Months Free

when you subscribe for 12 Months

SAVE OVER £41

SEE OVERLEAF FOR DETAILS

www.millsand███n.██.uk/subscripti█ns

'I want to set a date. And I want it to be soon.'

'For Florence?'

'For all of us, because until we're married, we can't be together when she's there, and I'm an impatient man, I've realised. So—how quickly can we organise a wedding?'

She smiled. 'Very quickly. I have two experts lined up who've just done it. I'll pick their brains.'

'Good.' He topped up her champagne and held the glass out to her, clinking it gently with his. 'Here's to us.'

'Mmm,' she said, smiling, and sipped it. 'This is the first time I've drunk champagne in a hay barn.'

He chuckled. 'Me, too. I could grow to like it.'

'Does Florence know?'

'No. I expect my parents have worked it out. They heard us rehearsing the song. And there was champagne in the fridge.'

'Maybe they were expecting to share it with us.'

'They can have some for breakfast,' he said, and taking the glass away from her, he laid her back against the blanket and took her in his arms...

The wedding was planned for the second weekend in September.

They booked a local venue, a hotel and leisure club that had been refurbished a few years ago and had an excellent reputation, and they'd had a cancellation. They could offer everything—the entire wedding package at a substantial discount.

They didn't care about the discount. What they cared about was that the timing was perfect—and that was dictated as much as anything by the delivery date of the MCMA twins.

'I can't go until they're 32 weeks,' he said. 'If they're still OK then, we'll grab a few days away and I'll make sure Matt's here until we get back, so if anything happens over the weekend, he can deliver them. And we'll have a proper honeymoon later.'

Daisy just smiled at that. She loved him for so many reasons, but his dedication to his patients was definitely one of them, and she was more than happy to fall in with his plans, because she'd become so involved with Mel Grieves and her babies that she wanted to be there when they were born.

She was, but only just.

It was the night before the wedding, and Ben rang her at eleven. Amy was staying with her, and they were still up putting the finishing touches to her headdress when he called.

'One of the twins is struggling. I'm going in with Matt to deliver them.'

'I'm coming!' she yelled, and threw the phone down and ran out of the door, leaping into his car as they pulled away.

'Will we be in time?' she asked desperately, and he shrugged.

'Don't know. Hope so. I can't go any quicker.'

They were in time, Ben on one side, her on the other and Matt standing by, happy to let her play her part. The heartbeats had recovered, but one of the twins had been compromised for a few minutes and she didn't know what they'd find.

Two healthy little girls, was the answer. Very small, but both a good colour, and her eyes filled with tears. Mel had had steroids a few days before, to prepare their lungs, and as they took their first breaths they pinked up beautifully and cried—not loud, not much, but enough that Ben gave a laughing sob as he handed the second one over to the SCBU nurse who was waiting.

Mel was sobbing uncontrollably, so was her husband, and Ben's smiling eyes met Daisy's across the table and he said, 'How's that for a wedding present?'

Wedding! she thought, and glanced up at the clock.

It was ten to twelve, and she looked at him and bit her lip. 'Are you superstitious?'

He glanced at the clock and smiled again. 'Not even slightly, but I'm not doing anything to jinx this marriage. Go home, darling. I'll see you tomorrow.'

'Have a great day,' Mel said, and Daisy stripped off her gloves and hugged her.

'You, too. Congratulations!'

And then she ran.

He was standing there waiting for her, turned towards her with Matt at his side, and even down the length of the crowded room she could see the love in his eyes.

Her father walked her down the aisle between all their family and friends, Florence following behind her with Amy in charge.

Amy, she thought with a flicker of worry, but then she was at Ben's side, and her hand was in his, and she could feel the love radiating from him and warming her heart. 'OK?' he asked softly.

OK? She was marrying the man she loved—the only man she'd ever truly loved. He'd given her so much, taken away the pain and hurt that was her constant companion, and he and Florence had filled her life with love and laughter. It was, quite simply, the best day of her life.

She turned and looked up at him, at the love shining

in his eyes, the incredible depth of kindness, the tenderness, the passion. OK?

'Very OK,' she said, and smiled.

* * * * *

THE FIANCÉE
HE CAN'T FORGET

BY
CAROLINE ANDERSON

All the characters in this book have no existence outside the imagination of the author, and have no relation whatsoever to anyone bearing the same name or names. They are not even distantly inspired by any individual known or unknown to the author, and all the incidents are pure invention.

First published in Great Britain 2011
by Mills & Boon, an imprint of Harlequin (UK) Limited.
Harlequin (UK) Limited, Eton House, 18-24 Paradise Road,
Richmond, Surrey TW9 1SR

ISBN: 978 0 263 88609 2

Harlequin (UK) policy is to use papers that are natural, renewable and recyclable products and made from wood grown in sustainable forests. The logging and manufacturing process conform to the legal environmental regulations of the country of origin.

Printed and bound in Spain
by Blackprint CPI, Barcelona

Caroline Anderson has the mind of a butterfly. She's been a nurse, a secretary, a teacher, run her own soft-furnishing business, and now she's settled on writing. She says, 'I was looking for that elusive something. I finally realised it was variety, and now I have it in abundance. Every book brings new horizons and new friends, and in between books I have learned to be a juggler. My teacher husband John and I have two beautiful and talented daughters, Sarah and Hannah, umpteen pets, and several acres of Suffolk that nature tries to reclaim every time we turn our backs!' Caroline also writes for Mills & Boon® Cherish™.

Recent titles by the same author:

Medical™ Romance

ST PIRANS: WEDDING OF THE YEAR
THE SURGEON'S MIRACLE
THE VALTIERI MARRIAGE DEAL

Mills & Boon® Cherish™

THE BABY SWAP MIRACLE
MOTHER OF THE BRIDE

**More praise for
Caroline Anderson:**

'Photojournalist Maisie Douglas and
businessman Robert Mackenzie have been
more or less amicably divorced for almost two
decades, but the upcoming marriage of their daughter,
Jenni, stirs up old emotions on both sides. Very
young when she married him, Maisie—pregnant and
disowned by her family—was miserable living in
Scotland with Rob's judgmental parents, and left after
little more than a year. Maisie hasn't found another
partner, and neither has Rob. Can they find a way to
trust each other again, after all this time? This lovely
reunion romance is rich with emotion and humour,
and all of the characters are exquisitely rendered.'
—*RT Book Reviews* on
MOTHER OF THE BRIDE

CHAPTER ONE

'ARE you OK?'

Was she?

She wasn't sure. Her heart was pounding, her legs felt like jelly and her stomach was rebelling, but it was Daisy's wedding day, so Amy dug around and dredged up some kind of a smile.

'I'm fine.'

'Sure?'

'Absolutely!' she lied, and tried to make the smile look more convincing. She didn't even need to ask how Daisy was. She was lit up from inside with a serene joy that was radiantly, blindingly obvious. Amy's smile wavered. She'd felt like that once, lifetimes ago.

She tweaked Daisy's dress for something to do and stood back. 'Are you ready?'

Her smile glowed brighter still. 'Oh, yes,' Daisy said softly. 'Do I look OK?'

Amy laughed indulgently and hugged her. 'You look stunning. Ben will be blown away.'

'I hope not, I want him here!' Daisy glanced down at Florence, fizzing silently on the end of Amy's arm, on her very best behaviour. She looked like a fairy in her pretty little dress and she was so excited Amy thought she was going to pop.

'OK, darling?' Daisy asked.

Florence nodded, her eyes like saucers, and for a second she looked so like Ben—so like Matt—that Amy's heart squeezed painfully with the ache of loss.

'Let's go then,' Daisy said, stooping to kiss her about-to-be stepdaughter, and with a quick, supportive hug for Amy that nearly unravelled her, she turned and took her father's arm.

As they gave the signal for the processional music, Amy sucked in a deep, slow breath.

You can do this, she told herself desperately. *Ignore him. Just keep your eyes on Daisy's back, and you'll be fine.*

And then with Florence at her side, she fell in behind them, her eyes glued on Daisy as they walked slowly down between the rows of guests to where Ben was waiting.

Ben, and Matt.

Don't look...

Matt's hair was slightly longer than his twin's, more tousled, the dark, silky strands so familiar that her fingers still remembered the feel of them. His back was ramrod straight, his shoulders broad, square, uncompromising.

She shouldn't have looked. She should have kept her eyes on Daisy, but they wouldn't obey her and her heart was pounding so hard she was sure he'd hear it.

Please don't turn round...

He didn't move a muscle.

He couldn't see her, but he could feel her there, getting closer. She was behind him, over his left shoulder, and there was no way he was turning round to look. Just getting through the ceremony was going to be hard enough, without making it harder by rubbing salt into the wound her presence here had ripped wide open.

Not that it had ever really healed.

Ben's hand brushed his, their fingers tangling and gripping for a second in a quick, wordless exchange.

You OK?

Sure. You?

Never better, and you're lying, but thanks for being here.

You're welcome. Wouldn't have it any other way.

Out of the corner of his eye Matt saw Daisy draw level with Ben, saw him reach out to her. He could feel their love like a halo around them, the huge depth of caring and emotion threatening to swamp him. The sort of love he'd felt for Amy...

Hang on in there. You can do it. It won't take long.

He heard Ben murmur something to Daisy, heard her murmur back, but he had no idea what they said. All his senses were trained on the woman standing behind Daisy. He could hear the rustle of her dress, feel the tension radiating off her, smell the slight drift of her achingly familiar perfume.

How could he be so aware of her? He closed his eyes, taking a moment to calm his thoughts, to settle it all down, to get the lid back on the box. There. He was fine. He could do this.

The ceremony began, and then it was his turn. All he had to do was to take the rings from his pocket and hand them over. Which meant he had to move, to turn— not far, but just far enough to see—

Amy...

The lid blew off the box with the force of an explosion, and he dropped the rings in Ben's outstretched hand and stepped sharply back to his place, his emotions reeling.

He had to concentrate on Ben and Daisy. This was their day, and he and Amy were in the past. Gone.

But not, apparently, forgotten.

Not by a long way.

The ceremony was interminable.

Her whole body was shaking and she was finding it really hard to concentrate on anything but Matt. Crazy, since she worked with Ben almost every day and they were scarily alike. The most identical of identical twins, with one huge difference—she loved Matt with all her broken, guarded heart, and today was the first time she'd had to face him in four years—

Don't go there!

She felt Florence wriggle at the end of her arm, and glanced down.

'You's squeezing me!' she whispered, and she realised she had a death grip on the little girl's hand. 'Sorry,' she mouthed, wincing, but Florence smiled up at her and patted her hand.

''S OK, Amy, I know you's scared,' she replied in a stage whisper that made several of the guests smile, and in the row beside her Amy heard Florence's mother give a quiet, despairing chuckle.

But then the ceremony was over, and Ben was kissing Daisy while everyone clapped and cheered, and Florence wriggled out of Amy's loosened grip and ran to them. Laughing, Ben scooped her up and kissed her, too, and as Amy watched Matt turned slowly towards her and their eyes met and locked.

Time stopped. She felt the room start to swim, and she dragged in a quick breath, then another. Matt frowned, then moved swiftly, his fingers gripping her elbow. 'Are you all right?' he murmured, his voice low, gruff and painfully familiar.

She swayed against him. All right? Not in a million years, but she wasn't telling him that. She straightened up.

'I'm fine. Low blood sugar,' she lied, and with a slight frown he let her go. Not that it made any difference. The skin of her arm was tingling from the touch of his fingers, her highly sensitised flesh branded by each one.

'We have to sign the register,' he said, and she nodded. They did. They should have done it years ago, but not like this. Not as witnesses…

'OK now?'

'Fine,' she said shortly, and took that vital and symbolic step away from him before she gave into the urge to turn her face into his chest and howl.

He thought it would never end.

The smiling, the greeting of old friends and family, the meeting of new people. And of course there were people there who'd known Amy. People who should have been at their wedding.

'Isn't that…?'

'Yes—small world, isn't it? She and Daisy are old friends. How are you? It's good to see you again…'

And on, and on, until he was ready to scream.

He drank rather more than was sensible, considering he had to make a speech, but every time he caught sight of Amy it was as if he'd been drenched in iced water and he felt stone cold sober. They sat down to eat at last, strung out in a line with Ben and Daisy and two sets of parents between them, and he was glad that his brother and his new sister-in-law had opted for a long top table instead of a round one.

Or maybe that was why they had, thinking ahead to this moment.

Florence was with Jane and Peter at another table, and he winked at her and she winked back, her little face screwing up as she tried to shut just one eye. It made him laugh, in an odd, detached way.

And then finally the food was eaten, the champagne glasses were filled and it was time for the speeches.

Amy didn't want to listen to his speech, but she had little choice. None, in fact, but she loved Daisy and she'd grown increasingly fond of Ben, and this was their wedding and she wanted to be here for it. And Matt wasn't going to spoil it for her, she told herself firmly as Daisy's father got to his feet.

He welcomed Ben to their family with a warmth in his voice that made Daisy cry, then Ben gave a funny, tender and rather endearing speech about Daisy and the change she'd made to his life, thanked everyone for coming to share their day, and then with a grin at Matt he said, 'Now, before I hand you over to my clone for the ritual character assassination I'm sure I've got coming, I'd like you to raise your glasses to two very special and beautiful women. One is my wife's dearest friend, Amy, and the other is my precious daughter, Florence. I know Daisy's appreciated their support and their help in giving us such a wonderful day to enjoy together. Amy particularly has worked absolutely tirelessly on the arrangements, and I think she's done a brilliant job. And Florence has painstakingly decorated and filled the little favour boxes for you all, so we hope you enjoy them. Ladies and gentlemen, the bridesmaids!'

She was grateful to little Florence, who was kneeling up on her chair giggling and attracting all the eyes in the room, because it meant fewer people were looking at her while she struggled with her prickling eyes and the rising tide of colour on her cheeks.

And then it was Matt's turn, and he was smiling engagingly at everyone as if he did this kind of thing all the time. He probably did, she thought. He'd always had a way with words.

'You'll have to forgive my deluded brother,' he began drily. 'Being the firstborn just makes him the prototype, and we all know they need refining, but I'm very pleased to be here today because after thirty-four years of arguments, black eyes, mind-blowingly foolish stunts and some underhanded, downright cheating, it's been settled. I am officially the best man, and now we can move on with our lives!'

There was a ripple of laughter round the room, but then he went on, 'On the subject of twins, we didn't get to bed very early last night. Ben, Daisy and I ended up delivering two rather special babies shortly before midnight, and I found myself wondering, will those little girls have as much fun growing up as we did? Because it wasn't all fights. I always had a friend, a playmate, someone to lean on. Someone to swap with. We did that quite a lot—in fact, Daisy, are you sure that's Ben? You wouldn't be the first person to fall for it. I think Jenny Wainwright's still confused.'

'No, I'm quite sure, he's much more good-looking!' Daisy said, laughing and hugging Ben.

It sounded silly, but Amy absolutely understood how she felt. The similarities were obvious. The differences were more subtle but they were definitely there, not only in their looks but in their characters, and her reaction to them was utterly different.

Ben could talk to her and she just heard his words. Matt talked, and her soul seemed to tune into his—but right now, she didn't need that spiritual connection that seemed to call to every cell in her body. She didn't need to feel the rich tones of his deep, warm voice swirling round her, that slight Yorkshire accent teasing at her senses, and with an effort she made herself listen to what he was saying.

She was glad she did. He was very, very funny, but also very moving. He told tales of their childhood escapades, but also their closeness, their enduring friendship, and finally he wound up, and she felt her heart hammer because she knew—she just knew—he was going to look at her and she was going to have to smile.

'Now, my job—as the best man,' he added with a grin, 'is to thank Ben for his kind remarks about Daisy's beautiful bridesmaids, and I have to say he's right, Florence is the cutest little bridesmaid I've ever seen. And as for Amy...' He turned to face her, as she'd known he would, and his smile twisted a little. 'Well, it's my duty and privilege to escort this beautiful woman for the rest of the day, so sorry, guys, you'll have to find someone else to dance with. She's all mine. There have to be some perks to the job.'

Amy tried to smile as he tilted his glass to her, drained it and sat down to cheers and applause, but it was a feeble attempt.

She was dreading the rest of the party. She would *have* to dance with him, and there was no getting out of it. As chief bridesmaid and best man, that was their role, but the irony wasn't lost on her.

As far as she was concerned, Matt wasn't the best man—he was the only man.

And when the chips were down, when she'd needed him most, he'd walked away.

'Good wedding—the hotel have looked after you well. It's a great venue.'

Ben smiled. 'Isn't it? We were really lucky to get it at such short notice. Good speech, by the way. Thank you.'

Matt frowned slightly, feeling another stab of guilt. 'Don't thank me. I wasn't there for you last time. I should have been.'

'No. You were absolutely right at the time, neither of us should have been there. I shouldn't have married Jane, and you weren't exactly in the right place to worry about me. You had enough going on with Amy. Matt, are you really OK with this?'

Matt met Ben's eyes briefly and looked away. 'Yeah, I'm fine.'

'Amy's not.'

'I know.'

'She still loves you.'

He snorted rudely and drained his glass. 'Hardly. I think she's finding it a little awkward, that's all. She'll be fine.'

Or she would as long as he kept avoiding her.

Ben made a soft, disbelieving noise and caught Daisy's eye. He nodded and looked back at Matt, his eyes seeing far too much for comfort. 'We're going to cut the cake now, and then have the first dance. And then—'

'I know.' He pretended to straighten Ben's cravat. 'Don't worry, I won't renege on my duties.'

'I wasn't suggesting you would. I was just going to say be kind to Amy.'

He looked up at Ben again, his older brother by mere moments, and laughed. 'What—like she was kind to me?'

'She was hurting.'

'And I wasn't?' He gave a harsh sigh and rammed a hand through his hair. 'Don't worry. I'll be good. You go and cut your cake and have your dance, and I'll play my part. I won't let you down.'

'It's not me I'm worried about,' Ben muttered, but Matt pushed him towards his wife and turned away. He didn't need to scan the room for Amy. His radar hadn't let him down. She was right there, by the French doors out onto the terrace, talking to two women that he didn't recognise.

One was visibly pregnant, the other had a baby in her arms, and for a moment his heart squeezed with pain. *Ahh, Amy...*

She could feel him watching her, the little hairs on the back of her neck standing to attention.

He was getting closer, she knew it. She'd managed to avoid him up to now, and she'd known it was too good to last.

'Excuse me, Amy—they're going to cut the cake and then have the first dance.'

And then it would be time for the second dance, the one she'd been dreading, and she'd have to dance with him and look—well, civilised would be a good thing to try for, she thought as she turned round to face him.

'OK. I'll come over. Give me a moment.'

She turned back to Katie and Laura, and after a second she felt him move away, and her shoulders sagged a fraction.

'Amy, are you all right, honey?' Katie asked, juggling the baby with one arm so she could hug her.

She returned the hug briefly and straightened up, easing away. 'I'm fine.'

'Well, you don't look fine,' Laura said, her eyes narrowing. 'Are you sick? You're awfully pale.'

'I'm just tired. It's been a busy week. I'd better go.'

She left them, letting out a soft sigh as she walked away. She'd never told them about Matt, and she'd asked Daisy not to discuss it. The fewer people at the wedding who knew they had history, the better. It was hard enough facing his mother, who'd given her a swift, gentle hug and patted her back as if she was soothing a child.

She'd nearly cried. She'd loved Liz. She'd been endlessly kind to her, incredibly welcoming, and she hadn't seen her since—

'Amy, we're going to— Gosh, sweetheart, are you all right?'

Daisy's face was puckered with concern, and Amy rolled her eyes.

'Daisy, don't fuss, I'm just tired. We didn't go to bed till nearly one and the cat was walking all over me all night. And we've been up for hours, if you remember.'

'I know. I just—'

'I'm fine,' she said firmly. 'Matt said you're going to cut the cake.'

'We are. Amy, are you sure you can do this? If you want to leave—'

'I don't want to leave! It's your wedding! Go and cut the cake, and we can have champagne and cake and dancing and it'll be wonderful. Now shoo.'

Amy turned her round and pushed her towards her husband, who held his hand out to her and drew her into his arms for yet another kiss.

'They do seem genuinely happy together.'

She froze. How had he crept up on her? She hadn't felt him approaching—maybe because she'd been so intensely aware of him all day that her senses were overloaded.

'They are,' she said, her voice a little ragged. 'They're wonderful together.'

'She's very fond of you.'

'It's mutual. She's lovely. She's been through a lot, and she's been a really good friend to me.'

'Which is why you're here, when you'd rather be almost anywhere else in the world.'

'Speak for yourself.'

He gave a soft huff of laughter, teasing the hair on the back of her neck. 'I was,' he answered, and despite the laugh, his voice had a hollow ring to it. 'Still, needs must. Right, here we go. I think Ben's going to make a bit of a speech to welcome the evening guests before they cut the cake.'

He was still standing behind her, slightly to one side, and she could feel his breath against her bare shoulder, feel the warmth radiating from his big, solid body.

The temptation to lean back into him—to rest her head against his cheek, to feel him curve his hand round her hip and ease her closer as he would have done before—nearly overwhelmed her. Instead, she stepped away slightly, pretending to shift so she could see them better, but in fact she could see perfectly well, and he must have realised that.

She heard him sigh, and for some crazy reason it made her feel sad. Crazy, because it had been him that

had left her, walking away just when she needed him
the most, so why on earth should she feel sad for him?
So he was still alone, according to Ben. So what? So
was she. There were worse things than being alone. At
least it was safe.

'Daisy chose the music for our first dance,' Ben was
saying, his smile wry. 'It has a special meaning for
us. While we're dancing, I'd like you to imagine the
moment we met—just about thirty seconds after the
kitchen ceiling and half a bath of water came down on
my head.'

And with that, they cut the cake, the lights were
dimmed and the band started playing 'The First Time
Ever I Saw Your Face'.

There was a ripple of laughter and applause, but then
they all went quiet as Ben, still smiling, drew Daisy into
his arms as if she was the most precious thing he'd ever
held.

Damn, Amy thought, sniffing hard, and then a tissue
arrived in her hand, on a drift of cologne that brought
back so many memories she felt the tears well even
faster.

'OK?'

No, she wasn't. She was far from OK, she thought
crossly, and she wished everyone would stop asking her
that.

'I'm fine.'

He sighed softly. 'Look, Amy, I know this is awkward, but we just have to get through it for their sakes.
I don't want to do it any more than you do, but it's not
for long.'

Long enough. A second in his arms would be long
enough to tear her heart wide open—

The dance was over, the music moved on and without

hesitation Matt took her hand, the one with the tissue still clutched firmly in it, led her onto the dance floor and turned her into his arms.

'Just pretend you don't hate me,' he told her, with a smile that didn't reach his eyes, and she breathed in, needing oxygen, and found nothing but that cologne again.

Holding her was torture.

A duty and a privilege, as he'd said in his speech?

Or just an agonising reminder of all he'd lost?

She had one hand on his shoulder, the other cradled in his left, and his right hand was resting lightly against her waist, so he could feel the slender column of her spine beneath his splayed fingers, the shift of her ribs as she breathed, the flex of the muscles as she moved in time to the music. She felt thinner, he thought. Well, she would. The last time he'd held her, he thought with a wave of sadness, she'd been pregnant with their child.

One dance merged into another, and then another. He eased her closer, and with a sigh that seemed to shudder through her body, she rested her head on his shoulder and yielded to the gentle pressure of his hand. Her thighs brushed his, and he felt heat flicker along his veins. Oh, Amy. He'd never forgotten her, never moved on. Not really.

And as he cradled her against his chest, her pale gold hair soft under his cheek, he realised he'd been treading water for years, just waiting for the moment when he could hold her again.

He sighed, and she felt his warm breath tease her hair, sending tiny shivers running through her like fairies dancing over her skin. It made her feel light-headed again, and she stepped back.

'I need some air,' she mumbled, and tried to walk away, but her hand was still firmly wrapped in his, and he followed her, ushering her through the crowd and out of the French doors into the softly lit courtyard. Groups of people were standing around talking quietly, laughing, and she breathed in the cooler air with a sigh of relief.

'Better?'

She nodded. 'Yes. Thanks.'

'Don't thank me. You look white as a sheet. Have you eaten today?'

'We just had a meal.'

'And you hardly touched it. My guess is you didn't have lunch, either, and you probably skipped breakfast. No wonder you had low blood sugar earlier. Come on, let's go and raid the buffet. I didn't eat much, either, and I'm starving.'

He was right on all counts. She *was* hungry, and she *had* skipped lunch, but only because she'd lost her breakfast. She never could eat when she was nervous, and she'd been so, so nervous for the last few days her stomach had been in knots, and this morning it had rebelled. And that dizzy spell could well have been low blood sugar, now she came to think about it.

'It's probably not a bad idea,' she conceded, and let him lead her to the buffet table. She put a little spoonful of something on her plate, and he growled, shoved his plate in her other hand and loaded them both up.

'I can't eat all that!' she protested, but he speared her with a look from those implacable blue eyes and she gave up. He could put it on the plate. Didn't mean she had to eat it.

'I'll help you. Come on, let's find a quiet corner.'

He scooped up two sets of cutlery, put them in his

top pocket, snagged a couple of glasses of wine off a passing waiter and shepherded her across the floor and back out to the courtyard.

'OK out here, or is it too cold for you in that dress?'

'It's lovely. It's a bit warm in there.'

'Right. Here, look, there's a bench.'

He steered her towards it, handed her a glass and sat back, one ankle on the other knee and the plate balanced on his hand while he attacked the food with his fork.

He'd always eaten like that, but that was medicine for you, eating on the run. Maybe he thought they should get it over with and then he could slide off and drink with the boys. Well, if the truth be told he didn't have to hang around for her.

'You're not eating.'

'I'm too busy wondering why you don't have chronic indigestion, the speed you're shovelling that down.'

He gave a short chuckle. 'Sorry. Force of habit. And I was starving.' He put the plate down for a moment and picked up his glass. 'So, how are you, really?'

Really? She hesitated, the fork halfway to her mouth. Did he honestly want to know? Probably not.

'I'm fine.'

'How's the job?'

'OK. I like it. As with any job it has its ups and downs. Mostly ups. The hospital's a good place to work.'

'Yes, so Ben says.' He stared pensively down into his glass, swirling it slowly. 'You didn't have to leave London, you know. We were never going to bump into each other at different hospitals.'

No? She wasn't sure—not sure enough, at least, that she'd felt comfortable staying there. Up here, she'd been able to relax—until Ben had arrived. Ever since then she'd been waiting for Matt to turn up unexpectedly on the ward to visit his brother, and the monoamniotic twins they'd delivered last night had been something he'd taken a special interest in, so once Melanie Grieves had been admitted, she'd been on tenterhooks all the time. Waiting for the other shoe to drop.

Well, now it had, and it was every bit as bad as she'd expected.

'I like it here, it was a good move for me,' she said, and then changed the subject firmly. 'Who's Jenny Wainwright?'

He laughed, a soft, warm chuckle that told her a funny story was coming. 'Ben's first girlfriend. We were thirteen or so. They'd been dating for weeks, and she wouldn't let him kiss her, so I talked him into letting me take his place on the next date, to see if I had more luck.'

'And did you?'

His mouth twisted into a wry smile. 'No. Not that time. I did about two years later, though, at a party, and she told me he kissed better, so I went and practised on someone else.'

She laughed, as he'd wanted her to, but all she could think was that whoever he'd practised on had taught him well. She ought to thank her—except of course he wasn't hers to kiss any more. Regret swamped her, and as she looked across and met his eyes, she saw tenderness in them and a gentle, puzzled sadness. 'I've missed you,' he said softly, and she gulped down a sudden, convulsive little sob.

'I've missed you, too,' she admitted, her voice unsteady.

He stared at her searchingly, then glanced down. 'Are you all done with that food?'

Food? She looked at her plate. She'd eaten far more

than she'd thought she would, to her surprise, and she was feeling much better. 'Yes. Do you want the rest?'

'No, I'm fine, but I'm supposed to be entertaining you, so let's go and dance.'

Out of duty? Or because he wanted to? She hesitated for a second, then stood up, raising an eyebrow at him. Whichever, she wanted to dance with him, and she wasn't going to get another chance.

'Come on, then, if you really want to.'

Oh, yes. He wanted. He got to his feet and led her back to the dance floor.

She'd always loved dancing, and he loved dancing with her, loved the feel of her body, the lithe, supple limbs, the sleek curves, the warmth of her against him.

He didn't get to hold her, though, not at first. The tempo was fast—too fast, he decided, after a couple of dances, so he reeled her in and halved the beat, cherishing the moment because he knew it wouldn't last. How could it, with all they had behind them? But now—he had her now, in his arms, against his heart, and his body ached for her.

The tempo slowed, moving seamlessly from one unashamedly romantic, seductive number to another, until they were swaying against each other, her arms draped around his neck, his hands splayed against her back, the fingers of one hand resting lightly on the warm, soft skin above the back of her dress, the other hand lower, so all he had to do was slip it down a fraction and he could cup the firm swell of her bottom and ease her closer...

She felt his hand move, felt him draw her in so she could feel every move he made. Their legs had somehow meshed together so his thigh was between hers, nudg-

ing gently with every slight shift of his body, brushing
the soft silk of her dress against her legs and driving
out all her common sense.

She knew him so well, had danced with him so many
times, and it was so easy to rest against him, to lay her
head against his chest and listen to the deep, steady
thud of his heart, to slide her fingers through his hair
and sift the silky strands that she remembered so well.

Easier, still, to turn her head, to feel the graze of
stubble against her temple and tilt her face towards him,
to feel the soft warmth of his lips as they took hers in
a tentative, questioning kiss.

I love you...

Had he said that? Had she?

She lifted her head and touched her lips to his again,
and his breath seared over her skin in a shuddering sigh.

'Amy—'

'Matt...'

He lifted his head and stared down at her in the dim
light on the edge of the dance floor, their eyes locked
as each of them battled against the need raging within
them. She could feel him fighting it, feel herself losing just as he closed his eyes and unclasped her hands
from behind his neck, sliding his hand down her arm
and linking their fingers as he led her off the dance
floor and up the broad, sweeping staircase to the floor
above in a tense, brittle silence.

They didn't speak to anyone. They passed people in
the hall, people on the stairs—they didn't stop, didn't
look left or right, until the door of his room was opened
and closed again behind them, and then he cradled her
face and stared down into her eyes once more.

Still he didn't speak, and neither did she. What was
there to say? Nothing that would make any sense.

Slowly, with infinite tenderness, he touched his lips to hers again, and she whimpered softly and clutched at him, desperate for the feel of him, for his body on her, in her, surrounding and filling her.

'Please,' she whispered silently, but he heard her and took a step back, stripping without finesse, heeling off his beautiful handmade shoes, his hired suit hitting the floor and crumpling in a heap. After a brief fight with his cufflinks the shirt followed, then the boxers, the socks, and he spun her and searched blindly for the zip.

'Here.' She lifted her arm so he could find it, sucking her breath in as he tugged it down and the dress fell to the floor, puddling round her ankles and leaving her standing there in nothing but a tiny scrap of lace.

A rough groan was torn from his throat and he lifted her in his arms and lowered her carefully to the middle of the bed. Fingers shaking, he hooked his fingers into the lace at her hips, easing it away, following its path down the length of her legs with his lips, the slight roughness of his stubble grazing the sensitive skin as he inched his way to her feet, driving her to the edge.

He turned his head, looked back at her, and his eyes were black with need. She whimpered, her legs twitching under his warm, firm hands, and he moved, nudging her thighs apart, so nearly there—and then he froze, his face agonised.

'Amy, we can't—I haven't—'

'I'm on the Pill.'

The breath sighed out of him in a rush, and he gathered her into his arms, held her for a moment, and then his lips found hers again and he was there, filling her, bringing a sob of relief from her as his body slid home and she tightened around him.

'Matt...'

'Oh, God, Amy, I've missed you,' he whispered, and then he started to move, his body shaking with control until she was sick of waiting and arched under him, her hands tugging at him, begging for more.

And he gave her more, pulling out all the stops, driving her higher and higher until she came apart in his arms, her reserve splintering under the onslaught of his unleashed passion.

Then he held her, his body shuddering in release, his heart slamming against his ribs so hard he thought they'd break, until gradually it slowed and he rolled to his side, taking her with him, their bodies still locked together as the aftershocks of their lovemaking faded slowly away into the night.

CHAPTER TWO

HE MADE love to her again in the night, reaching for her in the darkness, bringing her body slowly awake with sure, gentle hands and whispered kisses. She laid her hand tenderly against his cheek, savouring the rasp of stubble against her palm, her thumb dragging softly over the firm fullness of his lower lip.

He opened his mouth, drawing her thumb inside and sucking it deeply, his tongue exploring it, his teeth nipping lightly and making the breath catch in her throat. She shifted so she could reach him, her hands running over him now, checking for changes and finding only sweet, familiar memories. He moved on, his mouth warm and moist against her skin, and she joined in, their lips tracing tender trails across each other's bodies. They were taking their time now for leisurely explorations, the darkness shielding them from emotions they couldn't bear to expose—emotions too dark, too painful to consider.

That wasn't what this night was about, Amy thought later as she lay awake beside him listening to the deep, even rhythm of his breathing. It was for old times' sake, no-longer lovers reaching out to touch fleetingly what had once been theirs to love.

She was under no illusions. After the wedding, Matt

would be going back to London, and she'd be staying here, nursing her still-broken heart but with a little more tenderness, a little more forgiveness in her soul. He wasn't indifferent. Clearly not. But their lives had moved on, gone in different directions, and maybe it was for the best.

Maybe this was the way forward, for both of them. A little healing salve smeared gently over their wounds, kissing each other better.

She shifted slightly, seeking the warmth of his body, and he reached for her again in his sleep, drawing her closer, their legs tangled, her head pillowed on his shoulder as she slept, until the first light of dawn crept round the edges of the curtains.

He woke her gently, his voice a soft murmur in her ear.

'Amy?'

'Mmm.'

'Amy, it's morning.'

'Mmm.'

'You're in my room.'

'Mmm. I know.'

'Sweetheart, *everyone* will know soon.'

Her eyes flew open, and she sucked in a breath, the night coming back to her in a flood of memory and sudden awkwardness. 'Oh, rats. Damn. Um—Matt, help me get dressed.'

She threw the quilt off and starting searching for her underwear. Stupid, stupid... 'Where the hell are my pants?'

Pants? He nearly laughed. Try cobwebs.

'Take the dressing gown on the back of the door—have you got your room key?'

'Yes, of course. It's—'

In her clutch bag, which was—somewhere. She flopped back down onto the edge of the bed, dragging the quilt back over herself to hide her body from his eyes. Pointless, after he'd explored it so thoroughly, knew it so well in any case, but she was suddenly smitten with shyness. 'It's in my clutch bag,' she admitted.

'Which is…?'

Good question. 'Downstairs?'

He groaned and rolled away from her, vanishing into the bathroom and emerging a few minutes later damp, tousled and unshaven. And stark naked, the water drops still clinging to his body gleaming in the spill of light from the bathroom door and drawing her hungry eyes. He flipped open his overnight bag, pulled out some jeans and boxers and a shirt, dressed quickly and took the room key out of the door lock.

'What's your bag look like?' he asked briskly, and she dragged her mind off his body and tried to concentrate.

'Cream satin, about so big, little bronzy chain. It's got a lipstick, a tissue and the room key in it.'

'Any ideas where?'

She shrugged. 'The edge of the dance floor? I put it down at one point.'

He left her there, hugging her knees in the middle of the bed, looking rumpled and gorgeous and filled with regret.

He knew all about that one. How could he have been so stupid?

And why was she on the Pill, for heaven's sake? Was she in a relationship? Or did she do this kind of thing all the time?

Hell, he hoped not. The thought of his Amy casually—

He swallowed hard and ran downstairs, to find that

staff were already starting the mammoth clean-up operation.

'I'm looking for a cream satin evening bag,' he told someone, and was directed to the night porter's office.

'This the one?'

He wasn't sure, so he opened it and found exactly what she'd said inside. Well, if the room key fitted...

He went to it, and it gave him immediate access. Her case was there, unopened, inside the unused room, and he carried it back to her.

'Oh, Matt, you're a star. Thank you.'

'Anything to spare a lady's blushes. I'll go to your room,' he said, 'and if anyone knocks on the door, just ignore them. It'll only be Ben or my parents, and they'll ring me if it's anything important.'

He slipped his mobile into his pocket, picked up his wallet and did the same, then gave Amy an awkward smile. 'I guess I'll see you at breakfast.'

She nodded, looking embarrassed now, her grey eyes clouded with something that could have been shame, and without dragging it out he left her there and went to the room that should have been hers, lay on the bed and let his breath out on a long, ragged sigh.

What a fool. All he'd done, all he'd proved, was that he'd never stopped loving her. Well, hell, he'd known that before. It had hardly needed underlining.

He rolled to his side, thumped the pillow into the side of his neck and tried to sleep.

How could she have been so stupid?

She'd known seeing him again would be dangerous to her, but she hadn't realised how dangerous. She pulled the hotel gown tighter round her waist and moved to the chair by the window. She had a view over the courtyard where they'd had their buffet supper, could see the bench if she craned her neck.

Sudden unexpected tears glazed her eyes, and she swiped them away and sniffed hard. She'd done some stupid things in her life, most of them with Matt, and this was just the icing on the cake.

She got up and put the little kettle on to make tea, and found her pills in her washbag and popped one out. Thank God for synthetic hormones, she thought drily as she swallowed the pill. Or maybe not, because without the medication to control her irregular periods, they would never have spent the night together.

Which would have been a *good* thing, she told herself firmly. But telling him she was on the Pill was a two-edged sword. He probably thought she was a slut.

'I don't care what he thinks, it's none of his damn business and at least I won't get pregnant again,' she said to the kettle, and made herself a cup of tea and sat cradling it and staring down into the courtyard until it was stone cold.

And then she nearly dropped it, because Matt was there, outside in the courtyard garden just below her, sitting on the bench with a cup in his hand and checking something on his phone.

He made a call, then put the cup down and walked swiftly across the courtyard out of sight. One of his patients in London needing his attention? Or Melanie Grieves, mother of the little twins they'd delivered on Friday night?

Or just coming inside to see whoever he'd spoken to—his parents, maybe?

Moments later, there was a soft knock at the door.

'Amy? It's Matt.'

She let him in reluctantly and tried to look normal and less like an awkward teenager. 'Everything OK?'

'Yes. I'm going to see Melanie Grieves. Ben asked me to keep an eye on her.'

She nodded. 'Are you coming back for breakfast and to say goodbye to everyone?'

'Yes. I don't want to be lynched. Let me take my stuff, and I'll get out of your way. Here's your room key. Hang onto mine as well for now. I'll get it off you later.' He scooped up the suit, the shirt, the underwear, throwing them in the bag any old how and zipping it, and then he hesitated. For a second she thought he was about to kiss her, but then he just picked up his bag and left without a backward glance.

Amy let out the breath she'd been holding since he'd come in, and sat down on the end of the bed. There was no point in hanging around in his room, she thought. She'd shower and dress, and go downstairs and see if anyone was around.

Unlikely. The party had gone on long after they'd left it, and everyone was probably still in bed—where she would be, in her own room, if she had a grain of sense.

Well, she'd proved beyond any reasonable doubt that she didn't, she thought, and felt the tears welling again.

Damn him. Damn him for being so—so—just so *irresistible*. Well, never again. Without his body beside her, without the feel of his warmth, the tenderness of his touch, it all seemed like a thoroughly bad idea, and she knew the aftermath of it would haunt her for ages.

Years.

Forever?

Melanie Grieves was fine.

Her wound was healing, her little twins were doing

very well and apart from a bit of pain she was over the moon. He hadn't really needed to come and see her, he'd just had enough of sitting around in the hotel beating himself up about Amy.

Not that he shouldn't be doing that. He'd been a total idiot, and she really, really didn't need him falling all over her like he had last night. And leaving the dance floor like that—God knows what everyone had thought of them. He hadn't even asked her, just dragged her up the stairs and into his room like some kind of caveman.

He growled in frustration and slammed the car door shut. He'd better go back, better show his face and try and lie his way out of it. Better still, find Amy and get their story straight before his mother got her side of it and bent his ear. She'd always taken Amy's side.

Oh, hell.

He dropped his head forwards and knocked it gently against the hard, leatherbound steering wheel. Such a fool. And his head hurt. Good. It would remind him not to drink so much in future. He'd thought he was sober enough, but obviously not. If he'd been sober—

His phone rang and he pulled it out of his pocket and stared at the screen. Ben. Damn.

He ignored it. He'd talk to Amy first—if he got to her before they did. If only he had her number. She'd probably changed it, but maybe not. He dialled it anyway as he turned into the hotel car park, and she answered on the second ring.

'Hello?'

'Amy, it's Matt. We need to talk—we will have been seen last night. Where are you now?'

'Oh, damn. In the courtyard. Bring coffee.'

Stressed as he was, he smiled at that. He found a

breakfast waitress and ordered a pot of coffee and a basket of bacon rolls, then went and found her.

She was waiting, her heart speeding up as she caught sight of him, her nerves on edge. She couldn't believe what she'd done, couldn't believe she was going to sit here with him and concoct some cock-and-bull story to tell his family. Her friends. Oh, lord...

'How's Mel?' she asked, sticking to something safe.

'Fine. The babies are both doing well.'

'Good. Ben and Daisy'll be pleased.'

Silence. Of course there was, she thought. What was there to say, for heaven's sake? *Thank you for the best sex I've had in over four years? Not to say the only...?*

'Any sign of the others?' he asked after the silence had stretched out into the hereafter, and she shook her head.

'No. I put my bag in the car. Here's your room key. So—what's the story?'

'We wanted to talk?'

'We didn't talk, Matt,' she reminded him bluntly.

Pity they hadn't, she thought for the thousandth time. If they'd talked, they might have had more sense.

'You were feeling sick?' he suggested.

'What—from all that champagne?'

'It's not impossible.'

'I had less than you.'

'I think it's probably fair to say we both had more than was sensible,' he said drily, and she had to agree, but not out loud. She wasn't feeling that magnanimous.

'Maybe nobody noticed?' she said without any real conviction, and he gave a short, disbelieving laugh.

'Dream on, Amy. I dragged you off the dance floor and up the stairs in full view of everyone. I think someone will have noticed.'

She groaned and put her face in her hands, and then he started to laugh again, a soft, despairing sound that made her lift her head and meet his eyes. 'What?'

'I have some vague recollection of passing my parents in the hall.'

She groaned again. It just got better and better.

'Maybe you thought I needed to lie down?' she suggested wildly. 'Perhaps I'd told you I was feeling rough? It's not so unlikely, and it's beginning to look like the best option.'

'We could always tell them the truth.'

If we knew what it was, she thought, but the waitress arrived then with the tray of coffee and bacon rolls, and she seized one and sank her teeth into it and groaned. 'Oh, good choice,' she mumbled, and he laughed.

'Our default hangover food,' he said, bringing the memories crashing back. 'Want some ketchup?'

'That's disgusting,' she said, watching him squirt a dollop into his bacon roll and then demolish it in three bites before reaching for another. The times they'd done that, woken up on the morning after the night before and he'd cooked her bacon rolls and made her coffee.

He'd done that after their first night together, she remembered. And when she'd come out of hospital after—

She put the roll down and reached for her coffee, her appetite evaporating.

'So when are you off?' she asked.

'Tuesday morning,' he said, surprising her. 'Things are quiet at work at the moment, so I said I'd keep an eye on Mel till Ben and Daisy get back. They're only away for two nights.'

'Are you staying here?'

'No. I'm going back to Ben's.'

She nodded. It made sense, but she wasn't thrilled.

She'd be tripping over him in the hospital at random times, bumping into him at Daisy's house when she went to feed Tabitha—because if he was next door at Ben's, there was no way she was going to stay there, as she'd half thought she might, to keep the cat company.

Or moving in and renting it as they'd suggested, come to that. Not after last night's folly. The last thing she wanted was to be bumping into Ben's brother every time he came up to visit them.

Daisy had stayed in her own house adjoining Ben's until the wedding because of Florence, but she'd be moving into his half when they came back, and they'd offered her Daisy's house. They wanted a tenant they could trust, and her lease was coming up for renewal, and it was a lot nicer than her flat for all sorts of reasons.

It had off-road parking, a garden, a lovely conservatory—and the best neighbours in the world. She'd been debating whether to take it, because of the danger of bumping into Matt who was bound to be coming back and forth to visit them, but after this—well, how could she relax?

She couldn't. It would have been bad enough before.

'Why don't we just tell them to mind their own business?' she suggested at last. 'It really is nothing to do with them if we chose to—'

She broke off, and he raised a brow thoughtfully.

'Chose to—?'

But his phone rang, and he scanned the screen and answered it, pulling a face.

'Hi, Ben.'

'Is that a private party over there, or can we join you?'

He looked up, and saw his brother and brand-new

sister-in-law standing in the doorway watching them across the courtyard.

Amy followed the direction of his eyes, and sighed.

'Stand by to be grilled like a kipper,' she muttered, and stood up to hug Daisy. 'Well, good morning. How's the head?'

Daisy smiled smugly, looking very pleased with her-self. 'Clear as a bell. In case you didn't notice, I wasn't drinking.'

Amy frowned, then looked from one to the other and felt the bottom fall out of her stomach. Ben's eyes were shining, and there was a smile he couldn't quite hide. 'Oh—that's wonderful,' she said softly, and then to her utter humiliation her eyes welled over. She hugged Daisy hard, then turned to Ben—just in time to see Matt release him with a look in his eyes she hadn't seen since—

'Congratulations, that's amazing,' he said gruffly, and gathered Daisy up and hugged her, too, his expression carefully veiled now.

Except that Amy could still see it, lingering in the back of his eyes, a fleeting echo of a grief once so raw it had torn them apart.

'So, when's it due?' he asked, going through the motions. Not that he wasn't interested, but today of all days...

'The tenth of May. It's very, very early on,' Daisy said wryly. 'I did the test this morning.'

'Right after she threw up.'

Matt gave a soft huff of sympathetic laughter. 'Poor Daisy. It passes, I'm reliably informed by my patients.' *That's right, keep it impersonal...*

'It's a good sign,' Amy said, her voice slightly strained to his ears. 'Means the pregnancy's secure.'

Unlike hers. Oh, God, beam me up...

'Changing the subject, it's none of my business, but—' Ben began, but Matt knew exactly where this was going and cut him off.

'You're right, it's not. We needed to talk, there were a lot of people about. Amy slept in my room, and I went to hers.'

At a quarter to six this morning, but they didn't need to know that, and he was darned sure they wouldn't have been up and about that early. But someone was.

'Yeah, Mum said she saw you coming out of your room and going to another one at some ungodly hour.'

Damn. Of all the people...

'I went to get my phone so I could ring the hospital,' he lied, but he'd never been able to lie convincingly to Ben, and as their eyes met he saw Ben clock the lie and yet say nothing.

As he'd said himself, it was none of his business, and he obviously realised he'd overstepped the mark. He'd back him up, though, if their mother said any more, of that Matt was sure. 'So how is Mel?' Ben asked, moving smoothly on, and Matt let out a slight sigh of relief.

'Fine. They're all fine. I've been in to see them, and they're all doing really well. She was keen to hear all about the wedding. I promised I'd take her some cake—unless you want to do it when you come back?'

'No, you go for it. I'm glad she's well. Thanks for going in.'

'My pleasure. Did you order coffee or do you want me to do it?'

Daisy pulled a face. 'Can we have something less smelly, and something to eat? I really don't think I can wait till breakfast.'

'Sure. I'll order decaf tea. What about bacon rolls?'

'Oh, yes-s-s-s!' she said fervently. 'Amazing! Matt, you're a genius.'

He smiled, glancing across at Amy and sensing, rather than seeing, the sadness that lingered in her. She was smiling at Daisy, but underneath it all was grief, no longer raw and untamed, maybe, but there for all that.

Would it ever get easier? Ever truly go away?

He hoped so, but he was very much afraid that he was wrong.

'Well, hello, Mummy Grieves! Are you up for visitors?'

'Oh, yes! Hello, Amy, how are you? How was the wedding? Did Daisy look beautiful?'

'Utterly gorgeous, but I bet she wasn't as gorgeous as your little girls. Aren't you going to introduce me?'

'Of course. I hope you don't mind, but we've called them Daisy and Amy, because you two have been so kind and we really love the names.'

'Oh, that's so sweet of you, thank you,' Amy said, her eyes filling. In a rare complication, the twins had shared the same amniotic sac, and the danger of their cords tangling had meant Mel had been monitored as an inpatient for several weeks, and she and Daisy had got to know Mel very well. And this... She blinked hard and sniffed, and Mel hugged her.

'Thank *you*,' she corrected. 'So, this is Amy. Want a cuddle?'

'I'd better not—infection risk,' she lied. That was why she'd gone on her way in, so her clothes were clean, but the last thing she wanted was to hold them. Delivering babies was one thing. Going out of her way to cuddle them—well, she just didn't.

She admired them both, though, Amy first, then Daisy, their perfect little features so very alike and yet slightly different. 'Can you tell them apart yet?' she asked Mel, and she smiled and nodded.

'Oh, yes. I could see the differences straight away. Adrian can't always, but he'll learn, I expect. And Mr Walker and his brother—they're very alike, too, aren't they, but I can tell the difference. There's just something.'

Amy swallowed. Oh, yes. Ben didn't have the ability to turn her into a total basket case just by walking into the room, and just to prove it, Matt strolled in then and she felt her stomach drop to the floor and her heart lurch.

'Talk of the Devil,' she said brightly, and saying goodbye to Mel, she slipped past him, trying not to breath in the faint, lingering scent of soap and cologne, but it drifted after her on the air.

Just one more day. He'll be gone tomorrow.

It couldn't come soon enough…

He found her, the next day, working in the ward office filling out patient records on the computer.

'I'm off,' he said, and she looked up and wondered why, when she'd been so keen to see him go, she should feel a pang of sadness that she was losing him.

Ridiculous. She wasn't losing him, he wasn't hers! And anyway, since the wedding they'd hardly seen each other. But that didn't mean they hadn't both been painfully, desperately aware. Yet he hadn't once, in all that time, suggested they repeat the folly of Saturday night—

'Got time for a coffee?'

She glanced up at the clock. Actually, she had plenty of time. There was nothing going on, for once, and although no doubt now she'd thought that all hell would break loose, for the minute, anyway, it was quiet.

Did she *want* to make time for a coffee? Totally different question.

'I can spare five minutes,' she said, logging off the computer and sliding back her chair.

He ushered her through the door first, his hand resting lightly on the small of her back, and she felt the warmth, the security of it all the way through to her bones. Except it was a false sense of security.

'We ought to talk,' he said quietly, once they were seated in the café.

She stirred her coffee, chasing the froth round the top, frowning at it as if it held the answers. 'Is there anything to say?'

He laughed, a short, harsh sound that cut the air. 'Amy, we spent the *night* together,' he said—unnecessarily, since she'd hardly forgotten.

'For old times' sake,' she pointed out. 'That was all.'

'Was it? Was it really?'

'Yes. It really was.'

He stared at her, searching her eyes for the longest moment, and then the expression in them was carefully banked and he looked away. 'OK. If that's what you want.'

It wasn't. She wanted *him*, but she couldn't trust him, because when her world had disintegrated and she'd needed him more than she'd ever needed anybody in her life, he'd turned his back on her.

She wasn't going through that again, not for him, not for anybody.

'It is what I want,' she lied. 'It didn't work, Matt, and there's no use harking back to it. We need to let it go.'

His eyes speared her. 'Have you?'

Let it go? *Let her baby go?*

She sucked in a breath and looked away.

'I didn't think so,' he said softly. 'Well, if it helps you any, neither have I. And I haven't forgotten you, Amy.'

She closed her eyes, wishing he would go, wishing he could stay. She heard the scrape of a chair, felt the touch of his hand on her shoulder.

'You know where I am if you change your mind.'

'I won't,' she vowed. She couldn't. She didn't dare. She simply wasn't strong enough to survive a second time.

He bent, tipped her head back with his fingers and dropped the gentlest, sweetest, saddest kiss on her lips.

'Goodbye, Amy. Take care of yourself.'

And then he was gone, walking swiftly away, leaving her there alone in the middle of the crowded café. She wanted to get up, to run after him, to yell at him to stop, she was sorry, she didn't mean it, please stay. But she didn't.

Somehow, just barely, she managed to stop herself, and no doubt one day she'd be grateful for that.

But right now, she felt as if she'd just thrown away her last chance at happiness, and all she wanted to do was cry.

CHAPTER THREE

IT TOOK her weeks to work out what was going on.

Weeks in which Matt was in her head morning, noon and night. She kept telling herself she'd done the right thing, that not seeing him again was sensible, but it wasn't easy to convince herself. Not easy at all, and Daisy and Ben being so blissfully happy didn't help.

She ached for him so much it was physical, but she'd done the right thing, sending him away. She had. She couldn't rely on him, couldn't trust him again with her heart. And she was genuinely relieved when her period came right on cue, because although she might want *him*, the thought of going through another pregnancy terrified her, and for the first time since the wedding she felt herself letting go of an inner tension she hadn't even been aware of.

She could move on now. They'd said their goodbyes, and it was done.

Finished.

The autumn came and went, and December arrived with a vengeance. It rained, and when it wasn't raining, it was sleeting, and then it dried up and didn't thaw for days. And her boiler broke down in her flat.

Marvellous, she thought. Just what she needed. She

contacted her landlord, but it would be three weeks before it could be replaced—more, maybe, because plumbers were rushed off their feet after the freeze—and so she gave in to Ben and Daisy's gentle nagging, and moved into Daisy's house just ten days before Christmas.

'It's only temporary, till my boiler's fixed,' she told them firmly, but they just smiled and nodded and re-fused to take any rent on the grounds that it was better for the house to be occupied.

Then Daisy had her twenty-week scan, and of course she asked to see the photo. What else could she do? And she thought she'd be fine, she saw them all the time in her work, but it really got to her. Because of the link to Matt? She had no idea, but it haunted her that day and the next, popping up in every quiet moment and bring-ing with it a rush of grief that threatened to undermine her. She and Matt had been so happy, so deliriously overjoyed back then. And then, so shortly before her scan was due—

A laugh jerked her out of her thoughts, a laugh so like Matt's that it could so easily have been him, and she felt her heart squeeze. Stupid. She *knew* it was Ben. She heard him laugh all the time. And every time, she felt pain like a solid ball wedged in her chest.

She *missed* him. So, so much.

'Oh, Amy, great, I was hoping I'd find you here. New admission—thirty-four weeks, slight show last night, mild contractions which could just be Braxton Hicks'. Have you got time to admit her for me, please? She's just moved to the area last week, so we haven't seen her before but she's got her hand-held notes.'

She swiped the tears from her cheeks surreptitiously while she pretended to stifle a yawn. 'Sure. I could do with a break from this tedious admin. I'll just log off and I'll be with you. What's her name?'

'Helen Kendall. She's in the assessment room.'

Amy found her sitting on the edge of the chair looking worried and guilty, and she introduced herself.

'I'm so sorry to just come in,' Helen said, 'but I was worried because I've been really overdoing it with the move and I'm just so *tired*,' she blurted out, and then she started to cry.

'Oh, Helen,' Amy said, sitting down next to her and rubbing her back soothingly. 'You're exhausted—come on, let's get you into a gown and into bed, and let us take care of you.'

'It's all my fault, I shouldn't have let him talk me into it, we should have waited and now the baby's going to be too early,' she sobbed. Oh, she could understand the guilt all too well, but thirty-four weeks wasn't too early. Not like eighteen weeks…

'It's not your fault,' she said with a calm she didn't feel, 'and thirty-four weeks is quite manageable if it comes to that. It may well not. Come on, chin up, and let's find out what's going on.'

She handed Helen a gown, then left her alone for a few minutes to change and do a urine sample while she took the time to get her emotions back in order. What was the *matter* with her? She didn't think about her baby at all, normally. It was seeing that picture of Daisy's baby, and thinking about Matt again—always Matt.

She pulled herself together and went back to Helen.

This was her first pregnancy, it had been utterly straightforward and uncomplicated to this point, and there was no reason to suspect that anything would go wrong even if she did give birth early. The baby was moving normally, its heartbeat was loud and strong, and Helen relaxed visibly when she heard it.

'Oh, that's so reassuring,' she said, her eyes filling, and she was still caressing her bump with a gentle, contented smile on her face when Ben arrived.

'OK, Helen, let's have a look at this baby and see how we're doing,' he said, and Amy watched the monitor.

The baby was a good size for her dates, there was no thinning of Helen's uterus as yet, and her contractions might well stop at this point, if she was lucky. Not everyone was.

She sucked in a breath and stepped back, and Ben glanced up at her and frowned.

'You OK?'

'Just giving you a bit more room,' she lied.

He grunted. It was a sound she understood. Matt used to do the same thing when he knew she was lying. Maybe they were more alike than she'd realised.

'Right, Helen, I'm happy with that. We'll monitor you, but I'm pretty sure they're just Braxton Hicks' and this will all settle down. We'll give you drugs to halt it if we can and steroids to mature the baby's lungs just to be on the safe side, and then if it's all stable and there's no change overnight, you can go home tomorrow.'

She swallowed. 'That's so reassuring. Thanks. I feel an idiot now, but I didn't know what to do.'

'Don't worry, you've done the right thing coming in,' Amy assured her. 'Why don't you try and have a sleep? I might have to disturb you from time to time, but I think a rest will do you good.'

She followed Ben out into the corridor. 'Any special instructions?'

'Yes. Come for dinner. Daisy's worried about you—she thinks the scan upset you.'

She forced a smile. 'Don't be silly, of course it didn't.'

That grunt again. 'Humour her, Amy, for my sake if nothing else. You know what she's like when she's got a bee in her bonnet about something. So—seven o'clock all right?'

She wasn't going to get out of it without a fuss, Amy realised, so she gave in. 'Seven will be fine. I'll see you there—and I'll keep you up to speed with Helen in the meantime.'

She picked up some flowers for Daisy from the supermarket on her way home. And it really did feel like home, she thought as she showered and dressed.

Odd, how easily she'd settled into the little house, but she'd been lucky it had been available. Or maybe they'd deliberately kept it that way? She had a feeling they weren't exactly busting a gut to get a tenant and she wouldn't have put it past them to have caused the jinx in her boiler, but not even Daisy could make something rust through with the sheer force of her will.

It was a pity it was only temporary, but with their baby coming—well, thrilled though she was for them, it would be hard enough seeing Ben at work strutting around and showing off photos, without having it rammed down her throat at home.

At seven o'clock on the dot, she went out of the front door, stepped over the little low iron fence between the front gardens and rang their doorbell, and Daisy opened it instantly.

'Oh, flowers, thank you! Oh, you shouldn't,' Daisy said, hugging her as she stepped inside. 'I'm *so* glad you've come. I really thought I'd upset you...'

Her eyes were filling, and Amy sighed and hugged her back. 'Don't be silly. It was lovely seeing the picture

and I'm really glad everything's all right.' She eased
away and sniffed the air. 'Gosh, something smells wonderful. I've been starving recently. I think it's the cold,
but I'm going to have to stop it. People keep bringing
chocolates in.'

'Oh, tell me about it!' Daisy laughed. 'Come on
through. Ben's cooking up a storm in the kitchen. He
says it's a warming winter casserole, but all I know is
it's taking a long time!'

It was delicious, and she would have eaten more, but
her jeans were too tight and they were putting pressure
on her bladder. That would teach her to stuff the patients' chocolates, she thought.

They cleared the table, and she excused herself and
went up to the bathroom, but then had to hunt for toilet
paper in the little cupboard under the sink.

A box fell out onto the floor, a slim rectangular box.
She picked it up to put it back, and then stopped.

A pregnancy test, one of a twin pack...

Everything seemed to slow down for a moment, and
then her heart lurched and started to race.

No. Don't be silly. You can't be.

Or could she? She'd thought her jeans were tight because she'd been such a pig recently, but she was feeling bloated—and her period was overdue. Only by a
day, but the others...

'Amy? I've just remembered the loo paper's run out.
I've got some here, I meant to bring it up.'

She opened the door, the pregnancy test in her hand,
and Daisy stared down at it, her jaw dropping.

'Amy?' she murmured.

'I—um—I was looking for loo paper, and it fell out,
and—Daisy, what if I'm...?'

She looked into Daisy's worried eyes, unable to say the word, but it hung there in the air between them.

'What makes you think you could be? I thought you were on the Pill? I mean, surely you've had periods?'

'Yes.' Yes, of course she had. Thank God. She leant against the wall, weak with relief. She'd just overeaten.

'And you weren't ill, were you, before the wedding?'

Ill? Alarm bells began to ring again. Not *ill*, exactly, but thinking back she'd been sick in the morning with the thought of seeing Matt, and her stomach had played up all the previous week with nerves. And it was only a low-dose pill, so timing was crucial if you were using it for contraception—which she wasn't, so maybe she'd just taken it for granted. What if...?

'I can't be, Daisy, it was only one night, and I've had three periods...' She trailed off.

Scant ones. Lighter than normal. Shorter—and this one was late.

Oh, how could she have been so dense? The signs were all there.

'Just use the pregnancy test,' Daisy offered tentatively, putting it back in her hand. 'It's going begging, and it would answer the question.'

Did she want it answered? The wedding was months ago, so she'd be almost 16 weeks—four weeks behind Daisy. Only two weeks to...

She felt bile rising in her throat again, and swallowed hard. 'Um...'

'Go on. I'll wait outside.'

She left the door open a crack, and the moment the loo flushed, she was back in there, holding Amy's hand while they stared at the little window. One line—then the other. Clear as a bell.

Amy sat down on the floor as if her strings had been

cut, just as Ben appeared in the doorway behind Daisy. 'Are you girls OK?' he asked, looking from one to the other, and then he glanced down and saw the pregnancy test in Amy's lifeless hand, and she saw the penny drop.

'Oh, Amy,' he said softly, and as she stared at him blankly, the reality of her situation sank in and she began to shake.

'Ben, I can't—I can't do this again,' she said, her voice shuddering as fear engulfed her. 'Tell me I don't have to do this again! I can't—I'm so scared. No, please, no, not again, I can't...'

'Amy, shhh, it's OK,' Daisy said, gathering her up in her arms and rocking her against her chest. 'Hush now, sweetheart, it's all right, we'll take care of you. Don't be scared, it'll be all right.'

But it wasn't all right, and it wouldn't be, not ever again, she thought hysterically. She could hear herself gibbering, feel the panic and terror clawing at her, and underneath it, below it all, the agonising grief for the baby she'd loved and lost, too small to have any hope of surviving, and yet so much loved, so infinitely precious, so perfect—so agonisingly, dreadfully missed.

Her empty arms ached to hold him, her soul wept for his loss. Every Christmas, every birthday, every anniversary of the miscarriage—each one branded on her heart.

She couldn't bear it if it happened again...

They ended up in a row propped against the bathroom wall, her in the middle, Ben on one side, Daisy on the other, both of them holding her as she tried so very hard to push it all back down where it belonged.

And finally it was back there, safely locked away in the deepest recesses of her broken heart, and she could breathe again. Just about.

Ben let her go and shifted so he could see her face. 'Do you want me to help you tell him?' he asked, and she felt her eyes widen in shock.

Matt! Matt, who'd withdrawn into himself and isolated her in her grief, and then left her to deal with the loss of their baby alone. She hadn't even given him a thought, but—

'No! No, you can't!' she said frantically, clutching at Ben. 'I don't want him to know!'

Ben frowned. 'Well, of course he has to know, Amy, it's his baby. He needs to know—and you'll need him with you for all sorts of reasons. He should take some responsibility for this. He should have known better than to get you pregnant. I could kill him.'

She shook her head and drew her legs up, hugging her knees. 'No. Ben, I was on the Pill, I told him that. It's not his fault—not his responsibility. And I don't need him. I won't rely on him ever again, I can't. If anything goes wrong…'

'It won't.'

'It might! Ben, please! He can't deal with it, and I can't cope with all that again. I'd rather do it alone. You mustn't tell him. Please, Ben, promise me you won't tell him.'

Ben closed his eyes and let his breath out on a harsh sigh. For an age he said nothing, then he opened his eyes again and nodded. 'OK. I don't agree with you, and I think he should know, but I won't tell him yet—but you *have* to tell him at some point, Amy. He has the right to know—and the sooner the better.'

She opened her mouth to argue, but then shut it. She had the pregnancy to get through yet, and that was by no means a foregone conclusion.

'I'll tell him when it's over,' she said woodenly. 'Either way.'

'Amy, just because you've lost a baby in the past doesn't mean you're going to lose this one,' Ben said firmly, but he didn't understand. He hadn't been there, and even if he had…

'You can't say that. We didn't know why it happened, it could have been anything,' she told him, not sure what Matt had told him but needing to explain, to him and to Daisy, too, because she'd never really told her what had happened. 'I was eighteen weeks pregnant, I was fit and well, there was no bleeding, no pain, nothing, and the baby was…'

She shut her eyes tight. Perfect. Beautiful. And just too small, too frail, too unready for the world. She couldn't say it, couldn't let herself picture him, couldn't go back there.

As if he understood, Ben took her hands in his and held them firmly. 'We'll look after you. I'll get your old notes sent, and we'll make sure you're OK. We'll watch you like a hawk.'

'I was in Harrogate,' she said, her voice clogged with tears. 'With Matt—planning the wedding…'

He nodded. 'I know. Don't worry, Amy. We'll take care of you—but there's one condition.'

'I *can't* tell him yet!'

'It's not that, it's about you. You stay next door, so we can look after you properly and be there for you, or I *will* tell him. That's the deal,' he said flatly, and she looked into his eyes—Matt's eyes—and gave in. There was no arguing with the Walker men when they had that look in their eyes. And anyway, the last thing she wanted was to be alone in this, whatever she might have said.

'OK,' she agreed shakily. 'And I will tell him, but in my own way, in my own time. He'll smother me, and I can't cope with it yet. I just need to get through the next few weeks.'

Just until the baby was viable.

She couldn't say the words, but they understood, and Ben hugged her briefly and pulled her to her feet.

'I'll let you tell him. And I'll look after you. We'll look after you. It'll be OK.'

She smiled at him, feeling some of the terror dissipating in the friendly face of their support. She wasn't alone. And Ben and Daisy wouldn't desert her. So maybe she could do this, after all...

'So how are things?'

'Oh, you know how it is,' Ben said. 'How about you?'

Matt frowned. His brother sounded evasive. Odd, in only a handful of words over the telephone, but there was something there, something guarded. Something he wasn't telling him.

'Ditto. How's Daisy?'

'Better. Growing,' he said. 'She's finally stopped being sick and she's looking well. We did her twenty-week scan and everything's fine.'

'And Amy?' he asked carefully, and there was a pause.

'Amy's fine,' Ben replied, and he definitely sounded guarded now. So it wasn't that Ben was walking round him on eggshells because of Daisy being pregnant. It was Amy who was the problem.

'She—uh—she didn't want to see me again,' he admitted softly.

Matt heard Ben let out a soft sigh. 'Yeah. Well, she doesn't seem to have changed her mind. I'm sorry.'

Well, that was him told. He swallowed hard, staring sightlessly out of his sitting room window at the bleak winter garden of his small mews cottage. It had taken a bit of winding himself up to ask after her, and he wished he hadn't bothered.

Hell, he should just forget about her and move on, as she'd said, but...

'Look af—' His voice cracked a little, and he cleared his throat. 'Look after her for me.'

'We are. She's moved in next door, actually, into Daisy's house. Her boiler broke and it seemed to make sense.'

He had the totally irrational urge to jump in the car and come up and visit them. She'd be next door, just through the wall, and if he listened he'd hear her moving around—

Idiot. 'Give her my love,' he said gruffly. 'And Daisy and Florence. I'll try and see you sometime in the next couple of weeks. What are you doing over Christmas?'

'I don't know. I had thought we might go to Yorkshire, but I'm working. What about you?'

'I'm working Christmas Day and Boxing Day,' he said, and had a sudden longing for his mother's home cooking and his father's quiet, sage advice. But in the absence of that... 'Look, I've got to go, but I might try and get up between Christmas and New Year. Maybe on the twenty-seventh.'

'That'd be good. Let's see how it goes.'

'OK. You take care.'

'And you.'

He ended the call and watched a blackbird scratching in the fallen leaves under the bird feeder. Winter was setting in, the nights cold and frosty, even here in London.

He turned the television on and put his feet up, but he couldn't rest. Talking about Amy had unsettled him, and he'd suggested going up there—to see her?

Idiot. Idiot! It had taken him weeks to get over seeing her last time, so why on earth did he think it would be a good idea to go up to Yoxburgh in the hope of seeing her again?

He must be nuts. What the hell did he hope to achieve?

Maybe she's pregnant.

He stamped on that one hard. If she was pregnant, she would have told him weeks ago. Or Ben would. Yeah, Ben definitely would. Anyway, she was on the Pill, and she'd probably moved on, got herself another lover. He ignored the burn of acid at the thought. Maybe he should do the same, he told himself firmly. There was a new midwife who'd been flirting with him the past few weeks. He could take her out for dinner, see where it went.

But she's not Amy.

'You've lost Amy, get over it,' he growled. He had work he could do at the hospital, and anything was better than sitting here going over this again and again and again, so he turned the television off again, pulled on his coat and headed out of the door.

'Matt sends you his love.'

Amy felt herself stiffen. 'You didn't tell him?'

'No, of course I didn't tell him. I promised you I wouldn't.'

She let her breath out, and asked the question she'd been longing to ask. 'How is he?'

'OK, I think. We didn't talk for long. He asked how you were.'

'And what did you say?'

He smiled wryly. 'I told him you were fine and didn't want to see him again.'

It wasn't quite true. She'd been thinking about little else for the past two days, but he was right, she didn't want to see him again at the moment, because if she did, she'd have to tell him, and then...

'We were talking about Christmas,' Ben went on. 'We're both working on Christmas Day and we've got Florence on Boxing Day, but he might come up afterwards. What are you doing?'

He might come up afterwards...

'I haven't decided. They want me to work, so I'll probably do the day shift—'

'So spend Christmas night with us,' Daisy urged. 'We'll have a great time.'

It was tempting, but she shook her head. 'You want to be on your own—it's the last time you'll be able to. I'll be fine, really. Christmas Day is usually a lovely shift.'

And it would stop her worrying about her baby.

Ben scanned her the next day. They'd gone down to the big scanner in a quiet moment, and for the first time she actually acknowledged her baby's existence, dared to think about it, to see it as a real baby.

She watched the beating heart, saw the little arms and legs flailing around wildly, counted hands and feet, saw the fine, delicate column of its spine, the bridge of its nose, the placenta firmly fixed near the top of her uterus.

My baby, she thought, reaching out her hand and touching the image tenderly, and through her tears, she smiled at it and fell in love.

She pressed her hand to her mouth and closed her eyes as Ben turned off the scanner. 'Thank you,' she murmured.

'My pleasure,' he said, his voice roughened, and she realised he was moved, too, because this was his brother's baby, and he must have felt the loss of their first one keenly for Matt.

'Did you take a photo?' she asked, not sure she could bear to look at it. She still had the photo—

'Of course I did. I took one for us, as well, and one for Matt. To give him later,' he added hastily when she frowned.

She nodded. 'Thank you,' she said again, and took the tissue from him to wipe the gloop off her tummy. She'd started to show already, she realised. No wonder her jeans were tight.

Just eleven more days to go…

'You aren't going to lose this baby, Amy,' Ben said firmly, as if he'd read her mind. 'I'm not going to let you.'

'You may not be able to stop it.'

'I'd like to scan your cervix weekly from now on. Matt seemed to think—'

'Have you been talking to him?' she asked, horrified, but he shook his head.

'No. No, of course not. I promised I wouldn't. This was years ago, the only time we've talked about it. It was right after you lost the baby, and he was distraught. He thought it was your cervix. He was talking about monitoring you much more closely for the next pregnancy.'

She swung her legs down off the edge of the couch and stood up, straightening her clothes automatically. 'What next pregnancy?' she asked—fairly ridiculously, under the circumstances, she thought with a touch of hysteria, but if it hadn't been for the wedding she wouldn't have seen him again. 'He walked away, Ben. I told him I couldn't cope, that I needed time to get over it, and he walked away. He almost seemed relieved.'

'Amy, you're wrong,' he said, frowning, but she knew she wasn't. He'd been cold, remote. He'd hardly talked to her. He'd grieved for the baby, but he hadn't been able to support her, and he had rebuffed any attempt by her to support him.

'Ben, drop it. Please. You weren't there, you didn't see him. You can monitor me as closely as you like, but if it's all the same with you I'll take it one day at a time. I refuse to get my hopes up.'

'Because you feel guilty?'

She stared at him. Did she? Was that the reason she'd been so slow to realise that she was pregnant, and so reluctant to recognise this child? Because she didn't feel she deserved it? Because she'd gone for that walk with Matt the day before, and got overtired and then—?

'Ben, can we leave this?' she asked a little desperately, shutting the memories away before they could swamp her.

'Sure. I'm sorry. Here, your photo.' He handed her the little image in its white card mount, and she slipped it into her bag.

'I'd better get back to work. And—thank you, Ben. I really do appreciate all you're doing for me.'

'Don't mention it.'

She was doing fine.

There was nothing—nothing at all, from any test or examination—to indicate that she might lose this baby. Just as there hadn't been last time.

She put it out of her mind, and carried on as if noth-

ing was any different. Apart from taking the usual pre-
cautions and supplements, she carried on as normal and
tried not to think about it—or Matt—too much.

She worked the day shift on Christmas Day, and in
the end she went round to Ben and Daisy's in the evening, just to eat. She didn't stay long, though. Daisy
was looking tired, and it was their last Christmas alone
together, so she left them to it after they'd eaten, and
went home and thought about Matt.

Was he alone? It was all right for her, she'd had a
great day at work, and she'd had a lovely dinner with
Ben and Daisy. But Matt—who did he have?

She could phone him. Say Happy Christmas, and tell
him he was going to be a father.

No. It was still too early, but she would tell him soon.
She would.

CHAPTER FOUR

HE STOOD on the pavement outside, staring at the front door of Daisy's house and fighting indecision.

Amy was in. He could see the light from the kitchen shining down the hall, and he saw a shadow move across as if she'd walked into the dining room. She wasn't expecting him—none of them were, and he could see from the lack of lights that Ben and Daisy were out. So—to knock, or not to knock?

Instinct told him he wouldn't be welcome. Need told him to knock on the door anyway, to give her the benefit of the doubt, to try again, just one more time, to see if he could convince her to give their relationship another go.

He still hesitated, then with a sharp shake of his head, he walked firmly up the path and rapped on the door.

'Amy, it's Matt.'

Why had he done that? If he'd kept quiet, she would have come to the door, but instead there was silence. He resisted the urge to bend down and peer through the letter box. She was entitled to ignore him if she wanted to, and anyway there was a holly wreath hanging over it and it would probably stab him in the eye.

But she didn't ignore him. The porch light came on,

and he heard footsteps and the door swung inwards to reveal her standing there unsmiling.

'Hello, Matt,' she said quietly, and his heart turned over.

She looked—gorgeous. Her grey eyes were wary, her fair hair scrunched back in a ponytail as if she'd only just finished work and she was dressed in some shapeless rag of a jumper, but she looked warm and cosy and very, very dear, and he wanted to haul her into his arms and hold her.

As if she knew it, she hugged her arms defensively, so he forced himself to make do with a smile. 'Hi, there. Happy Christmas—or should that be Happy New Year?'

She ignored both. 'I didn't think Ben and Daisy were expecting you,' she said, her voice a little tight. 'You hadn't rung to confirm.'

'No. It was only tentative—a spur-of-the-moment thing.' Very spur of the moment. Two hours ago he'd been sitting in his house staring at the bird feeder and trying to talk himself out of it. He probably should have done.

'Oh. Well, they're out.'

'Will they be long?' Hell, they were talking like strangers.

'I don't know—why don't you come in? You can't stand out there for hours.'

'Will they be hours?' he asked, following her down the hall and eyeing her bottom thoughtfully. Had she put on a little weight? He thought so. It suited her.

'I don't know. Possibly. They're looking at baby stuff in the sales.'

Why had she said that? Why bring it up? She could have kicked herself, because absolutely the *last* thing she wanted to talk about with Matt was babies, although she knew that conversation was coming sometime soon.

'I was just making tea. Do you want some?'

'Yeah, that would be good. Thank you.'

So formal. So polite and distant. If he had any idea...

'You look well.'

She felt heat climb her cheeks. 'I am well.' *Very well, and pregnant with your child.* 'Have you eaten?'

'Yes—I had lunch, but don't mind me if you haven't.'

The stilted conversation was going to make her scream, but what was the alternative? *'Oh, incidentally, while I think of it, I'm having your baby'* didn't seem quite the right opener!

And anyway, she wasn't past the danger point yet. A few more days, maybe weeks—perhaps then.

She set a mug of tea down in front of him at the table, and finished making herself a sandwich. She was still starving, still eating anything she could lay her hands on—

'I thought you hated peanut butter?'

Damn. Trust him to notice. The only time she'd eaten it had been when she was pregnant, and any second now he'd guess.

'It goes in phases,' she said truthfully, and sat in a chair across the table and up from him, so she didn't have to look straight at him, didn't have to meet those searching blue eyes and risk blurting out the truth.

He gave a soft sigh and leant back. 'I'm sorry, I should have called you, but I thought you'd probably tell me to go to hell.'

'So why come?'

His smile was wry and rather sad. 'Why do you think, Amy?' he asked softly, and she swallowed.

'I don't— Matt, I told you before...'

He sighed softly. 'I know. That night was just for old times' sake. Laying our love to rest, I guess. I'd hoped it might turn out to be more than that. Might still turn out to be more.'

Oh, so much more. You have no idea.

'Matt, we've talked about this. We clearly didn't have what it takes, and if—'

She broke off, wary of straying into dangerous territory, but Matt had no such fear.

'If you hadn't got pregnant, our relationship would have fizzled out?'

Fizzled out? She'd said she couldn't cope with the wedding so soon after she'd lost her baby, and he'd heaved a sigh of relief and cancelled their entire relationship, so—yes, clearly he would have lost interest sooner or later, if he hadn't already done so.

She shrugged, and he shook his head slowly and gave a rueful smile.

'OK. I get that you think that, even if I don't agree, but—you seemed keen enough at the wedding, so what changed?'

What changed? *What changed?* She nearly laughed out loud at that. 'At the wedding I'd had a bit too much to drink,' she said bluntly, 'or I wouldn't have done anything so stupid. I would have thought better of it.'

'I've thought about very little since,' he said softly, and her heart contracted.

Oh, Matt.

She opened her mouth to tell him, but bottled out and changed the subject, asking instead how his parents were.

He gave a knowing little smile and let it go. 'Fine. They've got snow up there at the moment, but they're OK, they've got plenty of food in and Dad can still get to the farms for emergencies, but it's supposed to be thawing this week.'

Oh, for God's sake, just tell her you love her! Tell her you want her! Tell her you want to try again, and this time you'll make it work. She's said we didn't have what it takes, but does anybody? For what happened to us, does anybody have what it takes?

He was opening his mouth when there was a sharp knock on the door. She got up and opened it, and he heard her murmur his name as Ben strode in.

'You were going to phone!' he said, hugging him and slapping his back. 'Come on, let's get you out of Amy's hair and you can give me a hand to unload the car. Daisy's been shopping with a vengeance.'

Maybe he didn't want to go? Maybe Amy was happy with him there? Maybe he hadn't finished what he'd come for?

But then he looked at her, composed, controlled but not exactly overjoyed, and he let out his breath on a quiet sigh and moved towards the door.

'Sure. Thanks for the tea, Amy. It was good to see you again.'

She smiled, but it didn't reach her eyes. 'Happy New Year, Matt.'

And she shut the door gently but firmly behind them, and went back to the table, her hands shaking.

She had to tell him sometime. Why not now? Why on earth hadn't she taken the opportunity?

She sighed. She knew why—knew that until this week was over, at least, she couldn't share it with him, but she would tell him. Ben was right, he needed to know, and she wanted their child to have him in its life. He was a good man, and he'd be a wonderful father.

What she couldn't deal with again, if anything went wrong, was his grief on top of her own.

No. Better not to have told him yet—and Ben had promised not to. She just hoped she could rely on him.

He was there until the following evening, and she spent as much time as possible at the hospital.

It wasn't hard. They were busy and short-staffed, and delighted to have her.

She'd put herself down for the night shift on New Year's Eve—better to keep busy, because she was eighteen weeks on that day, and if she hadn't been busy she would have gone out of her mind.

Her phone beeped a couple of times—Happy New Year messages from people, she thought, but she was too busy to check it, so she carried on filling in the notes and went back to her mums to check on them.

But when her night shift finished and she went home in the cold, bright crisp air of the morning, she finally checked her phone and found a text from a friend and a voicemail message.

From Matt.

'Hi, Amy, it's Matt. Sorry to miss you, I expect you're working. I just wanted to say Happy New Year, and it was good to see you again the other day. I'm sorry it was so brief. Maybe next time…' There was a pause, then he added, 'Well, you know where I am if you want me.'

If she wanted him?

She sat down on the sofa in her sitting room, and played his hesitant, reluctant message again and again and again.

Of course she wanted him. She wanted him so much it was unbearable, today of all days, the exact stage to the day that she'd lost their first baby. She laid her hand over the tidy little bump—hardly a bump at all. If you didn't know, you wouldn't guess, but assuming it made it, and it was a big assumption, this baby was going to cause havoc in her life.

And in Matt's.

She had to tell him. Ben was right, she couldn't just keep relying on them, and he had the right to know about his child. She took the two-week-old scan photo out of her bag and stared at it, tracing the tiny face with her finger. It would be bigger now. As big as Samuel...

Lord, even the name hurt. She sucked in a breath, the images crowding in on her—the midwife's eyes so full of compassion as she wrapped his tiny body in a blanket and placed it in Matt's arms. The tears in his eyes, the searing agony she could see in every line of his body as he stared down at his son.

He'd lifted the baby to his lips, kissed his tiny head, shuddered with grief. It had broken him—broken both of them—and their relationship, like their son, had been too fragile, too young to survive.

She almost rang him. Her finger hovered over the call button, but then she turned the phone off and told herself to stop being so ridiculous. She'd decided not to tell him until after the twenty-week scan. Maybe longer. Maybe not until it was viable. He'd been so gutted last time, so deeply distressed, that he'd been unreachable, and she—she just *knew*—he'd be a nightmare if she told him. He'd probably have her admitted so he could scan her three times a day, but she wasn't having any of it. It was utterly unnecessary, and thinking about it all the time just made it all so much worse.

So she didn't ring him, and then she was past the time of the miscarriage, into the nineteenth week. Then the twentieth, and the big scan, which she could hardly bear to look at she was so nervous.

But it was normal, and it looked much more like a baby now, every feature clearly defined. It was sucking its thumb, and Amy felt a huge tug of love towards this tiny, vulnerable child—Matt's child. 'Do you want to know what it is?' the ultrasonographer asked her, but she shook her head.

'No.' Knowing would make it harder to remain detached, and she'd been careful not to look—but the baby was moving vigorously, and she could feel it all the time now, so real, so alive, so very, very strong that finally, at last, she began to allow a tiny glimmer of hope to emerge.

Was it possible that this baby would be all right?

She wanted to share it, to tell everyone in the world, but she was still a little afraid she might jinx it, so she took the photo home, propped it up on the bedside table next to her so she could see it when she woke, and fell asleep with a smile on her face and her hand curved protectively over her child...

She went shopping the following week with Daisy, and she talked Amy into getting some pretty clothes.

'You can't just wear scrubs and jog bottoms and baggy jumpers for the rest of your pregnancy,' she scolded, and handed her all sorts of things, all of which Amy thought made her look shockingly pregnant.

Shockingly, because she'd still not really taken it on board. It was still too early, the baby wasn't yet viable, and she felt a little quiver of nerves.

'Daisy, I really don't think—'

'No. Don't think. You think altogether too much. You're fine, Amy. You're well. Everything's OK.'

'I was well last time,' she said woodenly, and Daisy dropped the clothes she was carrying and hugged her.

'Oh, sweetheart, you'll be fine. Come on, Ben says everything's looking really good. It's time to be happy.'

Happy? Maybe, she thought, as Daisy took her to a café and plied her with hot chocolate and common sense, and gradually she relaxed. She was being silly. She could buy a few clothes—just enough. That wasn't tempting fate, was it? And her bras *were* strangling her. They finished their hot chocolate and went back to the shops.

And gradually, as the weeks passed and she got nearer to her due date, she began to dare to believe it might all be all right. She was beginning to feel excited, to look forward to the birth—except, of course, she'd be alone.

Unless she told Matt.

She felt her stomach knot at the thought. It was the beginning of April and Daisy had just started her maternity leave, five weeks before her baby was due, and nine weeks before Amy's. Gosh, 31 weeks, Amy thought, stunned, and bit her lip. There was no excuse now not to tell him and she was being unfair. He'd need time to get his head round it, and he was going to give her hell for keeping it quiet, but it had gone on for so long now that she wasn't sure how to broach the subject.

The baby was kicking her vigorously all night now. She'd never felt Samuel move—well, maybe a flutter, just before the end, but not like this, not so you could see it from the outside.

Matt would love to feel it…

Oh, how to tell him? Because she knew she had to, knew he had a right to know, and she was sharing the things she should have been sharing with him with Ben and Daisy, so much so that it was unfair.

Just how unfair was brought home to her two weeks later, when she was in their nursery looking at all the baby things and she'd jokingly talked about Ben delivering her and asked Daisy if she could borrow him. They exchanged a glance, and Ben sighed softly. 'Amy, I'm not my brother,' he said, his voice gentle. 'I'm happy to help, you know that, but it isn't me you need, and I can't take his place. And it isn't fair of you to ask me to. It isn't fair on any of us, especially not Matt.'

She felt hot colour flood her face, and turned blindly and went out of the room, stumbling downstairs and out into the garden. She hadn't thought of it from his side, but of course it was an imposition, and she'd been thoughtless, taken Ben and Daisy for granted, cheated Matt—but—

'Amy, wait!'

He stopped her just before she went through the gate in the fence, his hand on her arm gentle but firm.

'Amy. Please don't walk away. I don't mean to hurt you, but it's not my baby, sweetheart. Your baby needs its proper father—and he needs to know.'

She nodded, scrubbing away the tears. 'You're right. I know you're right. I'll do it soon, I promise. I'm just being silly. I just don't know how...'

'Do you want me to help you?'

She shook her head. 'No. I'll do it. I'll call him.'

'Promise me?'

She nodded, swallowing a sob. 'I promise.'

She escaped then, and let herself into her house and cried her heart out in the conservatory where they couldn't hear her through the wall.

She was mortified, but more than that, she was

afraid. She'd been leaning on Ben, she realised, not only because he was Matt's twin, but because he was reliable and kind and generous and decent, and because he'd let her.

And all the time it had been Matt she'd wanted, Matt she'd needed, Matt she still needed and always would. But this baby was going to make life so complicated, and it dawned on her in a moment of clarity that she'd been stalling because the status quo was far easier to deal with than the reality of sharing a child with a man who didn't really love her, even if he liked to think he might.

And that, she realised at last, was at the heart of her reluctance. They'd had a great time together at first, and the sex had always been brilliant, but Matt didn't love her, not enough to cope with the worst things life could thrust at them, and she didn't want him doing what he'd done before and offering to marry her just because they were having a child.

No, that was wrong, they'd already talked about marriage last time, made half-plans for the future. He hadn't officially proposed, but they were heading that way, drifting into it, and she wondered if they would have drifted all the way to a wedding if she hadn't got pregnant. But she had, of course, because they'd been careless with contraception on the grounds that it wouldn't have been a disaster if she'd got pregnant, at the time they'd both been anticipating a future together

Except it had been—a disaster that had left shockwaves still rippling around her life now over four years later.

She went round to see Daisy the following day and apologised for being an idiot, and they both ended up in tears. She talked about Matt, about how she felt, and then looked at all the stuff in the nursery and felt utterly overwhelmed.

She was having this baby in just seven weeks, maybe less, and she'd been so busy fretting about Matt she'd done nothing to prepare for it. 'I need to go and buy some basics,' she said to Daisy, and she rolled her eyes.

'Finally! Otherwise you know what'll happen, you'll have it two weeks early and you'll have no baby stuff at all!'

She was wrong. It wasn't Amy who had her baby two weeks early, it was Daisy herself.

She'd come into the hospital on Wednesday morning to see them all because she was bored and restless and sick of housework, and she was sitting in the office chatting to Amy in a quiet moment when her eyes widened and then squeezed tight shut.

Then she gave an exasperated sigh. 'Oh, I can't believe I've been so *stupid*! I had backache all day yesterday, but I've been cleaning. The kitchen was absolutely pigging, and—Amy, this isn't funny, stop laughing at me and get Ben!'

'Get Ben why?' Ben asked, walking in, and then he looked at Daisy and his jaw dropped.

'What's the matter?' Amy teased with a grin. 'Never seen a woman in labour before?'

It was a textbook labour, if a little fast, and Amy made it quite clear to Ben that she was in control.

'You're on paternity leave as of now, so don't even think about interfering,' she told him as she checked Daisy between contractions. Her body was doing a wonderful job, and Amy was happy to let nature take its course.

It was just another delivery, her professional mask was in place, and she was doing fine until the baby was born, but once she'd lifted their son and laid him on Daisy's chest against her heart, she let Ben take over.

It was Ben who told her it was a boy, Ben who covered him with a warmed towel as Daisy said hello to their little son, Ben who cleared his mouth of mucus with a gentle finger and stimulated that first, heart-warming cry, because Amy was transfixed, her eyes flooded with tears, her whole body quivering.

She wanted Matt with her when she gave birth in a few weeks, Matt to take their baby from the midwife and lay him—her?—on her chest, and gaze down at them both with love and wonder in his eyes. If only things were different...

But they weren't different, they were what they were, and she'd be alone, not only for the delivery but for the whole business of motherhood, and her confidence suddenly deserted her.

I can't do it alone! I can't be that strong. I'm not that brave. Matt, why can't you love me enough? I need you—

No, she didn't! She stopped herself in her tracks, and took a long, slow, steadying breath. She was getting way ahead of herself. One day at a time, she reminded herself. She was getting through her pregnancy like that. She could get through motherhood in the same way. The last thing she needed was a man who didn't love her enough to ride out the hard times, who when the crunch came would walk away, however much he might think he wanted her.

And right now, Daisy and Ben and their new little son were her priority.

'Let's give them a minute,' she said to Sue, the midwife assisting her, and stripping off her gloves, she turned and walked blindly out of the door and down the corridor to the stairwell.

Nobody would find her there. She could hide here for a minute, get herself together. Think about what Ben had said.

Should Matt be there with her when she gave birth? Even if they weren't together?

Yes, if it was like this, but if anything went wrong...

He'd been there last time, distant and unreachable, his eyes filled with pain. She couldn't cope with that again, couldn't handle his pain as well as her own. The last thing she needed during her labour was a man she couldn't rely on if anything went wrong, a man who couldn't talk about his feelings or hers.

But she needed him...

No! No, she didn't! She was made of sterner stuff than that, and she could cope alone. She could. She knew all the midwives here, she'd have plenty of support during her labour. She didn't need Matt.

She got to her feet and went back to them, to find Ben sitting in the chair cuddling his tiny son with a tender smile on his face that wasn't going to fade any time soon.

Lucky little boy, she thought. So, so lucky. Her baby would have a father who loved him like that, she knew, but it wouldn't have two parents sharing its life on a daily basis, supporting each other through thick and thin.

Her hand slid down over her baby in an unconscious caress. If only...

She helped Ben get the house ready after her shift finished at three.

He was bringing Daisy and Thomas home that evening, and they were almost done.

'Gosh, I've never seen it so clean and tidy,' she said with a laugh, and he just rolled his eyes and sighed.

'Silly girl. I should have smelled a rat when I got home last night and found the place sparkling. I can't believe I was so dense.' He gave the quilt cover one last tug into place, straightened up and met Amy's eyes.

'Matt should be with you when you have the baby, Amy. Labour can be a tough and lonely place. You're going to need support.'

'Ben, it's OK,' she said softly. 'I'll be all right.'

'And what about Matt? What about my brother, Amy? He lost a baby too, you know. He needs this to put things right for him, to balance the books a bit. You can't deny him the experience of seeing his child born. This is going to happen. You can't keep ignoring it.'

She swallowed and nodded. 'No. You're right, I know you're right. I'll discuss it with him when I tell him— just maybe not tonight. You'll want to talk to him tonight, tell him your news. There are things we'll need to sort out anyway, and I've only got five weeks to go. Nothing's going to go wrong now.'

Oh, foolish, foolish words.

She woke on Friday morning with a slight headache, and went downstairs and poured herself a tall glass of fruit juice and iced water, and sat in the conservatory listening to the birds.

Gosh, her head was thumping, she thought, and went and had a shower, washed her hair and let it air dry while she had another drink.

She must be dehydrated. Too busy yesterday to drink much. Too busy, and too stressed because Matt was coming up for the weekend and she was going to tell him. She'd tried to phone him last night from the hospital but she hadn't got hold of him, and she would have tried again when she got home, but she'd worked till nine and she'd been too tired, and today she was starting at seven. She'd try again this afternoon, before he left London—not that it seemed right to do it like that, over the phone, but she couldn't exactly do it face to face. He didn't need to be an obstetrician to work it out, so there'd be no subtlety, no putting it gently.

No 'You remember that night you made love to me, and I told you it was all right because I was on the Pill? Well, there's something I need to tell you.' Nothing so easy as that—although, to be fair, it couldn't be easier than just opening the door to him. That would be pretty straightforward, she thought with a wry grimace.

She dressed for work, wriggling her feet into her shoes and sighing because even they were getting tighter. Everything was, but it was pointless buying things at this stage.

It was ludicrously busy at work, of course, and she began to think she ought to consider taking maternity leave sooner than she'd allowed.

She had two more weeks to go, come Monday, and she was working today and tomorrow. Just as well, since Matt was going to be around, although she'd have to talk to him face to face in the end.

She found time for lunch somewhere between one and two—a quick sandwich eaten on the run, which gave her vicious indigestion, but she needed something in her stomach so she could take some paracetamol for her headache.

She sat down in the office for a moment and eased her shoes off. Pregnancy was the pits, she decided, and vowed to be nicer to her mums when they complained about it in future. Really, men didn't know how lucky they were—and that's if they were even there!

No. She mustn't be unfair. She hadn't given Matt the chance to be there.

'Amy, can you come? I've got a mum about to deliver.'

'Sure.'

She squirmed her feet back into her shoes, winced and followed Angie, one of the other midwives, down the corridor to the delivery room. Roll on nine o'clock, she thought. Why on earth had she agreed to do a double shift? It was a good job Ben wasn't here to see her, or Daisy. They'd skin her, but there hadn't been anyone else available at the last minute and at least it would mean she'd be out when Matt arrived.

Any other day, she thought, and tried to smile brightly at their patient. 'Hiya, I'm Amy,' she said, and threw herself into the fray.

Matt's car was outside, and just the thought that he was there made her heart pound, her throat dry and her chest ache.

She hadn't been able to ring him that afternoon. Should she ring him tonight?

No. Tonight should be for Ben and Daisy, for him to meet his little nephew, although judging by the sounds coming through their front door, Thomas was well and truly met.

She could just picture him holding the tiny baby in those big, capable hands.

She closed her eyes to shut out the image and squeezed them tight shut. Oh, they ached. Everything ached. Her head, her eyes, her feet...

She looked down, and blinked. Her feet were swollen. Not just the normal swollen feet of pregnancy, but a more sinister kind of swollen. And her fingers felt tight, and her head was splitting. She could feel her heartbeat in her eyeballs, even, and as she mentally listed the symptoms, she closed her eyes and leant against her front door, stunned.

Pre-eclampsia? Just like that? But she'd been fine up to now. Ben had been monitoring her minute by minute until Thomas had been born, but that was only two days ago, and she'd had no symptoms at all.

Except the headache this morning, and the tight shoes and clothes, and the epigastric pain she'd put down to indigestion—

Lord, she felt dreadful.

Matt. I need Matt.

She could hear voices through their front door, and the baby was quiet now. If she called out— Oh, her head ached so much, and she moaned. It was so far to the door...

She stepped over the little fence, arm outstretched towards the bellpush, but then she stumbled and half fell, half slid down the door with a little yelp. Oh, her head. She heard a voice, heard running footsteps, then felt the door open as she slid sideways across the step and came to rest.

There was a startled exclamation, and gentle hands touched her face.

Matt...!

CHAPTER FIVE

'WHAT was that?'

Ben frowned at him. 'I don't know. Amy? Are you all right?' he called, and there was a muffled cry and a crash against the door.

'What the hell—?' Matt thrust his nephew at Daisy and ran down the hall, turning the door handle and then catching the door as it was forced inwards.

'Matt, she's…' Ben began, as the door swung open and Amy tumbled over at his feet.

He knelt beside her, cupping her face in his hand and turning her towards him so he could check her pupils.

The doctor in him was registering her symptoms. The man was in shock, and deeply, furiously angry, because Amy was pregnant, and none of them had told him—unless it wasn't his?

'It's yours,' he heard Ben say, but he didn't answer. He was too damned angry with him and too worried about Amy to deal with that now, and the fear just ramped up a notch.

'Amy? Amy, it's Matt, talk to me!' he said urgently, his eyes scanning her. How the hell had she got like this? Her feet were swollen, her face was puffy, her eyes—her eyes were opening, searching for him.

'Matt.' She lifted her hand and rested it against his

cheek, and worry flickered in her eyes. 'I've been try-ing to phone you. I've got something I have to tell you.'

He laid his hand over hers and squeezed it. 'It's OK, sweetheart. Don't talk now.'

'But I have to. I have to tell you—'

'Amy, it's all right, I know about the baby. You just close your eyes and rest, let me look after you.'

Her fingers fluttered against his cheek, and he pressed his lips to her palm and folded her hand over to keep it safe. It made her smile, a weak, fragile smile that tore his heart wide open. 'I'm so glad you're here...'

'Me too,' he said softly, his voice choked, and turned his head. 'She's about to fit, we need an ambulance,' he snapped at Ben, but he'd gone and Daisy, standing there with Thomas in her arms and shock in her eyes, answered him.

'He's getting the car—he said there wasn't time for an ambulance. I'll get the emergency team to meet you there.'

'We'll need a theatre.'

'I know. Ben's outside with the car. You need to go.'

They did. She was barely conscious now, her eyes rolling back in her head, and he felt sick with fear. He scooped her up, ran down the path and got into the back of the car behind Ben, Amy on his lap.

Please be all right. Please let the baby be all right. Don't let it happen again. I can't do this again. Amy can't do this again. Please be all right...

They screeched into the hospital, pulled up outside Maternity and left the car there with the doors hang-ing open. Ben threw the keys at the reception clerk and asked her to deal with it, and a waiting team took over.

Matt dumped her on the trolley and they had her in the lift and on oxygen instantly, a line was going in each hand and an infusion of magnesium sulphate was started while they were still on the move.

'I'm scrubbing,' he said, and earned himself a hard stare.

'No way. By all means get gowned up, but I'm doing this, not you,' Ben said flatly, and filled the team in. 'Pre-eclampsia, sudden onset, partial loss of consciousness, she hasn't fitted as far as we know but she might have done,' he told them, but they were already on it, primed by Daisy, and as Ben went to scrub they were preparing her for surgery.

There was no job for Matt, so he stepped back out of the way. Someone fed his arms into a gown and tied it up, put a cap on his head, a mask over his face, and he stood there, his heart in his mouth, and watched as his brother brought his son into the world.

A boy. A perfect, beautiful boy, but still and silent, his body blue, his chest unmoving.

Please, no, not again...!

Matt was frozen to the spot, his eyes fixed on the little chest, begging it to move.

'Come on, baby,' the midwife was saying, sucking his mouth out, rubbing his back, flicking his feet. 'Come on, you can do it.'

When the cry came, he thought his legs would give way under him. He dragged in a huge breath, then another, and pressed his fist to his mouth to keep in the sob.

'Go and meet your baby,' Ben said gently, and he went over on legs that were not quite steady and reached out a finger and touched his baby's hand. Tiny, transparent pink fingers clenched around his fingertip, and another sob wrestled free from his chest.

He stroked the fingers, oh, so gently with his thumb,

afraid for the fragile, friable skin, but he was past that stage. Thirty-five weeks was OK. He'd be OK. The relief, for a child he didn't even know he was having until half an hour ago, was enormous.

It had plagued him, all the what ifs, the regrets that not once but twice he'd let her send him away without putting up a fight, the hope that she might contact him and tell him she was pregnant that had flickered and then died. He'd even seen her at Christmas, thought she looked well, had even put on a little weight, for heaven's sake, and all the time...

He turned his head. 'How is she?' he asked hoarsely.

'Stable. We'll know more when she comes round. The neurologist is coming to have a look at her and we're moving her to Maternity HDU.'

He swallowed the fear and turned back to his son.

'Hello, my little man,' he murmured softly, his hands trembling but his voice gentle with reassurance. 'Your mummy's not very well, but she'll be OK, and so will you. Daddy's here now and I'm going nowhere,' he promised.

'Want to hold him?' the midwife asked gently.

He nodded, and she wrapped him in a soft cotton blanket and placed him in Matt's arms. 'He needs to go to SCBU for a while, just to make sure he's OK and his lungs are coping, but he's looking good so far. He's 2.1 kilos. That's a good weight for a preemie—over four and a half pounds.'

He nodded. He could feel him, knew he was a good size, but that wasn't what he was seeing.

He was seeing another child in his arms, far smaller, too small to make it in this world, a child he'd never had the chance to love. His heart ached with the love he'd never been able to give, would never be able to give that child, and now he had another child, a child whose mother might not recover from this. God, how much more—?

Ben appeared at his side, and he felt an arm around his shoulders. 'He's going to be all right, Matt,' he said softly, and there was a catch in his voice.

He nodded. 'He is. Ben, how did she get like this?'

'I have no idea. I've had her under a microscope, and I'll be going over her notes again with a fine-toothed comb, to see if there's anything I've missed, but she hasn't even had high blood pressure.'

'What is it now?'

'Two thirty-five over 170.'

'*What*?' He felt his legs buckle slightly and jammed his knees back hard. That was high. Too high. Ludicrously high. She could still fit, still end up with brain damage—

'Don't go there, Matt. She's in good hands.'

He nodded, handed the baby back to the midwife and turned to watch Amy being wheeled out of Theatre. 'I need to be with her.'

'Yes, you do. I'm sorry. If I hadn't been off on paternity leave for the past two days, I would have spotted this coming on. Someone's just told me she did a double shift today, and she was supposed to be working tomorrow.'

'That's crazy!' he said under his breath. 'What the hell was she thinking about? Or was she keeping out of my way?'

'I don't know,' Ben said heavily. 'She wasn't booked to do the double shift. I think they were short-staffed, but if I'd been here I wouldn't have let her do it.'

The anger, so carefully banked, broke free again. 'Nor would I, but I didn't get that choice, did I? Why didn't any of you tell me she was pregnant? How could you *keep* that from me? For God's sake, Ben, I'm your *brother*!'

They were following the trolley, and Ben paused and met his eyes. 'You think I don't know that? I've been trying to get her to tell you since the day she found out.'

'*You* could have told me.'

'No. I promised her I wouldn't. I said I'd look after her.'

He made a harsh sound in his throat. 'If you'd told me, I would have been looking after her, and this wouldn't have happened.'

'Oh, for God's sake, man, if you're that bothered, why did you let her go in the first place? And it wasn't me who got her pregnant,' Ben snapped impatiently, and with a rough sigh he stalked off after the trolley, leaving Matt to follow or not.

He followed, his thoughts reeling, and they walked the rest of the way in an uncomfortable silence.

She fitted in the night, and Matt stood at the end of the bed with his heart in his mouth while all hell broke loose and drugs were pumped into her and the team struggled to control her blood pressure.

He clenched his fists and forced himself to keep out of it, to let them do their jobs, but in fairness they were doing exactly what he would have done if he'd been in charge, so he watched the monitor, and he waited, and finally it started to come down as her kidneys kicked in again, and he watched the numbers on the monitor drop gradually to sensible levels.

He felt his own blood pressure slowly return to something in the normal range, and then once he could get near her again he sagged back into the chair beside the

bed and took her puffy, bloated hand in his. He stroked
the back of it gently with his thumb, the rhythm soothing him, the contact with her warmth giving him hope.

She'd survived, and she was breathing. For now, that
was all he could think about. All he could let himself
think about.

'It's OK, Amy,' he murmured, trying to inject some
conviction into his voice. 'You'll be all right, my love.
Just hang in there. I'm right here, and I'm not leaving.
You'll be OK, don't worry. The baby's fine. He's going
to be fine, and so are you...'

His voice cracked, and he broke off, dragging in a
deep breath and staring up at the ceiling.

Who was he trying to convince? Her, or himself?
Empty words, the sort of platitudes he heard desperate
relatives telling their loved ones all the time in the face
of insurmountable odds.

Were they insurmountable? He forced himself to be
realistic. He treated women with pre-eclampsia all the
time, and usually it was fine, but rarely—very rarely—
it came on so fast, like Amy's, that it caught them by
surprise, and then it could spiral out of control with
shocking speed. Sometimes there were no symptoms at
all, the woman went straight into eclampsia and began
fitting, and then the symptoms might follow later.

The outcome then was dependent on many factors—
what had caused the fit, what damage it had done, how
bad the multi-system failure was—and it was impossible to second-guess it.

She might have had a stroke, or got irreversible kid-
ney or liver damage, he thought, and stopped himself
running through the list. He didn't need to borrow trouble. Time would tell, and until then he'd look on the
bright side. She was alive. She was breathing for her-

self, her kidneys were starting to work again, her blood results were in the manageable range and he just had to wait. It often got worse before it got better. He knew that.

The time, though, seemed to stand still, punctuated only by the regular visits of the nursing and medical staff every few minutes until it all became a blur.

Underneath the worry for Amy, though, concern for the baby was nagging at him incessantly. All the staff were busy, but even so they'd given him a couple of reassuring updates. It wasn't the same as seeing him, though. He wanted to watch over him as he was watching over Amy, to will him to live, to tell him he loved him.

But Amy needed him more, so he sat there feeling torn in half, part of him desperate to go and see his tiny son, the other, bigger part unable to drag himself away from Amy's bedside until he was entirely confident of her recovery.

Then Ben came in, at some ungodly hour of the morning, and stood behind him, hands on his shoulders, the weight so reassuring, anchoring him, somehow.

'How is she?' he asked softly.

Matt shook his head.

'I don't know. She fitted. They couldn't get her blood pressure down for a while. It's down now, it's looking better but she's sedated at the moment. We've just got to wait.'

He felt Ben's hand squeeze his shoulder. 'I'm sorry.'

'Don't be,' he said, his voice clogged. 'It wasn't your fault, you weren't even supposed to be working. I was just stressed and I shouldn't have taken it out on you. I know it happens.'

'I'm still sorry. I should have made sure someone kept an eye on her. I should have done it myself.'

'No. If she was fine, you couldn't have foreseen this, and you know how quickly it can happen, and she's a midwife. She should have recognised the signs. As you say, it must have been really sudden.' He put his hand over Ben's and gripped it, leaning back against him, taking strength from his brother while he voiced his fears. 'What am I going to do if she's not all right?' he asked unevenly, and he felt Ben's hand tighten.

'She'll be all right. Have faith.'

He dropped his hand abruptly. 'Sorry. I don't have faith any longer. I used it all up last time.'

'This isn't like that.'

'No. No, it isn't. This time I've got the baby, and I might lose the woman I love. I don't know which is worse.'

'You won't lose her.'

'There's more than one way to lose someone, Ben. She might have brain damage.'

'She's responding to pain.'

'Earthworms respond to pain,' he said bluntly, and Ben sighed softly, letting go of his shoulders and moving away slightly, leaving him in a vacuum.

'Have you had a break yet? Gone for a walk, stretched your legs? Eaten anything?'

He shook his head. 'I don't want anything—except to know how the baby is.'

'He's doing well. I rang from home, and they said he's fine, he's breathing on his own and looking good. They've put a tube in and given him some colostrum from the milk bank and they're happy with him.'

He nodded, his eyes fixed on Amy, and felt a little more of the tension ease. He glanced at the clock, then up at his brother with a frown. 'It's the middle of the night. You should be with Daisy. She's only just given birth.'

'She's fine, and I've got my mobile. I promised I wouldn't be long, but I couldn't sleep, so I thought I'd come back and see how it was going, make sure you were OK. Get you to eat something, maybe.'

'I'm not hungry.'

'Come and see the baby, at least, then, to put your mind at rest. Amy's stable, and we won't be far away. They'll ring me if they want us.'

How did he know that only seeing him with his own eyes would be good enough?

Stupid question. His brother knew everything about him. He got to his feet, stiff and aching from the hard plastic chair, and walked the short distance to SCBU.

The last time he'd been in here was to see the Grieves twins, back in September. Now it was the end of April, and he was here to see his own child, experiencing at first hand the hope and fear felt by the parents of a premature baby.

He washed his hands thoroughly, doused them in alcohol gel and introduced himself to the staff.

The neonatal unit manager, Rachel, remembered him from September, and she smiled at him encouragingly. 'He's doing really well. Come and say hello,' she said, and led him over to the clear plastic crib.

Ben had left him to it, giving him space. He wasn't sure he wanted it, but he was talking to a woman in a dressing gown sitting tearfully by a crib, and he glanced across and winked at Matt.

You can do it. Go and say hello to your son.

He nodded, and took the last few steps to the side of the crib. He was used to seeing babies in them, but not *his* baby, and he blew his breath out slowly at the impact. He seemed so small, so vulnerable, so incredibly fragile.

It was quite irrational. As a twin specialist he was used to delivering babies much smaller than him, sometimes as much as nine weeks younger, on the very edge of viability, but age wasn't everything and their baby wasn't out of the woods yet, he knew.

'Hi, little guy,' he said softly, and threading his hands through the ports, he cradled his sleeping son's head tenderly with one hand, the other cupping the tiny, wrinkly little feet. They fascinated him. The toes were so tiny, the nails perfectly formed, the skinny little legs so frail and yet so strong.

He looked like Ben and Daisy's Thomas, he thought. Not surprisingly, since half their DNA pool was identical. They were practically half-brothers, he realised, and smiled. They'd grow up together, be friends. That was good.

He studied the tiny nose with its pinpoint white spots on the skin, the creased-up little eyes tight shut, the mouth working slightly. There was a tube up his nose taped to his cheek, and a clip on his finger leading to the monitor, but he didn't need to look at it. He watched the scrawny, ribby little chest going up and down, up and down as he breathed unaided, and felt more of the tension leave him.

He was a tiny, living miracle, and Matt swallowed a huge lump in his throat as he stared down at the sleeping baby.

'He's doing really well,' Rachel said matter-of-factly. 'We put the tube in to get his feeding off to a good start, because he's a little light for his dates, but he's great. Just a bit skinny, really.'

Matt nodded. He was. At a guess her placenta had been failing for a couple of weeks, and although he was a good size, he was still slightly behind what he should have been. Whatever, he'd catch up quickly enough now, and he was clearly in good hands.

'He's looking good,' Ben said quietly from beside him, and he nodded again. It seemed easier than talking, while his throat was clogged with emotion and his chest didn't seem to be working properly.

He eased away from the crib with a shaky sigh and, asking Rachel to keep in touch, he headed out of the unit with Ben.

'How about coming down to the canteen?'

'I want to get back to Amy,' he said, even though he could murder a drink, now he thought about it.

'Can I get you anything, then? Tea, coffee, bacon roll?'

'Coffee and a bacon roll would be good,' he said, but when it came he could hardly eat it. Sitting there outside the high dependency unit and fretting about Amy did nothing for the appetite, he discovered, and the bacon roll only brought back memories—the morning after the wedding, when he'd spent the night with her, trying to convey with actions rather than words how much he loved her; the mornings they'd woken in his London apartment and she'd snuggled up to him and told him she was hungry and he'd left her there, warm and sleepy, and made her breakfast.

They'd been halcyon days, but they'd ended abruptly when she'd lost Samuel.

Odd. He always thought of him as Samuel, although they'd never talked about it since that awful day. They'd talked about names before, argued endlessly about girls' names but agreed instantly on Sam.

He tipped his head back with a sigh, resting it against the wall behind the hard plastic chair in the waiting area outside the HDU. Ben had brought the bacon roll and coffee up to him and then gone back to Daisy and their own tiny baby, and now he sat there, staring at the roll in his hand while he remembered the past and wondered what the future held.

Once, it had seemed so bright, so cut and dried and full of joy. Now, over four years later, Amy was lying there motionless, possibly brain injured, their newborn son was in SCBU, and Matt had no idea what lay ahead for the three of them.

He swallowed the last of the cold coffee, threw the roll into the bin and went back to Amy's side. Could the sheer force of his willpower pull her through? He didn't know, but he'd give it a damn good try.

He picked up her lifeless hand, and stopped. Was he clutching at straws, or was it less swollen? He looked at it thoughtfully, wondering if he was imagining it. No. He didn't think so. It *was* improving, slowly. *She* was improving.

Shaking with relief, knowing it was still early days, trying to find a balance between sheer blind optimism and drenching fear, he cradled the hand in his, pressed it to his cheek and closed his eyes.

She was floating.

No, not floating. Drowning. Drowning in thick, sticky fog and awash with pain.

There were noises—bleeps and tweets, hisses and sighs. People talking, alarms going off, laughter in the distance.

Hospital? It sounded like the hospital. Smelt like the

hospital. But she was lying down, floating on the fog—or water? Drowning again. It felt like water—

She coughed, and felt her hand squeezed. Odd. Someone was there, holding it. Talking to her in a soothing voice.

Matt? He was saying something about a baby, over and over. 'The baby's all right…he's going to be all right—'

But her baby was—

She felt herself recoil from the pain. It hurt too much to think, to work it all out. She tried to open her eyes, to argue, but it was too bright, too difficult, so she shut them again and let the fog close over her…

'She woke for a moment. She coughed, and she tried to open her eyes.'

'OK, well, that's good. Let's have a look. Amy? Amy, wake up, please, open your eyes. Come on.'

The doctor squeezed her ear, pressing his nail into the lobe, and she moaned slightly but she didn't open her eyes or react in any other way.

He checked her reflexes, scanned the monitor, listened to her chest, checked her notes for urine output and fluid balance, and nodded.

'She's shifting a lot of fluid, which is good. Have you noticed any change?'

'Her hand's thinner.'

He picked it up, pressed it, nodded again, had a look at her incision and covered her, but not before Matt had seen it. He smiled. It was neat. Very neat, for all the hurry. Ben had done a good job. She wouldn't have unsightly scars to trouble her.

'I gather the baby's doing well.'

'Yes, he is. I went to see him. He's beautiful. Amazing. Really strong.'

'Well, she's resting now if you want to go and see him again. I don't think she's about to wake up.'

He nodded. It wasn't what he wanted to hear. He wanted to be told she was lightening, that any minute now she'd drift out of the fog and open her eyes and smile, but he knew it was a vain hope.

Nevertheless, he took the advice and went to see their baby, and as he walked in, he was assailed by fear. He was exhausted, worried sick and for the first time understanding just what all the parents of sick and preterm babies went through.

And it wasn't great.

The shifts had changed, of course, and Rachel wasn't there, but there was another nurse who he'd met before, in September, and she greeted him with a smile. 'Matt, come and see him, he's doing really well. Do you want to hold him?'

He nodded. 'Could I?'

'Of course.' She sat him down, lifted the baby out of the crib and placed him carefully in Matt's arms. Well, hands, really. He was too tiny for arms. With his head in the crook of his arm, his little feet barely reached Matt's wrist, and those skinny, naked feet got to him again. He bent his wrist up and cupped them in his hand, keeping them warm, feeling them flex and wriggle a little as he snuggled them.

He pressed a fingertip to the baby's open palm, and his hand closed, gripping him fiercely. It made him smile. So did the enormous yawn, and then to his delight the baby opened his eyes and stared straight up at him.

'Hello, my gorgeous boy,' he said softly, and then he

lost eye contact because his own flooded with a whole range of emotions too huge, too tumultuous to analyse. He sniffed hard, and found a tissue in his hand.

'Thought I might find you here.'

'Are you checking up on me?' he asked gruffly, and Ben dropped into a chair beside him with an understanding smile.

'No, checking up on your son. Daisy wants to see photos, if that's OK?'

'Of course it is. I've been thinking about that. I took one on my phone and sent it to Mum and Dad, but it's not the same.'

'No. I've got my camera, I'll take some and print them. Does he have a name yet, by the way?'

He shook his head. 'I thought you might be able to tell me. I have no idea what Amy was thinking. Not Samuel...' His voice cracked, and he broke off, squeezing his eyes shut and breathing slowly.

Ben squeezed his shoulder, and gave him a moment before going on. 'She'd talked about Joshua—Josh. But Daisy said she thought Amy was going to ask you about names.'

'She *was* going to tell me about him, then?'

'Oh, God, yes! She said she'd tell you when—'

'What?' he asked, when Ben broke off. 'When what?'

He sighed. 'She said she'd tell you when it was over, one way or the other. That was right at the beginning, when she first found out. She was sixteen weeks pregnant, and I don't think she expected to get this far.'

'I wish you'd been able to tell me.'

'I wish I could have done. I so nearly did, so many times.'

The nurse came back. 'Want to try feeding him? We

gave him a bottle an hour ago, and he took a few mils. You could have a go, if you like?'

He took the bottle—a tiny little thing, with not much more than a few spoonfuls in it—and brushed the teat against the baby's cheek. He turned his head towards it, the reflex working perfectly, and Matt slipped the teat between his tiny rosebud lips.

He swallowed reflexively, and then again, and again, and in the end he took most of the small feed while Ben took photos.

How could something so simple be so momentous? The satisfaction was out of all proportion to the task, and Matt grinned victoriously and felt like Superman.

'You need to burp him,' Ben said, pointing the camera at him, and he laughed.

'What, and bring it all up again?'

'That's the way it is. Fairly crazy system but it sort of works.'

Matt shifted the baby so he was against his shoulder, resting on a clean blanket the nurse had draped over him. 'So how's my nephew doing?' he asked as he rubbed the little back gently.

'Really well. He's terrific. Daisy's in her element. Feeding's going really well, and she's feeling stronger by the hour, and it's good.'

'Does he sleep?'

Ben's smile was wry. 'I have no idea what he did last night. I was either here or out for the count. But Daisy was still smiling this morning.'

'That's a good sign.'

The nurse reappeared and asked Ben to have a word with the lady he'd seen in here before, then she turned to him with a smile. 'All gone? Brilliant. Has he burped?'

'Yup.'

'Nappy?'

He laughed quietly. 'I'll give it a go, now my brother's not here taking photos to taunt me with, but don't abandon me. I might stick it on the wrong way up.'

He didn't. He wiped the funny, skinny, wrinkly little bottom dry, got the nappy back onto him without sticking the tabs on his skin or cutting off his circulation or leaving massive gaps, and, feeling ridiculously pleased with himself, he went with Ben to see how Amy was doing.

There was still no change, so after talking to the staff so Ben could catch up on her general progress, they went for a coffee and something to eat, just because he knew he had to keep his strength up, but the moment it was finished he was twitching.

'I need to get back to her,' he said, and draining his coffee, he pushed the chair back and stood up.

'Want company?'

He shook his head. 'Not really. Do you mind? It's good to touch base and I really appreciate your support, but—I just want to talk to her, say all the things I've never said.'

Ben's hand gripped his shoulder. 'You go for it,' he said softly, and with a gentle smile, he left him to make his own way back. 'I'll bring you the photos. Keep in touch,' he called, turning as he walked away, and Matt nodded.

He would. Just as soon as there was anything to say...

He was there again.

She could hear him talking, his voice soft, wrapping round her and cradling her in a soft cocoon. She couldn't hear the words. Not really, not well enough to make them out, but it was lovely to hear his voice.

She tried to move, and felt a searing pain low down on her abdomen, and she gasped, the blissful cocoon vanishing. It hurt—everything hurt, and someone was holding her, gripping her hands.

'Amy? Amy, it's Matt. It's OK. You're safe, and the baby's safe. He's doing well. It's OK, my darling. You're all right. You're much better and you're going to be OK now.'

She lay still, sifting through the words with her fuddled brain, trying to claw through the fog. Something was wrong. Something...

The baby's safe...he's doing well...

But he wasn't. He wasn't safe at all! Why was Matt telling her that? He knew she'd lost him, he knew that, so why was he lying to her?

She heard a strange noise, like someone crying, a long, long way away, and then the fog closed over her again...

'She woke up. I was telling her everything was all right, and she started crying, and then she was gone again.'

'Don't worry. She could just be in pain,' the doctor said, and he stepped outside for a minute to stretch his legs and give them room to get to her. God, he needed Ben, but he couldn't ask.

He went back inside. They were nearly finished. They'd topped up her pain relief and checked her thoroughly. She was coming up now, hovering just under the surface of consciousness, and he was feeling sick with dread. This was the time he'd find out just how bad she was, how much brain damage she might have sustained during the fit, or in fact before it, causing it.

A part of him didn't want to know, but the other part,

the part that still, incredibly, dared to believe, wanted her to wake.

And then finally, what seemed like hours later, when he was getting desperate, she opened her eyes.

'Amy? Amy, it's Matt.'

His face swam, coming briefly into focus. So it *was* him there with her. She'd thought so. Emotion threatened to choke her, and as if he knew that he leant forwards, gripping her hand.

'How are you feeling?'

'Sore,' she said hoarsely, answering the question because it was easier than thinking about why he was there by her side in hospital. 'My head's sore. And—everywhere, really. Why do I feel like this?'

'You went into pre-eclampsia, and you had a fit,' he told her gently, her hand wrapped firmly in his. 'Ben had to deliver the baby, but he's OK. He's doing really well.'

She shook her head, slowly at first, then more urgently, because he was wrong and she had to tell him. 'No. Ben wasn't there.'

'Yes, he was. He delivered you, Amy. We found you on the floor.'

Yes. She remembered the floor. Remembered crumpling to the floor, someone coming to her, lifting her up, calling Matt. Telling him she was losing the baby…

She closed her eyes against the images, but they followed her, tearing her apart. 'I lost him. I'm sorry…'

'No, Amy.' He was insistent, confusing her. 'Amy, he's fine. He's going to be fine. He's all right.'

'No,' she whispered. 'No. I've lost him. I saw him, Matt! I saw him! Why are you lying to me?' she asked frantically, feeling panic and the raw, awful pain of loss sweeping over her and deluging her with emotion. She brushed his hands away, desperate to be rid of the feel of him, hanging onto her and lying, lying.

'Don't lie to me! He's dead—you know he's dead!'

He had her hands again, his grip inescapable, still lying to her. 'Amy, no! Listen, please listen, you're confused, I'm not lying to you, he's alive.'

'Stop it! Don't lie to me! Stop it!' she screamed, pressing her hands to her ears to block out the sound of his voice, but she could still hear him, over and over again, lying to her, the sound ringing in her head and driving her mad with grief.

'He's alive...alive...alive...'

'No-o-o-o—! Go away! I hate you! Leave me alone, don't do this.'

'Shh, Amy, it's all right, hush now, go back to sleep,' a firm, gentle voice told her. 'It's all right. Easy now.'

'Ben?' she whispered, her voice slurring. She struggled to get the words out, but they wouldn't come. 'Ben, he's lying, get him away from me! Get him away.'

'Hush, Amy, it's OK. He's gone. You go to sleep. Everything's all right.'

She wanted to argue, to tell him it wasn't all right. It was really important to tell them, but she felt herself sliding back down, felt the pain slip away as the fog wrapped her again in gentle, mindless oblivion...

Ben caught up with him in the loo off the corridor. The door was hanging open as he'd left it, and he was shaking.

He felt a gentle hand on his back. 'You all right?' Ben asked softly, and Matt straightened and leant back against the wall, shuddering.

'Ben, I can't take it. I can't do this.'

Ben shoved a tissue into his hand. 'Yes, you can. She'll be all right. She's just confused, but it'll pass. It's the sedation and the pressure on her brain from the fluid, not to mention the other drugs, the painkillers, the magnesium sulphate.' Matt lifted a hand to ward off the words, and Ben flushed the loo. 'Wash your face and hands, and come and sit down and talk this through with me. You know what's going on. She's having flash-backs, but she'll come out of it.'

'Will she? I'm not so sure,' he said, and swallowed hard as bile rose in his throat again.

'I'm sure. Come on. Sort yourself out and we'll go for a walk. You could use some fresh air.'

Fresh air? He could think of plenty of things he needed. Fresh air wasn't one of them. What he needed was a miracle, but in the absence of that, his brother's support was the next best thing.

He washed his face and hands, took a long, deep breath and went.

CHAPTER SIX

IT WAS quiet when she woke again.

Quiet, and calm.

Well, calm for the hospital, anyway. There were still the bleeps and tweets and hissings of the machines, the ringing phones in the distance, the sound of hurrying feet, someone talking, but there was a quietness about it.

Night-time, she realised.

She opened her eyes and looked around, slightly stunned. HDU? Wow. She was hooked up to all sorts of things, and Matt was asleep in the chair beside her, his top half slumped on the bottom of the bed, his head resting on one arm and the other hand lying loosely on hers. She couldn't see his face, it was hidden by a fold in the bedcover, but she knew it was him.

She thought he'd been there all the time—had a feeling she'd heard his voice in the distance. Oh. So hard. She blinked to clear her vision, to clear her mind, but it felt like glue.

She tried moving—carefully, just a little, because she was feeling sore. Something momentous had happened, but she couldn't remember what.

Samuel, her mind said, but she knew that was wrong. Samuel was years ago, and she could feel the sadness for him, the ache that never left her, but stronger now for some reason, and tinged with fear.

She eased her hand away from Matt's and felt her tummy. Soft, flabby—and tender, low down. A—dressing? A post-op dressing?

A section? Why had she had a section? Oh, think! she told herself. There was something there, just hovering out of reach, and she tried again.

Yes. She'd had a headache. It was a dreadful headache. She'd had it all day, getting worse, but when she'd got home it was awful. And then—

'Oh!'

Her soft gasp jerked Matt awake, and he sat up with a grunt, grabbing his neck and rubbing it, his head rotating, easing out the kinks. His smile was tired and—wary? 'Amy. You're awake. Are you OK?'

She nodded. He looked awful. He hadn't shaved, his clothes were crumpled and his eyes were red-rimmed. From exhaustion? Or crying? He'd looked like this before…

'Matt, what happened?' she asked, not sure if she wanted to know the answer. His face…

'You had pre-eclampsia,' he said carefully. 'Do you remember that?'

She nodded slowly, trying to think, trying to suppress the niggle of fear. 'Yes. Sort of. I had a dreadful headache. Were you there? I've got this vague recollection of you carrying me…'

His face crumpled for a moment, so she thought something terrible had happened. He looked so drained, and she felt her heart rate start to pick up. The baby…

'Yes, I was there. I'd come up to see Ben and Daisy's baby for the weekend. We heard you at the door, and when I opened it you'd collapsed on the floor. That was when I carried you. We brought you to the hospital.'

He waited, and she thought about it. Yes, she remembered that—not the hospital, but before then, his face looming over her, his arms round her, making her feel safe. And Ben and Daisy's baby. Of course. She'd delivered Thomas—when? Recently. Very recently. But—

'I had a section,' she said, not daring to ask and yet she could hear his voice in her head, saying he was all right, it was OK, the baby was fine. But there was something else, about him lying to her, some little niggle…

He smiled, his eyes lighting with a tender joy. 'Yes. We had a boy, Amy,' he told her, his voice shaking slightly. 'He's fine. He's a little small, but he's doing really well, he's a proper fighter. Ben took some photos for you.'

He held them out to her, and she saw a baby almost lost in Matt's arms. There was a clip on his finger, and leads trailing from his tiny chest, and the nappy seemed to drown him, but he looked pink and well and—alive?

She sucked in a breath, and then another, hardly daring to believe it as the hope turned to joy. 'Is he—is that really…?'

'It's our baby, Amy,' he said softly, his eyes bright. 'He's in SCBU and he's doing really well.'

He showed her another photo, a close-up just of the baby, and she traced the features with her finger, wondering at them. Amazing. So, so amazing…

'Can I see him? I want to see him. Can you take me?'

He shook his head. 'You can't leave the ward yet, sweetheart. You're still on the magnesium sulphate infusion, and you've been really ill.'

'I want to see him. I want to hold him,' she said, and she started to cry, because she'd been so afraid for so long, and there was still something there, something lurking in the fringes of the fog behind her, something terrifying that she didn't understand. 'Please let me hold him.'

'OK, OK, sweetheart, don't cry, I'll go and get him. I'll bring him to you.' She felt him gather her up in his arms, his face next to hers, the stubble rough and oddly reassuring against her cheek. 'Hush now,' he murmured gently. 'Come on, lie back and rest. It's all right. Just relax—'

His voice cracked, and she wanted to cry again, but for him this time. He'd had no warning of this. She'd been going to tell him, to explain, but she'd run out of time, and for him to find her like that—

'It's OK, Matt, I'm all right,' she said, reassuring him hastily. 'I'm fine. Please, just bring him to me. Let me see him. I need to see him with my own eyes. I need to know he's all right.'

'He's all right, I promise you, Amy, and I'm not lying. I'll get him—give me five minutes. I'll get someone to come and see you while I fetch him.'

He hesitated, then carefully, as if he was afraid to hurt her, he lifted her hand to his lips and pressed a gentle kiss to her palm, then folded her fingers over it to keep it safe while he was gone.

Her eyes flooded with tears. He'd always done that, right since their first date. The last time he'd done it was after Samuel died…

'Amy, it's good to see you awake. How are you?'

She blinked away the tears and smiled up at the nurse who was both friend and colleague in another life. 'I don't know, Kate. OK, I think. My head hurts, and my tummy's sore, but—Matt's gone to get the baby…?' she said, ending it almost as a question, but Kate smiled widely.

'Yes, he has. We can't let you off the ward yet, not till your magnesium sulphate infusion's finished, but he can come to you for a little while. You'll feel so much better when you've had a cuddle. Let's get you a little wash and sit you up. You'll feel better when you've cleaned your teeth, too.'

She'd feel better when she'd seen her baby, Amy thought, but she let Kate help her up, let her wash her and comb her hair, and she cleaned her teeth—Kate was right, it did feel better when her teeth were clean—and then she was ready, her heart pounding, every second an hour as she waited to hold her little son for the first time.

'He's gorgeous,' Kate said, smiling and tidying up. 'Ben's been in flashing photos of both of them, and he's just like their baby. Smaller, of course, but lovely. So cute. Oh, look, here he comes, the little man!'

Matt was trundling the clear plastic crib, and Amy scooted up the bed a bit more, Kate helping her and tutting and rearranging her pillows, and with a crooked smile Matt lifted his tiny, precious cargo out of the crib and laid him in her waiting arms.

Gosh, he was so small! He weighed next to nothing, his feet hardly reaching her hand, his little head perfectly round, but he was breathing, his chest moving, one arm flailing in his sleep.

She lifted him to her face, kissed him, inhaled the scent of his skin and felt calm steal over her. This was her child, here in her arms where he belonged, alive and well and safe. The last cobwebs of her nightmare were torn aside as she looked at him, taking in each feature, watching his little mouth working, his eyelids flicker as he screwed up his button nose, and she laughed softly in delight.

'He's so tiny!' she breathed, staring down at him in wonder. She took his hand, and the fingers closed on her thumb, bringing a huge lump to her throat, but then his eyes opened and locked with hers, and she felt everything right itself, the agonising suspense of the last six months wiped out in a moment. 'Hello, baby,' she said softly, her voice rising naturally to a pitch he could hear. 'Oh, aren't you so beautiful? My gorgeous, gorgeous boy...'

'He's due a feed,' Matt said softly, after a moment. 'They've given me a bottle for you to give him, if you want to.'

She felt shocked. 'A bottle?'

'Of breast milk, from the bank. Just until you're well enough, and because he's suffered a setback with the pre-eclampsia, so he needs to catch up. But if you want to try...'

She did. She desperately wanted to feel him against her skin, to touch him, nurse him, hold him.

They pulled the screens round her, and Kate eased the gown off her shoulders and then put the baby back into her arms. He was only wearing a nappy, and she felt his skin against her breasts, so soft, so thin it was almost transparent.

'He's too sleepy.'

'No, he's not. His mouth's working, look. He'll wake up if you stroke your nipple against his cheek.'

Oh, genius child! He knew exactly what to do. She touched his soft, delicate cheek with her nipple, and he turned his head, rosebud lips open, and as she'd done countless times with other mothers, she pressed the baby's head against the breast and he latched on. And just like that, he was suckling.

Relief poured through her, because so often if babies suffered a setback at this stage and had to be bottle fed for the first days or weeks, it could become almost impossible to establish breast feeding. Not so with her baby, she thought with a flurry of maternal pride.

'He's amazing,' she said contentedly. 'So clever.'

'He is,' Matt agreed, tucking a blanket gently round them to keep him warm. 'He's incredible. So are you.' He stared down at them both, at the little jaws working hard, the milk-beaded lips around her nipple, her finger firmly held by the tiny hand of this miracle that was their child.

It had taken them twenty-seven hours, but finally, mother and son were getting acquainted, her crisis had passed and they could look to the future—a brighter future than he'd dared to imagine.

Where it would take them, though, he still had no idea...

Amy didn't quite know what to do with Matt.

He'd taken the baby back to the neonatal unit after she'd finished feeding him, and once he'd changed his nappy and he was settled, he came back to see her.

She was lying down again, exhausted with emotion and effort, and the first thing he did was stick up the photos of the baby on the side of her locker right in front of her, so she could see them.

'OK now?' he asked gently, and she nodded tiredly.

'I'm fine. Bit sore. I could do with going to sleep, and you look as if you could, too. Why don't you go back to Ben and Daisy's and get your head down? Or mine,' she added, and then wondered if that was really such a good idea, but he latched onto it instantly.

'That might be better. They're getting little enough sleep as it is. I think Thomas has his own idea of a schedule and I don't think night-time features yet.'

She smiled at that. 'Babies don't do schedules—well, not at three days old or whatever he is now.'

'Day three today, which started about half an hour ago. It's just after midnight on Sunday. You had the baby on Friday night.'

She frowned. 'So long ago? How long was I out?'

'A long time. Over twenty-four hours.'

She reached out her hand, and he took it, his fingers wrapping firmly round hers and squeezing gently. 'That must have been awful for you,' she murmured, and his mouth twitched into a fleeting smile.

'I don't think you were enjoying it much either.'

She frowned again. 'No.'

'You're OK now, and so's he. And you're right, I could do with getting my head down. It's been a tough week at work and I haven't had any sleep to speak of since Thursday morning.'

He got to his feet, and hesitated. 'Are you sure you're all right if I leave you?'

'Absolutely sure,' she promised, really tired now. 'I need to sleep, too. My head's killing me.'

'It'll be better soon. Give it another few hours. You sleep well, and I'll see you in the morning. Get them to call my mobile if there's anything you want—anything at all.'

And as if he knew the only thing she really wanted was a hug, he leant over and gave her one, a gentle squeeze as his stubble brushed her cheek and he dropped a feather-light kiss on the corner of her mouth.

'Sleep tight,' he murmured, and kissing her hand again, he folded up her fingers and left her alone with her thoughts.

When he got back to the hospital in the morning, it was to find that Amy had been moved out of HDU into a single room on the postnatal ward, and he went to find her.

'Hi there,' he said, tapping on the door and pushing it open with a smile. 'How are you?'

'Much better. My hands and feet feel as if they might be mine again, and my headache's easing.' She frowned, and tipped her head on one side, eyeing him searchingly. 'Just how bad was it, Matt? Nobody seems to want to tell me and the consultant's not around, conveniently.'

'No. Well, I think Ben's sort of overseeing your care.'

'You mean you aren't?' she asked, only half joking.

Curiously, he hadn't felt the need to interfere, and he told her so. 'I think it's because I was keeping a pretty close eye on what was going on, and they were doing what I would have done, so there was no need.'

'You haven't answered the first question,' she pointed out, and he grunted softly and sat down on the chair beside her.

'You—uh—you fitted. In HDU, after the delivery.'

Amy was stunned. 'I fitted?' she said, thinking that it explained a lot about her headache. 'So what was my blood pressure?'

'At its highest? It went up to 240 over 180.'

She felt her jaw drop, and she shut her mouth and swallowed. Hard. 'Wow.'

'Do you know what it is now?'

She shook her head, and he checked on the chart in the rack by the door. 'One-sixty over 80. Still high, but coming down well. What's your baseline?'

'One-twenty over 70. I can't believe that. That's shocking!'

'Yes. It wasn't great,' he said drily.

'Were you there?'

He nodded. 'I was, pretty much all the time. Ben dragged me away for a few minutes a couple of times in the first twenty-four hours, but mostly I was there, and—well, it wasn't great spectator sport, let's put it like that. I'd rather be on the other side organising the treatment any day.'

She looked down, fiddling with the edge of the sheet. 'There's something I can't— Did we have a row? It's really foggy, I'm not sure if I dreamed it or what, but— did I accuse you of lying to me?'

His eyebrows scrunched up slightly, and he gave a reluctant nod. 'Yes. Yes, you did, but—'

'About the baby?'

'You were drugged up to the eyeballs, Amy. You didn't know what was going on.'

'I thought he was dead, didn't I?' she said slowly, sifting through the snippets of memory lurking in the fog, and then she looked up and met his eyes. 'I thought it was—last time,' she said softly. 'Didn't I?'

He nodded slowly, his eyes pained. 'Yes. You muddled them up, and thought I was lying when I said he was all right.'

Her eyes filled with tears, and she looked away. 'It still seems wrong that this baby's OK and—' She broke off, then carried on, 'We need a name for him. We can't just keep calling him the baby.'

'Daisy said you liked Joshua.'

'I do, but I wanted to ask you. He's your baby, too. Do you like it?'

'It's fine—yes, I do. It's a good name.' He hesitated,

not sure how to say this, how it would land. 'I thought—maybe we could call him Joshua Samuel.'

Her breath caught on a tiny sob. 'That's lovely,' she said, and biting her lip, she turned away.

Joshua Samuel. Both her boys.

Oh, lord.

She started to cry, broken, hiccupping little sobs, and found herself cradled tenderly against a broad, firm chest. 'I miss him,' she wept, and she felt him tense under her hands.

'I know, sweetheart, I know,' he murmured gruffly. 'I miss him, too.'

'Why did he have to die?' she asked, sniffing back the tears and pulling away. Her hands scrubbed at her face, swiping the tears aside, but fresh ones took their place and he reached for a tissue and handed it to her.

'I don't know. We'll never know. There didn't seem to be anything wrong with him, or you. It was just one of those things.'

'We went for a walk—the day before. A long one.'

'Yes. We did. But we often walked, Amy. It was what we did. We walked miles all the time, so it was nothing new. And you know that. You can't blame yourself, it wasn't your fault, or anything you or anybody else did. I braked sharply in the car on the way home, on the motorway. It could have been that, but it's unlikely. It was just one of those unexplained tragedies that happen in obstetrics. You know we don't have the answer to all of them. Sometimes things just happen.'

She nodded, and looked up at the clock on the wall. 'I need to feed him. They said if he's gained weight, I can have him with me here, and then we can go home together in a few days. They're really pleased with him.'

'Good.' His smile was wry. 'I'm really pleased with

him, too. I would have liked to have been here with you, to have known you were pregnant, to have shared it.'

She swallowed the guilt. It was too late to do anything about it, but even if she could, she wouldn't have told him until after 26 weeks, at least. 'I'm sorry. I just—'

'Couldn't let yourself believe it would be all right?'

Her smile was sad. 'Something like that,' she admitted.

'So what do we do now, Amy?' he asked, his voice soft. 'What happens next?'

The real question was too hard to answer, so she didn't even try.

'Now, we feed the baby,' she said, and started the slow and uncomfortable process of getting out of bed.

She had a rest later, and Ben came in and they went outside in the grounds with a coffee.

'So what happens now?' Ben asked quietly, echoing his own words to Amy, and Matt felt himself frown.

'I don't know. It all depends on Amy, on what she feels about my involvement.'

'Are you taking paternity leave?'

He gave a short huff of laughter. 'I have no idea. I haven't really had time to consider it. It's not a good time at work, but then it never is, is it? I've got some twins I don't really want to delegate—I need to be backwards and forwards. But if Amy will let me, I want to be around, and I'm certainly going to be part of his life.'

'I didn't doubt it for a moment,' Ben said drily. 'I just wonder if Amy's thought it through, or if she never let herself get that far. She hasn't bought any baby equipment according to Daisy. Not so much as a nappy.'

He frowned again. She really had been blanking it

out. He wondered why. Was it simply because she didn't think it would be all right? Or was it because she'd never really grieved for Samuel and hadn't moved on? Their relationship had fallen apart so soon after she lost him that Matt had no idea how she'd dealt with it. Now, he was beginning to wonder if she'd dealt with it at all.

He wasn't sure how well he'd dealt with it—not well at the time, certainly, and the thought of his first son left a hollow ache in his chest even now. But this was Joshua's time, he told himself firmly, and wondered how much of him he'd see, in reality.

Should he take paternity leave? Instinct said yes, but Amy might have other ideas. He'd talk to her about it, but he'd certainly investigate the possibility.

They kept her in for the rest of the week, and it felt like the busiest week of his life.

He had twins he was monitoring at the unit in London, and his specialist registrar called on Monday night to say they were concerned, so he drove down, weighed up all the results, added in his gut feeling and delivered them at four in the morning, then went into his office and cleared his outstanding paperwork. By the time HR were in at nine, he'd delegated responsibility for his cases, divvied them out according to severity, written a short—very short—list of patients he insisted on seeing himself, and was ready to go back.

The time he'd been away had enabled him to make one decision, at least. He phoned HR, told them he was taking paternity leave, notified them of the cover arrangements he'd put in place, and after a short detour to his house to pack some things, he was back in Suffolk by Amy's side before lunch.

'Gosh, you look tired.'

He laughed softly. 'Yeah. Been a bit busy. Some twins decided they'd had enough.'

'In London?'

He nodded. 'They were only twenty-seven weeks, but they were already struggling and they hadn't grown for five days. They're OK, but they were tiny.'

'They would be,' she said softly. 'Heavens. And I'm worried about our Josh.'

'Are you?' he asked instantly, and she shook her head.

'No. Not any more. Sorry, that was a bad choice of words. It's just that I mostly deliver babies that are term, and anything as small as those twins must be...'

Brings back Samuel, he thought, understanding instantly, and he wondered how she did her job, how she coped with stillbirths and labours so early that the babies couldn't be viable. By blanking it out? Well, it worked for him. More or less.

'How's the feeding going?' he asked, sticking to a safe topic, and her face softened into a smile.

'Great. He's doing really well. I think they're going to say we can go home in a day or two.' The smile faded, and she bit her lip.

'What?' he said quietly.

'I've been a bit silly,' she admitted. It was easy to say it, now he was all right, but before—well it had been hard to plan ahead. 'I haven't bought anything for him. No clothes, nappies, cot—nothing. I was going to do it as soon as I started maternity leave.' If she'd got that far. Well, she certainly had now, she thought wryly. 'I wonder how long things take to come if you order them over the internet. Sometimes it's quite quick.'

'Or you could write me a list. I'll just get the basic

stuff in ready for you to bring him home, and you can have all the fun of the cute, pretty stuff with Daisy once you're a bit stronger.'

It was so tempting. Just hand it all over to him and sit back and concentrate on Joshua. Which of course was what she should be doing, she realised. 'Would you mind? And it really needn't be a lot. I'll move some money into your bank account—'

'I hardly think it's necessary for you to refund me for basic purchases I make for my own child,' he said with that quiet implacability she was beginning to realise she couldn't argue with. Well, not and win, anyway. Pointless trying, so she vowed to keep the list as short as possible and do the bulk of the shopping once he'd gone back. He couldn't take much longer off work, surely?

'Incidentally, I'm on paternity leave,' he told her, as if he'd read her mind. 'Except for a few days here and there. I still need to go back a couple of days a week and I'm on standby for emergencies in my trickier cases, but otherwise I'll be here, giving you a hand until you're back on your feet.'

He wasn't asking, she noticed, and she wondered if she ought to mind, but in fact it was a relief. She'd been dreading going home, having to cope alone or, her reluctant alternative in an emergency, troubling Ben and Daisy.

She was sure they wouldn't mind. They'd been brilliant. Daisy had been in twice, Ben was always popping in because, like Matt, there were cases he didn't feel he could hand over, but they had their own new baby to worry about, and she didn't want to get in the way of that joyful time.

And now, she wouldn't have to, because she'd have the baby's father there staking his claim—

No! Stop it! Of course he has rights, and you want him to be there for your baby!

'If you're sure you can spare the time, that would be really helpful for a few days,' she said.

A few days.

He'd had in mind a lifetime, but after the road they'd travelled in the last four years, he'd settle for a few days as an opener.

'Let's write your list,' he said, pulling out his phone. It doubled as a notebook, so he keyed in the items as she thought of them, and when she was done he closed it and put it back in his pocket.

'I think it's time for a cuddle,' he said, standing up and peeling back the little blanket carefully, and sliding his hands under him he picked Joshua up without disturbing him at all.

She watched him, loving the sure, confident way he handled his son, knowing he was safe. She'd always loved watching him with babies. When she'd first worked with him, six years ago, she'd known he'd be good with his own. That had been one of the hardest things about losing Samuel—watching Matt holding him, the gentleness of his hands as he'd cradled the much-too-tiny baby, kissed him, before laying him tenderly on the white cloth, covering him...

She'd never seen him cry for Samuel, but she'd heard him. She'd envied him, because she hadn't been able to, not then, not for a long time.

But now—now he was holding Joshua, and his hands were just as gentle, just as sure, and the love in his eyes was just as certain.

If only he loved her. If only she could trust that love.

No. She wanted him in Josh's life, and she could trust him with her son without a doubt. She just wasn't sure she could trust him with herself.

CHAPTER SEVEN

HE WENT back to see her that evening, and found several of her colleagues standing around her, laughing and talking.

The moment he walked in, however, they stopped dead, smiled at him and left. 'Don't mind me,' he said, holding up his hands, but they went anyway, and he shook his head, slightly bemused, and sat down next to Amy.

'Was it something I said?'

'No, of course not. They're just—they don't really know what to say to you.'

'Hello would be a good start,' he said drily, and she chuckled, but then she pulled a face.

'One of the advantages of giving birth in your workplace is that you get spoilt to bits, but the disadvantage is that they think of you as public property, and there's only been one question on all their minds since they realised I was pregnant, and they've just found out the answer's you. That's why they can't talk to you. I think they feel a bit awkward, with you being Ben's brother.'

He was puzzled. 'Didn't they know I was the father?'

'No, of course not. I hadn't said anything about you, and I actively discouraged curious questions, but I suppose now I'm on the mend, and the baby's all right, they've stopped worrying about us and I can just *hear* the cogs turning. You know what hospitals are like.'

'You don't think they'd worked it out before?'

She shrugged. 'Maybe. Several of them were there for the evening do at the wedding, so it's quite possible someone saw us together and worked it out. Nobody really seems surprised, I guess.'

'No. I imagine they just want to know all the gory details.'

'Well, they aren't getting them from me,' she said firmly. 'I hate being the object of curiosity.'

'Yeah, me too. How's Josh?'

'OK. He's under the UV light. I thought he was looking a bit jaundiced when I changed his nappy, so they called the paediatrician. I thought they would have told you.'

'They did. It's quite common, nothing to worry about.'

He didn't know why he was reassuring her, except that she looked a little glum, and she tried to smile.

'I know that,' she said. 'It just seems odd without him here.'

'It's not for long.'

'I know.'

He frowned. There was something in her voice, something that didn't feel quite right, and he got up and went over to her, perching on the edge of the bed and looking down at her searchingly.

'Hey, what's up?' he asked softly, brushing her cheek with his knuckles, and just like that tears slid down her cheek.

'Oh, Amy,' he murmured, and easing her into his arms, he cradled her against his shoulder and rocked her gently. 'What's up, sweetheart? Are you worried about him? You don't need to be.'

She shook her head. 'No. I just miss him being here. It scares me,' she said, hiccupping on a sob. 'I don't like it when I can't see him, and I need to feed him, and my milk's come in and I feel as if I've got rocks on my chest and everything hurts—'

She broke off, sobbing in earnest now, and he shushed her gently and smoothed her hair.

'You've got the four-day blues, ' he said tenderly. 'All those hormones sloshing around. It'll soon pass. Do you want to go down there and feed him?'

She sniffed and nodded, and he got off the bed and handed her a hot, wrung-out face flannel to wipe away her tears, and then he helped her out of bed and walked her down to the neonatal unit. She was steady on her feet now, but he walked with his arm round her—just in case there was anyone there left in any doubt that he was Josh's father and definitely in the picture—and he handed Josh to her and sat beside her while she was feeding him.

'Ow, they're too full, it hurts,' she said, her eyes welling again, and he gave her another hug.

'It'll soon be easier. Give it a minute and you'll be fine, and it'll get better. You'd rather it was this way than you didn't have enough.'

'Do you have to be right about everything?' she sniped tearfully, and he blew out his breath slowly and took his arm away.

'Sorry. I was only trying to help.'

'Well, don't. I know all that. I don't need to be told—'

She broke off, knowing full well she was being unreasonable, but...

'Do you want me to go home?' he asked quietly, and

she thought, *Home? As in your home, in London, or my home?* The answer was the same, whatever. She shook her head.

'No. I'm sorry, I'm just tired,' she said. 'Tired and fed up and I want to go home myself.'

He gave a short sigh and put his arm round her again. To hell with it. She needed comforting, and he was right here, and the person who arguably should be doing it. Who else, for heaven's sake?

'You can come home soon,' he murmured soothingly. 'You could come home tonight, if you wanted. You're well enough. It's only the feeding, and you could spend the days here and stay at home for the nights. You could express the milk—'

She shook her head. 'I can't leave him, Matt. I can't leave my baby all night. I can't…'

Poor Amy. She'd been on an emotional rollercoaster for the last few months, and it wasn't over yet, he knew. They had so many unresolved issues, and if nothing else, they had to build a working relationship for the future.

'Stay, then, but I think you should restrict your visitors. They're wearing you out.'

She sighed and leant into him, her head finding its natural resting place on his shoulder. 'But they're lovely to me,' she said wearily. 'They've brought all sorts of presents, and they make me laugh and they're so kind, really.'

'I know they are, but you're tired, Amy. You need some rest. Come on, let me take him and deal with him now, and you go back to bed and get some rest.'

She nodded, and he took Josh, resting him against his shoulder where Amy's head had just been. He was getting good at winding him—he'd been practising on

Thomas in between times, and he'd got it down to a fine art now.

He put him back under the UV light with his eye-shade on, changed his nappy and left him to sleep. He fussed for a moment and then settled, and Matt went back to Amy and found her curled on her side in the bed, clutching a handful of tissues and sniffing.

'Can I have a cuddle?' she asked tearfully, so he tipped the blinds in the door, turned down the lights and lay down beside her, easing her into his arms.

'You've really been through the mill, haven't you?' he murmured, holding her close, and she sniffed again and burrowed closer. 'It's OK, I've got you. You're all right,' he said softly, and gradually the little shuddering sobs died away, and he felt her body relax, her breathing slowing as she slid into sleep.

He stayed there for an hour, until there was a quiet tap on the door and it opened to reveal Rachel, the nurse from SCBU.

'How is she?'

'Asleep,' he mouthed. 'Problem?'

'He's brought up his feed and he's hungry again. Shall I bring him to her, just for a minute? Don't move her. She's been a bit weepy today. I think she missed you while you were away.'

Had she? He woke her gently. 'Sweetheart, the baby needs feeding again, but you don't have to move. Rachel's bringing him.'

She made a sleepy little sound of protest, opened her eyes and breathed in shakily. 'Oh, I'm so tired, Matt. I can't do this.'

'Yes, you can. Just feed him. All you have to do is sit there. We'll do the rest.'

She let him help her up against the pillows, and

stared at him searchingly. 'Why are you doing all of this for me?' she asked, sounding genuinely perplexed, and he gave a soft laugh.

'Because I love you—both of you,' he replied, as if it was obvious, and then Rachel came in and there wasn't time to say any more.

But it stayed with her all night, the words keeping her company every time she woke to feed the baby or go to the loo or just to turn over, and although she wasn't sure if she could trust them, still they comforted her.

It might be true, she thought. Or at least, if he hung around long enough, maybe it would become true. People did learn to love each other, given time.

One day at a time, she told herself, just as she had through her pregnancy. One day at a time...

She went home with Joshua two days later.

Her blood pressure was much closer to normal, her hands and feet and face were her own again, and his jaundice had cleared up, so they were to be allowed out, and it couldn't come soon enough for her.

Matt came to fetch her, armed with a couple of bags. He was a few minutes late, but he'd been busy, he said. On the phone, probably, she thought, sorting out one of his cases in London, but he produced some clothes for her and the baby.

'They'll probably drown him,' he said, 'but they were supposed to be for babies of his weight.'

He looked out of his depth—strangely, for a man so at home with babies, but they were usually either still tucked up inside their mothers or slippery and screaming when he handled them, so all things considered he was doing well, and she smiled at him.

'I'm sure they'll be fine. Better too big than too small.'

'They won't be too small,' he assured her.

They weren't. She had to turn back the cuffs, and when he bent his legs his little feet disappeared, but he'd soon grow out of the first size. They always did.

'He looks really cute,' she said, smiling at Josh. 'Don't you, my gorgeous?'

The baby stared at her with startlingly blue eyes, so thoughtful.

'I wonder what he makes of us?' Matt said softly.

'I don't know. I wonder if he knows I'm his mother?'

'Of course he does. He'll know your voice.'

It was a lovely thought. She'd said as much to many mums over the years, but this time it was her baby, and she was the mother, and the thought was curiously centring.

'Right, all set?'

She nodded. 'I've packed my things—oh, Matt, we'll need a car seat! I didn't even think of it!'

'All done,' he said calmly. 'It's in the car.'

She had a committee to see her off. 'Isn't anybody in labour?' she asked wryly, as one by one they all hugged her and said goodbye.

'Go on, off you go, and keep in touch,' said Rosie, one of the midwives, hugging her again, and Matt closed the car door, got into the front and drove her home.

Bliss, she thought as he pulled up in the car port at the back and helped her out. She could sit in the garden and listen to the birds, and spend time in the conservatory soaking up the sun with Josh at her side.

They went through the conservatory into the kitchen, and she walked slowly in and looked around. In the middle of the dining table was a huge bunch of flowers in a tall vase, and they stopped her in her tracks.

'Oh, they're lovely! Who are they from?'

He put the baby seat and her bags down on the floor and gave her a wry smile. 'Me—just to welcome you home.'

'Oh, Matt—thank you. Thank you for everything...'

She hugged him, letting her head rest against his chest for a few moments, but it wasn't fair to hold him at arm's length for months and then lean on him when it suited her, so she straightened up and moved away, walking slowly through her house, touching it as if she was making sure it was still here, grounding herself.

'I bought a few things for the baby,' he said. 'They're upstairs.'

She made her way up there, and found Matt had made himself thoroughly at home.

She'd seen his laptop in the sitting room as she'd put her head in, and his wash things were in the bathroom, set out neatly on the window sill above the basin, and he'd taken over the back bedroom.

He obviously meant what he'd said about being around for her, she realised, and the implications of sharing her house with him, even in the short term, began to dawn on her.

She went into her bedroom, and found he'd changed the sheets on her bed—or someone had. Daisy? Surely not, so soon after having Thomas, but maybe she'd just suggested it and supervised. Daisy had got good at supervising towards the end of her pregnancy, she thought with a smile.

Whatever, it meant she was coming home to clean, crisp linen on the bed, and she had a sudden longing to climb into it and sleep for hours.

And then she looked beyond the bed, and spotted the pretty Moses basket draped with white embroidered cotton by the far side.

'Oh, Matt!' She trailed her fingers lightly over it, and her eyes filled. 'This is lovely—really pretty. Thank you. And all these clothes!' She stared at the little pile of baby clothes and accessories on the chest of drawers, touching them as if she didn't quite believe they were real. She'd put it off for so long, been so afraid to take this pregnancy for granted, and he'd just calmly come in right at the end and picked up all the pieces. He didn't need to do that, and she'd had no right to ask…

She felt a tear spill over and trickle down her cheek, and she brushed it away. 'Thank you so much.'

'Don't be silly, it's nothing. I didn't get many clothes. I didn't want to overdo it and you're bound to be deluged with presents, so they're only the basic vests and sleep suits and things to start him off, but he'll have grown out of them in five minutes anyway.'

She nodded. She had already been given some clothes, cute little things for him to grow into, and she knew he was right. 'They're just perfect. Thank you, you haven't overdone it at all, it's just what I would have got if I'd been a bit more proactive.'

He gave her a wry smile. 'I can quite see why you weren't, it's a bit overwhelming in there, isn't it? And as for the pram business,' he went on, rolling his eyes, 'I spent an hour in there being given a guided tour of how they fold and what clips on what and how they come apart and turn round and zip together, and some have pram inserts and car seats and face this way or that—by the time she'd finished I was utterly confused, so I just bought a seat and a base to put in my car for today, and whatever else you want you'll have to sort out yourself because frankly I think it's going to be down to personal choice and what you need it for, and I have *no* idea where you would even start!'

She bit her lip, picturing him in a sea of dismantled pushchairs, and she just wanted to hug him. Or laugh.

She ended up doing both, and he wrapped his arms round her and hugged her back, and for a moment they just stood there in each other's arms and held each other.

She could have stayed there forever, but that really wasn't wise or practical, so she let him go and stepped back, before she got too used to it, and looked at the Moses basket again.

'This is so pretty.'

'It won't last long, he'll outgrow it in a few months. I nearly got a crib, but I thought you could carry this downstairs and put him out in the garden in it, or in the conservatory, or in the sitting room in the evening, even take him round to see Daisy—it seemed to have all sorts of possibilities that the crib just didn't, and it doesn't stop you having a crib later, or even now if you wanted to. You could just use it downstairs. And, yeah, I thought it looked the part,' he added with a wry grin.

His talk of taking it downstairs held huge appeal. 'Can we take it downstairs and put him in it now? It's such a lovely day, and I've really missed the sunshine, being trapped in the hospital. It would be lovely to sit in the conservatory with the doors open and just enjoy the fresh air, really.'

'Sure. It's easy.' He looked pleased, as if he was glad his idea had met with her approval, and he lifted the basket, folded the stand and carried them both down.

She followed him more slowly, still a little tender, and by the time she'd taken Joshua out of the car seat and followed Matt through to the conservatory he was setting it up.

'Here, out of the sun?' he asked, and she nodded.

'That's lovely. Thank you.'

She laid the baby in it, and he stretched and yawned, his little arms flopped up by his head, the hat askew. 'He looks pretty chilled,' she said with a smile, and Matt laughed.

'Daddy's boy,' he said with a ridiculously proud grin. 'I always used to lie like that, if the photos can be believed. Cup of tea?'

'Oh, that would be brilliant.' She sat down on the chair carefully, her stitches pulling a little, and watched her baby sleeping. It was turning into her favourite occupation, she thought with a smile.

'Better now?'

He was lounging in the doorway, arms folded, one leg crossed over the other, looking utterly at home, and she realised it would be only too easy to get used to having him around.

'So much better,' she said, her words heartfelt. 'Matt, I'm so grateful to you for all you've done this last week. You just dropped everything, and I never expected you to—

'You didn't offer me the chance to discuss what I wanted to do, what role I wanted in your lives,' he pointed out gently, trying to keep the simmering anger under control. Now wasn't the time. 'I would have been here for you all along, Amy, if you'd given me the chance, but you always did like to go it alone.'

She looked down at her hands. 'Not really. I just didn't know how to deal with it—after the night of Ben and Daisy's wedding it all seemed so complicated.'

Oh, yes. He was with her on that. 'I wish I'd known.

I would never have left you alone to cope, and you shouldn't have allowed me to.'

'You didn't leave me alone to cope, I sent you away.'

He gave a wry laugh. 'Yeah, you're good at that, aren't you?'

She frowned at him, puzzled. 'What do you mean?'

'When you were ill—out of it, really, and you thought it was Samuel, not Josh—you told me to go away then.'

She bit her lip; her memories of that time were so patchy and veiled in layers of what seemed like fog, but through it all she knew he'd been there, and she wasn't sure she could have coped without him.

'I didn't mean it. I was so confused. I'm glad you didn't, I didn't really want you to go.'

'Didn't you? It sounded like it. You sounded desperate, Amy. And I've heard you saying it before, don't forget, when things were about as bad as they could be. I left you alone then, too, and I shouldn't have done.'

She swallowed. 'I didn't mean it then, either. Not really, not in that way. I just couldn't cope with your grief as well as mine, and the thought of a wedding so soon after we'd lost him—I just couldn't handle it. How could we have a party then, Matt? It felt so wrong. And if we'd known each other well enough, if we'd really known each other, we could have dealt with it, but we didn't, we retreated into our grief and took the easy way out.'

'Easy?'

She tried to smile. 'No, not easy. Nothing about it was easy, but it was easier than talking to a stranger about something I couldn't even bring myself to think about. And you were a stranger, relatively. We'd only worked in the same department for less than a year before I got pregnant, and we were hardly ever on the same shift or working together because I was on the midwifery-led unit and you were in the high risk unit. We hardly ever met up at work, and because we were working shifts we didn't always see each other at night, either, so even when we were living together we were like ships in the night. It was no wonder we struggled to communicate when we were grieving.'

It was true, he thought. They'd thought they'd known each other, they'd certainly wanted each other and talked about getting married, but they *had* been relative strangers, and yet they'd been expected to cope with the loss of their baby. No wonder it had all fallen apart for them. But now...

'Can we start again?' he said quietly, and she looked up at him, propping up the doorframe and looking rugged and kind and troubled, and she felt a flicker of apprehension.

If she said yes, if she let him back into her life, she'd run the risk of losing him again.

And if she didn't, she realised, she'd lose him now.

She took a deep breath.

'We can try,' she said carefully, and something flared in his eyes, something he quickly banked. 'I'm sorry I didn't tell you I was pregnant, but I was so afraid things would go wrong again.'

'Yeah. Ben said you had no confidence in your pregnancy.'

'Would you have done, in my shoes?'

He smiled wryly. 'Probably not. In my own shoes, had I known, had you told me, I like to think I'd have been rational about it.'

'Are you saying I was irrational?' she asked with an edge to her voice, and he sighed and crouched down beside her.

'No, Amy, I'm not saying that at all. Your reaction was perfectly natural and understandable, but maybe if I'd been with you I could have helped to reassure you.'

'And if it had happened again? If we'd lost Josh?'

His eyes flicked to the baby, and a spasm of pain showed on his face.

'No. I didn't think so. We didn't cope with this before, Matt, and there was nothing to suggest we'd cope with it any better a second time.'

He nodded. 'I'm sorry. I'm not very good at sharing my feelings.'

She laughed at that, a sad little hiccup of laughter that twisted his heart, and he straightened up and moved away, giving them both space. This wasn't going to be as easy as he'd imagined, he realised. No dropping seamlessly back into their old relationship, as if they'd just cut out the last five years and joined the ends together.

'About the next few weeks,' he said, getting back to practicalities because it was far easier than pursuing the other topic. 'I don't want to overcrowd you, and I don't want you to feel abandoned, either. I have to go back to London on Monday for a couple of days, and then I'll be back, and we can see how it goes. I'll try and give you space, and help with Joshua, and if it all gets too much you can kick me out and I can go and see Ben and Daisy and Thomas, or I can go back to London for the night and give you room. We'll play it by ear. Deal?'

She searched his eyes, and found only sincerity and a genuine desire to make this work. The rest could wait.

'Deal,' she said, and she smiled. 'Can we have that tea now? I'm parched.'

* * *

Ben and Daisy came round a little later, bearing plates of food and bottles of sparkling water.

'Just because we ought to have something fizzy to wet the babies' heads, and half of us can't drink,' Daisy explained, hugging Amy and bending over Josh and making besotted noises.

'He's so tiny! He's like a mini-Thomas! Oh, I want a cuddle. Hurry up and wake up!'

'No! He's only just gone back to sleep!' Amy said sternly. 'You leave him alone this minute and come and tell me all about Thomas. I feel dreadful abandoning you just after you had him.'

'Oh, Amy.'

She hugged her, told Ben to open the fizzy water and Matt to find glasses, and Amy sat there and cuddled Thomas and wondered how much better it could get.

Two days ago, she'd been in the depths of despair. Now, she was back home, her closest, dearest friends were with her, and she and Matt were going to see if they could make their relationship work.

That still filled her with a certain amount of trepidation, but she knew half of the butterflies were excitement at the prospect, and she tried to forget about it, to put it on one side and concentrate on enjoying the moment.

One day at a time, she told herself yet again, and took a glass of fizzy water from Ben and they toasted the babies. And as she lifted her glass, she met Matt's eyes over the top of it and he winked at her, and she thought, *It's going to be all right. We can do this. We can.*

'That was my parents. They send their love.'

Ben and Daisy had gone home with Thomas and

she'd just settled Josh in his crib when Matt came back into the sitting room, slipping his phone into his pocket. She'd heard it ring, and she frowned at what he said. 'They know you're with me?'

'Well, of course they do. Why wouldn't they?'

Why not, indeed? 'Have you told them about the baby?'

He gave a soft, disbelieving laugh. 'Amy, I've just become a father. Of *course* I've told them. I told them days ago.'

Well, of course he had. How stupid of her. They were a very close family, and Ben had just had a baby, too, which they would have been eagerly anticipating, and so they would all have been on the phone frequently. He was lucky to have them. So lucky...

He sat down on the sofa opposite her and searched her eyes. 'Amy, I know you've lost both of your parents, but have you told any members of your family?' he asked gently, and she shook her head.

'Not yet. I didn't want any of them to come over and have hysterics when they saw me, I just didn't need it. It's not as if I ever see my aunt or my cousins. I thought it would be better to tell them when it was all settling down and we knew the baby was all right.'

Not to mention her, he thought, because he'd had a few hours there where having hysterics wouldn't have been out of the way. 'You have a point. You looked pretty rough at first.'

She laughed, to his surprise. '*I* looked rough? Did you not look in a mirror?'

He smiled acknowledgement. 'Touché,' he said. 'I needed a few hours' sleep and a shave, but you—Amy, you worried me.' His smile faded as he remembered the sheer blind terror that had gripped him when he'd thought she might die.

'Was it really that bad? That close?'

He nodded, and swallowed hard. 'Yes, it was really that close, my love. You scared me half to death. I thought I was going to lose you.'

No wonder she'd been so out of it, she thought. She hadn't realised it had been that bad—although if she'd been thinking clearly she would have worked it out for herself from the state of him and the time that had elapsed and how high her blood pressure had risen.

'Oh, Matt,' she said softly, and he got up and came over to her and sat beside her, tucking his arm round her and dropping a light kiss on her hair.

'It's OK. It's over now, and you're getting better. I'm sorry, I shouldn't have told you. I didn't want to worry you.'

'You didn't—not for me. I know I was in good hands. You and Ben wouldn't have let anything happen to me.'

They might not have had any choice, of course. They both knew that, but by tacit agreement the subject was dropped. Joshua was asleep, Matt had put soft music on and she rested her head against his shoulder and let herself enjoy the moment.

CHAPTER EIGHT

JOSH woke at three.

Amy had fed him at eleven, and Matt had changed his nappy, put him in a clean sleepsuit and tucked him up next to her bed in the Moses basket while she'd used the bathroom.

And now he was awake again.

Prising his eyes open, Matt threw off the quilt and went into Amy's room. She was just stirring, about to get out of bed, but she looked sore and uncomfortable, and he tutted and eased her legs back up onto the bed and handed her the baby, tucking a stray lock of hair behind her ear with gentle fingers.

'You feed him, I'll get you a drink. Do you want decaf tea or herbal something, or just cold water?'

She gazed at him a little blankly. 'Tea?' she said hopefully, after a moment. 'Tea would be fabulous if you can be bothered, but you don't have to—'

'Don't argue, Amy. You've had far too much your own way. Now it's my turn to do the worrying.'

He left her alone with the baby, and she stared down at him while he suckled, his eyes firmly fixed on her in the dim light from the landing, his tiny hand splayed across her breast. She slid her thumb under it and it closed around her, and she stroked the back of his hand with her fingers, smiling down at him in wonder.

She was getting used to him now, getting used to how small he was and yet how determined and how very, very good at getting his way.

Just like his father, she thought wryly, and looked up as Matt came into the room and put the tea down on her bedside table.

He hovered for a moment, another cup in his hand, and she sensed he was waiting for the invitation, so she shifted her feet across and patted the edge of the bed. 'Stay,' she said softly, and he smiled, a fleeting quirk of his lips, and sat down at the end of the bed, watching her thoughtfully.

'How's the feeding going?'

'Well. Considering the start he had, he's amazing.'

She tucked her little finger in the corner of his mouth and eased him off, then held him out to Matt.

'Here you are, little one, go to Daddy. Want to wind him? Since you're so good at it,' she added with a smile, so he put his tea down and took the baby, and she shuffled up the bed a bit more and drank her own tea while he walked up and down, rubbing the baby's back. And as he walked, she watched him longingly.

He was dressed—if you could call it that—in soft jersey boxers, and the baby was propped against his bare shoulder, looking impossibly tiny against that broad chest. One large hand was holding him in place, the other stroking his back gently, and the tenderness of the gesture brought tears to her eyes. 'That's my little lager lout,' he said proudly as the baby burped, and she chuckled and blinked the tears away.

Matt turned and caught her eye, still smiling, and then he surprised her.

'Thank you,' he said, serious now, the smile gone, and she frowned at him in confusion.

'For what?'

'For having him? For going through all that alone, when you must have been so frightened. For mistakenly, misguidedly trying to spare me if things had gone wrong again. But not thank you for keeping me out of the loop, because I would have been here for you all along, Amy, if you'd only given me the chance.'

She felt another stab of guilt, but she'd done it for the best reasons and there was no point going over it again. 'Don't be daft, you work in London, you would have just been down there worrying and bullying Ben for hourly updates.'

He smiled wryly and brought the baby back to her side.

'You might be right, but you still should have told me.' The smile faded, and he gave a heavy sigh and ran his hand through his hair, spiking it wildly. He looked tousled and sexy and unbearably dear to her, and she took Josh from him and settled him at the other breast, suddenly self-conscious under his searching gaze.

Not because of the feeding, but because her hair must be all over the place, she had dark bags under her eyes and her tummy still looked like a bag of jelly.

But he didn't look as if he cared. He didn't look as if he was seeing any of that. Instead he gave a fleeting frown, picked up the cups and headed for the door.

'Call me when you're done, I'll change him and put him down for you,' he said, and left her alone.

He took the cups down to the kitchen, put them in the dishwasher and rested his head against the wall cupboard above it, his hands braced on the edge of the worktop.

He wanted her. Not like that, not at the moment, because she was still recovering from the eclampsia and the surgery. But he was overcome with longing—the longing to get into bed beside her and ease her into his arms and hold her, just hold her while she slept. He'd held her last night, on the sofa, her head on his shoulder and her soft breath teasing his chest in the open neck of his shirt.

It had felt so good to have her in his arms again, so right. But there was still a gulf between them, a wariness on both sides because of all the heartache and grief they'd shared and yet not really shared—and they still hadn't.

They had a long way to go before they could pick up the threads of their old life together, and he knew that, but he was impatient. They had so much going for them, and so much depended on the success of their relationship.

Not least the happiness and well-being of their son.

He heard the boards creak, and with a heavy sigh he pushed away from the worktop and headed upstairs. This he could do. The rest—the rest would come.

They just had to give it time.

Daisy took her stitches out on Saturday morning, which made her a lot more comfortable.

Matt had offered, but somehow it seemed extraordinarily intimate, and Ben was hardly any better, even if he'd put them there after the section and had a professional interest in his handiwork. She still felt uncomfortable about it, so Daisy did it for her, and then they had coffee together in the garden with the babies at their sides. And for the first time in years she felt like a normal woman again, doing the things that normal women did instead of standing on the outside looking in.

There was still a core of pain inside her for the loss of Samuel, and she supposed there always would be, but that was fine. She wouldn't have it any other way. He was still her son, always would be, and she was entitled to her grief.

Thomas started to fuss, so Daisy took him home and Amy left Matt with Josh in his Moses basket and went upstairs and had a look through the things Matt had bought—on her instructions. It seemed she hadn't been thinking quite as clearly as she'd imagined, because it had soon became obvious that the list she'd given him had some vital elements missing.

One of the most important, as Matt had pointed out, was a pram. She was still feeling tender, still walking carefully, but it was a beautiful day, and it would have been a good day for taking him out for a little stroll to the park nearby, only they didn't have a pram.

She. She didn't have a pram. They weren't a 'they' yet and might not ever be, so she'd be crazy to let herself start thinking like that.

There were also other things—very personal things—that she needed, and there was no way she was asking him, obstetrician or not! And it wasn't fair to keep asking Daisy…

He appeared in the doorway, tapping lightly and sticking his head round. 'Somebody needs his mum,' he began, and then took one look at her and said, 'What's the matter?'

'What makes you think something's the matter?' she asked, taking the baby from him, and he laughed.

'The look on your face? You're like an open book, Amy. So come on, let's have it.'

'I need to go shopping.'

His eyebrows shot up. 'Shopping?'

'For baby stuff. I was thinking, it would be nice to go out for a walk with the baby, but we don't have a pram.'

He rolled his eyes and sat down on the bed, sprawling back against the pillows as if he belonged there. Sadly not...

'You're going to take me pram shopping, aren't you?' he said faintly, and she started to laugh.

'You great big wuss, you can cope with it!'

'Twice? Dear God. I tell you, I shall have a lot more respect for women in future!' He tipped his head on one side and his face gentled. 'Are you sure you're up to it?' he asked softly. 'It's only been eight days.'

'I think so. I'll be careful.'

'Too right you'll be careful. I'll make sure of it. So when do you want to go?'

She sighed. 'I'd say as soon as I've fed him, but that seems to be pretty unreliable as an indicator of how long we've got before he wants more.'

'He's hungry. He's catching up.'

'Well, at least he eats like you and doesn't pick at his food!' she teased. 'Head down, get on with it, get it over.'

He smiled. 'It's only because I've spent so many years in hospitals and if you want hot food you have to grab the chance. So, if you feed him now and I make us something to eat while you do that, and then we make a dash for it as soon as he's done, we've probably got long enough to get part-way through the first pram demonstration—'

She threw a pillow at him, which was silly because it hurt her incision, but it was satisfying.

He caught it, put it down and shook his head.

'Steady, now. No pillow fights.'

Her breath hitched. They'd had a pillow fight once, and she'd lost—if you could call it that. She'd ended up under him, pinned to the bed by his long, solid leg across her, her hands manacled above her head by his firm, strong fingers, and he'd slowly and thoroughly plundered her body.

Matt watched her from the bed, his heart thudding slowly, the memory that was written clearly across her face still fresh in his mind. He'd held her down, and slowly and thoroughly explored every inch of her, and she'd loved every second of it—

Josh began to cry in earnest, yanking him back to reality, and he got off the bed and headed for the door. 'Why don't you feed him and I'll make you a drink and something to eat, and then we can go.'

He left her to it, getting out before he said or did something inappropriate, and as he reached the bottom of the stairs he heard her door close softly. He let his breath out, went into the kitchen and put the kettle on, and stared blankly into the fridge.

They needed a supermarket shop—and he needed an urgent appointment with a psychiatrist. Thinking about Amy lying naked beneath him was hardly the most sensible or intelligent thing for him to focus on at the moment—or ever, possibly.

He made some sandwiches—cheese and pickle, because that was about all there was and she could do with the calcium—and then carried them up to her.

He'd seen her breastfeeding loads of times, but suddenly—because of the pillow fight remark?—it took on a whole new dimension. He put the plate and cup down on the bedside table next to her and left her to it, taking his out into the conservatory so he could try to focus on something other than Amy and her body.

The pram shopping was every bit as mind-boggling and confusing as it had been the first time, but Amy took it in her stride. It seemed to make sense to her—women, he thought, must be hard-wired to that kind of stuff—and within an hour she'd chosen a travel system that seemed to do everything except fold itself.

And it had a baby seat that used the same base he had for his car, which meant greater flexibility. Excellent. It would be delivered on Monday morning, and all they needed now were the other things on her list, so she sent him off with Josh to browse.

'I need some things for me,' she said, colouring slightly in an endearing way that made him want to smile. He restrained himself until he'd turned away, just nodded and left her to it, the baby seat hanging from his hand. He was getting used to it, to the looks they were getting, the oohs and aahs because Josh was so tiny—and such a beautiful baby. Or was that just paternal pride? He looked down and met those staggering blue eyes staring up at him, and beamed. Nah. He was gorgeous. The pride was justified.

He glanced back and saw her examining a nursing bra, and he closed his eyes and tried not to think about her body. Inappropriate. Concentrate.

He took Josh to look at cots instead—travel cots, for starters, so they could take him down to London with them and stay in his house there on occasions. He hadn't discussed it with Amy, but he knew it was a possibility, so he found the same assistant who'd been so helpful over the buggy and was talked through the folding cots.

And it dawned on him very rapidly that this baby, tiny though he might be, was going to make a significant difference to his life. Starting with his car.

He sighed. He'd only had it four months, but it simply wouldn't fit all the paraphernalia of a baby on the move.

He glanced across at the underwear department and spotted her at the till. Good, because they had a lot to do. Or he did. Starting with the joys of the supermarket, and leading on to a little light surfing of estate cars on the internet.

His phone beeped at him, and he slid it out of his pocket and frowned at the screen. It was a text from Ben, telling him that their parents were coming down tomorrow for a flying visit. He blew out his breath, estate cars forgotten. He'd thought they were leaving it till next weekend, but apparently not. He glanced across at Amy again. He wasn't sure if she was up to such an emotional and stressful day. Not yet, but if they were coming down especially...

And then just to complicate it even further, Josh started to cry. He swung the baby seat by the handle, long slow swings to rock him off again, but he wasn't having any and Matt gave in.

'Come along, little man, let's go and find your mummy,' he said, and headed towards the tills.

She heard them coming, the new-baby cry going straight to her breasts and making them prickle. Damn. She'd forgotten breast pads. 'Over there,' the assistant said, and she grabbed a box and put it on the pile.

'I've just had a text from my parents,' he said as he arrived from her side, and she felt a sudden flurry of nerves. She hadn't seen them since Ben and Daisy's wedding, she hadn't spoken to them yet, and she wasn't at all sure she could cope with it.

'Where are they staying? You're in my spare room and Ben and Daisy have got Florence for the weekend.'

'I don't know that they are. I think it's a flying visit, because they have to have someone to look after the dogs. I think they were talking about coming down to see Thomas next weekend, but they've obviously just brought it forwards.'

'I didn't even know it was on the cards,' she pointed out, and he smiled wryly.

'Nor did I, really. Mum just sprang it on me. It'll be OK, though, I'll get some biscuits or something while I'm at the supermarket and you can just sit there and drink tea and let them admire him. They're thrilled, Amy, really thrilled, and you won't have to do anything.'

Was that what he thought? That she was worried about having to do things? She wasn't, not at all, but apart from a brief hug and a fleeting exchange at the wedding, the last conversation she'd had with his mother had been after she'd lost Samuel, and for all his reassurance that they were thrilled, she wondered if it would be a little awkward because she'd kept Josh a secret.

Oh, this was so hard! She thanked the assistant, scooped up her shopping and headed for the door, Matt at her side with the now-screaming baby. She fed him in the back of the car, sitting in the car park, and then they drove straight home and he dropped her off with Josh and went shopping, leaving her alone.

It was the first time he'd left her since she'd come out of hospital, she realised, except for odd trips to the corner shop, and she was glad to have a little peace and quiet.

Not that he was noisy, exactly, but having him there

was just—disturbing? As if there was an electric current running through her all the time, making her tingle.

She changed Josh's nappy, and the baby, full and contented, didn't even stir as she put him in the Moses basket. And the bed looked so inviting. Could she snatch half an hour?

Sure she could. Why not?

She slipped off her shoes, climbed onto the bed fully clothed and fell straight asleep.

The house was in silence when he got back. He'd put the car in the car port at the back, and carried the shopping through to the kitchen via the conservatory, so he hadn't used the front door, which was right under her bedroom.

Maybe she hadn't heard him come in—and maybe she was resting?

He crept upstairs as quietly as he could and stuck his head round the door, to find her lying curled on the bed, fast asleep, the baby flat out in the Moses basket next to her. It made him smile, but it brought a lump to his throat as well.

How was it possible to love someone so small so very, very much? And so soon? Or still to love a woman for all these years, even though she'd made it clear she didn't want to spend her life with him? Or hadn't. Maybe now it would be different, but maybe only because of Josh.

Maybe if she changed her mind now, it would be for practical reasons, perhaps the same reasons she'd agreed to marry him last time? And as soon as that reason had no longer existed, she'd called off the wedding.

She surely wouldn't have done that if she'd loved him.

He backed out of the room and went downstairs, his

heart suddenly heavy. He'd managed to convince himself that it was going to be wonderful, but now he felt a flicker of doubt.

Well, more than a flicker. Oh, hell.

He needed to *do* something, something concrete rather than wandering around on a knife edge. If the garden hadn't been largely paved, he'd go and dig it or mow the lawn or something, but there was nothing to do.

But there was something he could do, something he needed to do, no matter what happened with him and Amy, because he had a son, regardless, and that was already making its impact felt.

He'd put the kettle on already, so he made himself tea, went out into the conservatory with his laptop and started researching estate cars.

They heard his parents arrive the next day—the sound of the doorbell ringing faintly in the distance, the cries of delight as they went through to the garden and found Daisy there with the baby.

She met Matt's eyes, and he smiled reassuringly and gave her hand a quick squeeze.

'It'll be fine,' he promised her.

It was. He gave them twenty minutes, then got to his feet and headed for the garden, dropping a fleeting kiss on her head in passing. She could see him as he stuck his head over the fence and grinned. 'Permission to come aboard?' he asked, and Ben opened the gate in the fence to let him through.

She could hear them laughing, hear the warmth of their greeting from her seat in the conservatory, and her palms felt suddenly prickly with nerves. She hoped—

she desperately hoped—that they wouldn't come as a tribe, all the Walker clan in force to overwhelm her.

She should have known Liz, of all people, would have had more common sense. Matt's mother slipped quietly through the gate on her own, came into the conservatory and bent to gather Amy into her arms for a motherly hug.

'Oh, it's so good to see you,' she said softly, then let her go and sat beside her, holding her hand. 'How are you? Matthew said you'd had a dreadful time.'

She gave a quiet laugh. 'Apparently. I don't really remember very much about it.'

Liz smiled. 'Lucky you, from what I gather. You had both my boys worried there. And are you OK now?'

She nodded. 'I think so. Getting there.'

'And the baby?'

'Pick him up, see for yourself. He's about to wake up anyway.'

'Sure?'

She smiled, feeling herself relax. Liz was a midwife, too, and she knew she could trust her absolutely with her precious son. 'Sure,' she echoed, and Liz turned back the little cover and pressed her fingers to her lips, her eyes flooding.

'Oh, he's so tiny! Oh, bless his little heart, what a beautiful baby. Oh, Amy. You must be overjoyed.'

She nodded, but then for some inexplicable reason she started to cry, and Liz crouched beside her, rubbing her back and making soothing noises.

'Oh, sweetheart,' she murmured. 'It must have been so scary for you on your own—you're a silly girl, you should have told us, we could have looked after you. I could have come down.'

She sniffed and stared at her, the tears welling again at her kindness. 'Why would you do that?'

'Oh, poppet, do you need to ask? You were going to be my daughter, and I've never forgotten you. I've worried about you all these years, and I worried about you at the wedding, too. I could see how strong the pull was between you—and to be honest I never believed that cock-and-bull story of Matthew's about getting something from his room. A blind man could have seen the way it was with you that night, and it was only going to end one way. It was what might happen afterwards that worried me most, because I thought it had the capacity to hurt you both dreadfully, and I wasn't sure who I was most worried about, you or him.'

'Why would you worry about me? He's your son.'

'Because you left so much unfinished business between you,' she said quietly. 'So much sorrow and pain. And I don't know about you, but I don't think Matthew's ever really dealt with it.'

She nodded. 'I think you're right. I don't think either of us have really dealt with it.'

'You need to. And Joshua will help you—he'll help to heal you.'

'He already is,' she said, her eyes going automatically to her little son. His legs were starting to go, his arms flailing, and any moment now he'd begin to wail. 'I think he needs a cuddle with his grannie,' she said softly, and Liz got to her feet again and picked him up, crooning to him as she cradled him in her arms and introduced herself to him.

'Oh, he's so like Matthew.'

'Not Ben?'

She laughed. 'Not so much, no. They were different, even at Josh's age—but only I could see it. He lies in the same way, with his arms flung up. Ben never did that.'

He started to grizzle and turn his head towards her, and Liz smiled and held him out to her. 'Yours, I think,' she said, and handed him over. 'That's the wonderful thing about being a grandmother, so I'm told. You just hand them back when they need attention.'

Why on earth had she worried?

They were lovely. The visit was only short, and they all ended up having lunch under the tree in Ben and Daisy's garden, the two proud grandparents cuddling the babies in turn while Amy sat with Daisy and enjoyed the luxury of being redundant for a few hours.

Florence was there, too, pushing her own 'baby' round in its buggy, and she announced that Mummy was having a new baby for her, so she'd have two brothers soon. She seemed utterly delighted at the idea, and she was sweet with the babies, and with Daisy.

And there it was again, the knowledge that Samuel was missing from the scene. He would have been a little older than Florence, and Amy could imagine them playing, the four children growing up together. But it would never be…

'What's up?'

Matt's voice was soft in her ear, and she turned her head and found him crouched behind her, her eyes searching. 'Nothing,' she lied, but his smile told her he knew she was lying.

'Can I get you anything?'

She shook her head. 'Actually, I think I might have a lie down. I'm feeling tired.'

He laughed softly. 'Me, too. These ruptured nights are a bit wearing.'

'Ruptured?' she said with a smile, and he smiled back and leant over and kissed her cheek.

'You know what I mean,' he said, and straightened up. 'I'll take him, Dad. I think he probably needs feeding, and Amy's ready for a rest, so we'll leave you to it. Thanks for coming, it's been lovely to see you.'

'Come up soon,' his mother said, and he nodded, but he wasn't making any promises. It all depended on Amy, and Harrogate—well, Harrogate held all manner of memories.

They were hugged and kissed, and then they made their escape. And somehow, after she'd fed him and Matt had put him back in the Moses basket in the bedroom, he ended up lying down on the bed next to her, the soft sound of his breathing somehow soothing.

'I'm glad they came,' she murmured. 'It was so nice to see them again. Your mother was lovely to me.'

He turned his head. 'Why wouldn't she be?'

'No reason. She's been worried about me, apparently.'

'Of course she has. We all have.'

'She's worried about you, too.'

He sighed. 'She's got a point, Amy. We're both in limbo, have been for years.'

He turned so he was facing her, lying on his side just inches away, his head propped on his hand. 'Why don't you come back with me to London tomorrow for a couple of days? I only have to pop into the hospital for a short while, and you could sit in my garden and watch the birds while I'm out, and then we can take Josh for a walk in the park.'

She frowned. 'You don't have a garden.'

'Yes, I do—I don't live in the flat any more. I thought

you realised that. I moved to a mews cottage just a few doors from Rob.'

That surprised her. They'd often visited his friend, and she'd always said how much she loved his house. It wasn't large, but it had a garage and a garden, unusually for London, and the little cobbled lane that ran between two streets was filled with flowers and potted plants outside the houses.

They'd even talked about moving there, but then she'd lost the baby and everything had stopped.

Except he'd done it, anyway, bought one of the houses and was living their dream alone.

Why?

Because it had made economic sense, or because he hadn't been able to let the dream go?

Only one way to find out.

'That sounds lovely,' she said, feeling—excited? Maybe. She hadn't felt excited about anything in this way for years, and she smiled at him. 'Really lovely. How did you know I had cabin fever?'

He smiled back and reached out a hand, touching her face. It was the lightest touch, the merest whisper of his fingers over her cheek, but it set all her senses on fire, and for a breathless, endless moment she was frozen there, eyes locked with his, her entire body motionless.

And then he dropped his hand and rolled off the bed.

'I'll leave you to rest. I've got things to do. Give me a call if you need anything.'

Only you, she thought, but she said nothing.

It was too soon, and this time, she was going to make absolutely sure of what she was doing before she committed herself to Matt again.

CHAPTER NINE

THEY left for London after the travel system was delivered.

Matt spent an hour trying to work out how to put it all together, then eventually, temper fraying, managed to get the frame and the carrycot into the boot of his car. There was no room for their luggage except on the back seat beside the baby, and he frowned at it.

There was nowhere else he could put it, so he made sure there was nothing heavy loose in the cabin, squashed their bags behind the seats and resolved to get an estate car at the first possible opportunity.

Tomorrow would be good.

Then as soon as he was fed and changed, they strapped Josh into the car seat and set off.

'It's like going on an expedition to the Antarctic,' he grumbled, sounding so exasperated and confused that Amy laughed.

He shot her a dirty look, sighed and then joined in, his bad mood evaporating rapidly. Why would he be grumpy? The woman he loved was in the seat beside him, his baby son was in the back, and they were going to see the house where he hoped—please God not in vain—that they'd live together.

No. He wasn't grumpy. He was just driving the

wrong car. Easily fixable. The accommodation issue was far harder, and he ran his eye mentally over the house. Was it clean? Tidy? He'd issued the invitation without a thought, but he couldn't remember how he'd left it and his cleaner came in once a fortnight. Had she been?

No idea. The days since Josh had burst into his life had blurred together so he didn't have a clue where he was any more. With Josh and Amy, he told himself. That was the only thing that mattered. The state of the house was irrelevant.

The house was lovely.

It was just a few doors from Rob's, and it was bigger, the one they'd often talked about because it looked tatty and run-down and in need of love.

Well, not any more. It looked immaculate, the sash windows all renovated, by the look of it, the brass on the front door gleaming, and she couldn't wait to see what he'd done to it, especially the garden. It had had the most amazing wisteria, she remembered, sprawling all over the garden. Had he been able to save it? He pressed a button on his key fob and the roller-shutter on his garage door slid quietly up out of the way, and he drove in and cut the engine.

'Home,' he said with satisfaction, and she felt a strange and disorientating sense of loss. How odd. She had a home. Except of course it wasn't hers, not really. She was only living there on a temporary basis, on Ben's insistence, but now that Matt was back in her life, there was no need for that.

'What's up?'

She opened her mouth to tell him, and thought better

of it. 'Nothing,' she said. 'It's the house we used to talk about. You didn't tell me that. It took me by surprise.'

'It didn't look like a very nice surprise,' he said quietly, and she realised he sounded—what? Disappointed?

'It's a lovely surprise,' she assured him. 'I can't wait to see it.'

'I can't guarantee what it's like, it might be a tip,' he warned, unclipping Josh's seat and heading for a door. 'Come on in.'

It was beautiful. They went straight into the kitchen, a light and airy room with doors out into the garden. There was a sofa at one end, and a television, and she guessed he used this room more than any other. She could see why, with the garden just there, and it looked lovely. Far less overgrown, of course, but lush and inviting, a real oasis in the middle of the city. It was a little smaller than Daisy's, and the painted brick walls that surrounded it gave it a delightfully secret feel.

He opened the doors and they went out, and she could hear birds singing and smell the most heavenly scent—from the old wisteria scrambling up the back wall of the house.

'You saved it!'

His mouth twisted into a smile, and he reached out a hand and touched her cheek. 'I had to keep it after everything you'd said about it. It reminded me of you.'

What could she say to that? Nothing. She was picking her way through a minefield again, and she felt suddenly slightly nervous. 'Can I see the rest?'

'Sure.'

He left the doors open, and they went past a cloakroom and upstairs to the hall. The front door came in there, accessed from the mews by old stone steps that she'd noticed were covered in pots, and off the front of the hall was a study, and behind it a sitting room.

'You haven't got a dining room,' she said, and he gave a wry smile.

'I don't really need one. I've got a breakfast bar, and I eat there. I don't really entertain like that. Come and see the bedrooms.'

She followed him up and found three rooms, two small ones over the front, and a larger one, obviously his, next to the bathroom at the back.

'It's lovely, Matt. Really, really nice. I love the colours.'

'Yes, they're your sort of colours,' he said softly, and she noticed he wasn't smiling. Why? And why put it like that, as if he'd chosen the colours because she'd like them—unless…?

'I'm glad you like it. I was sort of hoping that maybe one day you might—' He broke off, shrugged and turned away, heading back down the stairs. 'Tea?'

'Sounds lovely.' *Might what?* She followed him thoughtfully.

'Why don't you have a potter round the kitchen and make us some tea while I bring in all the luggage?' he suggested, putting Josh down on the floor by the sofa, and she filled the kettle and searched through the cupboards.

It was logically organised, as she might have expected from Matt. Mugs over the kettle, tea and coffee beside them in the next cupboard, cutlery in the drawer underneath.

Nice mugs, she thought. Plain white bone china. She looked around, frowning slightly. The kitchen was the sort of kitchen she'd fantasised about, a hand-built painted Shaker kitchen, with granite worktops and integrated appliances. The garden was heavy with the scent of the wisteria she'd said she loved. Everything about it—*everything*—was how she would have done it.

Had he done it for her? she wondered, and she felt her eyes fill with tears.

'You haven't got very far with the tea.'

She switched the kettle on to boil again and reached for the mugs. 'When did you buy the house?' she asked,turning to look at him, and he went still.

'Um—it came on the market just after…'

'After we lost Samuel,' she finished for him softly.

He nodded. 'I thought…' He shook his head. 'It doesn't matter.'

'I think it does. I think it matters a lot.'

He let his breath out very slowly, and turned to face her, his eyes wary and yet revealing. 'I hoped—one day—that you might come back to me. That we might live here, together, as we'd talked about. Build a new life, start again. Then I realised it wasn't going to happen, but I finished it anyway, because it was handy for the hospital and—well, I loved it.'

She didn't know what to say, because it hadn't been an invitation, as such, more a statement of why and how he'd done it. And she wasn't sure if it was still current, if the hope was still alive. And if it was, she wasn't sure what her answer would be, so she just nodded slowly, and turned her back on him and made the tea, and by the time she'd finished, he'd found some biscuits and taken Josh out into the garden so they could sit near the wisteria and soak up the last of the sunshine.

The subject was dropped, and he talked instead about work, about the people she'd known and what they were doing, that Rob was married now and had a child, a little girl of one, and another on the way, and how Tina, one of the other midwives, had finally convinced her registrar boyfriend to marry her—lightweight gossip that distracted her from the delicate subject of their relationship.

Then Josh woke, starving hungry and indignant, and she fed him, the sudden blissful silence broken only by the twittering of the birds and the muted hum of the traffic in the distance.

'I need to do some work,' Matt said suddenly, getting up. 'Make yourself at home. I'll be down in a while.'

She nodded, but he'd already gone, heading upstairs to his study, no doubt, and leaving her alone to ponder on his motivation and what, if anything, this new information might mean to her.

He stood upstairs at the sitting room window, staring down at her and wondering why he'd brought her here.

He'd been longing to, for years now, but at least before he couldn't actually picture her here. Now, though, her image would be everywhere, her presence almost tangible in every room. If this didn't work out…

It had to work out. There was no acceptable alternative—at least not to him. Not one he could live with.

He dialled the hospital number and asked them to page his registrar and get him to call him, then he stood there staring broodingly down at her until the phone rang. Only then did he take his eyes off her, go into the study, shut the door and concentrate on work. At least that was something he had some control over.

They stayed in London for two days, and for Amy they were idyllic.

She spent a lot of time in the garden with Josh, and

when Matt was there they walked to the little park just two streets away. It had a playground for little children, and she found herself imagining bringing Josh here when he was older.

Which was silly, because she lived in Suffolk, not London. It was where her job was, and just because Matt had hoped she'd come back to him five years ago didn't mean they were going to make it work now.

Which meant Matt would be bringing Josh here on his own at the weekends, she realised, and felt suddenly incredibly sad.

He'd been taking photos of her with the baby in the park, sitting under the trees and strolling with the buggy, and she took the camera from him and photographed them together, the two men in her life—except Matt might not be.

There was still a wariness about him, a distance from her, and she wasn't sure why it was. Protecting himself from further hurt? She could understand that, but the image of him playing here alone with his son was too awful to contemplate.

Going back to Yoxburgh was strange, and not necessarily in a good way.

They quickly settled, though, and Matt went back to London in the middle of Saturday night because they'd had a multiple pregnancy admitted and the staff were worried about the babies.

He came back on Tuesday, having delivered the triplets, and he was sombre.

'We lost one,' he told her, when she asked, and she wished she hadn't—which was ridiculous, because she worked as a midwife, she knew these things happened.

But he looked gutted, and for the first time really she

wondered how *he* dealt with stillbirth, not from the patients' viewpoint but his own.

'I'm sorry,' she said, hugging him, and he held her close for a moment, his head rested against hers, drawing strength from her. God, he needed her. He'd missed her, the last few days interminable without her and Josh, and sad though he was, it was good to be home.

Home? he thought. This wasn't home! This was Amy's home, and he had to remember that. He was getting too comfortable. Too settled.

And in too deep.

They went backwards and forwards between London and Yoxburgh for the next three weeks, the journey being made much easier by the fact that he'd changed his car for an estate version, so at least she knew he was serious about being a hands-on father. Very hands on. He got up in the night almost without fail and made her tea, staying to chat while she fed Josh and then change him and settle him again, and when she was exhausted he sent her back to bed in the day and did everything except the breast feeds. And gradually she grew stronger and fitter, her incision felt almost normal and she started talking about going back to work.

Matt was astounded. 'You can't! How can you do that? You've been ill—you've had a section!'

'Matt, I'm fine! I'm all right now, and I have no choice. If I don't work, I've got no way of paying my living expenses.'

'I'll pay you maintenance.'

'Why should you?'

'Because he's my son?'

She shook her head. 'That's different, but I need to

earn a living for me. I don't need maintenance from you for that, I can cope on my salary—'

'Only because Ben and Daisy aren't charging you the proper rent for this house.'

She stared at him, stunned. 'Matt, they won't take it! I've offered, but they won't take any more.'

'Only because they know you haven't got it, and that's unfair, Amy, it's taking advantage of their friendship and good nature, and it's costing them hundreds of pounds every month.'

She felt her mouth hanging open, and shut it. Of course it was—she knew that, but she'd avoided thinking about it. Now he'd brought it so forcibly to her attention, she was gutted. They'd seemed to want her there so much—and because she'd needed the house, she hadn't challenged it hard enough, she'd taken their argument about being choosy about their tenant at face value.

'They said they wanted me,' she said, shocked, and he shrugged.

'They do, and they can have you. They can have you, Amy, but at the proper rent, and I'll pay you maintenance so you can afford to live here. But what about Josh? You haven't answered that one yet. What'll happen to him when you go back to work?'

'I'll put him in the crèche.'

'Have you booked? Because places are usually tight, and it's tricky with shift work. And childcare is hideously expensive. Are you sure you can afford it? Have you looked into the costs?'

No, of course she hadn't. She hadn't done any of it because she hadn't dared to believe it would be all right, and now she felt sick with worry and shame and guilt towards Ben and Daisy. She bit her lip, and he shook his head and sighed.

'Amy, do you *really* want to go back to work so soon? Or is this a purely economic decision? Because if it is, you don't have to work if you don't want to. I can afford to support you, but I want to be part of his life, and part of yours. And if you moved back to London, we could do all of that. It would be amazing. You've said you like my house, and we could live there and you could be at home with him and enjoy his babyhood, and I'd get to see him growing up.'

It was the obvious answer, of course. If she lived with him, it would cost him hardly anything to support her, and he'd be with his son. But how much of it was to do with her and how much he loved her?

Because he'd never said those words, in all these weeks of talking and getting to know each other again. Never once had he said he loved her, or tried in any way to touch her, kiss her, hold her in anything other than a supportive way.

And she realised she had no idea at all where she stood.

'What happens when something goes wrong, Matt? If I leave behind my job, my home, my friends—I'd have to start again. I've done that once. Believe me, I don't want to do it again.'

'What makes you think anything would go wrong?'

'Experience,' she said quietly, and to her relief Josh woke at that moment and she had a legitimate excuse to leave the room.

He didn't say any more about it that day, and the following day he left her in Suffolk and went back to London on his own. Maybe, he thought, it was time to let her cope alone for a while, ease himself out of her life and let her see what it was like.

He was helping her with all nappy changing and bathing, he did all the shopping, all the housework, he watered the garden and weeded the flowerbeds and washed her car and cleaned the windows—mostly to fill the time between feeds because he didn't trust himself not to rush her if he was alone with her. She'd been so ill, was still getting over major surgery, whatever she might say to the contrary, and the last thing she needed was him coming on to her.

So he took himself off out of her life, and rattled round his house alone and missed her every single minute he wasn't at work.

And then he got to work one morning and checked the calendar.

It was the date they'd lost Samuel, he realised with shock. He'd never forgotten it before, never overlooked it. He was always in Harrogate on that day, always took flowers to the cemetery, but this time he had Amy to think about, and maybe it was time they confronted this issue together, today of all days.

He cleared his workload, delegated his clinics and left London, arriving back at Amy's house in Yoxburgh without warning and finding her sitting in the conservatory in tears. He'd let himself in with his keys, and he wondered if he should have done or if she minded.

'Hey,' he said softly, crouching down and touching her face with a gentle hand. 'It's OK, I'm here now.'

'I'm all right,' she lied, and he knew she wasn't, because her face was blotched and tearstained and her eyes were swollen and she was in a sea of soggy tissues.

He knew just how she felt. He'd done the same thing every year, but this year he'd been more worried about her, and he scooped her up and carried her into the sitting room and cradled her on his lap as she cried.

Then finally she sniffed to halt and tried to sit up, but he wouldn't let her, just held her against his chest and she gave in and rested her head on his shoulder and laid her hand over his heart.

Could she feel that it was broken?

She looked up at him, and with a soft sigh she wiped away his tears. 'When is it going to end?'

He kissed her gently, his lips tasting the salt of her tears, and he sighed quietly.

'I don't know. I don't know if it'll ever truly go.'

She closed her eyes, and the welling tears slid down her cheeks, breaking his heart still further. 'I just wish I had somewhere to go—a focus for my grief. Somewhere I could go and remember him, once in a while. All I've got is the scan photo and my armband from the hospital. Nothing else.'

'There is something else,' he said softly, kicking himself for never thinking of it, never telling her, never sharing their grief. If only he'd known how she felt, if only he'd thought about it. 'I asked the hospital to arrange his cremation, and I went to the...' He couldn't say funeral. 'To the service,' he went on, after a moment. 'The hospital chaplain said a few words, and they scattered his ashes in the garden there. I go every year and put flowers in the garden, but they wrote his name in the Book of Remembrance, and I'm sure you can view it. I'm so sorry, I should have told you, but I'd just put it out of my mind.'

She stared at him blankly. 'There's a book with his name in it? Can we see it?'

He nodded. 'I think so. I'm pretty sure you can. I'll have to phone, but I think so.'

'Phone them now. Please, Matt, phone them now! It's only eleven o'clock. Maybe we could go today.'

He used his phone to find the number, and rang. Half an hour later they were heading north on their way to Yorkshire, the baby fed, Amy's clothes packed haphazardly, but that wasn't what mattered. What mattered was that they were together, today, and anything else was irrelevant.

The book was open at the date, and she ran her finger down the page and found the entry.

Samuel Radcliffe Walker, beloved son of Amy and Matthew. Always in our hearts.

The words swam in front of her eyes, and she sagged against Matt, his arm firmly around her, supporting her. Joshua was on his chest in a baby sling, fast asleep against his father's heart, next to the cherished memory of their other son, and she laid her hand against the baby's back, making the connection.

'I thought he'd been forgotten,' she whispered.

His arm tightened slightly, and she felt his lips brush her hair. 'No. No, Amy, he'll never be forgotten. He'll always be our first son.'

She nodded, her finger tracing the words once more, and then she nodded again and turned away.

'Thank you—thank you so much,' she said to the kindly man who'd shown them the book. He was hovering quietly behind them, giving them space, and Matt shook his hand and thanked him, and led her back outside into the sunshine.

'Where are his ashes?' she asked unsteadily, and Matt showed her the place. He'd never seen the book, but every year he'd brought beautiful cottage garden flowers from a lady who sold them from a little barrow outside her cottage just down the road—real flowers, not a stiff arrangement of scentless hothouse blooms.

They'd bought some on the way here today, and Amy kissed them, then laid them on the grass, taking a moment to remember him and say goodbye, then she straightened up and snuggled against Matt's side, his arm automatically going around her holding her close. He pressed his lips to her hair, and she rested her head against his shoulder as they stood for a moment staring at them, and then she sighed and turned away and they strolled quietly along the paths in the sunshine, arms around each other, hanging on.

They found a bench and sat down, by tacit agreement, not quite ready to leave just yet.

'Are you all right?' he asked softly.

'Mmm. You?'

He smiled wryly. 'I'll do.'

'Thank you—for bringing me here, for coming to see me. I'm not normally that bad. It seemed worse this year, somehow.'

'Mmm. Maybe it's having Josh. It sort of underlines what we've lost,' he said, his voice unsteady, and she nodded.

'I'm so glad we came. I feel so much better now—as if I've done something I've been waiting all these years to do. And I'm glad you were there for his funeral. How did you do that?' she asked, bewildered. 'I wouldn't have been strong enough. How did you cope?'

He gave a hollow little laugh. 'I didn't really. Mum offered to come, but I wanted to do it alone. I didn't want anyone seeing me like that. I was in denial, and if nobody saw me, I could pretend it wasn't happening.'

'That was why I ran away to India,' she admitted. 'So nobody I knew would see me as I fell apart.'

'You were in India?'

'Yes. I went backpacking on my own. Probably not the most sensible thing, but while I was there I spent a couple of weeks living on the fringe of a village where the child mortality rate was dreadful, so it put it in perspective.'

'I'll bet. Amy, I had no idea. I thought you were somewhere in London, one of the other hospitals. I didn't try to find out, either. I thought, if you didn't want me, there was no point in pursuing it.'

She turned and looked at him, seeing the pain in his eyes, and she shook her head slowly. 'It wasn't that I didn't want you, it was that I felt you didn't want me.'

He gave a soft grunt of laughter. 'Oh, I wanted you, Amy. I've never stopped wanting you. I just didn't know how to talk to you, how to deal with it. Mum suggested bereavement counselling, but I turned it down flat because I didn't want to be made to think about it.' He touched her face, his fingers gentle, and his eyes were filled with sorrow.

'I let you down. I'm sorry.'

'I let you down, too. I should have stayed in England, talked to you instead of letting you shut yourself away. I never wanted to end our relationship, Matt, I just couldn't cope with the idea of a party. That great big wedding, with all our family and friends all gathered there just weeks after we'd lost him—it seemed wrong, somehow. It would have been wrong.'

He nodded. 'It would, but I wasn't sure then if it would ever be right, or if we'd lost each other as well along the way. And then you disappeared off the face of the earth, and I bought the house, in case you changed your mind and decided you wanted me after all, but you never did. You'd handed in your notice, and you were gone.'

'You could have found me. I'm a registered midwife, you could have tracked me down.'

He smiled. 'Probably not legally, but I wasn't sure I wanted to. You knew where I was. I thought, when you were ready, you'd come back to me, but you never did, and I gave up hope.'

'And then Ben met Daisy, and there you were again in my life,' she said softly. 'And now we have another son.'

'We do, and I have a feeling he has rising damp,' he said with a smile.

She laughed quietly and felt the edge of his little shorts. 'Oops. I think you might be right.'

'Can you cope with my parents?' he asked, his eyes concerned, and she smiled and nodded.

'Yes. Yes, I can cope with them. I'd love to see them. Can they cope with us, though?'

'I'm sure they can.'

They were overjoyed to see them.

There were more tears, and tea, and lots of hugs, and then they offered to babysit so Matt could take Amy out for dinner.

'Go and have a quiet meal somewhere by yourselves. We can cope. You can express some milk and we can feed him if he wakes.'

'We haven't got any bottles,' Amy said, but Liz had an answer.

'Ben and Daisy have been up here and they brought a steriliser and some bottles with them so we could look after Thomas. Now what else are you going to come up with as an excuse?' she teased, and Amy laughed.

'Nothing. Thank you. Dinner out with Matt would be lovely.'

'In which case, if you'll excuse me, I have a phone call to make,' Matt said, and he dropped a kiss in Amy's palm, closed her fingers over it to keep it safe and with a little wink he walked out with a spring in his stride she hadn't seen for years.

'Right. Let's get these bottles sterilised,' Liz said. 'I don't want you two having any excuses for coming home early.'

CHAPTER TEN

'WHICH rooms do you want us to have?'

His mother searched his eyes, and he lifted his shoulders in an almost invisible shrug, but she understood, it seemed, because she just smiled.

'Yours and Ben's are already made up, and the crib's in Ben's already.'

He nodded. They had a communicating door, which would mean he could help Amy with Josh in the night— and if things went the way he hoped, they'd only need his room.

He took the luggage up, opened the windows and stood staring out over the familiar countryside and breathing in the glorious fresh air. He loved London, loved his job, but it was good to come home.

'Matt?'

He turned and smiled at Amy. 'Hi. I've put your things in Ben's room with Josh's. There's a changing mat in there, and the crib, which might make life easier.'

She looked at the crib, rocking it gently with one finger, memories washing over her. It was one of two that Matt's father had made for their boys, and Liz had shown them to her when she'd been pregnant with Samuel. 'The baby will be able to sleep in one when you come and stay,' she'd said, only Samuel had never needed a crib, and now his brother and his cousin would be sleeping in them.

She waited for the wave of pain, but there was only a gentle sorrow, a quiet acceptance that this was the way things were, and now she could move on, with Josh—and Matt?

She felt a tingle of anticipation, and turned to find him standing in the doorway, watching her.

'OK?'

She nodded. 'Yes. So—where are we going for dinner?'

He smiled. 'A place Ben recommended. It's—um—it's quite smart,' he said, 'but you're about the same size as Mum. I wonder if she's got anything you could borrow?'

She looked down at her baggy jersey dress and leggings, soft and comfortable and easy to wear, but not exactly smart dining. 'Let's hope so or you might be cancelling the reservation!' she said lightly, and went to find Liz.

'Oh, gosh—right. Um—come and see. I'm sure I've got something.'

She had. A lovely black lace dress, soft and stretchy and elegant, and although her tummy was still a little bigger than she would have liked, the dress fitted beautifully and she wasn't ashamed in any way of her post-pregnancy figure.

'It's lovely, Liz. Are you sure?'

'Of course I'm sure. How about a little pashmina? I've got one that I wear with it to keep the chill off, and it might get cold later.'

She borrowed them both, but stuck to her little flat black pumps. They had sparkly gems on the toe and they fitted, more to the point.

She showered and then tipped out her bag, hunting through the things she'd thrown into it in haste on the way up, and then wailed.

'What's up?'

Matt appeared in the doorway, and she pulled the borrowed dressing gown tighter round her. 'No knickers.'

'Ah.' He disappeared, and came back a moment later dangling a scrap of cream lace from one finger.

She frowned and snatched them from his fingertip. 'They're mine!'

'Yup. I must have scooped them up with the suit and things the morning after the wedding. I didn't exactly pack carefully.'

'No.' He hadn't. He scooped everything up and shoved it in the bag, and she hadn't been able to find the tiny lace shorts. 'So what are they doing here?'

'They were in my case—in the pocket. I found them and washed them—I meant to give them back to you ages ago, but I shoved them in the case and just forgot. You talking about it reminded me.'

'Thanks. They'll go a treat with the nursing bra.'

He started to laugh, and then he pulled her into his arms and hugged her close, pressing a kiss to her forehead. 'You're gorgeous, Amy. You don't need sexy underwear to turn me on.'

And just like that, with those few words, her body came alive in his arms. Her breath caught in her throat, her heart speeded up, and she took a shaky step back and met his eyes. 'Shoo,' she said, more firmly than she felt. 'I need to feed Josh and express some more milk before we go, and I don't need an audience. If you want to do something useful, you can make me a cup of tea.'

He went, humming softly as he walked away, and she

shut the door and put on the little shorts. They looked all right, she thought, even though she'd gained a little weight. She'd been too thin at the wedding—worrying about seeing him again.

Now, she couldn't wait to be alone with him, and she put on the borrowed makeup—a touch of concealer over the bags under her eyes from the disturbed nights, a streak of eyeshadow over her lids, a flick of mascara. Nothing more. She'd eat the lipstick off in moments, and anyway Matt didn't like kissing lipstick, and she really, really hoped he'd end up kissing her goodnight.

At the very least…

'Mr Walker! Welcome back, sir.'

Matt smiled. 'Sorry—wrong Mr Walker. You're thinking of my twin brother,' he explained with a grin. 'I'm not two-timing Daisy.'

'My apologies, sir—I must say I'm relieved to hear it.' The maitre d' beamed and showed them to their table, set in a quiet alcove. 'I've put you at their favourite table. He caused quite a stir in here the night he proposed to Mrs Walker. How are they?'

'Very well. They had a boy.'

'Ah. I wondered. Well, please give them our congratulations. May I get you a drink?'

'Yes—thank you. Could we have sparkling water?'

'Of course.'

He faded away, and Amy smiled. 'Don't you ever get sick of that happening?'

He grinned. 'No, not really. I'm used to it. It's a bit more complicated when we're working together. We used to wear colour-coded scrubs and shirts to give the staff a clue, but the patients found it confusing.'

'I've never found it confusing.'

'That's because you love me,' he said, and then let his breath out on a sigh and smiled wryly. 'Sorry. Ignore me.'

It was on the tip of her tongue to say yes, he was right, but she didn't, and a waiter appeared with their sparkling water and menus, and they ordered their food. Eventually.

'I can't decide,' she'd said, and he grinned.

'Neither can I. Let's share, then we can have two dishes from each course.'

So they did, swapping plates halfway through, or a little more than half in Matt's case because he was bigger than her and it was only fair, but the food was gorgeous and she was reluctant to let it go.

'I want everything,' she said, and he just laughed and swapped the plates.

'We'll come again,' he said, and she felt a little flutter in her chest.

'Yes, let's.' She looked away to break the tension, and scanned the room with her eyes. 'It's lovely in here, a real find. I can see why Ben and Daisy like it so much.'

'Yes, so can I.'

She sighed softly, her face thoughtful. 'It's so nice being alone with you like this. It seems forever since we did it.'

'It is. The last time we had dinner together was before Samuel.'

She smiled sadly, twisting his heart. 'And all I wanted was peanut butter.'

He nodded. 'I've thought about that. I should have realised at Christmas when you were eating that sandwich.'

'I should have told you. I wanted to, but I was blocking it out, too afraid of what might come out if I let go, and I wanted to protect you, just in case.'

His hand found hers lying on the table, his thumb tracing circles on the soft skin. 'I didn't need protecting, Amy,' he said softly. 'I just needed to share it with you, whatever it was. Promise me you'll never do that again, whatever happens, whatever you're worried about, whatever you're afraid of. Tell me the truth. And I'll do the same. We need to learn to open up to each other, to talk about the things that really matter. And it won't always be easy. It never is, but we have to.'

She nodded. 'I agree.' She hesitated for a moment, then took the first step on that road. 'Can I ask you something about the house?'

He gave a slightly puzzled frown. 'Sure. What about it?'

'Why did you do it like that?'

'Like what?'

'All of it—the kitchen I'd said I liked, the colours, the granite—you even kept the wisteria, and a lawn. We'd talked about needing a lawn for children to play on, although you'd talked about having a modern low-maintenance garden.'

'It is low maintenance. It's mostly paved, and I found I wanted a piece of lawn—just a little bit of home, I suppose,' he said, but then remembered what he'd said about telling the truth, and he smiled wryly. 'And I suppose I hoped that you'd come back to me, that one day we might have another child to play on the lawn. And yeah, I did the kitchen for you, and painted it all for you in your favourite colours. I told you that.'

'But you didn't really say why.'

'For you. I did all of it for you. I wanted you back, Amy, and I still do. I've told you that.'

'You said you wanted me to come and live with you with Josh. I thought—'

She broke off, and he prompted her. 'You thought…?'

'I thought you wanted Josh with you, and it was the easiest way. And the cheapest, if you were talking about paying my rent so I didn't have to worry about money. It would be cheaper and easier and more convenient to have me with you.'

'And you really thought that was why I wanted you to come back to me?' he asked, genuinely shocked. His hand tightened on hers. 'Oh, Amy. I didn't even give the money a thought. I just—it seemed a way to convince you to come back to me. It was nothing to do with Josh, nothing at all. Of course I want to be near him, but I would have moved, would have found a way like Ben did to be near Florence. But I want *you*, Amy. I love you, I always have, I always will, and I don't want to be without you. Josh is amazing, and having him in my life is wonderful, but the thought of my life without you in it is untenable.'

'Really?' She stared at him for ages, and then her eyes filled. 'Oh, Matt. I love you, too. I thought you didn't love me, I thought losing Samuel gave you a way out of a relationship that you hadn't asked for and came to realise you didn't want.'

'Of course I wanted it! Why would I want a way out, Amy? I love you. I'll always love you. I thought four years would be enough to get over you, but I realised at the wedding that I wasn't over you at all, I'd just been marking time.'

'Me, too.' Her smile was gentle, her eyes filled with tears, and suddenly he wanted to be alone with her—completely alone, so he could hold her, touch her, love her.

And lovely though the restaurant was, he'd had enough of it. He glanced up and caught the waiter's eye, and asked for the bill.

'Is everything all right, sir?' he asked worriedly, and Matt smiled.

'Everything's fine. Thank you.'

'Matt?'

He stroked her wrist with his thumb again, tracing the pulse point, feeling it leap. 'I just want to be alone with you,' he said a little gruffly, and her eyes widened slightly. And then she smiled, and ran the tip of her tongue lightly over her lips. He groaned softly and closed his eyes.

'Stop it,' he murmured, as the waiter came back with the bill and the card machine. He didn't even glance at the bill, just keyed in his PIN and left a couple of notes on the table as he ushered Amy out.

They walked to the car in silence, hand in hand, and he drove home as fast as was sensible.

The house was quiet when they got in, a note on the kitchen table. 'All well. Josh is in with us. Sleep well.'

He met her eyes, slid his fingers through hers and led her upstairs to his room. There wasn't a sound in the house except the ticking of the clock, and he closed the door of his room and turned to Amy in the moonlight.

'Come here,' he said gruffly, and wrapped her in his arms, his mouth coming down on hers tentatively, searchingly. He hadn't kissed her since the wedding, not like this, and he wasn't entirely sure of how she'd react. It was still only weeks since Josh's birth, and although she seemed well...

He needn't have worried. She slid her arms around his neck, leant into him and kissed him back with the pent-up longing of all those years without him, and with a groan of satisfaction he let instinct guide him and plundered her mouth with his.

She stopped him after a moment, easing away and looking up at him regretfully. 'Matt, we can't. What if I get pregnant?'

He smiled. 'Don't worry. My brother's a good boy scout. I checked his bedside locker. They've just been to stay.'

'And?'

'And I may have raided it.'

She smiled back, her lips parting on a soft laugh and her eyes creasing. 'Well done,' she said, and went back into his arms.

'So how do you feel about coming back to London to live with me?'

She was propped up against the headboard feeding Joshua, Matt beside her with his arm around her shoulders, and she turned her head and met his eyes.

'It sounds lovely. I'll miss being near Ben and Daisy, but it's not far from them, we can see them often.'

'We can. They're talking of selling both houses and buying something bigger, so we'll be able to go and stay, and I'm sure we can squeeze them in here. And if you really want to work, I'm sure we can find room in the department for another midwife for a few shifts a week—especially if her name's Mrs Walker.'

She went still and searched his eyes. He was smiling, but his eyes were serious and thoughtful. 'I might want to keep my maiden name,' she said, fishing hard because she wasn't quite sure, and the smile spread to his eyes.

'They'll all gossip about us.'

'How will they know?'

'Because I can't keep my hands off you?' he murmured, and she laughed softly.

'Really, Mr Walker, that's so unprofessional.'

'I like to keep tabs on my staff.'

'Well, just make sure you're only keeping those sort of tabs on one member of staff, please,' she scolded, and he chuckled and hugged her closer.

'Absolutely. So—is that a yes?'

'Was that a proposal?'

He smiled wryly. 'I've already asked you once. And I haven't got a ring to give you.'

'I've still got the one you gave me. It's in my jewellery box, with Samuel's scan photo.'

His lips parted, and he let his breath out slowly and hugged her. 'Oh, sweetheart. I thought you would have sold it.'

'Why would I do that?'

He shrugged. 'To fund your trip to India?'

She smiled sadly. 'I could never have sold it, and I didn't need much money in India. All I did was walk along beaches and sleep under the stars and think.'

'On your own? That doesn't sound very safe.'

'I didn't care about safe, Matt, and it didn't cost a lot which was good, because I didn't have much. But I would never have sold your ring. It would be like selling part of myself.'

He picked up her hand, stroking her ring finger softly, his heart pounding. 'Will you wear it for me again?'

'You could ask me again, just so I know you mean it.'

'I just did, and you know I mean it, Amy,' he said, and then gave a rueful laugh and gave up. He wasn't going to get away with it, obviously, but he wasn't going down on one knee. That would mean letting her go and he didn't plan on doing that any time soon, so he shifted so he was facing her, still holding her hand, his eyes locked with hers.

'I love you, my darling, and I want to spend my life with you, and with Josh and any other children that might come along in due course, and I want to grow old with you, so you can trim the hair in my ears and buy me new slippers for Christmas and remind me of where I've left my glasses. So will you marry me? Share your life with me? I'll put your tights on for you when you can't bend over any more, and I promise I won't steal your false teeth.'

She started to laugh, but then her eyes filled with tears and she rested her head on his shoulder and sighed. 'That sounds lovely. So lovely.'

'Even the false teeth and the hair in my ears?' he laughed.

'I'll buy you one of those gadgets. And that's a yes, by the way. I'd love to marry you, as soon as you like, but—can we have a quiet wedding? Just family and a few friends.'

'Sure. Where?'

'Here? In the church where we were going to get married before? And maybe—if we got married on a Saturday, perhaps we could have Josh christened there on the Sunday, while the others are around?'

'That sounds lovely,' he said softly. 'In fact, if you want, maybe the vicar could say a few words before the service, to remember Samuel.'

Her eyes flooded with tears. 'Oh, yes. Oh, Matt, that would be—'

She broke off and he hugged her. 'Shh. Don't cry any more, my love. It's going to be all right.'

'Yes. Yes, it is.' She looked down at Josh, fast asleep at her breast, and smiled tenderly.

'It's all going to be all right.'

The wedding took place in September, on the anniversary weekend of Ben and Daisy's wedding, in the family's little parish church outside Harrogate. It was decorated with flowers from the lady who'd sold them the posy they'd taken to the cemetery, and it looked lovely.

So did Amy.

She was wearing a simple, elegant cream dress—not a wedding dress, because she'd refused to go down that route, and he hadn't wanted to argue with her. Not about their wedding. All he was doing this time was listening. And when he saw her as she walked towards him on his father's arm, carrying a posy of those lovely, natural flowers, Matt thought he'd never seen anyone more beautiful.

It was a short service, but heartfelt, and afterwards they took everyone to the restaurant for a meal to celebrate.

The staff had opened the restaurant specially for the afternoon, and it was a meal to remember. They pulled out all the stops, and the food was amazing, but there were not supposed to be any speeches. Matt said he wasn't going to give Ben a chance to get back at him, but there was some good-natured rivalry and a lot of love, and in the end Ben had his way.

'I don't have a lot to say,' he began, which made Matt laugh so hard he had tears running down his face, but

Ben waited him out with a patient smile, and then he started again.

'I just wanted to say how much this means to all of us, to see the two of you together again. I'm not going to make any cruel jokes about what a lousy brother you've been, because you haven't. You've supported me through some pretty tough times, and I wish I could have done more for you, but I don't suppose anyone could. However, I can take credit for bringing you together again a year ago tomorrow, even if you didn't appreciate it at the time, and the consequences are delightful!'

At that point Josh gave a shrill squeal and banged his rattle on the table in front of Liz, and everyone laughed.

'So, no bad jokes, just a few words to wish you well, and to say how glad we all are that this day has come for you at last. Ladies and gentlemen, can we please raise our glasses to Matt and Amy!'

'Matt and Amy!' they chorused, and Matt leant over and planted a lingering kiss on her lips. It was full of promise, and the smile in his eyes warmed her to the bottom of her heart.

They went back to the farmhouse for the night. As usual they were in Matt's room with Josh, with Ben and Daisy next door with Thomas, and Amy lay there in Matt's arms in blissful contentment.

'All right, my darling?' he murmured, and she made a soft sound of agreement and snuggled closer.

'It was a lovely day.'

'It was. You looked beautiful in that dress.'

She tipped her head and searched his eyes in the moonlight. 'It was only a simple little shift dress.'

'It was elegant and understated, and you looked amazing.'

She smiled. 'Thank you. You looked pretty amazing yourself, and Josh was so good. I was sure he'd scream all through the service.'

She saw his lips twitch. 'He's probably saving that for tomorrow, for the vicar.'

He wasn't. Josh and his cousin Thomas were both as good as gold for their christening, and the vicar remarked on how alike they were.

'It'll be hard to tell the difference between these two,' he said with a smile as he handed Josh back to Amy.

'No, it won't,' they all chorused, and then laughed. He was right, they were very alike, but there were differences, more so than between Ben and Matt, and to their parents and grandparents the differences were obvious.

They filed out into the sunshine, and Matt and Amy hung back behind the others for a moment, Josh squirming in Matt's arms.

'OK?'

She nodded. 'It was lovely. Just right.'

It had been. Before the ceremony, the vicar who'd married them had asked for a few moments of silence while they remembered Samuel.

They hadn't cried. Their tears had been shed, their love was stronger, and they were looking forward to their future together. It might not be untroubled, but it would be shared every step of the way, and whatever happened, they would always know that they were truly loved.

What more could they possibly ask for?

'Come on, you two, or we'll eat all the cake!' Ben yelled, and Matt laughed.

'He's not joking. Come on.'

And putting his arm round Amy and drawing her in close to his side, he walked her out of the churchyard with a smile...

* * * * *

A sneaky peek at next month...

Medical Romance™

CAPTIVATING MEDICAL DRAMA—WITH HEART

My wish list for next month's titles...

In stores from 4th November 2011:

❏ The Child Who Rescued Christmas – Jessica Matthews

❏ Firefighter With A Frozen Heart – Dianne Drake

❏ Mistletoe, Midwife...Miracle Baby – Anne Fraser

❏ How to Save a Marriage in a Million – Leonie Knight

❏ Swallowbrook's Winter Bride – Abigail Gordon

❏ Dynamite Doc or Christmas Dad? – Marion Lennox

Available at WHSmith, Tesco, Asda, Eason, Amazon and Apple

Just can't wait?

Visit us Online

You can buy our books online a month before they hit the shops! **www.millsandboon.co.uk**